LORD ROGUE

REBECCA HAGAN LEE

AMBER HOUSE BOOKS

Praise for Rebecca Hagan Lee

"Rebecca Hagan Lee warms my heart and touches my soul. She's a star in the making!" — Sabrina Jeffries, *New York Times* bestselling author

"Tender, enthralling romance straight from the heart!" — Eloisa James, *New York Times* bestselling author

"Rebecca Hagan Lee taps into every woman's fantasy!" — Christina Dodd, *New York Times* bestseller

"Rebecca Hagan Lee is a writer on the rise!" — *Romantic Times*

BOOKS BY REBECCA HAGAN LEE

The Charlotte Society

Lord Temptation

Lord Dare

Lord Rogue

Gold Coast Bride Series

The Treasure Bride

The Silk Bride

The Heiress Bride

The Irish Bride

Free Fellows League Series

Barely a Bride

Merely the Groom

Hardly a Husband

Truly a Wife

A Bachelor Still

Mistresses of the Marquess

Once a Mistress

Always a Lady

Ever a Princess

Borrowed Brides

Golden Chances

Harvest Moon

Something Borrowed

The Counterfeit Bride

Twice Blessed: A Borrowed Brides Novella

A Hint of Heather

Whisper Always

Copyright Info

ISBN: 978-1-943505-99-9

Cover design by Control Freak Productions

Cover Photo © Period Images

Cover Background © Unholy Vault Designs (Used under license from Shutterstock.com)

Published by Amber House Books, LLC

http://www.amberhousebooks.com

For more information, contact publisher@amberhousebooks.com

This book is dedicated to my sister-in-law,
Sandra Lee Stephenson
Thanks for the years of support and the interest
and for all the great book recommendations and conversations.
You brighten my life and expand my reading horizons and you buy books
and re-read them. Over and over again.

And for all the Dulcies in the world who overcome
overwhelming loss and go on to find the love they deserve.

And as always to Steve
who makes it all possible.
With love.

PROLOGUE

Raphaels character is his fate."
—Heraclitus, c.540-c.480 B.C.

Near Waterloo,
United Kingdom of the Netherlands
15 June 1815

"Hold!" Colonel Lord Cornelius Fenton shouted the order to the cavalry unit currently watching as a barrage of artillery from the French Middle Guard targeted their own troop of Royal Horse artillery aligned in the field below.

"Hold?" Major Lord Raphael Blackburn glared at the colonel. "We can't hold. Our artillery is being cut to ribbons, Colonel. We've got to retreat and regroup to flank the French Middle Guard or charge forward to provide cover so our artillery unit can relocate. What we cannot do is hold this position while the French blow our artillery to smithereens!"

"You have your orders, Major." Fenton refused to budge, more than willing to hold his position while seated on a magnificent white stallion he had purchased from a Prussian cavalry officer who had sworn it was a more suitable mount for a British colonel than the colonel's previous horse. And it appeared Cornelius Fenton was more than willing to watch the artillery men in his command come under attack and be needlessly slaughtered. "I expect you to obey them."

"I fear we shall both be disappointed, Colonel. For I expect you to lead," Rafe told him. "Those men currently under fire and facing the might of the Middle Guard, expect you to lead. Or, if you are unwilling, to order your officers to lead the charge in your stead." He fixed his gaze on the colonel. "What I do not expect to do is stay behind the lines, beyond the range of the French artillery, and watch you sacrifice more good men rather than lead the cavalry charge to save them."

"How dare you, Major!" Fenton's face darkened with rage.

"I dare because your arrogance, utter incompetence, and willingness to sacrifice the men you command in order to protect yourself have already cost me one good man. I'm not going to allow you to cost me any more."

"You are relieved of duty, Major."

Rafe met Fenton's glare without flinching. "And you are derelict in yours, Colonel. By your cowardice in refusing to engage the enemy to aid men in your command."

Colonel Fenton turned to his aide-de-camp and ordered, "Captain Cornish, escort Major Blackburn from this field of battle and see that he is confined to quarters under guard until a military court of inquiry can be convened."

"Sir?" Captain Cornish was ambitious and eager to please his superior officer, but he was a cavalry officer first. A cavalry officer without a trace of cowardice. "Our artillery battery is under siege. Every man will be needed for this battle. That means Major Lord Blackburn and I will be needed. Someone has to lead the charge."

"There isn't going to be a charge," Fenton insisted. "We hold our position here until the French exhaust their ordnance. I gave you an order. Follow it. Or you'll stand beside Blackburn as defendants in a military court of inquiry."

"Behind the lines, sir?"

"Of course, behind the lines," Fenton snapped. "Where we are safely out of artillery range."

Raphael pinned the captain with his gaze. "Are you going to watch the slaughter? Or help me prevent it?" Without waiting for Cornish's answer, he gathered his mount's reins in hand. But before he could send the horse lunging forward, the French Imperial Guard released another artillery barrage.

Shells exploded on the field in front of them, enveloping them in a thick cloud of black smoke, showering them with burning debris from trees and brush in the paths of the mortars. Cornelius Fenton's mount squealed as bits of rock and fiery greenery peppered him. Flattening his ears and rolling his eyes in stark terror, the horse shied, then reared on his hind legs in a classical *courbette* before lowering his head and bucking several times in quick succession, successfully ridding himself of his rider and galloping away to safety.

The colonel hit the marshy ground with a thud. Scrambling to get to his feet, Fenton grabbed for Raphael's reins.

Rafe snatched his rein out of Fenton's reach and spurred his mount into action. His horse charged, knocking the colonel aside as he did so. Rafe drew his sword, raised it high, and led the charge across the field of battle while the Middle Guard hurried to reload. Captain Cornish and the dozen cavalrymen under his command followed, leaving Colonel Lord Cornelius Fenton to fend for himself.

RAFE LED THE FIRST CHARGE, A SECOND, AND THEN MADE A FINAL DASH across the field, successfully covering the realignment of the scattered troop of Royal Horse artillery. A round of huzzahs filled the air around him as the bombardment came to an abrupt halt. The battle was over. The combined remnants of Troops C and G of the Royal Horse Artillery hailed Rafe and Captain Cornish as saviors of the troop by forcing the French guard to flee the field.

Rafe acknowledged the cheers of the men, then immediately began the task of seeing to the welfare of the wounded artillerymen and his own cavalrymen.

At the conclusion of the battle, Rafe was summoned to the Duke of Wellington's headquarters to brief Wellington on his actions. Rafe carefully recounted the events of the day in full as well as he remembered them, including the incident that had compelled him to lead the first charge and concluding with a report on the injuries suffered by the men of the troops of the Royal Horse Artillery and those of his cavalry unit. The Duke of Wellington commended him for "his personal determination to do his duty as he saw fit and for exemplifying extraordinary bravery and courage under fire in leading the charge that saved the men of the Royal Horse." Rafe was toasted by the duke and his staff officers and invited to share their evening meal before returning to his duties.

"My word as a gentleman, I'll be keeping my eye on you, Major Lord Blackburn," the duke told him, a twinkle in his blue eyes, as he raised his glass of after dinner port to his lips. "Never doubt it."

"Thank you, Your Grace." Raphael met the duke's gaze. "I appreciate it."

Wellington gave a brief nod of dismissal. "Now, if you will excuse us, Major Blackburn, my staff and I must return to our duties."

Rafe rose from his seat, thanked the duke and his fellow officers, and made his way across the recent field of battle, back to his quarters.

He was awakened at dawn by four rather beefy assistant deputies from the Provost Marshal Corps.

"What the devil?" Rafe demanded, as he was unceremoniously yanked from his bed.

"Major Lord Raphael Blackburn?" the largest of the four men barked.

"Yes."

"You are under arrest by order of Lieutenant Colonel Cornelius Fenton."

CHAPTER 1

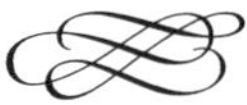

"The day shall not be up so soon as I
To try the fair adventure of tomorrow."
—William Shakespeare, 1564-1616

27 April 1816

"I was beginning to worry that you wouldn't make it," Dulcie Tennant said as soon as her close friend, Phoebe Osborne, entered her bedchamber. "And I would have to go alone. I've been on pins and needles all night."

Phoebe gave Dulcie a quick hug. "I'm sorry. It took longer to get away than I thought. But I couldn't let you go alone."

Dulcie had spent the night in Phoebe's bedchamber in Lady Augusta Nesbitt's home on Grosvenor Street. She and Phoebe and Serenity Blakenheath had accompanied Lady Nesbitt to Lady Middleton's masked ball, the first, and some said, the most important, ball of the Season. Phoebe had stayed at the ball to take part in the midnight buffet and the four o'clock breakfast, but Dulcie, Serenity, and Lady Nesbitt had left the ball before the buffet.

Phoebe and her widowed mother had lived with Lady Nesbitt for the past ten years. Dulcie lived with her Uncle Guilford Tennant, the current Viscount Tennant, and his wife, Mavis, in the home in which she had been born. And Serenity Blakenheath lived with her father, the fourth Viscount Blakenheath, across the park from Lady Nesbitt, who had graciously agreed to sponsor Serenity in her first Season.

Phoebe had elected to remain at the ball for the midnight buffet and the four o'clock breakfast, but Lady Nesbitt deemed it unseemly for a young lady in her first Season to attend the midnight buffet. She and Serenity had thanked their hostess and said their goodbyes after the last quadrille. Dulcie had decided to forego the buffet as well and accompany Lady Nesbitt and Serenity.

She and Phoebe had a very early appointment this morning and while Phoebe had been loath to leave the ball, Dulcie had been ready to call it a night.

Phoebe had just returned from the four o'clock breakfast and would have to hurry through her morning ablutions and do without sleep in order to chaperone Dulcie on her most important appointment.

"I ordered a bath for you a half hour ago," Dulcie said.

"Thank you." Gathering the clothes she'd laid out before dressing for the masked ball, Phoebe pulled the privacy screen around her and began stripping off her mermaid costume.

"It's probably cold. I thought you'd be here sooner." Dulcie chattered to hide her nervousness. "Isn't it funny that Lady Middleton's midnight buffets begin at eleven and the four a.m. breakfast begins at three and ends at four?" Hearing Phoebe suck in a quick breath as she stepped into the tub, Dulcie became concerned. "Gracious, Phebe, let me ring for some hot water. That water must be freezing by now."

"The bath is fine," Phoebe told her. "I'll be finished before the water gets here. I just need a quick wash to freshen up."

"The bath isn't fine," Dulcie said. "I can hear your teeth chattering."

"I don't plan to linger. I'll be finished in a moment…"

"And probably frozen." Dulcie stirred the coals in the fireplace and paced around the room, rubbing her hands up and down the arms of her new spencer as she listened to Phoebe splashing in the tub. "I'm ringing for hot chocolate and toast." Dulcie followed her words with deed, ordering chocolate and toast for two when the maid appeared. "I know you just came from a breakfast, but I doubt you ate very much, and I haven't eaten at all."

"Thanks, Dulce. That will be nice. And you're right. I was in such a hurry I didn't take time to eat breakfast," Phoebe explained. "I spent every moment I could in Alasdair's arms. But I wasn't about to make you late for your meeting." Phoebe's voice was muffled as she swallowed a yawn. "Mercy, but I'm tired." She sighed. "I haven't danced so much in years."

"Neither have I," Dulcie said. "It was fun, wasn't it?"

"Yes, it was," Phoebe said. But that was an understatement. Lady Middleton's ball had been more than fun. It had been magnificent. The masquerade ball had been everything she could have asked for and more than she'd ever imagined.

"I don't blame you for spending as much time as you could in Lord Sinclair's arms. Who wouldn't? He dances divinely." Dulcie wrinkled her brow and chewed on her bottom lip. "Tonight reminded me of how much I've missed dancing. I hope *my* soldier is equally adept on the dance floor."

"If he's a gentleman, like Geoff told you he was, he will be," Phoebe assured her.

"Serenity Blakenheath is a lady." Dulcie giggled. "And after months of lessons with an Italian dancing master, she still has two left feet."

"Dulcie!"

"I'm only speaking the truth. Ask any of the gentlemen who partnered her tonight if you don't believe me."

Dulcie heard more splashing from behind the screen before Phoebe spoke. "The *Honorable* Serenity Blakenheath and her two left feet aside, your soldier will probably be a perfect gentleman and an excellent dancer. And if he isn't, you can teach him."

Dulcie's most important appointment this morning was with the soldier she intended to adopt for The Charlotte Society. Today, she was meeting him for the very first time. Phoebe, acting as Dulcie's chaperone, was going to accompany her.

Choosing individual soldiers to sponsor was part of the plan she and Phoebe and Caroline had devised when they created the Charlotte Society. The Charlotte Society, named for their royal patroness, their beloved Queen Charlotte, was a charity devoted to helping soldiers returning from long years of war adjust to civilian life once again. Each of the three longtime friends and founding members had decided that rather than raise and donate money to help returning soldiers, they would each select an individual soldier to help.

Caroline Hardage, a widow whose elderly husband had died two years earlier, had adopted Major Lord Anthony Carlisle, third Earl of Carlisle, after learning that Carlisle, the man she'd thought had been killed in the Battle of Quatre Bras was badly injured, but very much alive.

Phoebe had chosen to adopt a surly highland Scot she'd met while helping Lady Nesbitt serve refreshments to the patients at the Returning Soldiers' Hospital. Phoebe's soldier had surprised her tonight by attending Lady Middleton's masked ball dressed as a gentleman pirate. He had swept Phoebe onto the dance floor after refusing to associate with her or any of his fellow English officers. Their relationship seemed quite promising. Dulcie smiled at the memory of Lord Sinclair dancing with every wallflower seated beyond the boundary of the dance floor—including herself—in order to dance a second dance with Phoebe, the only woman he seemed to really want to partner.

Dulcie's own choice of soldier had been made for her when her beloved brother, Geoffrey, had arranged for his friend, and fellow cavalryman, to assume responsibility for her should anything happen to him. Geoffrey had suffered a mortal injury while serving in the Peninsula Campaign and succumbed weeks later, leaving Dulcie in his friend's care.

Dulcie had known who she was going to adopt the moment she

and Caroline and Phoebe had formulated the idea for the Charlotte Society. Unfortunately, she had been unable to locate him and after visiting every hospital, inn, and boarding house for soldiers in London, Dulcie had asked Caroline, who was a marchioness in her own right, to use her connections to help Dulcie find him. In addition to a title, Caroline had a powerful godfather in Lord Trevor Weymouth, the Earl of Weymouth, also known around town as the Wizard of the War Office. No one was quite sure what Lord Weymouth did in the War Office or how much power he wielded, but everyone agreed that he had enormous influence in government.

After agreeing to help her, Lord Weymouth had somehow managed to find Dulcie's chosen soldier and had arranged to escort her to meet him. On the morning following Lady Middleton's masked ball.

This morning.

Phoebe sighed. "Everything is changing, Dulce. After today, I'm afraid our lives will never be the same." Stepping from behind the screen wearing a flannel chemise, drawers, and stockings, Phoebe pulled a pink calico gown over her head and smoothed it into place, then turned so Dulcie could button the row of buttons running down the back.

Dulcie handed her a brushed cotton spencer in a darker shade of pink and Phoebe gratefully put it on. "How do I look?"

"If you want to know the truth, you look tired. Tired and pensive," Dulcie answered honestly. "But that pink suits you and nobody else will notice the dark circles beneath your eyes. And if they do, you can truthfully blame it on Lady Middleton's ball."

Phoebe glanced at her reflection in the mirror, noting the shadows beneath her eyes Dulcie had pointed out. "It's a good thing *I'm* not going to meet the man I'm going to marry."

"That's because you already have," Dulcie said. "You'll see."

"I don't think so..." Phoebe's voice faded as she fought to keep her tears at bay. In the space of a week, everything had changed. Her friends were getting married and beginning lives of their own, while she was unsure of her own future.

"Nothing in life stays the same, Phoebe," Dulcie reminded her. "A month ago we could not have imagined that you would be dancing with your dashing buccaneer at Lady Middleton's masquerade ball or that I would be running away from home to meet the man who promised my brother he would marry me. Or that Caro would actually be *married* to Anthony Carlisle."

"I know nothing stays the same, Dulce, but I don't think I'm quite ready for everything to change at once."

Dulcie walked over to Phoebe and hugged her. "One thing that won't change, Phebe, is our friendship. We are friends for life. Nothing will change that. And not all change is bad. It was nice to not be a wallflower for one evening." She smiled. "Your Scottish buccaneer might normally be angry and churlish, but he was exceptionally gallant and kind last night. And as far as I could see, he only had eyes for you." Dulcie checked her reflection in the mirror, then turned to Phoebe. "What do you think? Will I pass muster?"

Dulcie was wearing a new ensemble. A spencer in green velvet and a muslin dress dyed a shade of green that complimented the darker green of the velvet jacket. With her russet-colored hair and big, brown eyes, Dulcie looked lovelier than Phoebe had ever seen her look before.

"You'll not only pass muster, Miss Tennant, but you'll also turn every head on the parade ground. You look beautiful, Dulcie. Rested and happy. You've lost that tense, pinched look you've been wearing ever since Mavis and Guilford moved in and took over your household."

Dulcie beamed. "You can thank your aunt Augusta for that. I'm so grateful to her for sponsoring me and inviting me to be her guest at the ball and in her house last night." She glanced down at her new dress. "It's not the wedding dress I would have chosen for today, but Lord Weymouth said to dress for a normal outing. And wearing the silk gown and jewelry I wore at Caro and Tony's wedding seemed a bit much since I might not be attending a wedding at all..."

"Did you pack the silk gown in your valise?" Phoebe asked.

Dulcie nodded.

"Then you'll have it if you get the chance to change."

"If I get the chance."

"It will be all right, Dulce. I'll be there with you and so will Lord Weymouth. Cheer up! It's supposed to be your wedding day."

THE MAN ARRANGING HER WEDDING DAY DROVE UP IN ONE OF THE EARL and Countess of Carlisle's unmarked coaches as Phoebe and Dulcie were finishing their hot chocolate and toast.

Hearing the sound of the coach's wheels rolling to a stop on the cobbled drive outside the house, Phoebe rose from her chair to glance out the window. "It's time, Dulcie." She turned to her dear friend. "Lord Weymouth has arrived to collect us."

"Are you certain?" A quaver of apprehension shook Dulcie's voice.

"It's Lord Weymouth," Phoebe assured her. "I recognize the coach and the driver. They're the ones Caroline sent for us to use on our last shopping trip." She gave Dulcie a reassuring smile. "Gather our things," she instructed. "We don't want to keep the earl waiting, do we?"

Dulcie sighed. "What if this was a terrible idea? What if my intended didn't want to be found? What if he doesn't want to meet me?"

"I'm sure Lord Weymouth asked himself those questions before he decided to arrange the meeting. And I'm sure he would not have done so if he thought your soldier wasn't interested in meeting you." Phoebe gave her a sympathetic look. "You're just nervous and having second thoughts."

"What if he's having second thoughts as well? What if he's changed his mind since he promised Geoffrey he would take care of me. Maybe that's why I couldn't locate him. Maybe he didn't *want* to be found."

Phoebe took a deep breath and slowly released it. "There's only one way to find out. And the means of finding out is waiting for us outside." She handed Dulcie her reticule, then linked her arm though Dulcie's and led her out of the bedchamber and toward the stairs."

"Let's not keep Lord Weymouth waiting any longer."

As they emerged from the house, Lord Weymouth didn't disembark from the vehicle. He simply doffed his hat and invited the ladies to join him.

The footman jumped down from his perch, opened the door, and helped Dulcie and Phoebe inside before closing the door behind them. "Good morning, ladies," Lord Weymouth said. "I trust you were able to get away without any undue trouble."

"None at all," Phoebe replied. "Aunt Augusta had everyone in the household otherwise engaged this morning. We didn't see anyone except the maid who brought our morning chocolate and toast."

"And you, Miss Tennant," Lord Weymouth inquired. "Did you encounter any resistance or difficulties from Lord and Lady Tennant regarding your attendance at Lady Middleton's masked ball last night or your planned stay with Lady Nesbitt?"

"No, Lord Weymouth." Dulcie shook her head. "Uncle Guilford seemed quite pleased that Lady Nesbitt has agreed to sponsor me for the Season. Neither he nor Aunt Mavis voiced any objection to my absence."

Weymouth's brow furrowed. "No objections at all?"

"None, my lord," Dulcie replied. "He even remarked that it was fortunate for me that Lady Nesbitt had taken a liking to me and could afford to bear the expense of all the new dresses and accoutrements necessary for a London Season." She met the man's steady, yet kind, gaze. "Please understand, Lord Weymouth, that I'm not a charity case." She bit her bottom lip. "At least, I shouldn't be. What Lady Nesbitt did, she did out of kindness to me. Not to accommodate my uncle because he's an inveterate and very bad gambler."

"I do understand, Miss Tennant," he assured her. "Your brother, like your father before him, left a very healthy and prosperous estate. And a number of people in very high positions have done what can be done to protect it from your uncle's excessive greed and folly."

"I don't want the man I'm about to meet to think he's getting a pauper. I couldn't bear it if he thought Geoff had deceived him. I have a dowry for my future husband and a personal income from my mother. It won't be released until I am legally wed. But I am not without means that my uncle cannot gamble away."

"There are rumors going around town that your uncle has mounting debts and that he owes some *very* dangerous and impatient people."

"Does *he* know?" Dulcie asked, feeling the color drain from her face.

Weymouth could tell from the inflection in Dulcie's voice that she was referring to her brother's friend rather than her uncle, Guildford Tennant. Reaching across the space between the seats, Weymouth patted Dulcie's hand. "He was completely aware of your brother's concerns regarding the current Viscount Tennant."

Dulcie sighed. "All right then. As long as he knows he isn't getting a pig in a poke."

Lord Weymouth laughed. "Hardly that, my dear. The gentleman in question held your brother in high esteem and is very fortunate to be getting you." He gave her hand another reassuring pat. "Now, you mustn't worry, Miss Tennant. Everything is going to be all right." Lord Weymouth settled back in his seat. "I've kept his identity secret to everyone except for my close associates who assist me in the work I do for the government."

"Dulcie has done the same," Phoebe told him. "Neither Caro nor I are privy to his name or status except that the late Lord Tennant considered him a friend and a gentleman."

"Good," Weymouth said. "It's vitally important that no one know his identity until he and Miss Tennant are safely wed."

Phoebe nodded.

"Now..." He rubbed his hands together. "Tell me about Lady Middleton's masked ball last night. I heard it was *quite* a show."

Dulcie realized he was deliberately changing the subject to take her mind off her upcoming meeting with the man who had been Geoff's friend and who would become her husband, but she pretended not to notice. "It was."

"Tell me about the costumes," he urged. "I'm always fascinated by the choices people make at those things." He smiled. "What did you go as, Miss Tennant?"

Dulcie wondered if Lord Weymouth was testing her veracity. The man had a reputation for knowing the answers before he asked the questions and for keeping tight-lipped about the information he ferreted from people. Whatever the reason for his question, Dulcie was fairly certain he already knew. "I was Little Bo Peep searching for my sheep."

"The only Little Bo Peep?" he asked.

Dulcie shook her head. "I had hoped to be unique, but Lady Nesbitt told me she mistook another Bo Peep for me." She shrugged. "But I didn't see any other shepherdesses searching for lost sheep in the crush."

"And your first dance partner?" he asked.

"A friar," Dulcie admitted.

Weymouth laughed. "So, you had something in common seeing as how you were both accustomed to tending to flocks."

Dulcie smiled.

"And you, Miss Osborne?" Weymouth pinned Phoebe with his gaze. "What role did you choose?"

"I was a mermaid," Phoebe said.

"Ah," Weymouth drawled. "A siren."

"More fish out of water," Phoebe told him, a wry smile playing around her lips. "It had been ages since I had been to a dance."

"And your first dance partner?"

Phoebe's face took on a dreamy expression. "A gentleman pirate who called himself a buccaneer."

"And was he?" Weymouth asked. "A *gentleman* pirate?"

Phoebe lifted her chin. "In every sense of the word."

They continued to discuss Lady Middleton's fabulous masquerade ball, repeating bits of overheard gossip, and speculating about the true identities of the guests who left before the official unmasking. Weymouth even surprised them by asking about decorations and the refreshments and who the ladies recognized and who they did not.

The light conversation helped pass the time as they travelled through London.

When the topic was exhausted, Weymouth settled back in his seat and said, "Thank you, ladies, for regaling me with the details of the ball. Your information has been invaluable. You see, Lady Weymouth and I make it a point to attend Lady Middleton's masked ball every Season. It's my countess's favorite event of the year. But with a new addition to our immediate family and the arrival of twins for my eldest son and his wife, we decided it was best for my wife, daughter-in-law, and the infants to remain in the country. Of course, those ladies will want to hear all the details and the gossip when I return home. And other than my visit with your friend and my goddaughter, Lady Carlisle, Lady Middleton's ball is one of the few things I can talk about."

"You're welcome, Lord Weymouth," Phoebe said. "Now, there's something we'd like you to answer for us."

"If I can."

"Where are we going?" Dulcie asked as they left the sprawling streets of the city behind.

"It's not far," Lord Weymouth assured them.

"That's not what she asked," Phoebe pointed out.

Weymouth smiled like a cat that had been into the cream. "I know."

CHAPTER 2

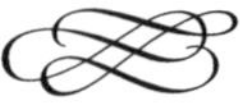

"The use of traveling is to regulate imagination by reality, and instead of thinking how things may be, to see them as they are."
—Samuel Johnson, 1709-1784

They made the journey to the Southwark docks in record time. Traffic was light on the Saturday morning following Lady Middleton's masked ball. The streets around the park were empty except for the night watchmen and a few stragglers. Most of the merrymakers who had attended the ball had made their way home to their beds after the breakfast. The only folks stirring were the milkmen and pie men beginning their routes and the fish mongers at Billingsgate preparing the early morning catch in time to open their stalls. Dulcie wrinkled her nose as the scent of freshly baked pies gave way to the strong fishy odor as they neared the busy open-air fish market.

Peeking around the edge of the heavy leather curtain covering the coach window, Dulcie caught sight of a sign marking the routes to the network of docks on the river. Dulcie sank back against the cushioned seat and gave an involuntary shudder at the thought of meeting her intended in one of the less than reputable inns or public houses surrounding the docks. "We're meeting him here?" She glanced at Lord Weymouth, her heart doubling its rhythm. "Is he awaiting us at one of the local establishments? Or aboard a ship bound for some foreign land?"

"No." Lord Weymouth shook his head. "He isn't going anywhere. *We* are." He opened the curtain on his window and nodded toward a sleek yacht berthed at one of the wharves. "We're sailing with the tide. On that."

Phoebe leaned over Dulcie's shoulder in order to look out the window. "Will you tell us where we're going, Lord Weymouth? Or is it to remain a secret until we arrive?"

"I'll be happy to tell you, Miss Osborne, once we're safely aboard ship. The fewer people who know, the better for you and for Miss Tennant. The docks are full of unsavory characters who might be willing to sell information about the comings and goings of this vehicle to equally unsavory peers who offer payment for it. I will not endanger your lives *or* your reputations."

"Davies Shipping, my lord. Wharf Twelve," the driver called out as he brought the coach to a stop.

"Davies Shipping?" Phoebe frowned, suddenly apprehensive about Dulcie's clandestine meeting with her intended. The need for secrecy had made the meeting seem like a grand adventure at first, but now, Phoebe was genuinely concerned about the mystery surrounding Dulcie's chosen soldier.

"Baron Davies is a family friend," Weymouth explained. "And a great patriot. He makes it possible for me to conduct necessary business for king and country by providing me with suitable vessels from his fleet and loyal, trustworthy captains and crews to man them whenever the need arises."

"And Dul"—Phoebe caught herself—"I mean, Miss Tennant's need qualifies as business for king and country?"

Weymouth smiled his inscrutable smile. "Indeed, it does."

Phoebe glanced at Dulcie for confirmation.

Dulcie nodded.

"And if it did not," Lord Weymouth added. "I would gladly reimburse Lord Davies for the use of his yacht in order to ensure your comfort and anonymity while we are engaged in these travels."

The door to the coach opened. "It's misting rain," the footman announced. "I took the liberty of breaking out the sealskin capes Lady Carlisle provided for your use, my lord."

"Thank you, Henson." Lord Weymouth swept out a hand, inviting Phoebe and Dulcie to precede him out of the vehicle. "Ladies, if you will allow Henson to assist you..."

Recalling Lord Weymouth's words about protecting their reputations and privacy, Phoebe exited first. She was taller than Dulcie and could provide cover for her. Unlike Dulcie, Phoebe had nothing to fear from her relatives. Her great aunt Augusta was a willing accomplice in the effort to guarantee Dulcie's ability to rendezvous with her betrothed. But Dulcie's Uncle Guilford would be livid if he got wind of Dulcie's intentions and would do everything in his power to thwart her.

The current Viscount Tennant had plans for his niece and a husband of her choosing was not a part of them. This way, Dulcie would be hidden between Phoebe and Lord Weymouth and blocked from view of any unsavory characters lurking about who might be persuaded to tattle.

The footman handed Phoebe down the coach steps, then helped her don the hooded sealskin cloak Caroline had thoughtfully provided. Phoebe didn't know if their friend and benefactor had been aware of their destination or if Caroline had simply prepared for inclement weather. Whatever her reasons, Phoebe was grateful for the warmth of the garment and the protection from the rain.

Dulcie followed close behind Phoebe, careful to keep her face averted from prying eyes as she stepped down from the coach and allowed Henson to assist her into the weatherproof cloak. She shivered involuntarily as she fumbled with the fasteners on the cloak, her hands and fingers icy cold inside her kid gloves. "I don't know if I'm shaking from nerves or the damp," she murmured to Phoebe as they waited for Lord Weymouth to finish issuing instructions to the coachman and footman and join them.

"Probably both," Phoebe said.

"I'm relieved to hear it." Dulcie's reply was rife with irony.

Phoebe glanced over her shoulder at Dulcie. "Sorry, but if it makes you feel any better, I'll admit I'm just as nervous as you are."

Dulcie was surprised. "Really?"

Phoebe nodded.

"Why?"

"I'm nervous for you," Phoebe admitted. "I'm nervous about leaving you alone with your betrothed."

"Oh, Phebe, I love you for caring so much about me," Dulcie hastened to reassure her friend. "But I'm sure you don't have to worry on my account. I know I'll be fine. I trust my brother's good judgment. And as you and Caro have reminded me time and again, Geoff would not have asked so great a favor from his friend if he hadn't been entirely certain the man was a completely honest and trustworthy gentleman. And if by some rare turn of events, Geoff happened to misjudge his friend's character, I'm convinced Lord Weymouth would not. He would never leave me in the care of someone who wasn't worthy of my brother's trust."

Glancing at their chaperone, Phoebe nodded. "I'm certain of that, too. After all, Lord Weymouth is a man who made and kept a solemn promise of his own when he promised Caroline's mother he would look out for her daughter." She gave Dulcie a smile. "He would never leave you here with a stranger if he didn't think your intended was a good man and a suitable husband for you."

"I've no doubt about it." Dulcie hoped she sounded more confident than she felt. "So there's no need for either one of us to be nervous about this adventure."

"Speak for yourself," Phoebe said. "You're a good sailor."

"So?"

"I don't want to disgrace myself," Phoebe said.

"You could never do that," Dulcie assured her.

"Oh, yes, I could." Phoebe fixed her gaze on the sleek yacht anchored at the end of the dock. "I've never been especially fond of boats—including the punts on the Serpentine in Hyde Park. And I haven't been on a boat of any kind in ages. Much less one meant to sail the open sea."

Dulcie followed Phoebe's gaze, then stuck her hands in the pockets of her cape and crossed her fingers against the fib she was about to tell. "No need to worry, Phebe. That's not a boat. It's a yacht. And sailing on a yacht is like being on land. You don't even know you're on the open sea."

Lord Weymouth joined them before Phoebe had a chance to reply to Dulcie's reassuring fable. "Well, ladies," he invited, ushering them toward the yacht. "Make yourselves comfortable. We'll be sailing for several hours before we reach our destination." He gifted them with a wry smile. "I do hope you're good sailors."

Dulcie hoped so, too. For Phoebe's sake.

~

As it turned out, Dulcie's wishes were granted. Phoebe's face paled, then turned a slight shade of green as the yacht set sail, but she gradually gained her sea legs and began to relax and enjoy the journey.

"Lord Weymouth, is it safe for you to tell us where we're going?" Phoebe asked once her stomach began to settle and she felt able to speak without fear of tossing her accounts.

Weymouth glanced around. He and the two ladies were the only souls on the private deck. "Our destination is the Isle of Wight. We'll be visiting the army garrison where the gentleman Miss Tennant is to meet is in temporary residence. While we are on the island, Miss Tennant will be Miss Susan Brown and you, Miss Osborne, will be Miss Anne Hall." He fixed his gaze on the two young ladies. "I'll introduce you as such as a precaution to protect your reputations. Understood?"

"Yes, Lord Weymouth," they answered in unison.

"What happens after their meeting?" Phoebe asked.

"That depends on Miss Tennant." He leveled his gaze at Dulcie. "If she decides to go through with the wedding, I've made the arrangements to have the necessary people present. I brought the letter the late Lord Tennant sent to Miss Tennant as well as the signed, witnessed, and sealed copy of the marriage contract he sent to her and she gave to me. And I have made arrangements for her dowry to be paid."

"My dowry?" Dulcie couldn't believe her ears. Was it possible Lord Weymouth had convinced her Uncle Guilford to relinquish it? "How did you get it?" She frowned as a sudden thought occurred. "Caroline —Lady Carlisle—didn't..."

"Oh, no, Miss Tennant." Lord Weymouth smiled his enigmatic smile once again. "I requested a meeting with your uncle. In my request I intimated that I was representing a party interested in pursuing you for the purpose of matrimony. Your uncle declined to speak with me about you or the possibility of a wedding or a dowry." He shrugged. "I suppose it's because he is aware that my elder son is happily married and my younger son is not of age."

Dulcie managed a tiny half-smile. Lord Weymouth's younger son was only a few months old. "I doubt you would be able to persuade Guilford to provide money for my dowry by the time your younger son comes of age."

Weymouth grinned.

Dulcie's uncle had already vowed not to part with a single farthing for her dowry unless she agreed to wed the suitor of his choosing. Dulcie couldn't imagine her uncle surrendering the amount of money Geoff had promised would be hers for a clandestine wedding to a man her uncle knew nothing about.

"No need for pessimism, my dear Miss Tennant. There are ways to get around your uncle's reluctance to part with funds on your behalf."

"I don't see how," Dulcie told him. "Unless you can persuade a highwayman to waylay him and demand that amount in ransom for his safe return."

"Or better yet, persuade a highwayman to dispatch him," Phoebe suggested.

Weymouth laughed aloud. "I don't think there is enough money in the city to convince any London highwayman to attempt a robbery of Guilford Tennant."

"Why not?" Dulcie asked.

"Because once he leaves the gaming tables at night, Guilford is devoid of any coin. He always loses. And no self-respecting highwayman would accept his chits." He glanced at Phoebe. "Or risk swinging from the end of a rope trying to ransom him when all he would get were promises of payment. Never any cash."

"But he might get paid if he promises to dispatch him…" Phoebe mused, an uncharacteristically bloodthirsty glint in her eye.

Weymouth pinned Phoebe with a stern gaze. "I wouldn't give it too much consideration, Miss Osborne. Murder for hire is a very dangerous and dirty business. Respectable young ladies should leave it to the professionals."

Phoebe blushed. "I wouldn't hire a murder done, Lord Weymouth. Even of a despicable man like Guilford. I wouldn't want *anyone's* murder on my soul, but I'll admit I wouldn't mourn Guilford's death if someone else decided to do it."

"I'm relieved to hear it," Weymouth said, a teasing note in his voice.

Dulcie turned her gaze on Lord Weymouth. "My uncle will never part with a single farthing of a gift for me unless I agree to marry the man of his choosing."

"That is generally the way guardianships work," Weymouth reminded her.

"But I couldn't accept my uncle's choice even if I wanted to. Because my brother had already chosen a husband for me. My betrothal or marriage to anyone else would be a breach of contract with Geoff's choice." She met Weymouth's penetrating gaze. "Not that I would agree to any man Uncle Guilford would choose for me. I trust my brother's judgment and his deep regard for my welfare far more than I trust Guilford's."

"And you are wise to do so," Weymouth confirmed.

"I don't want the gentleman I'm going to meet to refuse to honor the contract unless my dowry is paid. He made an honorable deal with my brother. He should receive what Geoff agreed to give him. He deserves some recompense for making such a sacrifice for us."

"Dulcie!" Phoebe exclaimed. "Any gentleman who gets you as a wife won't be making a sacrifice! He'll be most fortunate and will count his blessings every day. You must stop seeing yourself as a burden when you are nothing of the sort!"

Dulcie knew her friends, Phoebe and Caroline, loved her and valued her for her loyalty and character and her unwavering support and friendship. She knew they recognized her strengths and weaknesses and were privy to her doubts and fears. And she knew they wanted only the best for her. Dulcie wanted to believe Phoebe with all her heart, but the loss of her parents and brother and the loyal family retainers who had been with her all her life and who had been summarily dismissed when Guilford and Mavis had become her guardians and had moved into her house had taken a toll. Her self-confidence had begun to wither away beneath their constant fault-finding and scorn. Their disregard for her had planted a seed of doubt deep inside her.

The only place Dulcie could be herself—her old self—was with Caroline and Phoebe and she was terrified at the thought of losing them or of losing her access to them. The Charlotte Society had become her place of refuge. Its mission had become her reason for being and Dulcie didn't want to lessen Phoebe and Caroline's faith in her. Or her brother's choice of a husband for her. They believed in her. She could not—would not—disappoint them.

But she wouldn't fool herself either. She was going into her arranged marriage with eyes wide open and no illusions. While Caroline and Tony's marriage was a love match and Phoebe and her dashing Scotsman only had eyes for each other, Dulcie's marriage was strictly a means of fulfilling a marriage contract her brother had secured. It was a matter of honor for her intended and a means of escaping Guilford's machinations for her. Love had nothing to do with it. And because it was a legal obligation, Dulcie understood that she was getting the better end of the bargain and that the man she was going to marry would not only lose his freedom, but gain very little except the legal right to use her in order to produce an heir. And Dulcie had no way of knowing if she'd be successful at that.

"Phoebe, we both know how the marriage game works," Dulcie said. "The gentleman in question will be providing me with a good name and position in society. He has a right to expect something in return. As it is, I will be coming to him with nothing but the clothes on my back and in my valise. Because my guardian refuses to do the right thing."

"I agree with Miss Osborne," Weymouth said. "You are not a burden. And you shouldn't worry too much about your lack of a dowry. I assure you it's temporary. There are ways to collect what is owed to you and your intended. I am certain the gentleman in question didn't agree to your brother's request because he needed or wanted your dowry. It's simply a condition of a legal, binding contract. I feel certain the gentleman in question granted your brother's favor because it was the only thing he could do to ease his friend's worry and suffering. Because he admired Geoffrey Tennant and was honored to call him friend and to have that friend entrust him with his beloved sister's future."

Dulcie's face brightened at his words. "Do you really think so?"

Weymouth nodded. "I know so."

"How do you know?" she asked, struggling to conceal her desperate need to believe Lord Weymouth was right.

"I know because no man would consider granting such a favor if he didn't care deeply about his friend and want to help relieve his mind. The gentleman in question was well aware of what his friend was asking of him, and he gave his word of honor that he would live up to the terms of the contract and see that you were taken care of. A *dis*honorable man would ease his friend's mind by agreeing and then forget his obligation once his friend was dead and buried."

"That's what Guilford would do," Phoebe admitted.

"Exactly," Weymouth agreed. "Guilford has no honor. Your brother's friend is completely honorable." He patted Dulcie's hand. "Don't fret, my dear. Everything has been arranged. Trust me. Trust in your brother. He chose a worthy man to be your husband. It's all to the good for you."

Dulcie nodded. "Will you answer something else for me?"

"If I can."

"Will you tell me just how much in debt Guilford is?"

"I don't know the exact amount," Weymouth said. "But it's considerably more than he can pay."

"Has he mortgaged the London townhouse or our country estate? Has he frittered away the considerable family fortune my brother left behind?"

Weymouth didn't mince words. "Not yet. But he's well on his way. He owes a great many people. If they should call in his debts all at once, he'll be ruined. Fortunately, your brother made certain his heir could not sell or mortgage any of your family land or property. My associates have been keeping an eye on that and the local jewelers and pawn brokers."

"He wouldn't!"

Weymouth arched an eyebrow. "One would hope not, but he's raising cash somehow. It's only a matter of time before he begins selling jewelry and other family heirlooms. But I've made it known that anything of value he sells should be immediately redeemed by my trusted associates."

Dulcie breathed a sigh of relief. "Oh, Lord Weymouth, I don't know how to thank you."

"There's no need for you to thank me, my dear," he said. "I enjoy thwarting abject greed and treachery in wretchedly evil people. And I'm exceedingly good at it."

CHAPTER 3

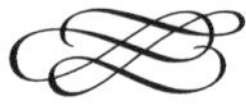

"We met as strangers."
—Christopher Marlowe, 1564-1593

"On your feet, you!"

Rafe jerked his head around as the door to his room opened with enough force to send it banging against the wall just seconds before Sergeant Amos Wilson, the sergeant assigned to the Cumberland Barracks, filled the doorway.

Rafe had been lying on his back with his head propped on his hands, contemplating the expanding spiderweb of cracks spreading across the plaster ceiling. His stockinged feet were propped on the footrail of a bunk ten or so inches too short to accommodate his height.

"I said, on your feet!"

Rafe rolled into a sitting position and placed his feet on the floor. He reached for his boots and pulled them on before pushing to his feet.

"Get into your tunic, mister."

Rafe gritted his teeth as he pulled on his red coat.

"Button that collar!"

A muscle in his jaw developed a noticeable tic, but Rafe fastened the hooks on his collar without comment.

"Let's go." The sergeant jerked his head in the direction of the door. "The commandant wants to see you. Don't keep him waiting any longer than necessary."

Rafe preceded the sergeant through the doorway and into the corridor. Turning left, he and the sergeant made their way toward the commandant's office, followed by the sounds of whistles and catcalls.

"Hey, Major! What's going on?"

"You leaving us so soon?"

"You're heading toward the commandant's office. Haven't you seen enough of him for one day?"

"Yes, but apparently the commandant hasn't seen enough of me," Rafe retorted. He wasn't inclined to answer the barrage of questions, but he was as curious as his comrades and their sudden interest in him gave Rafe the perfect opportunity to ask some questions of his own. He took a deep breath, then slowly exhaled it. "What does the commandant want with me? We spent over half the morning together. He could have said anything he wanted to say to me then."

The sergeant snorted. "I don't believe he wants any more to do with you than you want with him. But you have visitors."

"Visitors?"

"That's what I said," the sergeant snapped. "Or didn't I speak plain enough for you?"

"I heard you, Wilson," Rafe replied. "I'm simply not inclined to answer further questions from officers who have spent the entire war serving behind a desk or behind the lines rather than in the field of battle."

"These visitors came all the way from London to see you."

"Is it the Prince Regent? Or Wellington?"

"No, not the Regent," Sergeant Wilson told him. "Or Wellington."

"Then tell the commandant, I'm unavailable for further questioning." Rafe turned on his heel and headed back toward his room.

"They're not military." The sergeant warmed to the topic. "They're civilians. *Important* civilians."

Rafe stopped in his tracks and turned to look back at Wilson. "Who are they? What are their names?"

"I didn't catch the names," Wilson admitted. "But they look like quality folk. Two ladies and a gent."

"What sort of gentleman would bring two ladies here?"

"I don't know," Wilson said. "But they're expecting other folks to join them, and they informed the commandant they wouldn't leave until they'd had an opportunity to meet with you and discuss urgent business."

Rafe frowned. The people most important to him had no idea where he was. And wouldn't come here to visit him if they did. A military garrison was not the sort of place they would or *should* have to visit. There was only one man he truly wanted to see and Rafe certainly hadn't expected him to arrive this soon after his arrest. "I can't imagine who they could be."

"Maybe your prayers have been answered. Maybe the commandant decided to fulfill your request. After all, you're entitled to entertainment," Wilson speculated.

Rafe's frown deepened. "What entertainment?"

"Don't you remember, Major? At the conclusion of your inquiry when the commandant asked if you wanted anything special as entertainment, you told him that nothing less than a case of Scots whisky, a brass band, and a woman on each arm could possibly entertain you."

Rafe winced. He did recall saying that to the commandant, but he'd spoken the words in disgust and anger at the idiocy of the statement and the situation. He hadn't meant for the commandant to take them literally. Surely, it wasn't possible… Surely, the commandant hadn't arranged a bacchanal for him… "Bloody hell."

Turning back around, Rafe headed towards the commandant's office once again.

DULCIE JUMPED WHEN THE DOOR TO THE COMMANDANT'S antechamber, where she sat waiting for the most important meeting of her life, opened. She looked up from her lap and her breath caught in her throat at the sight of the man framed in the doorway.

He was neat in appearance despite the fact that he was unshaven, his cheeks shadowed by a two- or three-day growth of beard. He was dressed in the familiar red tunic, buff breeches, and tall boots of a cavalry officer. His hair was dark and thick and straight and much longer than was currently fashionable. He wore it combed back in a queue tied with a black ribbon that brushed the collar of his tunic whenever he moved. Staring at him, Dulcie was struck by the fact that in his red tunic, buff breeches, and boots, this man was a sight to behold. The epitome of the dashing, romantic horse soldier and every bit as handsome as Phoebe's Scottish buccaneer.

Their gazes locked.

He cleared his throat.

And the spell was broken.

Suddenly remembering her manners, Dulcie sprang out of her chair and onto her feet. The delicate linen handkerchief she'd spent the past quarter hour twisting into knots fell to the floor at her feet.

"Who are you?" the man demanded, glancing around the room. "There is only one man who would be bold enough to visit me here and you are most certainly *not* the Wizard of the War Office."

"No, I am not." Dulcie smiled at the Earl of Weymouth's familiar sobriquet. "However, Lord Weymouth did bring me here."

"Forgive me for pointing out the obvious, but you appear to be alone."

"I am alone. Lord Weymouth is waiting in the room next door." Dulcie's voice trembled ever so slightly as he focused the full force of his gaze on her. She couldn't determine the color of his eyes from where he stood just inside the doorway, but there was no doubt about their intense focus on her.

"My mistake." He took a step back as if to leave.

"No!" She straightened to her full height. "It isn't."

"Oh?" He arched one dark eyebrow in query, a trace of Scotland clearly evident in the way he pronounced the word. His burr wasn't as thick as Phoebe's Highlander's, but it was definitely there.

"You didn't make a mistake," she told him.

"Well, someone has," he retorted. "Why else would they escort me to this room if Weymouth is awaiting me in the one next door?"

She faced his scrutiny without flinching. "Because I asked them to."

He frowned. "For what purpose?"

"I asked Lord Weymouth to make it possible for me to meet with you in private before he and the others—"

"Others? The others who accompanied you and Weymouth?"

Dulcie shook her head. "My friend, Miss Hall, and I accompanied Lord Weymouth on the journey from London. The commandant sent for the other gentlemen upon our arrival at Lord Weymouth's request."

He winced. "Please tell me the other gentlemen aren't members of a brass band."

Dulcie gave him a quizzical look. "I wouldn't think so."

"I'm relieved to hear it."

She bit back a smile as she met his gaze once again. "I thought a few minutes alone might give us a chance to become better acquainted. But it's readily apparent you know nothing about me."

He drew his brows together. "If Weymouth has come all the way from the War Office, it can only be on a matter of utmost importance."

"He did." Dulcie nodded her agreement. "And it is.

His intimidating frown turned into a most intimidating scowl. "And you know this how?"

"Because *I* am the reason for Lord Weymouth's visit." She sighed. "Please, do come in while I explain."

He stepped over the threshold, closed the door behind him, and moved closer to get a better look at her face. "Have we met before?"

"No." Dulcie shook her head.

"You look familiar," he told her.

Dulcie beamed at him.

"But I don't remember your voice."

Her smile died on her lips.

His Scottish burr grew more pronounced. "And I'm not likely to forget the sound of it."

Dulcie wasn't sure if he meant what he said as a compliment or a criticism. She'd always been a bit self-conscious about the husky quality of her voice. Her governess had made her practice speaking in a higher register from the time she was nine until she turned fifteen without much success and Dulcie had gradually resigned herself to having an unladylike voice. As long as her friends didn't object to the way she sounded, Dulcie didn't care what society thought. But she found herself slightly disappointed in him. Somehow, she'd expected better. "I'm sorry you find the timbre of my voice disconcerting."

He frowned once again. "I didn't say I found your voice disconcerting..."

"You said..."

"I said," he interrupted, "that I wasn't likely to forget the sound of it. It's quite remarkable."

Dulcie shrugged. "I know it's not the voice a lady should have. In fact, my guardian's wife reminds me nearly every day that I would be best served to speak only when spoken to and never above a whisper. She finds it appalling that I should have the coarse voice of a fishwife."

"Your guardian's wife is undoubtedly tone deaf."

Dulcie tried to suppress an unladylike snort of laughter and failed. She'd had the exact same suspicion at every Sunday service when Mavis attempted to sing.

"See? I was correct in my assessment of the guardian's wife. She *is* tone deaf. For your voice is a musical sound if ever I've heard one, Miss...?" He smiled at her—a genuine smile that reached his eyes. Eyes, she realized, that were a rich, dark brown, rimmed by thick, black lashes beneath equally thick, black eyebrows. Eyes that crinkled at the corners when he smiled. "You haven't told me your name."

"I could say the same about you, sir," she pointed out. "I've come to meet a particular gentleman. How do I know if you're that man?"

"If you've come to meet Raphael Blackburn, seventh Earl of Blackburn, I'm your man."

Dulcie sighed. "I'm relieved to hear it."

"Are you now?

"More than I can say."

"Now that we've determined my identity, can you share your name, Miss? That's how introductions work." Bending down, he whisked the delicate lace handkerchief she had dropped off the floor. He fingered the fabric, noting the embroidered monogram.

"Susan Brown."

He arched an eyebrow at that. "Miss Brown with the initials 'DMRT' on her lacy handkerchief."

"Lord Weymouth introduced me to the commandant as Miss Susan Brown," she answered truthfully. "But my actual surname is Tennant."

"Tennant." He gazed down at her as if he couldn't quite believe his ears. Or his eyes. "Tennant." Rafe returned her handkerchief. "No wonder you look so familiar. You're Geoff's little sister—"

"Dulcie," she said. "Dulcinea Marjorie Rose Tennant."

"Dulcie," he breathed her name.

The sound of her name spoken in his deep voice, laced with a faint Scottish burr sent a tingle of awareness down Dulcie's spine. "And you are Geoff's friend, Raphael."

"I'm generally called Rafe. It sounds less—"

"Angelic?"

He gave an exaggerated grimace. "I was going to say biblical." Rafe rubbed his unshaven chin. "But biblical might be more apt today. I'm usually clean shaven, but in here I'm only allowed a shave every three days." He made another face. "Today was not the third day. I hope I haven't given offense by appearing in a less than presentable state."

Dulcie smiled at his reaction as she lowered her gaze and executed a perfect curtsey. "Not at all. How do you do, Lord Blackburn?"

He bowed before her, then took her hand. The current of electricity that shot through him at the contact surprised him. Glancing up, Rafe caught her gaze and saw that she'd felt it, too, and was just as surprised by it as he was.

Instead of releasing her hand, Rafe brushed his lips against her glove.

Their gazes met once again.

"How do you do, Miss Tennant?"

"Very well, thank you, Lord Blackburn."

"I'm pleased to hear it, Miss Tennant."

The knock at the door interrupted their flirtatious exchange. The Earl of Weymouth opened it just in time to hear Blackburn say her name.

Suddenly aware they were no longer alone, Rafe immediately released Dulcie's hand and stepped back, putting more than a respectable distance between them.

Noting his gentlemanly behavior, Weymouth acknowledged it with a nod of approval. "Oh, good. I see the two of you are getting acquainted. The vicar has arrived." He met Blackburn's gaze. "And your solicitor." Weymouth patted the front of his coat. "I have all the necessary documents for you to sign."

Blackburn glanced down at Dulcie. "I promised your brother I would see that you are taken care of. And I will."

"You didn't promise Geoff you would see that I am taken care of," she reminded him. "You promised him you would *marry* me. Have you changed your mind? Are you disappointed now that you've met me?"

"On the contrary, little one." Blackburn shook his head. "I'm not at all disappointed. You are exactly the way your brother described you." Ignoring Weymouth's presence, Rafe moved close enough to Dulcie to touch her. Reaching out, he traced her lower lip with the pad of his thumb and experienced the unsettling tingle once again. "He told me you were beautiful. But all brothers who love their sisters think they're beautiful. I'm ashamed I didn't quite believe him. I should have known Geoff would never lie."

Dulcie searched his face. "Is there someone else?"

"No."

"But you don't want to make me your countess..."

He shook his head. "It's not that I don't want to give you my name and make you my countess. It's that I don't want to make you my widow."

Dulcie blinked. "I don't understand..."

"They're hanging me tomorrow."

CHAPTER 4

"Wedding is destiny,
And hanging likewise."
—John Heywood, 1497-1580

"H*anging you?"*

Rafe nodded. "I'm afraid so."

Dulcie blinked up at him in disbelief. *"Tomorrow?"*

"Yes." He didn't mince words. "At dawn."

"No!" Dulcie's anguished cry pierced the air seconds before her knees buckled. She folded like a paper fan, collapsing into a heap of green velvet and muslin onto the floor.

Weymouth moved to catch her, but Rafe reached her first. Weymouth watched as he lifted Dulcie from the floor and cradled her against his chest.

Holding Dulcie close, Rafe barked, "Don't just stand there! Send for the surgeon!"

"She doesn't require the surgeon." Weymouth's reply was calm and measured. "She's fainted."

"Fainted?" Rafe repeated the word as if he'd never heard it before. He glared at Weymouth. "What do I do with her?"

Weymouth nodded toward the brocade sofa. "Place her on the sofa."

Gazing down at the girl in his arms, Rafe realized he was loath to let her go. She seemed so tiny and delicate and looked defenseless and as fragile as an injured sparrow. Holding her as he was, Rafe realized how diminutive she was. She couldn't weigh more than six or seven stones at most, but she'd still managed to surprise him with a jolt of awareness whenever he touched her that had set his body humming. He turned a jaundiced eye on the sofa. "It doesn't look very comfortable."

"It probably isn't," Weymouth agreed. "But she won't be there long enough to feel it. She'll come around in a moment or two."

Rafe frowned as he carefully laid her down in as comfortable a position as he could manage. "Shouldn't we do something? Burn feathers or find some smelling salts or some spirits or something?"

Weymouth, ever the pragmatist, gave Rafe a wry look. "Do you *have* any feathers or smelling salts?"

"No."

"Then there's nothing to be done until she comes around on her own."

"Except send for the surgeon, who should have feathers and smelling salts," Rafe insisted.

"Because there are so many young ladies in residence at this military garrison," Weymouth countered. "Remove her bonnet and unbutton her spencer. She'll come to when she's ready."

Rafe glanced down at Dulcie lying on the sofa. Her bonnet was askew, and the ribbons tied beneath her chin looked much too tight. He untied the ribbons, lifted her bonnet off her head, propped it on the arm of the sofa, and unfastened the frogs of her spencer so she'd be more comfortable. "I may not have feathers or smelling salts to help her, but I know the commandant keeps a flask of whisky in the bottom right drawer of that writing desk."

Weymouth shot Rafe a look. "Let her rest a bit longer," he

suggested. "She had a very late night last night and a very early morning this morning. She would never admit it, but she's been running on nervous energy since we left London."

"She told me she was the reason for your visit and that it was of the utmost importance."

"She spoke the truth. And the young lady might not require spirits right now, but we do." Going to the writing desk, Weymouth opened the drawer Rafe had indicated, brought out a heavy silver flask, then rummaged for a glass. Unable to locate one, he said, "There are no glasses. We'll have to make do with the cover." He gave Rafe a wry look before removing the silver shot cup that covered the cap on the flask. He poured a shot of whisky in the cup and handed it to Rafe. "I'm sure the commandant won't mind."

Rafe smiled. "I'm sure he will, but I'm equally sure he won't voice his displeasure to the Wizard of the War Office for fear of losing his comfortable billet here." He raised the cup to Weymouth. "We who are about to die salute you." He swallowed the whisky. It burned its way down his throat and stung his eyes. Rafe handed the cup to Weymouth.

"Another?" Weymouth asked.

Rafe held up his hand. "No, thanks. It's been a long time since I've tasted good whisky." He met Weymouth's gaze. "Or any whisky. I suppose I'll have to wait a bit longer for the good stuff."

"It will be worth the wait." Weymouth grimaced as he swallowed another mouthful of inferior whisky. "There's a distinct taste of gin in this whiskey."

Rafe glanced at the sofa. "So that's Geoff Tennant's younger sister…"

"Yes."

"There's a strong family resemblance. She favors him." Rafe was thoughtful.

"Then, you must have recognized her right away."

"Not as Miss Susan Brown."

Weymouth shrugged. "A precaution to protect the ladies' reputations until I know if we can trust the others with Miss Tennant and Miss Osborne's true identities."

"A sensible precaution. I recognized the name Tennant first, and then her resemblance to Geoff."

Weymouth arched an eyebrow in silent query.

"The only picture I'd seen of her was a pen and ink sketch done when she was about nine or ten. Geoff kept it with him for luck." Rafe managed a self-deprecating smile. "I expected a young girl."

"She's all grown up," Weymouth commented.

"She's filled out," Rafe corrected. "What she lacks in height, she gained in looks."

"She is a lovely young woman."

"She's a *beautiful* young woman," Rafe corrected once again. "Who doesn't seem to realize it."

Weymouth nodded. "And you have reservations about marrying her..."

"I gave her brother my word I would. I'm not going back on it," Rafe told him.

"I am pleased to hear it," Weymouth said. "It confirms what I was told about you."

"What was that?"

"That you were a man of his word. A man of integrity and conviction."

Rafe managed a slight smile. "If I wasn't before, I'm certainly a *convicted* man now."

Weymouth winced. "I apologize for my poor choice of words."

Rafe shrugged.

Weymouth's expression gave nothing away. "I had hoped to get here before your court of inquiry. I've heard some unsettling rumors around the War Office that you were being confined without benefit of a proper inquiry and that the superior officer was advocating that you be hanged for your crime. I planned to speak to Commandant Swindell on your behalf. Your treatment and confinement here is unprecedented. Belted earls cannot be executed for any offense except treason against king and country."

"I appreciate the thought and your good intentions, but I fear you would have been outranked, if not overmatched, had you been here."

"That bad?"

Rafe answered honestly. "I believe the result of this morning's inquiry was a foregone conclusion. Inducing a favorable outcome for me would have required nothing less than a duke to intercede on my behalf. Wellington or the Prince Regent, if not the King himself."

"The king would be of no use to you in his present state," Weymouth told him. "What did you do to incur the rancor of higher nobility?"

"I'm accused of striking a superior officer and disobeying orders."

"Are you guilty of the charges?"

Rafe rubbed his hand over his face. "I'm guilty of disobeying orders. I'm not guilty of striking a superior officer." His lips tilted up at the corners in a moment of private amusement. "I could make the argument that he was an *inferior* officer and if I had struck him, I would do just that." He met Weymouth's direct gaze. "But I didn't strike him. Ricky did."

Weymouth narrowed his gaze at the mention of the name. *"Ricky?"*

"My horse. A big, bay Trakehner stallion named Frederick the Great. Ricky for short."

Weymouth's interest was piqued by mention of horseflesh, as he, along with his elder son, Griffin, owned two of the finest private stables in Great Britain, equaled only by Griffin's father-in-law, Lord Tressingham's, stables. "A cavalry mount or your own?"

"He was originally a cavalry mount for our Prussian allies. I was offered a mount from the Prussian remounts when my first horse was killed. I chose Ricky because he was steady under fire and strong-willed." He met Weymouth's gaze. "He's a trained war horse who took exception when the superior officer grabbed at his reins from the ground. Ricky whirled about, bumped the colonel with his right haunch, and knocked him on his arse. I didn't stay to apologize." He grinned. "Neither did Ricky."

"Were there witnesses to the incident?" Weymouth asked.

"Eight of them."

"The men you led into battle." It wasn't a question, but a statement of fact.

"The same," Rafe confirmed.

"Didn't any of them speak for you at the inquiry?"

"All of them," Rafe said. "Captains Cornish, and Somersby and the five junior officers who followed me in the charge as well as Marbury, the young lieutenant commanding the artillery unit we rode in to protect. And Wellington sent a letter commending me for my actions. But the members of the court of inquiry were neither impressed nor convinced."

"Your reputation preceded you," Weymouth ventured.

"'Raging Raphael Blackburn.'" Rafe grimaced. "I was given the name following my first cavalry charge on the Peninsula during the fiercest fighting. My men claimed I was raging like an avenging angel." He scrubbed at his eyes with the heels of his hands. "In truth, I remember very little of the actual fighting. I only recall the sight of the carnage afterwards." He shuddered at the memory. "Unfortunately, today in my unshaven state, I probably look the part of a raging avenger."

"My son led a charge in that battle and was grievously wounded," Weymouth said. "You are fortunate to have escaped without injury."

"Aye," Rafe said, his eyes clouding at the memory. "We lost many good men that day."

"Were you raging before you led the charge at Waterloo?"

"No. I was angry and frustrated, but I kept my temper. I disobeyed the colonel's orders to prevent the massacre of the men in the artillery unit after the colonel ordered us to hold our positions behind the lines and allow the slaughter to take place." Rafe's hands were fisted, his knuckles white with strain. His Scots burr deepened as he spoke. "If I was raging once I entered the battle, it was to protect those men."

"There was no repeat of what occurred after the ambush that caused Geoffrey Tennant's death?" Weymouth asked.

"No," Rafe replied. "I led the charge, engaged and defeated the enemy, and returned to our encampment to face my punishment without incident."

"What about Ricky?" Weymouth changed the subject from human to horse to reduce the tension.

Rafe glanced at him, but the earl's face gave nothing away. "Well, he hasn't had to face a military inquiry yet," Rafe replied. "But it may come to that. And he'll be convicted. I doubt they'll hang him. But I'll wager they sentence him to a forced gelding."

"That *would* be a crime." Weymouth smiled. "Is he a sorrel bay?"

"No." Rafe shook his head. "Seal brown."

"Even better," Weymouth pronounced. "Did he come home with you?"

"Aye," Rafe said. "He's stabled here. At least, he's supposed to be. His stable fee has been added to my monthly account for food and board since we've been here."

"Anyone exercising him?"

"Nobody's ridden him since I last rode him." He pinned Weymouth with a puzzled gaze. "Why?"

"Because I believe we might be able to do some business together."

"Horse trading?"

Weymouth nodded. "I've been considering expanding my breeding stock to include breeds other than Thoroughbreds. For pleasure, not war."

"Your reputation as the Wizard of the War Office is only surpassed by your reputation as a horseman. Once we conclude our business pertaining to Miss Tennant, I'll have my solicitor add a codicil to my will leaving Ricky to you." He met Weymouth's concerned gaze. "Once my sentence is carried out, I won't be riding him anymore." Rafe swallowed hard.

"I wouldn't be so certain of that," came Weymouth's cryptic reply.

"I'll make the arrangements anyway," Rafe said. "I can't depend on a last-minute reprieve. And Ricky is an exceptional horse. He deserves an owner who appreciates his character, his history and his breed."

"I'll take excellent care of him," Weymouth promised. "And I appreciate your confidence in my ability to do so. If I can secure a suitable string of pedigreed mares, I'll use him for breeding, and I'll pay top price for the right to do so to you if my plan works or to your widow if it does not. Agreed?"

"Lord Weymouth, I am going to hang at dawn."

"Yes, you are," Weymouth agreed. "But you don't have to die from it."

"If I don't, they'll hang me again," Rafe reminded him. "If they're going to hang me, I prefer to get it over with the first time and not be compelled to repeat the ordeal."

"I understand completely, but I've been working on a plan since I learned of your situation. And we might as well implement it."

Rafe narrowed his gaze. "What sort of plan can you devise in an hour?"

"A plan that began as a negotiation for your unconditional release and is rapidly becoming a rescue that keeps you alive and living as someone else until the danger to you and to that young woman"—Weymouth pointed toward Dulcie—"is eliminated."

"Will I be apprised of the plan?" Rafe asked.

"No," Weymouth told him. "Only that there is one. Once you wake up, you'll be briefed on the next phase."

"And Miss Tennant?" Rafe asked. "I take it you brought her here to conclude the business Geoffrey Tennant and I began before my sentence is carried out and I go to meet my Maker."

Weymouth shook his head. "Not at all. I wasn't aware of your unjust sentence until we arrived."

Rafe was surprised.

"Commandant Swindell apprised me of the sentence while you were getting acquainted with Miss Tennant."

"What will happen to her if your plan doesn't work?" Rafe asked.

"She'll return to her life in London, hopefully not at the mercy of her uncle."

"Guilford," Rafe murmured.

"Yes." Weymouth sat up straighter in his chair. "Do you know him?"

Rafe shook his head. "I only know *of* him. Geoff feared what might happen to his sister if Guilford succeeded him. He suspected Guilford in the deaths of their parents, and I suspect he could have even arranged for Geoff's ambush and subsequent death."

His interest piqued, Weymouth frowned. "Have you any evidence of that?"

"None," Rafe replied.

"But you're still suspicious."

"Of course I am. Geoff's parents die in an accident while he's serving in Spain," Rafe elaborated, grateful to be able to share his suspicions with someone for the first time since the ambush. "His father's death elevates Geoff to viscount. A few months later, Geoff is waylaid while on patrol and mortally wounded."

"He *was* scouting for bands of mercenary guerillas who changed allegiance as often as they changed their shirts," Weymouth reminded him, playing devil's advocate.

"But he wasn't supposed to be leading the unit scouting *any* guerillas that morning," Rafe informed him. "Since we'd only just returned from midnight patrol less than two hours earlier, he was supposed to be asleep in his bed."

"What?" Weymouth came halfway out of his chair. "The report I read stated that Captain Tennant was—"

"The report you read was wrong," Rafe stated flatly. "Captain Tennant was assigned to the midnight patrol, not the morning one."

"How do you know?" Weymouth asked.

"He was my second in command. *I* assigned him to ride with me on midnight patrol. A higher-ranking officer changed my orders without consulting me. *He* ordered Captain Tennant to lead the dawn patrol."

"What higher-ranking officer?" Weymouth demanded.

"The same one I'm accused of striking at Waterloo."

"Who else knows the orders were changed?"

"The other men on that morning patrol. They knew Captain Woolridge had been assigned to lead the morning patrols. And they were present when Woolridge was ordered to stand down so Captain Tennant could take his place."

"What happened to the men in that patrol?"

"Two died in the ambush. Geoff saved the other five, but died of his own wounds a fortnight later."

"Where are the five survivors now?" Weymouth asked.

"I don't know," Rafe admitted. "My guess is that they became casualties after I was reassigned."

Weymouth ran his hand over his face, then pinched the bridge of his nose. "Why would you assume that?"

"Other than the sheer numbers of dead between the Peninsula and Belgium?"

"Yes," Weymouth said. "Other than that."

Rafe pinned him with a look. "Because none of those cavalry men were in the unit I commanded at Waterloo."

"*None* of them?" That news came as a surprise to Weymouth, who was rarely surprised. "Not even Woolridge?"

Rafe shook his head. "Check your reports from the Peninsular Campaign. You'll find that Woolridge was killed in an ambush two months after Geoffrey Tennant." He met Weymouth's troubled gaze. "And I fear the men who testified on my behalf have all signed their own death warrants."

"I'll need the names of all the men."

"Of course." Rafe named the men who had been in his cavalry unit in Spain, including Woolridge, and the names of the men in his cavalry unit in Belgium. "What are the odds? After waiting for months for a military inquiry, I get one and I'm charged with disobeying orders and striking a superior officer after being ordered to stand down and allow the artillery unit we were assigned to protect to be slaughtered in the field."

"Did you know any of the officers serving on the inquiry?"

"None of them. By name or reputation."

Weymouth looked Rafe in the eye. "You believed you were going to be charged either way. For disobeying orders and striking a superior officer or dereliction of duty by not engaging the enemy to protect the artillerymen."

"Aye," Rafe said.

"So you engaged the enemy and saved the artillery unit…"

"I recognized an ambush when I saw it."

Lord Weymouth nodded. "I'll also need the names of those officers who judged you."

Rafe nodded. "I wasn't given the names, but my solicitor has them."

Weymouth pursed his lips in thought. "Did Miss Tennant's brother tell her of his suspicions?"

"No." Rafe shook his head. "She may have suspicions of her own of which Geoff was unaware, but he told me he never discussed his suspicions with her. Because he didn't want to burden her with more worry and doubt."

Weymouth propped his chin on his thumb and began idly tapping his forefinger again his temple. "You and Miss Tennant have powerful enemies. But you also have powerful allies. I'll keep my eye on her and I'll ensure that her friends do the same."

"Does she know about your plan?"

"No," Weymouth answered truthfully. "We decided it was better that she not know about it."

"We?"

"My associates and I."

Rafe frowned. "How many associates?"

"Enough." Weymouth handed Rafe a small vial. "You'll need to give her two drops of this in the champagne I included in your wedding hamper before my associates arrive to fetch you in the morning. It will assure her a restful, calm sleep."

Rafe arched an eyebrow as he pocketed the vial.

"It's harmless. I would not give it to you otherwise," Weymouth assured him. "And I would not give it to you if it were not necessary. But we cannot risk her recognizing any of my associates who will be keeping an eye one her once she returns to London."

Rafe stole a glance at the sofa. Dulcie's features looked even more delicate in repose. "How much danger is she in?"

"It's hard to say. And we only have until the end of the Season to conclude our operation."

"What happens at the end of the Season?"

"Her uncle intends to marry her off to the highest bidder from among his gaming associates."

"And if I marry her today?"

"She'll resume her normal life unless it becomes necessary for her to produce her marriage lines at the end of the Season. If that's the case, she can claim to be in mourning or with child."

"She'll be a countess," Rafe pointed out. "She'll outrank her uncle. And she'll have my estate in Scotland and other property, including a townhouse in London. The law grants a widow nine months before a new heir assumes the title and the entailed property."

"True," Weymouth agreed. "But only after she produces proof of your clandestine marriage."

"When word gets out in town that she married a condemned man, she'll be mired in scandal." Rafe's frown deepened. The consequences of his actions at Waterloo would be a stain on his family's and his widow's reputation.

"She'll have the time remaining in her year of mourning and a widow's portion of your estate at the conclusion of it."

"If I still have an estate," Rafe reminded him. "I have been condemned. The crown could take it all."

"You won't lose your estate," Weymouth promised. "The crown won't penalize your heirs. And my associates and I will take steps to mitigate any scandal she might face for honoring her late brother's wishes by marrying the man of his choice instead of her guardian's."

"Her uncle will become a bigger threat to her," Rafe warned. "He won't be happy at having his plans thwarted and being made to look inconsequential at best and foolish at worst."

"Perhaps," Weymouth allowed. "But he won't be able to control her. Or have the marriage annulled."

"She'll face scandal either way," Rafe said. "There will be witnesses..."

"We want witnesses," Weymouth reminded him. "To a legal marriage."

"To the marriage, yes. But only witnesses we can trust and I don't want Swindell," Rafe said. "I don't trust him. I trust my solicitor and I assume Miss Hall is trustworthy or she wouldn't be here. That leaves you and the parson. I trust you. I don't know the parson."

"I do," Weymouth said. "He's a family friend. His late father attended university with me. He's entirely trustworthy, willing to marry you and keep a duplicate parish register in case anyone inquires about your marriage. Miss Tennant signs the actual parish registry with her name and the duplicate as Miss Susan Brown. Miss Osborne will do likewise as Miss Anne Hall."

"What about what comes after?" Rafe asked. "What about tonight? If you take her back to London with Miss Osborne, her uncle could force an annulment." Rafe sighed. "But allowing her to stay here in the barracks with me will cause more scandal and speculation."

"She won't be in the barracks," Weymouth assured him. "I've arranged for the two of you to have the use of a furnished cottage after the wedding. The landlord has promised to make it ready, supply the wedding hamper and champagne, and leave the door unlocked."

"Thank you," Rafe said. "My room is not suitable for a lady to visit, much less spend the night."

"The cottage I rented probably isn't what Miss Tennant is accustomed to either. But it was the best I could arrange on short notice. I'm told it is often used as a honeymoon cottage..."

Rafe arched an eyebrow.

"What you do or don't do there is between you and your bride. It will be guarded, of course," Weymouth explained, shaking his head in apology. "I couldn't persuade the commandant to accept your word as a gentleman that you wouldn't attempt to escape with your bride."

"In my current situation, I'm not at all certain *I* would accept my word as a gentleman," Rafe admitted. "I'm not certain, as time draws closer to my execution, that I wouldn't try to escape with my bride."

Rafe glanced at the sofa once again. Dulcie still appeared to be sleeping peacefully. "Shouldn't we see to the business of securing her future before we have to wake her?"

"Excellent idea." Weymouth pulled out the sheaf of documents he'd brought for Rafe to sign and spread them out on top of the commandant's writing desk.

After carefully reading each document Weymouth presented to him, Rafe scrawled his name at the bottom and affixed his seal with his signet ring. "I'll ask my solicitor to make the changes to my will regarding Frederick the Great if that meets with your approval."

Weymouth nodded.

"I'll sign it before my countess and I leave for the honeymoon cottage. I assume you've made arrangements for transportation?"

"Yes."

"Will you be here tomorrow when my sentence is carried out?"

"No," Weymouth told him. "It's best if I adhere to the plan and escort Miss Osborne back to London. But I need to contact the men who testified on your behalf. Do you know if they're still on the island?"

"They're lodging in the same establishment as my solicitor," Rafe said.

"Did you speak to them?"

"No," Rafe replied. "It wasn't allowed. I could only speak to my solicitor to make arrangements in the event I was convicted. He mentioned that the captains and the lieutenant were lodging at the same establishment."

"I'll need to have a word with your solicitor. With your permission, of course."

"Of course," Rafe consented.

"Good." Reaching into the pocket sewn into the inner lining of his coat, Weymouth pulled out a money pouch. "I almost forgot. Here's the dowry the late Lord Tennant agreed to settle on you. Twenty thousand pounds."

"We settled on fifteen thousand," Rafe corrected.

Weymouth grinned. "Guilford refused to bestow a dowry on Miss Tennant, so we devised a way to extract it, plus a bit extra for causing her unnecessary anxiety." He offered the money pouch to Rafe.

"Keep it for her in the event…"

"The dowry has to change hands," Weymouth reminded him.

Sighing, Rafe accepted the money pouch before returning it to Weymouth's safekeeping. Rafe offered Weymouth his hand.

Weymouth took it.

"It's been a privilege doing business with you, Lord Weymouth. Thank you for locating Miss Tennant and bringing her to me so I could keep my promise to her brother."

"You're welcome, Lord Blackburn," Weymouth told him. "But you are laboring under a rather large misconception…"

Rafe arched an eyebrow in query.

"I only made the arrangements and escorted her. The truth is Miss Tennant came to me for help after she and Miss Osborne, and my goddaughter, the former Marchioness of Blessing and current Countess of Carlisle, formed a charitable society in order to help soldiers returning from war. They call it The Charlotte Society, after the queen."

"What does a ladies' charitable society have to do with me?"

"Miss Tennant spent weeks searching newspaper casualty lists, haunting the War Office, and going to every hospital, inn, boarding house, coffee house, and street corner in London looking for *you*."

Rafe frowned. *"What?"*

"The Charlotte Society doesn't simply disperse goods or coin to help soldiers. It operates on a more personal level," Weymouth explained. "Each member of the society chooses a soldier to assist in his return to society. She becomes a personal advocate for him."

"Unmarried ladies?" Rafe's frown deepened.

"Yes," Weymouth said. "It's—"

"Unheard of," Rafe said.

"Unique," Weymouth corrected. "Miss Tennant chose you because her brother chose you. And because you signed a marriage contract proclaiming that you would marry her."

"I agreed to honor Geoff's request should he be killed in battle."

"He was and you shall. Miss Tennant was most determined to find you. No other man would do." He gave Rafe a meaningful look, then handed him the whisky flask. "Now, go wake up that remarkable young woman so we can see the two of you happily wed."

CHAPTER 5

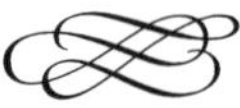

"Marriages are made in heaven
and consummated on earth."
—John Lyly, 1554-1606

"Sleeping Beauty, it's time to wake up." Rafe uncapped the whisky flask and waved it beneath Dulcie's nose.

She shoved his hand away. "Stop."

"I will when you open your eyes and look at me." He waved the flask beneath her nose once again.

Dulcie opened her eyes, saw Rafe leaning over her, and struggled to sit up. "What happened?"

"You fainted."

She blinked up at him. "*I* fainted?"

"Aye," Rafe nodded. "When I told you that I'm to hang tomorrow morning."

Dulcie felt the blood drain from her face once again. Rafe poured a measure of whisky into the silver cup and placed it against her lips. "Here—drink this before you faint again."

Dulcie wrinkled her nose at the smell. "What is it?"

"Whisky," Rafe told her.

"Spirits?" She sounded horrified. "Ladies do not drink spirits."

"Sure, they do," Rafe told her. "For medicinal purposes. In place of burnt feathers and smelling salts for rousing young ladies who faint dead away upon meeting their intended." He smiled a devilish smile. "Young ladies like you."

"I can't—" She opened her mouth to speak and Rafe deftly tipped the cup of whisky inside it. Dulcie had no choice but to swallow. It burned all the way down. She coughed and sputtered, but the whisky did its job and brought color back to her face. "That stuff is vile!"

"It's an acquired taste."

Dulcie coughed again. "I could never acquire a taste for it," she protested, glaring at the whisky flask as Rafe handed it to the waiting Lord Weymouth.

"I'm delighted to hear it," Rafe told her. "It means you won't develop the habit of tippling the bottle while you're mourning my early demise." He met her gaze. "Ladies really shouldn't drink spirits."

She studied his face. "And I didn't faint upon meeting you. I fainted when you told me you were going to hang. Is it true? Are they really going to hang you in the morning?"

"Yes, they really are."

"You're awfully cavalier for a man about to be hanged."

"And you're awfully out of sorts for a lady about to be married."

"Who wouldn't be out of sorts at learning she's going to be a widow a few hours after becoming a bride?" She turned to Lord Weymouth. "I wasn't prepared for that sort of news. Can't you do something to stop it?"

"No," Weymouth told her. "There's nothing I can do."

Dulcie shot to her feet, wobbled for an instant, then regained her equilibrium. "They don't call you the Wizard of the War Office for no reason, there must be something..."

"I'm sorry, but there isn't. I might have been able to intercede if we'd arrived before the conclusion of his inquiry, but there's nothing I can do once the judges have issued their verdict."

Dulcie clasped her trembling hands together to keep from wringing them. . "Well, there must be something I can do then. I refuse to become a widow before I'm a wife."

"You mean a countess," Rafe said.

She whirled around to face him. "I mean a *wife!* I lost my brother to the army. I don't intend to lose my husband as well. I didn't go to all this trouble to find you just to watch the army hang you. I'm not going to stand by and let it happen. All I have to do is think of something."

Rafe shot Weymouth a guarded look over Dulcie's head before turning his attention back to her. "All you have to do right now is get ready for your wedding." He placed his hands on her shoulders. Another spark of electricity shot through him at the touch. "While Lord Weymouth and I see to the legal details." He hesitated for a second. "That is if you still wish to marry me… I realize a good many young ladies would be fearful at the prospect of becoming a widow so soon. Marrying a condemned man is not for the faint of heart. If word of a lady like yourself marrying a disgraced soldier condemned to hang should reach the ton, the rumors and innuendo would be most unpleasant and you could become an object of pity and shame."

Dulcie inhaled sharply. "If word of *our* marriage and your unjust punishment reaches London, I shan't give it any credence. I'll hold my head high and will never allow myself to be shamed or pitiful. I'm neither fearful or faint-hearted. I'm a Tennant, just as my brother was, and I haven't a weak or fearful bone in my body."

"That's my little countess," Rafe leaned forward and brushed his lips against her hair. "Are you ready?"

"If you don't mind, I would like to change my gown." She tucked her chin in a sudden onset of shyness. "I brought another one more suitable for a countess."

"How long will it take?" Rafe asked.

"Not long if you'll ask Phoebe to bring my small valise."

"Your maid?"

"No," Dulcie shook her head. "My dearest friend."

~

"Oh, Dulce, is it true?" Phoebe rushed into the anteroom as soon as Rafe and Lord Weymouth left the antechamber to return to Commandant Swindell's office to conclude the legalities. She dropped Dulcie's small valise on the nearest chair and hurried to hug Dulcie.

"Is what true?" Dulcie asked.

"I was waiting in a little alcove while Lord Weymouth met with the commandant in private. I didn't mean to eavesdrop, but I overheard a sergeant and a corporal posted outside the commandant's door, talking about a Major Lord Blackburn's visitors. They were talking about us. *Us!* Is it true? Is Lord Raphael Blackburn, the Earl of Blackburn, your soldier?"

"Yes, it's true," Dulcie admitted.

"They were also saying that Lord Blackburn was convicted of striking a superior officer and disobeying orders and is scheduled to hang tomorrow. They called him 'Raging Rafe'. Is that true as well?"

"Of course not." Dulcie crossed her fingers behind her back as she lied to Phoebe for the first time since they had become friends. She didn't enjoy doing it, but she knew Phoebe well enough to know that Phoebe would never leave her alone on the island with a condemned man for a husband, no matter who the condemned man was. And Dulcie was determined to marry Raphael Blackburn no matter what. "There was another man—another major—who struck a superior officer while disobeying orders, but it wasn't Major Lord Blackburn. He's too much of a gentleman. He would never do anything to dishonor my brother's memory or Geoff's trust in him. And a gentleman like Lord Blackburn would never marry a young lady if he knew he was scheduled to hang. He would never risk sullying her good name by tying her to a condemned man."

"I'm so glad!" Phoebe heaved a sigh of relief. "I could have sworn the sergeant and the corporal said Major Blackburn."

"I was present when Lord Weymouth and Lord Blackburn were discussing what happened. The military inquiry investigating the incident found Lord Blackburn innocent of all charges." Dulcie forced herself to meet Phoebe's worried gaze without flinching. "There were two majors involved in similar incidents and there was considerable confusion about the facts of the cases because the names of the two majors were both Scottish and sounded so much alike. The investigator confused Major Blackburn with Major MacBurn and put the wrong man under house arrest." Dulcie invented the story as she went along, determined to convince Phoebe every word of it was true. "I nearly swooned at the mention of Lord Blackburn being under house arrest until I heard Lord Blackburn mention the impending execution of Major MacBurn. You must have misunderstood what you heard because Lord Weymouth made it quite clear Lord Blackburn's temporary stay here was a regrettable mistake."

Phoebe frowned, not looking entirely convinced. "I suppose it could have happened that way..."

"Of course, it could. After all, the army believed Lord Anthony Carlisle had died from the wounds he suffered at Quatre Bras. They even published his name and rank in the casualty rolls printed in *The Times*. And they were wrong. It was all a terrible mistake. Lord Temptation not only survived, he recovered well enough to marry Caroline."

"I was so worried about you and the situation," Phoebe admitted. "I want you to be happy and I could never, in good conscience, let you marry a man you only just met under those circumstances. I wouldn't be able to forever hold my peace or bear witness to your marriage. I would have to object to it."

"There's no need to worry," Dulcie assured her. "Lord Blackburn is a true gentleman. Geoff knew it and so do I."

"Then I'm thrilled for you, Dulce." Phoebe hugged her in a burst of genuine happiness. "When is the ceremony? No one has mentioned what time it's to take place."

"We'll start as soon as Lord Blackburn and Lord Weymouth finalize the marriage agreement and the transfer of my dowry. And as soon as I change my dress."

"Tell me, how did Lord Weymouth manage to get Guilford to release your dowry? I'm dying of curiosity. Did he finally give in to your pleas or to Lord Weymouth's legal arguments?" Phoebe was well aware of Guilford Tennant's reputation as a man who enjoyed being the viscount because it enabled him to spend his nights at the gaming tables and he no longer had to endure lectures about the money he lost from his older brother or his nephew. Guilford habitually spent money on his own pleasures and never spared a thought for anyone else. Especially his niece. Unless he needed to clear his gaming debts by selling his niece in marriage to the highest bidder. Dulcie was right to find the man who had been her brother's friend and marry him before Guilford chose a husband for her.

"I didn't manage to persuade Guilford to release the money Geoff promised for my dowry. And I don't know how Lord Weymouth managed it. He told me he couldn't persuade Guilford to speak with him about it, but he assured me he and his business associates had ways to manage it. Guilford has always refused to release it to me by saying I'm not old enough or responsible enough to control my own money." She sighed. "I suppose he's correct about that..."

"Oh, pish," Phoebe pronounced. "You don't while your time away drinking and losing at the gaming tables like your uncle does. Or spend money on frivolous pursuits like there's no tomorrow. You're much better with money than Guilford will ever be."

"I agree with you completely," Dulcie said. "But I'm not old enough yet. According to Papa's will, my money was to be released upon my marriage or upon my twenty-fifth birthday—whichever comes first."

"That was your father's will," Phoebe said. "What about your brother's?"

"Geoff's will had the same provisions for my dowry and inheritance. Both Papa's and Geoff's wills were more than generous to me, and I am terribly grateful that they loved me and provided for me. Unfortunately, Guilford isn't willing to part with coin on my behalf unless I agree to marry the man of his choosing."

"I shudder to think who Guilford might choose." Phoebe's words were punctuated by an involuntary shudder.

"So do I. That's why I chose Lord Blackburn as my Charlotte Society soldier. I have no idea how Lord Weymouth has managed to find a way to get the money from my uncle, but I'm grateful he did. Geoff chose Lord Blackburn for me, and I intend to marry him. It was my brother's dying wish. And Lord Blackburn agreed to fulfill it. I'm not going to let Guilford determine my future. *I'm* going to determine *my* future and I determine that it's going to be with Lord Blackburn."

"Then we'd better get on with it." Phoebe grabbed Dulcie's valise and set it on the sofa. "And get you dressed. Did you bring everything you need?"

Dulcie nodded. "I packed the green silk dress and shift, along with the necklace and earrings Caro and Tony gave me." She smiled at Phoebe. "I also packed a nightgown and wrap, and an extra shift, stockings, and extra hairpins and ribbons... and my dancing slippers." She shrugged. "I didn't know what else to bring. I couldn't bring too much since I was only supposed to be spending two nights at your aunt Augusta's."

Phoebe rummaged through Dulcie's things before removing a long white flannel nightgown. She unfolded it and frowned. "You won't be needing this." Rolling the garment into a tight roll, Phoebe stuffed it in the pocket of the traveling cloak she'd hung on a peg beside the door when they'd first arrived.

"Phoebe! It's the only nightgown I brought!"

"Tell me you didn't bring a night cap."

"You know I don't wear a night cap."

"I also know tonight is your wedding night, Dulce. And no bridegroom wants to find his bride buttoned up to her chin and hidden beneath yards of flannel."

"How do you know?" Dulcie challenged. "You've never been married before either."

"Madam Gabrielle confided it to me when I was choosing fabrics and notions for my trousseau for Freddy." Phoebe was talking about the trousseau she would have worn after her marriage to Freddy Ralston. Unfortunately, Freddy had died while serving in the cavalry on the Peninsula two months before their wedding.

"I'm sorry, Phebe. I spoke without thinking." After Freddy's death, Phoebe had left London and gone to stay with her aunt's family in the Lake District for the duration of the Season. Dulcie had feared Phoebe would never get over losing Freddy. She used to speak of him all the time, but in the past few weeks her conversations and reports at the Charlotte Society meetings had been all about her chosen soldier, a once churlish Scots Highlander named Lord Alasdair Sinclair, who had unexpectedly shown up last night at Lady Middleton's masked ball as a buccaneer and proceeded to sweep Phoebe off her feet.

"It's all right, Dulce. Freddy's at peace and so am I." Phoebe hugged her tightly. "Now, let's get you dressed for your wedding."

As Phoebe stepped away, Dulcie asked, "Phebe, what do I wear to bed if not my nightgown?"

Phoebe gave her a pointed look.

"Oh, no! I couldn't!"

"Then wear this." Phoebe held up a nearly transparent shift.

"Are you sure?"

"According to Madam Gabrielle."

"Very well then." Dulcie unhooked the two remaining frogs on her spencer, wondering how the top one had come unfastened, then slipped it off, and handed it to Phoebe, who draped it across the back of the sofa, then began unbuttoning the row of buttons down the back of Dulcie's dress.

Dulcie shimmied out of her muslin dress, removed her short stays and cotton shift, and snatched the one designed to be worn with her green silk dress and her stays out of Phoebe's hand. "Promise you'll leave me my wrapper or I'll die of mortification." Phoebe nodded as she gathered the green silk and dropped it over Dulcie's head. "I know I'm probably being vain and foolish." Dulcie glanced down at her muslin dress and velvet spencer she'd discarded. "There's nothing wrong with the muslin dress. It's new and becoming and perfectly suitable for a wedding, but I wanted to look like a countess."

"And so you shall," Phoebe pronounced as Dulcie presented her back. "We'll start the process by getting you fastened, coiffed, and adorned with jewels so you can become Blackburn's countess." She gave Dulcie a lopsided smile before handing her a pair of slippers "Here are your slippers, Countess."

Ten minutes later, Dulcie was splendidly dressed in her green silk gown, complemented by her peridot necklace and matching earrings, and ready to exchange vows with her chosen soldier.

Phoebe packed Dulcie's muslin dress, velvet spencer, and half boots in Dulcie's bag, propped her bonnet atop it, and stowed it on the bottom shelf of the table beside the door, where it would be ready for Dulcie to take with her when she and her husband left for their honeymoon. "All set?" She turned to ask Dulcie for permission to admit Lord Blackburn, Lord Weymouth, the local vicar, the Right Reverend Mister Matthew Kendrick, and Lord Blackburn's solicitor, Mr. Archibald Gunn.

Suddenly struck by the enormity of what she was about to do, Dulcie placed her hand on her heart and took a deep breath. "I may need a moment." She squeezed her eyes shut and willed the butterflies in her stomach to settle down. "I think I may be sick. Or faint again."

"No, you won't," Phoebe assured her sternly. "Just take a few breaths. There's no need for you to be afraid. You've done this before…"

Dulcie turned her startled gaze on Phoebe.

Phoebe gave her a reassuring smile. "As a *bridesmaid*. Earlier this week. You know what to do. You know the ceremony by heart. The only difference is this time, you're the bride."

"You're right, Phebe." Dulcie released the breath she'd been holding. "I do know how to do this." She smoothed her hands over her skirts one last time, checked that her necklace was positioned correctly, patted her hair into place, and nodded at Phoebe. "Let them in."

CHAPTER 6

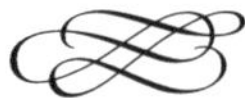

"Now join your hands, and with your hands, your hearts."
—William Shakespeare, 1564-1616

Rafe entered the antechamber, saw Dulcie standing before him in a green silk gown and matching jewels fit for a countess, and stopped dead in his tracks. Geoffrey Tennant's little sister had vanished and a beautiful young woman had taken her place. There wasn't much of her when compared to the tall, willowy blond standing beside her. Dulcie Tennant might be small of stature, but every inch of her was exquisitely displayed in the dress she was wearing. Her fashionably demure muslin frock and matching spencer was nowhere in sight. She looked like a countess any earl would be proud to call his own. She looked like the countess she was about to become. The Countess of Blackburn. *His* countess. Until death did them part…

Suddenly, Rafe was filled with regrets—not for leading the cavalry charge at Waterloo that had gotten him into this mess—but for allowing his horse to knock the colonel on his arse, instead of doing it himself. If he had to die for striking a superior officer, Rafe regretted not striking him.

Seeing the look of trepidation that crossed Rafe's face, the Earl of Weymouth ushered him into the room, allowing the other men in the party to follow them. Once they were all in, Weymouth turned to Dulcie. "Our host, Commandant Swindell, will not be joining us, Miss Tennant, so may I introduce the remainder of the wedding party?"

"Please do. The gentlemen in this room and my dear friend, Miss Osborne, are to be witnesses to the most important occasion of my life," Dulcie said. "And the fulfillment of my beloved brother's dying wish. I should very much like to make their acquaintance."

Lord Weymouth introduced them in turn, beginning with the clergyman, the Right Reverend Mister Matthew Kendrick.

Dulcie offered him her hand. "A pleasure to make your acquaintance Reverend Kendrick."

He shook her hand. "Likewise, Miss Tennant."

"The reverend will officiate," Weymouth explained. "And because you are being married by special license, which allows you to wed in any parish and at any time or place, Reverend Kendrick brought his parish register, and a duplicate, for you and Lord Blackburn and the wedding party to sign."

Dulcie gave Rafe a shy smile. "Special license?"

"Aye," Rafe replied. "There was no time for you to establish residence or have the banns read and a common license wasn't adequate to our situation, Lord Weymouth secured a special license on our behalf."

Special licenses were inordinately expensive and rather difficult to obtain. Most weddings Dulcie had attended had been sanctioned by the posting of banns or a common license. The exception was Caroline's wedding to Anthony Carlisle. They had been married by special license. The fact that she was also about to be married by special license filled Dulcie with the sense of worth she'd been lacking since Guilford and Mavis had usurped her position in the household. Perhaps she wasn't so ordinary after all. She turned to Lord

Weymouth. "Thank you, Lord Weymouth. I am in your debt once again."

"I don't consider it a debt, Miss Tennant. As it has been my very great pleasure to facilitate your nuptials," Weymouth replied with a slight bow.

"What of the marriage contracts my brother, the late viscount, negotiated with Lord Blackburn?"

"Lord Blackburn's solicitor, Mister Archibald Gunn"—he indicated the remaining gentleman—"reviewed the documents, ensured all terms were satisfactory, verified the signatures, and the amount of your dowry shortly after Lord Blackburn and your brother signed them. Mr. Gunn is here to attend to Lord Blackburn's other legal obligations and to witness the ceremony should there be any questions in the future as to its legality."

Dulcie offered the solicitor her hand. "Thank you for coming, Mister Gunn."

"My pleasure, miss." He took her hand and bowed over it.

"Now that everyone is acquainted with everyone..." Weymouth rubbed his palms together. "Shall we get on with the ceremony?"

Dulcie nodded.

Weymouth offered Dulcie his arm and gently accompanied her the few steps it took to reach Rafe's side. Leaving her beside her bridegroom, Weymouth stepped back beside Phoebe, and the reverend stepped forward to take his place in front of the bride and groom.

Opening his prayer book, Reverend Kendrick began, "Dearly beloved, we are gathered together here in the sight of God, and in the face of these witnesses, to join together this man and this woman in Holy Matrimony, which is an honorable estate, invented by God in the time of man's innocency, signifying unto us the mystical union that is betwixt Christ and his church, which holy estate Christ adorned and beautified with his presence, and first miracle that he wrought in Cana of Galilee..."

He turned first to Dulcie, then to Rafe. "I require and charge you both as you will answer at the dreadful day of judgment, when the secrets of all hearts shall be disclosed, that if either of you know any impediment why you may not be lawfully joined together in Matrimony, ye do now confess it."

Standing beside her, Rafe heard Dulcie's quick intake of breath, then waited, silently counting until she released it when he failed to confess his impediment to the marriage. He gazed at Dulcie's profile as she focused her whole attention on the words the clergyman was repeating. Rafe hadn't expected to have to fulfill his promise to Geoff one day before he was scheduled to hang. He had thought he'd have more time. The fact that he would hang in the morning was an impediment, but not enough of one to leave Dulcie unmarried and unprotected.

Rafe had decided long ago that five and thirty was a good age to marry. It was old enough to have experienced more than a single Grand Tour of Europe following matriculation from university. And old enough to have fallen in love at least once and to have had his heart broken. It was also old enough to understand the importance of family, tradition, and duty, and to have sown plenty of wild oats. His father had married at thirty-five and Rafe had expected to do the same.

He didn't regret promising to marry Geoff Tennant's younger sister. She was a tiny, little thing, but there was nothing childish about her. She was a woman grown. And beautiful. Rafe hadn't realized just how beautiful until he saw her in her wedding dress.

A corner of his mouth turned up in a half-smile as he recalled the pre-dawn hours of a morning in Spain as he and Geoff Tennant had led their cavalry unit back to camp after a midnight patrol and Geoff had talked of looking forward to introducing Rafe to his baby sister. Geoff had assured Rafe that he and Dulcie would get on quite well. Rafe hadn't been nearly as certain courting his best friend's baby sister was a good idea. But Geoff had been adamant. He'd even written to his father to ask him not to accept any offers of marriage for Dulcie until Geoff returned home and had the opportunity to introduce her to his friend, the seventh Earl of Blackburn. Six months later, Geoff had returned home to bury his father and mother, who had died during a freak storm while yachting. Geoff hadn't planned to return to Spain, but he'd been persuaded to return to the unit when Rafe suffered minor injuries and his second had been seriously wounded in battle. Geoff had returned to Spain to fulfill his obligation to the unit, Raphael Blackburn, and to the current Duke of Wellington. Four months after returning to the unit, Geoff had been ambushed and mortally wounded. He died a fortnight later.

Now, Rafe was standing beside Geoff's baby sister, plighting his troth to her, promising to protect her, knowing full well his protection would end a few moments after dawn. And he didn't regret anything, except not being able to spend more time with her.

"Raphael Simon John Blackburn, seventh Earl of Blackburn, twelfth Viscount Blackburn, wilt thou have this woman to thy wedded wife, to live together after God's ordinance in the holy estate of Matrimony? Wilt thou love her, comfort her, honor and keep her in sickness and in health; and forsaking all others, keep thee only unto her, so long as ye both shall live?"

"I will," Rafe vowed in a firm voice, just loud enough for Archibald Gunn, who was deaf in one ear, to hear. Sparing a brief glance for his long-time solicitor, Rafe saw Archie nod his approval.

"Dulcinea Marjorie Rose Tennant, wilt thou have this man to thy wedded husband, to live together after God's ordinance in the holy estate of Matrimony? Wilt thou obey him, love him, comfort him, honor and keep him in sickness and in health, and forsaking all others, keep thee only unto him, so long as ye both shall live?"

Dulcie's eyes shimmered with unshed tears as she gazed up at Rafe, her voice low and husky, as she pledged her vows to him. "I will."

"Let us pray."

Dulcie bowed her head, but she didn't close her eyes. Instead, she stole a sidelong look at Rafe from beneath her lashes as he stood with his head lowered and his eyes closed. He couldn't see it, but she smiled at him anyway. Simply because she wanted to. Raphael Blackburn didn't know her. Or anything about her except what her brother might have told him. Rafe had only just met her. He certainly didn't love her. Or even know if he liked her. He certainly hadn't planned to marry her. But he had proven himself to be a loyal friend and a man of honor. He had given his word to her brother and had signed his name on the marriage contracts, making everything legal and proper. And perhaps his most endearing trait was his determination to do everything in his power to protect her.

For as long as their marriage lasted, until death parted them, Raphael Simon John Blackburn, seventh Earl of Blackburn, was hers for the keeping. Although she had been an obedient child, Dulcie had found it difficult to blindly obey Guilford and Mavis since they had become her guardians. And in truth, she had also struggled to obey Geoff at times. Yet she had promised she would do her best to obey her husband and honor his wishes. Most of all, Dulcie was determined to make enough memories with him during their time together to last her a lifetime. However long or however brief their life together, Raphael Blackburn would never have cause to regret his decision to give her his name.

Reverend Kendrick concluded his prayer and focused his gaze on Raphael. "Lord Blackburn, face your bride and repeat after me." The minister spoke the vows and Rafe repeated them.

"I, Raphael, take thee, Dulcinea, to my wedded wife, to have and to hold from this day forward, for better for worse, for richer for poorer, in sickness and in health, to love and to cherish, till death us do part, according to God's holy ordinance; and thereto I plight thee my troth."

The reverend turned to Dulcie. "Miss Tennant, face your groom and repeat after me."

Dulcie's gaze never left Rafe's as she repeated her vows to him.

The clergyman cleared his throat before asking Rafe. "Have you a ring?"

Rafe glanced at Lord Weymouth.

Reaching into his jacket pocket, the Earl of Weymouth withdrew a slim gold band and handed it to the minister.

Having participated in Caroline and Tony's wedding earlier in the week, Dulcie prepared for the next part of the ceremony by removing her gloves and handing them to Phoebe.

The reverend held the gold band between his fingers as he

explained the significance of the wedding band in the marriage ceremony. He finished with another prayer, then presented the ring to Rafe. "Take her left hand in yours."

Rafe took Dulcie's left hand, noticing as he did so how small, and fragile her hand looked in his.

"Repeat after me," the reverend said. "And place the ring on her finger."

Rafe repeated the vows. "With this Ring, I thee wed, with my body I thee worship, and with all my worldly goods I thee endow in the Name of the Father, and of the Son, and of the Holy Ghost. Amen." He slipped the slim gold band onto her ring finger.

Fresh tears welled up in Dulcie's eyes as she gazed at the shiny, gold band encircling her ring finger.

Reverend Kendrick led them in the Lord's Prayer, then joined Rafe's and Dulcie's right hands together and prayed the marriage prayer, ending with the words, "Those whom God hath joined together let no man put asunder."

Dulcie and Raphael Blackburn were husband and wife.

After the register had been signed by all appropriate parties, they celebrated with champagne and wedding cake, though how or where Lord Weymouth had managed to procure them was a mystery to Dulcie. The Earl of Weymouth truly was the Wizard of the War Office. A month ago, Dulcie had despaired of ever finding Lord Blackburn and on this day, she had married him. And Lord Weymouth had made it all possible.

Before she knew it, the small celebration was at an end. The minister congratulated them on their wedding, then produced a second parish register and instructed Dulcie to sign the name Lord Weymouth had instructed her to use while on the island. Miss Susan Brown. Phoebe signed as Miss Anne Hall and the others signed their true names. The reverend wished them well and promised to pray for them both. Mr. Gunn stayed long enough to offer his felicitations to the new Lady Blackburn before asking Rafe for a private moment so that he might sign the last of the legal documents needed to finalize his will.

Rafe smiled at Dulcie. "If you'll excuse me for a few moments, my dear, I must attend to this business so Archie can make his way back to his lodging house for the night."

"Of course," Dulcie said. "I need to say goodbye to Phoebe and Lord Weymouth before they leave." She turned to Mr. Gunn and offered him her hand. "Thank you for sharing this day with us, Mr. Gunn. I'm honored by your presence."

"The honor is mine, Lady Blackburn," Gunn replied as he bowed over her hand. "May I offer you my sincere felicitations on your wedding?"

Dulcie beamed at the old man. "Thank you once again, Mr. Gunn." Dulcie was still smiling as she left to join Phoebe and the Earl of Weymouth.

~

"I DON'T HAVE ENOUGH WORDS TO THANK YOU FOR AGREEING TO TRAVEL all this way to come to my aid, Archie." Rafe shook hands with the man who had been his family's solicitor for as long as he could remember. "Or express my gratitude for all you've done for me—past and present."

"It's been a privilege, sir," Archibald Gunn replied. "I only wish I could have done more to put an end to this travesty of justice."

"You did everything you could, Archie. The die was cast when the inquiry ignored the circumstances surrounding the incident."

"Including the testimony of the witnesses who joined your charge to save the artillerymen. None of whom faced charges or were cashiered from the army. And the fact that you received a commendation for bravery in battle from Lord Wellington and the Prince Regent as well as commendations from General Blücher and the King of Prussia."

"No matter," Rafe told him. "My fate was sealed when I made a mortal enemy of the colonel. He has powerful allies."

"As I said, sir, it has been my very great privilege to have served you and your father and grandfather before you."

"And I hope young Simon to follow," Rafe reminded him.

He nodded. "Of course, sir."

"He'll need your guidance. I was one and twenty when I inherited. Simon has just turned nine. That means he'll inherit at ten." Rafe sighed. "I worry that he's so young, but I know you will guide him in his duty as you so wisely and skillfully did for me after my father's death. And if you're agreeable to the task, I would consider it a very great favor if you would agree to accompany Lady Blackburn back to London after my sentence is carried out tomorrow morning."

Gunn's eyes clouded. "I'm happy to do it, sir."

"Please see that the instructions I gave you for the only unentailed property I own in London are carried out. The deed is in the safe at Blackburn Abbey. The same goes for my unentailed property in Edinburgh. That deed and my instructions for the disposition of it are also in the safe at the Abbey. If you have any questions I haven't answered, consult with Lord Weymouth. I've made him aware of my plans."

"I'll take care of it, sir. Your wishes will be followed to the letter."

"Thank you, once again, Archie. I'll rest easy knowing that." Rafe's voice trembled ever so slightly as he said a final goodbye to his old friend. "Now, get some rest. Tomorrow will be a long day for you. And for Lady Blackburn." Rafe scanned the room until he located Dulcie still in conversation with Weymouth and her friend, Phoebe.

Yes, tomorrow would be a very long day for Archie and for Dulcie. And a very brief day for him.

"I'm going to miss you so much." Phoebe sucked in a breath to keep from crying when she hugged Dulcie. "But I'm very happy for you. A day ago, we were getting dressed for Lady Middleton's ball and today, you've become a married woman. The Countess of Blackburn, no less." Phoebe released Dulcie, then stepped back and curtseyed to her. "Lady Blackburn."

Dulcie took her by the hand and pulled Phoebe out of the curtsey. "Only on formal occasions," Dulcie told her. "And then, the briefest of all possible curtseys will do. We've been through too much together—the deaths of my parents, your fiancé, Freddy, and my brother, Geoff—and have been the dearest of friends for too long to let silly formalities get in the way." She smiled up at Phoebe through a sheen of unshed tears. "And should I ever get too full of my own importance as the Countess of Blackburn, I shall rely on my best friends to mock me soundly for it."

Phoebe laughed. "All we have to do is pay a visit to Caro. She may prefer to use her new title of Countess of Carlisle, but she's still the Marchioness of Blessing in her own right. We will both curtsey to her."

"As do I," Weymouth reminded them. "My goddaughter outranks me. As does my eldest son."

Dulcie met Lord Weymouth's gaze. "I don't think I truly understood the enormity of what I've done until Phoebe called me Lady Blackburn. Even after everything I've learned and everything you told me, part of me still believed I would return to London with you and Phoebe. But I'm *married* now, and my place is here by my husband's side. I won't be returning to London with you. Lord Weymouth, how are we going to explain my absence?"

"Lady Nesbitt knows you and Miss Osborne left with me in order to facilitate your clandestine marriage. She's agreed to send a message to your guardian and his wife informing them that you've come down with a case of the ague following Lady Middleton's ball. Most likely caused by becoming overheated during the dancing amid the crush of people and then chilled in the cool night air afterwards. She will tell them she's confined you to bed until the physician says otherwise."

"Do you think they'll believe it? What if they try to see me while I'm supposed to be at Lady Nesbitt's?" Dulcie asked. "I should hate for Phoebe and Lady Nesbitt to have trouble from my uncle."

Phoebe answered before Lord Weymouth could. "Dulce, you know better than that. If Mavis thinks you're ill, she won't come near you. She'll be relieved that you're in Aunt Augusta's house instead of yours. And Guilford will probably be hoping your fever and chills turn into a fatal case of pleurisy."

Weymouth smiled. "I'd say Miss Osborne has pegged the situation correctly. And if by some miracle your aunt and uncle should grow concerned about you, we'll find a way to deter their interest." He took her hand and brushed his lips against it. "Miss Tennant, it has been my very great pleasure to assist you in becoming Lady Blackburn. Now, not to worry. Everything will be all right. I'll see Miss Osborne back to London while you and your husband see to your honeymoon." He glanced from Phoebe to Dulcie and back again. "If you ladies will excuse me, I need a moment to say goodbye to Lord Blackburn and speak with his solicitor and to the commandant before we depart."

"Of course," Dulcie replied.

Phoebe waited until Lord Weymouth had left the room before she spoke. "I can't believe it. Both of my best friends are married and I..."

"Are madly in love with a Scotsman of your own," Dulcie finished for her.

"I am," Phoebe admitted, bravely lifting her chin. "But sadly, he's not madly in love with me."

"Are you sure of that?" Dulcie asked.

"Quite sure," Phoebe said. "Alasdair is still in love with his dead wife."

"The man who rushed me through two dances last night so he could meet his obligation and be free to dance another dance with *you* seemed very much engaged with the living," Dulcie suggested. "Not the dead."

"It may have seemed that way last night. But he let me go this morning. He let me walk out of his life and he never gave a single thought to coming after me."

"Then he'll regret it," Dulcie said with all of the conviction her friend was lacking. "If not today, then tomorrow. Because he couldn't keep his eyes off you last night."

Phoebe looked stunned.

"And, Phebe, when he comes after you, do me a favor and forgive him for taking so long to regain his senses," Dulcie said.

"Dulce..."

"I know something happened between you last night," Dulcie told her. "And I know you had been crying when you got home."

"I…"

"Don't bother to tell me otherwise." Dulcie gave her a shrewd look. "Your eyes are still red and puffy."

"I was up all night," Phoebe reminded her.

"Very well then. We won't argue about it. But promise me one thing, Phebe…"

"Anything."

"Promise me you'll give that stubborn Scotsman a chance to prove he loves you."

Phoebe crossed her heart. "I promise. Now," she drawled, "tell me, just when did you become so wise when it comes to matters of the heart?"

Dulcie's mouth turned up at the corners in a tremulous smile. *If only Phoebe knew how unwise she'd been to offer her heart to a man destined for the gallows in a few short hours. If only Phoebe knew…* Fighting back her fears, she managed a regal sniff that made Phoebe break into a smile of her own. "It came with the title."

CHAPTER 7

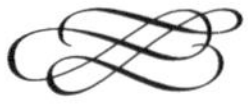

"This is the night
That either makes me or fordoes me quite."
—William Shakespeare, 1564-1616

"Dulcie."

Dulcie jumped and clapped a hand to her heart when Rafe spoke close to her ear. "Oh! I didn't realize you had returned."

"I didn't want to intrude while you were bidding your friend good-bye." He also didn't want her to know that he had been watching her as she gazed pensively at the door long after her friend had departed with the Earl of Weymouth. He wasn't certain if she even realized the rest of the wedding party had followed suit, leaving them alone.

The commandant opened the door to the antechamber. "Major Lord Blackburn."

Recognizing the impatience in Commandant Swindell's voice, Rafe shot him a look.

Ignoring Rafe's warning look, the commandant barked, "The

coach is here. Sergeant Wilson and Corporal Peavey are waiting to accompany you to your cottage."

"Dulcie, it's time to go," Rafe said, biting back a frustrated sigh. He had hoped to have more time to prepare her for their wedding night.

Just as he had feared, Dulcie's big, brown eyes widened in alarm. "I thought we were staying here. I thought you were confined to quarters.

"My quarters aren't suitable for a lady." Rafe managed a lopsided smile. His quarters weren't suitable for a lord either. They weren't suitable for anything except mice and other vermin, but Rafe had never bothered to complain. He'd always understood his quarters were temporary. He would be leaving one way or the other depending on which way the political winds were blowing. "Commandant Swindell has graciously granted me a brief reprieve. And Lord Weymouth took the liberty of securing a private cottage for us. We're going there now. Where's your valise?" Rafe asked.

"Phoebe put it on the shelf beneath that table by the door along with my bonnet." Her voice cracked on her friend's name, but Dulcie managed to maintain her composure as she pointed to the table beside the door.

Rafe collected her bag and bonnet and brought them back to Dulcie. He studied her thin silk gown with its cap sleeves and the creamy flesh visible above the scooped neckline. "Do you have a wrap to wear? It's misting rain again."

"I have a hooded cape in my bag."

Rafe removed her cape from the valise, draped it over her shoulders, and fastened it before carefully pulling her hood over the thick russet curls artfully piled atop her head. Carrying her valise and bonnet, Rafe gently rested his other hand against the small of her back.

Dulcie gave an involuntary shiver.

"Cold?" Rafe asked.

"No," she admitted, stealing a shy look up at him.

Rafe tried not to smile. He had suspected it was a shiver of awareness, not cold, because he had felt the same current shudder through his own body. He escorted her to the door, pausing to offer his hand to the waiting commandant. "Thank you, Commandant. I appreciate this consideration on behalf of my bride."

Commandant Swindell sneered down at Rafe's hand for a long moment before he deigned to shake it. "I was advised by the Earl of Weymouth and your solicitor that you have certain rights as a peer, Major Lord Blackburn. A wedding night is one of them."

Rafe acknowledged the commandant's meaning with a brisk nod. "Understood, Sir."

"You gave me your word, Major," Swindell reminded him, making no secret of the fact that he resented the way the Earl of Weymouth had used his considerable influence and power to gain concessions for a condemned man. "I expect you to be there when Sergeant Wilson and Corporal Peavey are relieved."

"I wouldn't be much of a man if I abandoned my bride on our wedding night in order to save myself, Commandant," Rafe said.

Dulcie sucked in a breath.

"Other men have," the commandant retorted.

"I'm not other men." Rafe looked Swindell in the eye. "I'm a man of my word. When I give it, it means something. And I gave Lord Weymouth my word." Placing his arm around Dulcie's back, Rafe guided her past the commandant and out the front door. As he helped her into the coach, he did not spare a glance for the soldiers waiting beside it.

Dulcie didn't speak until the coach started rolling. "I don't understand. What happened to the commandant? He was most cordial when Lord Weymouth introduced us. He gave me the use of his antechamber for a private meeting with you, allowed us to use the room for our wedding even though he chose not to attend. I thought he was a most congenial host."

"He didn't choose not to attend the wedding," Rafe said. "He wasn't invited."

"Why not?"

"Because I don't like him and Weymouth doesn't trust him."

"Oh."

"He was only a most congenial host until all the people he needed to impress left."

"You mean…" she began.

He nodded. "Yes. Weymouth, Miss Osborne, Archie Gunn, and the minister."

"Lord Weymouth most of all," Dulcie concluded. "Lord Weymouth does have a way of getting things done despite the obstacles." She gazed up at her new husband. "I suppose Commandant Swindell was opposed to me and to our wedding?"

Rafe shook his head. "I don't believe he opposed either."

"So…it's only you he opposes."

"And possibly Lord Weymouth at this point," Rafe admitted. "Since Weymouth was the one who requisitioned his office and antechamber on behalf of the War Office. But I've been a thorn in his side longer."

"How long?"

"Since the day I arrived at the garrison. The commandant is regular army. Being a soldier is his profession, and as far as he's concerned I'm a dilettante, an earl playing at being a soldier. He outranks me as a military man, but I outrank him in life by a stroke of good fortune by having been born into the peerage. And while Commandant Swindell was stuck on the Isle of Wight commanding a garrison of prisoners, other men were making names for themselves on the battlefield."

"Men like you," Dulcie said.

"And Geoff."

Dulcie's regard for her new husband deepened when he included her brother in that special group of men, recognizing that Geoff had been awarded an army gold medal for his gallantry in saving the men in his patrol following the ambush where he was mortally wounded. Captain Geoffrey Tennant had been posthumously awarded a battlefield promotion to major and the army gold medal. The letter confirming his promotion to major, and the gold medal, had been sent to Dulcie and were two of her most cherished possessions.

"They don't confer honors or give medals to the commandants of prisoner garrisons," Rafe explained.

She smiled at Rafe. "I suppose it's been helpful for you to understand why the commandant feels the way he feels."

"It wasn't helpful at all." Rafe returned her smile. "When I first arrived, I didn't understand why Swindell exhibited an inordinate animus towards me. Other than the fact that I was detained until such time when I would face a court of military inquiry to investigate the charges against me." He made a wry face. "I could understand a certain amount of animosity towards me for that. Commandants of military garrisons that house military prisoners naturally frown upon having an officer join the population."

"I suppose that's understandable," Dulcie said. "But I should think an officer and a gentleman—especially a noble gentleman—should be considered innocent of those charges unless proven guilty."

"I agree," Rafe said. "But it was my commanding officer's word against mine and he is surrounded by powerful allies and hopeful junior officers. And apparently a friend or an ally in the commandant."

"Do you think that's why you were posted here?"

"I do," Rafe told her. "There's no other explanation for it. Everything was preordained. I didn't receive any orders for the Isle of Wight. I wasn't posted here. I was brought here in chains. Most men in my position are temporarily confined to quarters or placed under guard in their private lodgings. I'd never met Swindell. Never heard his name mentioned, and as far as I know, I'd never caused him any harm. Yet his animosity towards me was apparent from the moment I arrived."

"How long have you been here?"

He thought for a moment. "I was brought here three days before my term of service in the cavalry expired on the thirty-first of July, eighteen hundred, fifteen."

"That was ten months ago." Frowning, Dulcie bit her bottom lip.

The unconscious gesture caught Rafe's attention. Her lips were plump, beautifully shaped, like the rosy-red lips carefully painted on the faces of porcelain dolls. The first word that came to mind was kissable. Rafe was suddenly obsessed with the idea of kissing them.

Obsessed with the idea of covering her mouth with his own and soothing the abrasions on her lower lip she'd made with her teeth.

Feeling the heat of his gaze, Dulcie looked up and caught him staring at her. "What is it? Have I cake crumbs from our wedding cake in the corner of my mouth? My friends will tell you that I have a terrible weakness for sweets. I only ate one slice of cake today, but I generally make a pig of myself. Phoebe and Caroline joke that I'll eat anything if it's coated in sugar icing." She ran her tongue over her lips, touching each corner with the tip of it, searching for cake crumbs.

That innocent gesture was nearly his undoing as Rafe realized she might be Geoff's little sister and a virtual stranger, but she was also his wife. And wearing his ring. She hadn't pulled on her gloves for the short walk to the coach and the thin gold band Weymouth had purchased for Rafe to give to her shone like a beacon on the fourth finger of her left hand. Rafe was reminded that they had exchanged vows. He'd plighted his troth and pledged to worship her with his body. And she'd done the same. Rafe didn't just want to soothe the abrasion on his bride's lower lip. He wanted to taste her, wanted to trace a path along her luscious lips with his tongue and tease and tempt while he explored every bit of her mouth and beyond.

"Lord Blackburn, why are you staring at me like that?"

He continued to stare at her.

"Lord Blackburn…"

"Rafe," he whispered as he closed the distance between her lips and his.

"What are you doing?"

"I'm sealing our deal."

"I don't understand," she began.

"Hasn't anyone ever kissed you?" he asked when his lips were a mere breath away from hers.

"No."

"Then allow me, your husband, to be the first…"

CHAPTER 8

"Make me immortal with a kiss."
—Christopher Marlowe, 1564-1593

Dulcie closed her eyes and puckered her lips in anticipation of her first kiss. The first touch of her husband's lips to hers. His kiss wasn't the quick peck on her lips she'd received from her mother and father when they greeted her in the mornings and visited the nursery each evening to tuck her into bed. Or the platonic brotherly kisses Geoff had given her to heal her childish scrapes and heartaches.

Raphael Blackburn's kiss was a new and thrilling experience.

The sensation was like nothing she had ever felt. Or had ever expected to feel. Warmth spread throughout her body as her bridegroom covered her mouth with his own. The feverish heat growing within her body had nothing to do with her thick velvet cloak or the close confines of the coach and everything to do with *him*. The surge of pleasure that swept through her took her by surprise and made it all but impossible for her to think of anything except the feel of Rafe close beside her—and the way his lips felt moving against hers.

He took her breath away, then gave it back to her in the most incredible way possible.

Dulcie sighed. She'd rarely engaged in conversation with unmarried men without a chaperone looking on. During the Season, the dance floor afforded a snippet of privacy now and then with the gentlemen who partnered her in the dances, but there had been no stolen kisses in dark alcoves or eager embraces during leisurely moonlit strolls in her hosts' gardens. The conversation she'd had with Lord Sinclair at Lady Middleton's ball last night had been the longest unchaperoned conversation she'd had with an eligible man in years. And although he was still unmarried, Lord Sinclair was Phoebe's choice, and had only danced with wallflowers like Dulcie to garner a second dance with Phoebe. Her brief exchange with Phoebe's masked Scottish buccaneer had begun with polite pleasantries and ended with her warning him to preserve his toes and refrain from dancing more than one dance with Serenity Blakenheath, who was a notoriously bad dancer.

She certainly hadn't exchanged witticisms and serious conversation with Lord Sinclair the way she had just done with Rafe. She'd never engaged in any manner of flirtation or verbal sparring with her dancing partners or any member of the opposite sex except her brother. And Geoff had been gone so long, she thought she had forgotten how. But something about Raphael Blackburn invited her to indulge. Sparring with him filled her with renewed self-confidence. He made her feel bolder and braver than she had felt in anyone's company except Phoebe's and Caroline's.

His kiss created a wonderful sort of tension in her, a delightful anticipation of something more. He fascinated her. Intrigued her. Excited her.

Rafe had awakened a hidden side of her, a side filled with a wild yearning for what could be. A thrilling, adventurous side that she'd never known existed. Never considered. Never thought possible. For her.

But raphael Blackburn, a tall, broad-shouldered, slim hipped, handsome man had just broadened her horizons. He might be a stranger, but he was her husband and entitled to take whatever he wanted from her. And Dulcie was increasingly inclined to give him whatever he wanted. It was part of their bargain. He'd kept his word to her brother and married her, sight unseen. He was permitted to use her body however he chose. That was the way arranged marriages worked. He gave her his name and title, pin money, and a home, and she gave him her dowry, her loyalty, her body, and an heir.

But she hadn't expected him to give pleasure rather than take it.

He was a stranger with absolute jurisdiction over her, yet he made her feel safe and beautiful. She, who hadn't felt safe since her brother had died in Spain and Guilford and Mavis had moved into her home and become her legal guardians, felt completely safe in his company. And when he kissed her and held her in his arms, she felt beautiful.

Dulcie knew she was attractive, even passably pretty, but she was a petite, brown-eyed, auburn-haired girl with a mass of unruly curls, and a low, husky voice in a world where tall, fair-haired, blue-eyed beauties with dulcet-toned voices were perpetually in vogue.

She would never be one of the *Incomparable Beauties* of the London Season. She didn't turn men's heads when she walked down the street or inspire them to pen romantic sonnets and although the dowry Geoffrey had put away for her was generous, she wasn't part of a powerful family with vast tracts of land, a great fortune, or a king's ransom in family jewels behind it. The title and the wealth her father had inherited had been modest, but he had skillfully increased their wealth through sound investments and devoted stewardship to the land. Her father had passed a greater wealth on to her brother to manage. But that wealth was rapidly diminishing in the hands of her uncle.

No one would consider her a great beauty or a great heiress, but when Rafe kissed her, she felt as if she were both. When he touched her, Dulcie became an *Incomparable.*

Wrapping her arms around his neck, she pulled him closer, loving the scrape of his unshaven face against hers, loving the hunger in his kisses.

~

Rafe responded to his new wife's urging by obliging her. He deepened his kiss, gently tracing the abrasion on her bottom lip with the tip of his tongue, before teasing the seam of her lips with it until she opened them and allowed him inside.

He rewarded her decision by raking his tongue inside her mouth. Dulcie had told him the truth. No man had ever kissed her. She was a complete innocent in the ways of seduction. But she was learning. Rafe groaned when she tentatively touched her tongue to his. The gesture sent a spark like a bolt of lightning surging through him. After initially pursing her lips like a child expecting a quick, dry peck, she'd progressed from allowing him deeper intimacy to demanding it. Rafe knew he was kissing a woman who had never been kissed the way he was kissing her—a woman who had never been kissed at all. He knew he should slow down and give her time to accustom herself to his kisses, knew he should pull away and end the kiss before he forgot she was an innocent and only remembered that they were married and that she was his for the taking.

It was the gentlemanly thing to do. And Rafe was an officer and a gentleman, but he couldn't seem to make himself do what he knew to be the proper thing to do. His sense of right and wrong failed him. Everything in him told him to end the kiss, apologize for his ungentlemanly behavior, and put some distance between them. But he was enthralled by the sensations his innocent bride had evoked. Rafe didn't want to end their kiss or put distance between them. He couldn't. He wasn't strong enough or disciplined enough to deny himself what he wanted any more than he could deny himself his next heartbeat. So Rafe took it farther, kissing her for all he was worth, making love to her mouth, showing her how a man kissed a woman he desired. Showing her how *he* kissed the woman he desired…

~

Overwhelmed by the onslaught of emotions, Dulcie feared her body wouldn't be able to contain the myriad of wondrous feelings he created inside her. She feared she might splinter into a thousand pieces and fly away or that she might faint from the sheer pleasure his kisses gave her and make a cake of herself for the second time in one day. For the second time in her life. She was out of her depth, over her head, on the verge of drowning in pure joy, and completely captivated. She had never experienced the intense tug of yearning he made her feel. She wasn't sure she'd ever been aware that it existed except in books. She knew she hadn't begun to understand its power. Until this moment.

Dulcie didn't know where it would lead. She only knew she never wanted it to end.

Suddenly, kissing him wasn't enough. Even as she met him stroke for stroke, even as she learned the taste and touch of him, even as her tongue tangled with his, she wanted more. More of him. More of everything he made her feel. More of everything he had to teach. Everything he had to share... She whimpered, giving voice to her need, and he abruptly broke the kiss.

Dulcie plummeted back to earth at his sudden desertion. She touched her fingers to her swollen lips. *A man had finally kissed her. Her husband had kissed her. And it was the most amazing feeling of her life because he kissed her as if she were the most beautiful and desirable woman in the world.* "Why did you stop?"

Rafe took a deep breath, giving them both time to recover from their feverishly spiraling desires before he released her. "I had to." His voice was deeper and his Scottish burr more pronounced than before.

"Why?" she asked, still pressed against his coat, still clinging to his neck.

"The coach has stopped," he said. "We've arrived at the cottage."

The cottage Lord Weymouth had rented for them was a mile or so away from the garrison's Cumberland barracks on a picturesque street with a view of the harbor. It was a traditional white-washed, cobblestone cottage crowned by a slate roof. The arched front door in the center of the ground floor was painted a brilliant royal blue and flanked by tall mullion-paned windows on either side, framed by heavy wooden shutters to keep the sea at bay during storms. A stone walkway led from the street through a small garden to the front door.

"It looks like a cottage in a fairytale!" Dulcie exclaimed as Rafe handed her down from the coach. "I can't wait to see the inside."

She would have hurried forward to investigate, but Rafe halted her by keeping his hand on her waist. Dulcie glanced up at him. *"Lord Blackburn?"*

Rafe stood on the cobblestone walkway, gazing up at the roof. His bride was right. It did resemble a fairytale cottage. There were masses of flowers growing along the low stone wall enclosing the front garden and topiary trees in massive stone pots beside the front door. The cottage bore such a strong resemblance to the pictures found in storybooks that it might have been constructed using the illustrations in *The Children's and Household Tales by the Brothers Grimm*. Looking at it, Rafe was immediately reminded of the architecture of the little house Hansel and Gretel had stumbled upon in the forest. The features that delighted Dulcie gave Rafe a measure of concern.

The cottage was perfectly suited to someone of Dulcie's size, but he was considerably taller and broad-shouldered. His room in the Cumberland barracks was small, but Rafe was willing to bet it was larger than any room in the cottage. It looked perfectly suitable for small folks, but entirely unsuitable for a giant. Rafe couldn't help but wonder if he would even be able to fit through the door, and if he did, would he be able to stand upright without banging his head against exposed beams? And what of the furniture? Any chair built for a diminutive person would be entirely too small for him. Would the chairs support a fully grown man who stood five inches over six feet and weighed close to fourteen stone? And what about the bed? Would it be made for tiny folk, too?

"Rafe? What's wrong? Aren't we going inside?"

Realizing he was standing in the center of the path staring at the house, he glanced down at Dulcie. "We are. But not before we observe the traditions."

Dulcie wrinkled her brow in puzzlement. "Traditions?"

"I believe it's customary for the groom to carry his bride over the threshold..."

Dulcie's cheeks took on a rosy hue as she beamed up at him. "I believe you're correct."

"Shall we, Lady Blackburn?" He presented her with a formal bow.

"My pleasure, Lord Blackburn." Her brown eyes were sparkling as she dropped into a brief curtsey.

Bending low, Rafe scooped her into his arms, then turned to his guards. "Corporal Peavey, if you would kindly follow with milady's things." He didn't wait for a response from the corporal before starting for the white, arched, front gate connecting the stone walls.

"You're in charge of gate latches and doors," he murmured to Dulcie as they reached the gate. "My hands are full."

"Of me." Dulcie giggled, a deep, throaty giggle that sent ripples of awareness through Rafe as he pretended to drop her when he bent low enough for her to unlatch the gate.

"There it is," he said.

"What?" Dulcie asked.

"The lovely, musical tones I heard when you first spoke to me."

"You are unique in your assessment of my voice," she said softly. "I like that about you."

"I am unique in many ways, my lady. You've only uncovered one of them." He flashed his most devastating smile at her. "You'll like me for those qualities, too."

Dulcie noted that he had perfectly straight teeth, except for one front lower tooth that was crooked and slightly out of line with the others. A small unremarkable imperfection. She made note of the solitary dimple on the right side of his mouth and the way the corners of his dark brown eyes crinkled when he smiled. Dulcie moistened her lips with the tip of her tongue. Her husband was wrong. In the time it had taken him to flash his devastatingly handsome smile, she had uncovered three more traits that made him unique.

Dulcie delighted in those discoveries and looked forward to uncovering more. Because every discovery would soon become a treasured memory, like perfect blooms from bouquets she'd received for special occasions, flowers she pressed between the pages of the heavy Greek and Latin volumes in the library at Tennant House. And the newspaper clippings that marked the course of the war in the Peninsula while Geoff was serving there, and the pages of casualty lists she'd clipped and pasted in her albums to memorialize family, friends, and acquaintances who had been lost in the war. Casualty lists she'd perused time and time again while searching for the name of Geoff's close friend and fellow cavalry officer, Raphael, seventh Earl of Blackburn. The man who had promised to marry her. The man who had kept that promise today.

Rafe carried her through the gate and up two steps to the blue front door before bending at the knees once again.

"Do you have the key?" Dulcie asked.

"The landlord promised Lord Weymouth it would be unlocked."

Dulcie reached out and turned the glass doorknob. "The landlord kept his promise," she said as she pushed the door open.

Rafe ducked to keep from braining himself on the lintel and inhaled the soft, musky, floral scent of soap and Dulcie. The fragrance ignited tiny sparks of awareness throughout his body and Rafe knew the scent of her would be permanently locked in his memory. He would forever recognize it as hers. It belonged to Dulcie Tennant. His wife. Turning sideways, Rafe maneuvered them through the doorway with bare inches to spare. The leather slipper on Dulcie's left foot bumped against the door frame as he carried her over the threshold. "Welcome to your honeymoon cottage, Lady Blackburn."

"Welcome to *our* honeymoon cottage, Lord Blackburn," Dulcie murmured, then tightened her hold around his neck and pressed her lips against his.

Rafe didn't set Dulcie on her feet, but held her close as he straightened to his full height. He had been kissed by women more skilled in the art of kissing, but he'd never been kissed by a woman with more genuine emotion or sheer wonder in her kiss. He remembered his first kiss with the Queen of the Harvest at the Autumn Festival. It had been magical. No one he'd ever kissed had made him feel the way his first kiss made him feel. Until now. And the woman kissing him wasn't experienced in the art. She wasn't Queen of the Harvest, an actress, a bar maid, a widow, an accomplished courtesan, or any of the other women he'd kissed. She was a mere slip of a girl—the younger sister of his close friend—who didn't know enough about kissing to keep her heart out of it. He was her husband and her first kiss and in a few short hours he was going to be her first heartbreak. And there was nothing he could do about it. And Rafe knew that soon he would never be able to feel anything again. Certainly not the kiss of his bride, whose experimentation and curiosity were driving him mad. So Raphael Blackburn ignored his nobler self and did what he wanted to do. He allowed her to kiss him all she wanted.

"I brought your lady's things, Major. Where do you want me to… Oh!"

Rafe turned toward the front door and saw Corporal Peavey standing in the opening with Dulcie's valise and bonnet in one hand and a food hamper in the other.

"Lord Blackburn," Dulcie murmured in his ear. "We're inside now. And we have an audience. You may put me down."

Rafe reluctantly lowered Dulcie to her feet. "Put them there." He pointed to the wing chair closest to Peavey. "And thank you, Corporal."

Corporal Peavey touched his forelock. "Sir. Ma'am." He set Dulcie's belonging in the chair and turned to leave, then stopped. "Me and Sergeant Wilson will be standing guard tonight, sir."

"That's not necessary, Corporal," Rafe assured him. "I gave the commandant my word. I'm not going anywhere."

"Just the same, sir," Peavey insisted. "Sergeant Wilson and me will be right outside the door. Felicitations on your wedding, ma'am. Good afternoon."

"Goodnight, Corporal."

Peavey frowned, clearly bewildered. "It's not night yet, sir."

"It is for you," Rafe told him. "We won't need anything else."

"Yes, sir." Peavey turned and walked out the door, leaving them alone.

Rafe smiled down at Dulcie. "Shall we continue where we left off?"

Color rose in her cheeks. She gave Rafe a shy look, then glanced at the front door, where the corporal would be standing guard right outside. "Would you mind terribly if we waited a bit?"

He minded quite a bit, but he did his best to hide it. "If we aren't going to resume our previous activity, we might as well explore the rest of the cottage."

Dulcie laughed. "There can't be much more to explore. It's rather small."

"Small?" Rafe echoed. "It's Lilliputian."

Dulcie widened her eyes at his reference to *Gulliver's Travels*. *"Lilliputian?"*

Rafe confirmed her question with a brisk nod. "When we're not engaged in battle or drilling and training for battle or taking care of our equipment and our mounts, cavalry officers spend a lot of time in their tents reading." He made a wry face. "At least, I did."

"My brother loved *Gulliver's Travels*. He took it from our library without Papa's permission and carried it with him when he left for the Peninsula."

"I know." Rafe nodded. "When I exhausted my small library, I read his."

Dulcie laughed. "I'll bet he didn't read yours."

"You would win that wager," Rafe replied. "He declined the opportunity to borrow Virgil and Homer and shuddered at the thought of Shakespeare. He said he'd had sufficient Latin and Greek and the Bard in school."

"Geoff didn't like to sit and read. He loved being outside doing things. He was always on the move. But my father loved reading," Dulcie remembered. "Maman used to complain that he'd rather stay at home and read than dress up and go out to parties and musicales and the opera or theater during the Season. But she and Geoff and I would gather around the fire in the library in the evenings when Papa and

Maman weren't attending a society function and listen while my father read aloud to us."

"Sounds like an enjoyable way to spend the evening."

"Not to my mother. She loved to dance and take part in the Season. She loved everything about it. Papa loved to stay in and read. Reading and sailing were his passions."

"A boat's a good place to relax and read."

"Not when you're racing," Dulcie replied. "The only thing Papa loved about the Season were the regattas and waltzing with my mother. He loved the feel of the wind in his face." She stopped suddenly and looked at Rafe. "I haven't thought about these things since I lost them. It hurt too much."

"They sound like happy memories of a close family," he said softly, his burr more pronounced.

"We were very close," Dulcie said. "In some ways, we were a rarity in the ton. My parents loved us, and they loved each other." She smiled. "Although Maman and Papa teased each other about being true opposites." She smiled up at Rafe. "Like us. We're opposites. You're Gulliver and I'm a Lilliputian. Of course, compared to you, I should think most people are Lilliputian. I was afraid we weren't going to make it through the front door. And if we did, I was afraid the ceiling would be too low for you."

"Thought of that, did you?" There was a teasing note in Rafe's voice.

"I didn't at first," she admitted. "But when you lifted me into your arms to carry me over the threshold as if I weighed nothing, it occurred to me that a cottage perfect for me might not suit you at all."

"It occurred to me, too." Rafe grinned at her. "As soon as I saw the place. I was quite relieved to find the high ceiling." He glanced up at the exposed beams far above his head in what would normally be the first-floor bedchambers, or an attic. The open area provided the illusion of space in what would otherwise be an unbearably small house. "I generally avoid Lilliputian cottages because they tend to have narrow doorways and low lintels and ceilings."

"And I've spent most of my life stretching and standing on tiptoe or climbing on furniture to reach my belongings."

"Speaking of tiptoes, how's your foot?"

Remembering how he'd accidentally bumped it against the doorframe as they entered the cottage, Dulcie extended her foot and flexed her ankle to show him her foot was undamaged. "I barely felt it. See? It's fine."

Rafe bent and took hold of it, encircling her slim ankle with his fingers before removing her slipper and testing each toe. "I feared you might have bruised it." He held her foot a moment longer before she slipped her shoe back on it.

"Is that why you didn't set me down right away?"

He shook his head. "Not entirely."

"Then why didn't you?"

He liked the way she refused to let him get away with half-truths. Rafe inhaled deeply, then slowly exhaled. "I enjoyed the tradition of carrying you over the threshold."

Dulcie blushed. "So did I."

"Is that *all* you enjoyed?"

"No." She blushed a deeper shade of pink. "I enjoyed what came before."

Rafe arched his eyebrow in query.

Dulcie raked her bottom lip with her teeth. "I enjoyed our kisses." She sighed. "Very much."

"So did I," Rafe echoed her sentiment in a voice that was gruffer than usual.

"Then we're in accord," she said.

"Indeed."

The look he gave her, and the way he pronounced the one word, sent more ripples of awareness through her body. "Why don't we explore the rest of the cottage?" she invited.

Rafe bit back a protest. As long as the ceiling was tall enough to accommodate his height, he didn't care about exploring the rest of the house. The only room he wanted to see contained a bed, and he was doing his best not to sweep her up his arms and find it. But Dulcie seemed to want to explore the rest of the house so Rafe hid his pronounced lack of enthusiasm in order to keep from disappointing her. He had to be patient and do his best not to rush her. Hefting the hamper, Rafe gestured for Dulcie to lead the way, then watched with great interest as she removed her cloak and draped it over the back of the sofa. "After you, my lady..."

His heart thumped against his chest and his body tightened in anticipation of her green silk dress joining her cloak, but her cloak was the only garment she removed.

Rafe squeezed his eyes shut and silently counted to ten, then followed his bride on a tour of their honeymoon cottage. "It's perfectly charming," Dulcie pronounced, scanning the interiors as they explored the rooms beyond the front parlor. "And lucky for us, it's larger than it appeared from the outside."

The little house was sparsely, but comfortably, furnished. The front room held an overstuffed sofa and two matching chairs arranged before a large fireplace occupying one wall. A cheery fire warmed most of the house, keeping the damp and chill outside at bay.

There were five rooms in all. A kitchen accented with decorative woodwork and filled with niches and cupboards, a stove, a worktable, and a dining table and four chairs. Rafe set the food hamper on the worktable.

Next to the kitchen was a small scullery with two sinks surrounded by shelves. A pump was affixed to the largest sink. Beside the scullery was a small bathing room that connected the scullery to the remaining room. The bathing room contained a large, enameled tub, a mirrored washstand and basin, commode chair, privacy screen, and a small linen chest.

"It's nice to have a room like this dedicated to bathing and such." Dulcie ran her hand along the rim of the enameled tub. "Look how deep and big it is! I could almost swim in it." Her eyes sparkled with delight at the thought. "At Tennant House, I have to ring for a footman to bring a tub up to my room. It's always a small one, and then I wait, shivering in my shift, for the maids to carry buckets and kettles of hot and cold water to fill it." She bit her bottom lip and looked away in embarrassment at the realization she'd shared such an intimate admission with a man she barely knew. "Of course, it isn't as private as my bedchamber. In a house this size, I'm sure the bathing room is shared…" She broke off.

Recognizing her mortification, Rafe said, "I can attend to my needs elsewhere."

"Oh, no, that won't be necessary," Dulcie said. "Besides, there is nowhere else."

"The scullery will suit me fine," he said. "And I'll be closer to the hot water for bathing." He shrugged. "I spent a great deal of the past four years living in tents. And the last ten months in a single room. I'm accustomed to improvising." He saw no need to remind her that the close quarters they currently shared would end at dawn. "As a lady, you require greater privacy than I do."

Opening the opposite door, Rafe ushered her forward, out of the close confines of the bathing room and into the last room in the house. The room he'd tried not to think about. The room dominated by a massive four-poster bed.

Rafe groaned his dismay at the sight. If the bed had proved to be too small for his height and size, he could have been noble and offered it to her in order to make do on the sofa before the fire. But this…

This massive bed beckoned him like a siren singing to a sailor. What possible excuse could he use to talk himself out of bedding his bride when every cell in his body urged him to do just that? If the room contained other furnishings, he didn't see them. His complete attention was focused on the bed.

Rushing forward, Dulcie pulled back the curtains then turned to Rafe. "Why are you groaning? It's big enough."

As Rafe stared at the bed, images of all he could do in that bed filled his brain. And every image he had was of what he could do in bed with her. Little Dulcie. Geoff's sister. "Big enough for what?" He thought, he *hoped,* for a moment that she'd read his mind.

"For you," she said. "I was afraid the bed would be the same size as the one I sleep in at home, but this bed is much bigger. You can sleep comfortably for the first time in years…"

For the last night of his life.

"There's plenty of room for the both of us without you worrying about your feet hanging over the edge," Dulcie concluded.

"My feet hang off the end of every bed I've ever slept in, except my own."

"They won't hang off the end of this one." Dulcie made use of the bedside steps and climbed up to see. She stretched out on the coverlet, then wiggled her way from the pillow to the foot of the bed as if she were an inchworm measuring it, before squirming her way back to the head of the bed, exposing her slim ankles and shapely calves and a tantalizing bit of sheer lawn fabric and delicate lace during the process. Patting the empty space beside her, Dulcie invited, "Come… try it for yourself."

Rafe dismissed the images of sheer lawn and delicate lace surrounding her shapely body that had suddenly imprinted themselves on his brain to focus on the living, breathing, beautiful, and provocative woman in the green silk evening gown lying on the bed half a step away, demanding that he join her.

CHAPTER 9

"Infinite riches in a little room."
—Christopher Marlowe, 1564-1593

"I'm not certain that's a good idea, my lady." Rafe didn't know how he managed to get the lie out without choking on it. *Lying on the bed beside Dulcie was a capital idea. It was the best idea he'd heard in ages. It was practically all he'd thought about since he'd realized the little beauty who had been waiting for him in the commandant's antechamber was Geoff's sister, the girl he'd promised his friend he'd marry. It was what he wanted to do. Exactly what his body had been urging him to do since he'd kissed her in the coach. And it was exactly what he knew he shouldn't do. Kissing her in the coach had been tempting enough.*

She wasn't trying to be seductive. Dulcie was genuinely delighted by the size of the bed. But gazing at her stretched out on the coverlet was almost more than he could bear. Rafe had been too long without female companionship—*any* female companionship—and dared not test his self-control on a woman he wanted.

"Why not?" Dulcie gazed up at him. "We're going to be staying the night. You should see if the bed is to your liking before you retire to it."

Her words sounded perfectly reasonable when they reached Rafe's ears, even as he recognized himself as a desperate man who was willing to latch onto any idea that matched his ultimate desires. He was more than willing to allow himself to be convinced. "It doesn't matter if my feet hang off the bed," he assured her. "As I mentioned before, I'm accustomed to it."

"I'm not." She pursed her lips in a stubborn show of determination.

"Dulcie..."

"What's wrong with trying the furniture on for size to see if it suits?" she asked. "Like sitting on the sofa or testing the chair cushions." She gave him an impish look. "There's nothing untoward about it. We're married. Besides, it's early afternoon. It isn't as if anything is likely to happen between us until it gets dark. It isn't our wedding night yet."

Rafe glanced at the weak light coming through the window, trying to gauge the hours of daylight left. *It isn't as if anything is likely to happen between us until it gets dark...* How little she knew! Or understood. Only a complete innocent would believe that. Or trust that a man would pay any heed to the time of day or wait for darkness. Rafe clamped his jaw shut. If he needed further evidence of Dulcie's virginal state, that statement provided it. His darling little bride was too inexperienced to know that lovemaking between men and women took place at all hours of the day and night and could be deliciously decadent in the early afternoon hours when the rest of the world was going about its workday. She was too innocent to realize what a temptation she was lying there on the bed bidding him to fulfill his fondest wish. Too innocent to realize he'd been grappling with the knowledge that they were legally married ever since he'd kissed her in the coach. He kept telling himself there was no reason he should refrain from taking his conjugal rights, but Rafe knew there were at least two reasons he shouldn't.

Dulcie was an innocent and the younger sister of one of the finest men he had ever known. And what kind of friend and gentleman would he be to spend the night seducing his bride only to abandon her at dawn? Rafe was struggling with his desires and his conscience to keep from making love to her in every way he knew for as long as he could. Dulcie had no idea how close he was to taking her in his arms and enveloping her in a conflagration of white-hot passion throughout the night and the devil take tomorrow.

She patted the coverlet once again. "Come join me, Rafe. Come see if the bed is to your liking."

"It doesn't matter if the bed is to my liking," he murmured. "The woman lying on it is to my liking."

"Am I?" Dulcie looked up at him from beneath the cover of her lashes.

"Aye." The affirmation came out as a low rumble. "You are very much to my liking."

She let out a husky giggle at the way he was starting to roll the *r*'s in his words. "How much?"

"Very much."

In for a penny, in for a pound. "Then, come lie beside me and hold me in your arms," she directed.

Rafe arched an eyebrow at that.

"I like the way you hold me."

Rafe's attempts at nobility deserted him. He had no defense against her when she asked him to hold her. He told himself that as long as they kept their clothing on, everything would be all right. As long as he kept the situation platonic, as long as all he offered was comfort and warmth, holding his wife in his arms would not be compromising his principles or his best intentions.

"Well," she drawled. "Are you or aren't you coming to try out the bed?"

"I am," he said, sounding more Scottish than she'd ever heard him. He toed off his boots. "But I think it's only fair to warn you, Lady Blackburn, that daylight won't protect you."

"I don't need protection from you, Lord Blackburn."

"Oh, yes, you do," he told her as he climbed onto the bed and leaned over her. "We were kissing in the coach in full daylight."

Dulcie's smile wasn't quite as innocent as it had been before. "Were we?"

Rafe arched his eyebrow at her once again.

Reaching up, Dulcie wrapped her arms around his neck and pulled him closer. "It's been so long, I've forgotten..."

~

"Are you feeling better now?" The Earl of Weymouth asked as Phoebe left her seat on *The Manx Princess* and approached him.

Phoebe managed a wan smile. "I fear I'm not a very good sailor. Or a very good travel companion for you."

"On the contrary," Weymouth told her. "I rarely have such delightful sailing companions." He looked up from the correspondence he'd been reading. "Won't you join me in a cup of tea?"

"I'd like that," Phoebe told him. "If you're willing to risk it..."

Weymouth let out a rare chuckle. "Lady Weymouth was ill nearly four months during her recent confinement. The mere mention of a cup of tea would upset her. So, you might say I've become something of an old hand at managing bouts of sickness. On the sea or otherwise." He gestured to the chair across the table from him, then signaled for the steward and ordered tea and toast for each of them.

Phoebe sat down at the table across from him as Lord Weymouth returned his papers to the leather pouches he was never without. "That's comforting."

"I was plagued with seasickness myself when I first started crossing and recrossing the channel. The crossings became so frequent, I eventually became accustomed to the motion and overcame the illness. And so will you. But I always carry this when I travel by boat. In case the need arises." Reaching inside his coat, Weymouth produced a bottle of clear liquid sealed with a cork stopper. A silver, doubled ended measuring spoon was tied around its neck. "My daughter-in-law makes it for me. It's an herbal remedy for *mal de mer.* A small dose settles the stomach. A double dose induces restful sleep.

Alyssa concocted this to help me since I'm often deprived of sleep as well. If you need it, I'll share."

Phoebe was surprised a man like Weymouth would admit to any weakness especially a weakness like *mal de mer*. "I think I'll be all right now. But thank you."

"You recovered much faster this time than on the way over. It won't be much longer before you gain your sea legs." A hint of a smile curved the corners of his mouth. "Or regain your mermaid's tail."

"I doubt I'll ever masquerade as a mermaid again," she confessed.

Weymouth was thoughtful. "And why is that, Miss Osborne?"

"I've discovered I'm not overly fond of the sea."

"And what of your Scottish buccaneer? You are fond of him, are you not?"

Phoebe shook her head. "No, I'm—"

The Earl of Weymouth didn't give her a chance to lie. "What will become of him if he has no mermaid to look out for him?"

A shadow crossed her face. "I suppose he'll give up masked balls and return to the Highlands." She lifted her chin, lying to herself this time. "He'll be fine."

Weymouth waited until the steward had served the tea and toast before he pinned Phoebe with his gaze and asked, "Will you?"

Phoebe read the genuine concern in the earl's eyes. "Of course. I have plenty to keep me busy. Helping Aunt Augusta at the Returning Soldiers' Hospital and helping Caroline—"

"Lady Carlisle is on her honeymoon," Weymouth reminded her.

"Of course, she is," Phoebe agreed. "But the work of the Charlotte Society continues and Dul—" She swallowed the lump in her throat when she remembered she and Lord Weymouth had left Dulcie on the Isle of Wight and were sailing for home. "I know she's on her honeymoon, too. Now. With Lord Blackburn. But I feel so guilty about leaving her there alone."

"Blackburn is a good man. The late Lord Tennant made an excellent choice when he chose Blackburn for his sister. And I've arranged for Lady Blackburn to return to London on tomorrow afternoon's tide."

Phoebe frowned in confusion. "Tomorrow afternoon's tide? Dulcie and Lord Blackburn are honeymooning. Why would you arrange for Dulcie to return?"

Weymouth winced at his uncharacteristic slip of the tongue. He rarely made mistakes when it came to discovering the secrets of others or keeping them, but he'd left himself with no choice but to acknowledge this blunder. "She didn't she tell you."

"Tell me what?" Phoebe demanded.

"Major Lord Blackburn's fate."

"Oh, no!" A look of abject horror crossed Phoebe's face. "I told her I'd overheard the corporal and the sergeant talking about Major Lord Blackburn being sentenced to hang at dawn tomorrow. Dulcie convinced me that I had misunderstood. She told me the inquiry had been a mistake. She told me Lord Blackburn had been confused with a Major MacBurn and cleared of all charges." Phoebe turned her accusing gaze on the earl. "There is no Major MacBurn, is there?"

Sighing, Weymouth shook his head sadly. "No."

"Dulcie *lied* to me." The realization hit Phoebe hard. Her breath caught in her throat, and she feared she was about to disgrace herself in front of Lord Weymouth by bursting into tears. "She's never lied to me. About anything. Ever. She's always been completely honest with me." She squeezed her eyes shut. "I should have known better. I should have known what she would do. And I should never have told her that I couldn't allow her to marry a condemned man. That I couldn't allow her to ruin her reputation by marrying a man who had been condemned to death. I even told her I was so relieved to hear MacBurn had been condemned to hang instead of Lord Blackburn because, otherwise, I would have to object to the marriage for her own good." Her despairing gaze met Weymouth's. "She lied to me so I wouldn't object. She lied so she could marry him." Phoebe covered her face with her hands. "Because she knew that had I known the truth, I would have never left her on that island alone."

Seeking to comfort her, Weymouth said, "Miss Tennant had every chance to change her mind about the wedding. Blackburn gave her several chances. She not only chose to marry him, but she was also *determined* to marry him."

"Please, can't you turn the boat around?"

"We cannot do that, Miss Osborne. As much I would like to accommodate your request, I have a schedule to keep. A return trip to the Isle of Wight is not part of it."

"We *must* go back to the isle." Phoebe glanced at the water, trying to gauge how far they'd traveled. "I can't leave Dulcie there alone."

"She's not alone, Miss Osborne," Weymouth reminded her. "Lady Blackburn is with her husband."

"What about tomorrow? What happens to her once his sentence is carried out?"

"Lord Blackburn has made provisions in his will for his wife and arranged a suitable escort for her. She'll return to London and resume her life with the knowledge that if her uncle tries to force her to take a husband not of her choosing, all she has to do is produce her marriage lines."

"But…"

"No need to fret, Miss Osborne," Weymouth assured her. "We've planned for all eventualities."

"*All* eventualities?" Phoebe demanded.

"Yes," Weymouth told her.

"What about the eventuality that Dulcie will be a widow pretending nothing has happened. She'll be secretly mourning for her husband while she's participating in the Season. What about Dulcie's broken heart, my lord? Did you plan for that eventuality?"

CHAPTER 10

"The slowest kiss makes too much haste."
—Thomas Middleton, 1580-1629

Dulcie kissed him.

Rafe slid down onto the bed and pulled her into his arms, marveling at her boldness even as he allowed himself to revel in the pleasure of having his bride kiss him. "What did I do to deserve that?" he asked when she ended the kiss.

"First, you married me," she whispered against his mouth. "And then, you graciously indulged me."

Genuinely perplexed by her answer, Rafe asked, "Indulged you how, my lady?"

She patted the coverlet between them. "You knew you would fit on this bed. You knew it the very moment you saw it. But you indulged me by allowing me to prove it."

"It was my pleasure, my lady," came his gallant reply. "Why shouldn't I indulge my bride on her wedding day?"

Dulcie moved closer to him, allowing the heat from his body to warm her. Shivering with delight at the sensation. "I can't think of a single reason." She brushed her lips against his, silently imploring him to indulge her once again.

Rafe obliged, indulging her while he indulged himself, kissing her open mouth without warning. He meant the kiss to be a light, flirtatious kiss, but the moment his lips touched hers, he ignited. There was nothing light or flirtatious about the way he kissed her. Rafe swallowed the soft sigh that escaped her lips along with his name as he took her in his arms and deepened the kiss, encouraging her to follow his lead and allow him further liberties as he swept his tongue past her teeth and into the deep recesses of her mouth, tasting her with his mouth while his hands roamed at will, exploring the hidden contours of her body through the soft silk of her dress.

Dulcie melted against him, shivering with a mix of delight and anticipation.

Rafe molded her to his body as she plastered herself against him. He kissed her senseless and just as he was about to roll her onto her back and cover her with his body, Rafe remembered that she had no experience beyond passionate kissing. He wanted to introduce her to the pleasures of lovemaking, but time was running out. They had only a single night to share. Rafe wanted to make love to her. He wanted to spend the last night of his time on earth pleasuring and being pleasured by a beautiful woman—by his beautiful bride. He wanted to take her to the pinnacle of pleasure and watch her as she reached fulfillment for the first time. He wanted to see her face, feel the heat of her skin pressed against his, and hear his name on her lips when she cried out. He wanted to be her first lover.

Her only lover.

But Rafe was torn between his desires and her welfare. He couldn't have Dulcie on his conscience. He couldn't meet his Maker knowing he'd taken advantage of her innocence and her desperation just to slake his own desires. While making love to Dulcie Tennant would give him tremendous gratification and release, doing so was not without consequences. And while Rafe wanted very much to leave something of himself behind to preserve his lineage, leaving Dulcie a widow with an infant was beyond the pale.

Funny how he had never given much thought to consequences before tonight. There had never been any reason to. The women he'd entertained as a bachelor had been experienced. They had all known what to expect when they shared his bed or when he shared theirs. One or two might have hoped for more, but Rafe had never made promises he could not keep. He had never promised love or marriage or any sort of permanent arrangement. He enjoyed their companionship, their bodies, and the pleasures they shared. He was a generous lover in bed and out, bestowing gifts as well as carnal pleasure. But he had never offered his heart. Had never spoken of love. Only passion. And Rafe had never lingered once the relationships had run their course. And until he'd met his bride, he had never regretted leaving a woman behind. But he couldn't help but regret leaving Dulcie behind. He couldn't help but regret that he wouldn't be the lover or the husband he wanted to be, and he regretted he would never have children or build a life with her.

But neither would he risk leaving her with his child.

Rafe understood better than most the difficulties that might pose for a woman left alone. His oldest sister had been left a widow before her son had celebrated his second natal day. She'd been twenty-six at the time, older than Dulcie was now, and although Micheline had since married the wealthy Viscount Ennisbrooke and had borne him a daughter and a son, during the early years of her widowhood, his sister and her infant son had relied on Rafe.

He had been one and twenty at the time and had just become the Earl of Blackburn. He would not allow what happened to his sister to happen to Dulcie. There was nothing Rafe could do to prevent her from becoming a widow, but he could prevent her from becoming a widow *and* a mother. She no longer had a brother she could rely on, and her uncle was a scoundrel—most likely, a murderous scoundrel. Rafe refused to besmirch Geoffrey Tennant's memory by leaving Dulcie alone and with child. His child. The child of a disgraced military hero who had been hanged for disobeying orders and striking a superior officer.

Rafe wanted to see Dulcie in all her naked splendor. He wanted to carry the memory of her curly, dark auburn hair lying against her soft, pale skin, wanted to measure the span of her slender waist with his hands, wanted to cup her unfettered breasts in the palms of his hands and taste the unique flavor of their tips on his tongue, and carry the memory of his exploration of her body with him to the grave. He ached to feel her naked flesh pressed against his, but he forced himself to rein in his passion and concentrate on what he *could* do.

He had lifted his bride from the floor when she had fainted and had cradled her against his chest. He had tasted her lips, felt her kisses, and heard the soft moans and mewling sounds she made in the coach when he did so. And he'd carried her across the threshold of their honeymoon cottage. Rafe would have memories to sustain him as he climbed the steps to the gallows at dawn, but he wanted—needed—more to carry with him when he met his Maker. Surely, God would understand that after Rafe had witnessed so much pain and suffering during four years of war and inflicted so much death and destruction, when the executioner placed the rope around his neck and the floor opened beneath his feet, Raphael Blackburn wanted to remember the unexpected beauty his friend had entrusted to his care.

Rafe moaned as Dulcie raked the interior of his mouth with her tongue. She abruptly broke the kiss and frowned up at him. "Did I do something wrong?"

He slowly shook his head. "No, sweet Dulcinea. You did everything right."

She smiled up at him. "Then why did you groan as if you were in pain?"

Because he was in pain. And the agony was exquisite. "Because I liked it verra much. Too much."

"You moan as if you're in pain because you liked the way I kissed you?" Dulcie drew the graceful wings of her brows together. "That doesn't make any sense, Raphael."

"It does if you're a man," he told her.

"I'm not a man," she began.

"And I'm grateful you aren't." Rafe brushed his lips against hers once again, then began nibbling a path over her chin, along her jaw to the exposed shell of her ear. He lightly traced the contours of her ear with the tip of his tongue, nipped the delicate lobe, then soothed the tiny bite by sucking it into his mouth. Biting the wire hook of her earring, Rafe tugged it out of her ear and dropped it in the valley between her breasts.

Dulcie shivered in delight as the cool peridot slid down the hot crevice between her breasts. "Are you going to retrieve that later?"

"Aye, my lady." His words held infinite promise.

She moistened her lips with the tip of her tongue. "My, aren't you a clever boy?"

Rafe felt that gesture throughout his entire body. "Clever, yes. Boy, no. I am a very clever *man*, my lady." As if to prove his point, he trailed his tongue along the edge of her decolletage.

"Good." She plunged her fingers into his hair. "Because it means you'll be able to explain what you meant."

"Kiss me again," he directed.

She pulled back just far enough to see his expression. "Are you trying to change the subject, Lord Blackburn?"

"No, Lady Blackburn," he assured her. "I'm trying to explain."

"All right, then." She moved to within a hair's breadth of his lips before whispering, "Explain it to me." But before he could try, she kissed him again.

Rafe allowed her license to kiss him as she pleased for as long as he could before he took control. He kissed her deeper and harder and with more finesse than he had before. He made love to her mouth the way he wanted to make love to the rest of her. He took her breath away, again and again, until she was writhing in his arms and moaning, expressing her need for whatever came next.

She whimpered her yearning for his touch and protested when he abruptly stopped kissing her once again.

"What you're feeling, sweet Dulcie, is passion. Desire. Longing. Need." Rafe was breathing hard, his chest heaving with the effort and his heart pounding so hard he could feel it in his ears. His body was tight with the strain of holding back and aching with the need to consummate their vows by burying himself deep inside of her.

Dulcie tightened her hold on him, pressing her body against his, sighing against his lips, experiencing the heat of passion for the first time, as she begged him to kiss her again. "Please…"

"Passion is a verra powerful emotion, my sweet," he explained, his Scots burr deepened once again by his own longing. "It overrules logic. It overrules everything except the deep primal urge to follow it wherever it leads. Passion throws caution to the wind and propels couples into scandal, gossip, and ruination without considering the consequences of their actions. The physical need to mate becomes all that matters." Rafe pressed his forehead to hers. "For men, the need for that physical release is most urgent and painful."

"Oh." She moved away from him, giving him room in an attempt to alleviate the pain she was causing him.

"Yes, oh." Rafe rolled to his side to face her. "I want you, sweet Dulcie. Make no mistake about that." He trailed his index finger along the slope of her nose. "I find you very desirable. At this moment, I want you more than I want my next breath. But I cannot allow us both to be swept along in the tide of passion unless you understand the consequences." He didn't sound convincing to his own ears, for his burr was more pronounced and quavered in places.

"There won't be any scandal, gossip, or ruination," she insisted. "We've exchanged vows. We're married, both in the eyes of society and in the eyes of God."

"We are legally married, but there will still be scandal and gossip and your reputation will suffer if word of it becomes known." He gazed into her brown eyes. "You eloped, Dulcie. You went behind your guardian's back and sneaked away to marry me."

"Because Geoff chose you," she reminded him. "I did what my brother wanted. I honored his last request." Her eyes sparkled with unshed tears. "And I don't regret it."

"Not at the moment," he warned her. "But you will."

Dulcie bristled at the thought that Rafe believed her to be that shallow. "Would you rather have me accept one of my uncle's choices?"

"No." He was adamant on that point. "Never. But that doesn't mean I'm not concerned. Your uncle has plans for you."

"Of course he does. He's my guardian. And his wife is about to present him with a child of his own. He proposes to marry me off to one of his friends, thereby relieving himself of the responsibility of providing for me. And if he profits from my marriage so much the better." She met Rafe's gaze. "I don't like my uncle's choice of friends. My brother's choice of friends is more to my liking."

"I'm heartened to hear it. But your uncle isn't going to appreciate your decision to disrupt his plans."

"I didn't appreciate his moving into our house and immediately dismissing all the people who had been with our family for decades..."

"Guilford pensioned off your staff and family retainers?"

She shook her head. "He dismissed them *without* pensions or references and replaced them with help hired from a staffing agency. Help who would be loyal to him instead of to me and the memories of my brother and my parents."

Rafe muttered a vicious curse beneath his breath. "None of the staff currently in residence at Tennant House worked for Geoff or your father?"

"No," she whispered. "Everyone I knew and loved is gone."

Rafe gritted his teeth so hard a muscle began to tic in his jaw. When he finally spoke, there was an angry urgency in his voice. "Dulcie, you cannot tell your aunt or uncle about our marriage. No matter what happens."

"No matter what happens?" She stared at him. "Even though he plans to marry me off at the end of the Season?"

Rafe felt the metallic taste of fear sweep through him, not for himself, but for her. "Go along with it," he urged her. "Don't fight him."

"I can't go along with it. That would be bigamy. I'm already married. To *you*."

Rafe clamped his jaw shut a second time while he considered what he was about to do. "Dulcie, you must."

"No."

Rafe wasn't sure if she was steadfast or simply stubborn. Or both. But he knew he had to change her mind and if it took sternness from him to accomplish it, so be it. "I'm asking while I'm still your husband, Lady Blackburn. Less than two hours ago you promised to obey me before both God and witnesses."

"I'm sure God will make an exception for me, if obeying you means committing bigamy."

"You won't be committing bigamy." Rafe didn't mince words. "Tomorrow, you'll be a widow. Once you return to London you'll continue your Season as if nothing ever happened. As if you'd never met me."

"And let Guilford choose a husband for me at the end of it?" She was clearly indignant.

"Yes."

"No." she insisted. "When Guilford makes his choice known, I'm going to produce my marriage lines. Once I prove I'm a widow, Guilford won't be able to force me to marry anyone."

"Dulcie, your uncle is a dangerous man."

"Guilford?" She scoffed. "He's greedy and selfish, but he's not dangerous."

"He's very dangerous," Rafe insisted. "Especially to you."

"Guilford has never laid a hand on me. He barely knows I'm alive and only speaks to me to inform me of the invitations I'm to accept and the parties I'm to attend."

"You've never interfered with his plans before."

"How do you know this? Did Lord Weymouth tell you about my uncle?"

"He didn't have to," Rafe said. "Geoff did."

CHAPTER 11

"In thy face I see
the map of honor, truth, and loyalty."
—William Shakespeare, 1564-1616

"*What?*" Dulcie looked stricken.

Rafe squeezed his eyes shut, blocking out the expression on her beautiful face.

"What did Geoff tell you?"

"He told me he believed Guilford lacked character and moral fiber, but was full of ruthlessness and greed. He told me he didn't want to leave you in Guilford's care. Geoff also confided that your father's solicitor, Mister..." Rafe paused, searching for the name.

"Merritt. Wiley Merritt," she finished for him. "Papa always called him a Wiley solicitor of Merritt." She smiled at the memory. "Papa was never very good at remembering names. He hated having to memorize Debrett's and used to make up little rhymes and sayings to help him."

"That's right. Mister Merritt." Rafe took a deep breath. "Merritt warned Geoff that Guilford Tennant was swimming in debt and desperately trying to keep his head above water."

"But how can that be? Papa always gave Guilford a generous allowance and paid all his bills at the first of every month."

"Not all of them," Rafe said. "Mister Merritt told Geoff your father paid your uncle's living expenses, but refused to pay your uncle's mountain of gaming debts to the gaming houses or to his gaming cronies." He caught Dulcie's gaze and held it. "Geoff continued your father's practice of paying his living expenses and his allowance, but not his gaming debts."

She gasped. "So Geoff made you promise to marry me in case he was killed in battle."

"He didn't make me, Little One," he said softly. "He *asked* me."

"And you readily agreed to marry a girl you'd never met. Sight unseen."

"Yes."

Her gaze didn't waver. "Why?"

He smiled a knowing smile. "For the same reason you were determined to find me and adopt me as your Charlotte Society soldier."

She clamped down on her bottom lip, then pulled it through her top teeth. "To thwart my uncle?"

Rafe snorted. "Partly. But mostly because I was fond of your brother. I admired him, aspired to be like him, and considered myself tremendously fortunate to have him as my friend." He inhaled. "And also, because I knew why Geoff asked me."

"Why did he ask you?"

"He thought we—" He smiled at her. "You and I. Would be a good match."

"He did?"

Rafe nodded. "Geoff wrote to your father during your first Season and asked him not to accept any offers for your hand until he had the opportunity to bring me to London to meet you."

"My brother was playing Cupid!" Dulcie breathed, sounding awestruck. "For the two of us."

"It seems so. He told me all about you. And shared bits of your letters on occasion." Geoffrey Tennant had shared almost all of his sister's letters with Rafe. Rafe even knew Dulcie's daily routine at Tennant House and at their country house in Hampshire from Geoff and Dulcie's descriptions. He knew their staffs and the layout and decor of the two Tennant residences almost as well as he knew his own homes. But he saw no need to share that information with her. No need to cause her to wonder and fret about the confidences she might have shared with her brother in those letters. "As I shared my letters from friends and family with him. But when he returned to Spain after your parents died, he wasn't simply playing Cupid. Geoff had another reason for asking."

"What was it?"

"Your parents were gone. He'd become Viscount Tennant. His responsibilities had increased tenfold. And the weight of those responsibilities took some getting used to. Until he went to war, Geoff had only ever had to be responsible for himself. Your father had always taken care of everything else. Suddenly, Geoff was the viscount. And he needed someone he could rely on to take care of you and his other responsibilities in the event of his untimely death."

"Geoff was worried about something happening to him?" Dulcie frowned. "That doesn't sound like the brother I knew. Geoff was always fearless. Invincible. He was never afraid of anybody or anything."

He smiled at her description. "Your memory sounds exactly like the Geoff I remember. If he was afraid, Geoff never showed it. We were in Spain and at war. Leading patrols in hostile territory day and night. Yet, Geoff never feared what might happen. He never believed anything *would* happen. Not even on midnight patrol. He was supremely confident in his ability to get the job done. No matter what it was. Until he returned from London."

"What changed?"

"Once your parents died, Geoff came to face to face with his responsibilities and his own mortality."

Her face clouded. "I'm not sure I like the idea that my brother thought of me as a responsibility."

"He didn't mean it as a slight," Rafe assured her. "He loved you very much. The sudden, crushing sense of responsibility happens to us all when our fathers die and we are suddenly thrust into the world of men with all the worry and responsibilities of inheriting a title and estates. We instantly become responsible for the livelihoods of hundreds of men and women." He met Dulcie's gaze. "Your brother was one of the bravest men I ever knew, but he was afraid of what would happen to you if he died before you were happily married and in possession of your inheritance. And he had every reason to be afraid for you." Rafe hesitated, as if measuring his next words with care. "Geoff was convinced your uncle Guilford was responsible for your parents' deaths."

Her first reaction was disbelief. The color drained from her face and Rafe feared she might faint again. But she quickly recovered. "My parents died in a yachting accident during a summer thunderstorm. I was supposed to have gone sailing with them, but I woke that morning with an earache and Maman didn't think I should be out on the ocean or in the wind." She bit her bottom lip. "I should have been with them."

"If you had, you wouldn't be here with me. Tonight." Leaning close, Rafe brushed her lips with his, kissing her softly, tenderly, reverently. "I know this isn't the time or place." He rolled into a sitting position and leaned against the headboard. "It's our wedding night. We should be celebrating it. Doing what newly married couples do. But things are different for us." He sighed. "I don't want to hurt you, Dulcie, or cause you more distress, but you need to know what your brother told me so you can be on your guard and protect yourself. And I've only one night to tell you."

Dulcie pushed herself into a sitting position, angling her body so she could see his face. "I'm listening."

"Your parents died while sailing on your father's yacht, but their deaths weren't the result of an accident," he said gently.

Frown lines marred the smooth skin of Dulcie's forehead. "How do you know what happened to my parents? Did Lord Weymouth tell you?"

"No, sweet Dulcie." Rafe reached over and tried to smooth her worry lines with the pad of his thumb. "Your brother did."

"But how? Nobody knows for sure what happened. And Geoff was in Spain when they died. By the time he got home, their bod—" Her voice cracked. She swallowed hard before continuing. "*They* had already been recovered from the wreckage of the *Amphitrite* and buried."

"That's all true," Rafe agreed. "There was no way Geoff could have known what happened if your father hadn't left him the letter."

"What letter?" Her frown lines deepened.

Rafe gently smoothed them out again. "Your father left a letter for your brother and entrusted it to Mister Merritt for safekeeping. It was to be opened in the event of Lord Tennant's death. In the letter, your father documented previous attempts on his life. He described an incident where he was nearly shot while making his quarterly visits to the tenants on your country estate. The shot grazed him on the cheek."

"I remember that afternoon. Papa returned home with a wound on his face from a rifle ball. He thought it must have been a stray shot from someone poaching game in the woodlands." She searched Rafe's face for confirmation. "Poaching was illegal, of course, but Papa turned a blind eye when times were hard."

Rafe nodded. "Your father was originally convinced that incident was an accident. He believed the culprit to be a poacher. But then he suffered several other close calls. His carriage was run off the road and overturned. He was set upon by ruffians, robbed, and stabbed after leaving his club one evening. He was thrown from his favorite mount and when his groom unsaddled the horse, he found a large thorn lodged beneath the saddle. He became very ill when no one else did and suspected someone had poisoned the brandy he kept in the library." Rafe sighed. "One stray bullet might be an accident, but a string of seemingly unrelated incidents within the span of a few months couldn't be dismissed, particularly since your father had never been prone to accidents before. Your father eventually concluded someone was trying to kill him and alerted the Bow Street

Runners. Your father included their report with the letter he wrote to Geoff."

Dulcie let out a shaky sigh. "What did Bow Street conclude?"

"That the only people who had anything to gain from your father's death were his heir and his younger brother."

"I remember when Papa had those accidents. He broke his arm in the carriage accident, but he was lucky. Shockley, the coachman, Newton, the footman, and two horses were killed. Papa twisted his ankle when he was thrown from Jupiter and was stabbed in the shoulder when he was robbed. Papa swore he'd have been a corpse if the two Robin Redbreasts patrolling St. James's Street hadn't rushed to his aid." She referenced the Bow Street mounted patrol nicknamed for the scarlet waistcoats they wore. "As for his illness, Papa claimed he must have eaten some bad oysters at his club, but none of us truly believed him."

Rafe frowned at her. "Why not?"

"Because Papa was a terrible liar," she said. "And you might as well know that I take after him. I'm a terrible liar, too. I never fool anyone, so I generally speak my mind."

"I appreciate a person who speaks his mind," he said.

"You appreciate a *man* who speaks his mind," she countered. "It's not as admirable a trait in a woman."

He arched his eyebrow at her once again.

"It's disconcerting. Especially when girls are taught that politeness is the mark of a true lady and that young ladies should keep their mouths closed and their thoughts to themselves..."

"That's not why they teach young ladies to keep their mouths closed." Rafe couldn't resist teasing her a bit.

Dulcie did her best to emulate his arched brow.

"They teach young ladies to keep their mouths shut so they won't get into trouble," he explained.

"Really?"

"Absolutely. Men rarely steal kisses from young ladies who keep their mouths closed. Closed-mouthed kisses aren't nearly as enjoyable as open-mouthed ones."

"That can't be true," Dulcie said.

"You seemed to enjoy our open-mouthed kisses," he reminded her.

"The open-mouthed kissing *is* more enjoyable. Much more enjoyable. You are right about that. But the other part can't be true because I'm forever having to apologize for not keeping my mouth shut. If your theory was true, I should have had a veritable army of young men lined up to steal kisses from me," Dulcie pointed out. "But you were the first."

"Disappointed?"

"Yes."

Rafe was taken aback by her brutally honest answer. "Because I was your first kiss?"

"Because you don't do it often enough."

He laughed. "If you say things like that when you speak your mind, you *will* have a veritable army of men lined up to kiss you."

"I don't want an army of men." Dulcie looked him in the eye. "I only want you."

He groaned. *"Dulcie..."*

"I told you, I take after my father. He was a terrible liar and so am I. I'd rather get in trouble for telling the truth than for telling lies no one believes. And it's better for my Recording Angel. He doesn't have to record the truth, only lies. And why should I have marks against me for doing something I'm terrible at?"

The corners of Rafe's mouth turned up at her bluntness. She was still such an innocent. She still worried about her Recording Angel enumerating her sins. Rafe hadn't thought of a Recording Angel since he was a boy. If he had one, his angel had recorded volumes of sins for which he would be judged soon enough. Tomorrow. Upon meeting his Maker. "You didn't tell me how you knew your father was lying about the oysters."

"You didn't kiss me."

Rafe gave her a quick kiss.

"That hardly counts," she protested.

"Two hours ago, you'd never been kissed. Now, you're complaining about the quality."

"Two hours ago, I didn't know you were so good at kissing." She smiled at him. "Or how much I would enjoy it."

"Serious business first. Pleasure after," he said.

Dulcie conceded with a sigh. "We knew he was lying because Papa never ate oysters prepared by anyone other than our cook. Papa didn't trust them." She met Rafe's gaze. "I agree with Bow Street that someone must have been trying to do grievous harm to my father. When you hear all of his accidents listed that way instead of spread out over a period of weeks and months, it makes perfect sense. Papa wasn't simply having a run of bad luck. Someone was trying to kill him. But I cannot agree that it was family." Her husky voice held an indignant note that matched the fierce look in her eyes. "And certainly not his heir! Geoff would never cause my father harm. The Runners are wrong about that. And Geoff would never hire ruffians to do it for him, either."

"No, he wouldn't," Rafe agreed. "It wasn't in Geoff's character. And even if it had been, he had no reason to. Since he was the heir, Geoff understood that everything that belonged to the seventh Viscount Tennant would one day belong to the eighth. And because he wasn't a gambler or a wastrel, Geoff wasn't in urgent need of his inheritance. He was content to wait for it." Rafe captured Dulcie's gaze and held it. "But Guilford is selfish and greedy. Guilford *was* in urgent need of money to pay his gaming debts. And willing to do whatever it took to get it." Rafe continued. "The Bow Street Runners noted in the report they sent to your father that Geoff was serving in Spain when the incidents occurred. But Guilford was in residence at the country house when the first incident occurred and in London thereafter."

She gasped. "Reading their report must have broken poor Papa's heart. Guilford is my father's younger brother. Papa loved him." She blinked back the tears stinging her eyes. "I can't believe Guilford would..."

Dulcie squeezed her eyes shut. If she was being honest with herself, after living under her uncle's rule and seeing how he behaved toward her and his callous disregard for the feelings of the loyal Tennant House family retainers, she *could* believe Guilford was capable of killing her father or hiring it done. She had been struggling for months to reconcile *that* man with the loving uncle she had once believed him to be. "But what would he gain with Papa dead? Papa was the one who supported him." She opened her eyes and fixed her gaze on Rafe's face. "Guilford wasn't going to inherit upon Papa's death. He wasn't the heir."

"No, Geoff was," Rafe said. "And less than a year after your parents perished, Geoff died from injuries suffered during an ambush while on a patrol he wasn't scheduled to make. Leaving Guilford to become the ninth viscount and your guardian." Rafe took her by the shoulders and looked her in the eye. "Dulcie, that's not coincidence any more than your father's 'accidents' were coincidences. It's cold-blooded murder."

CHAPTER 12

"Other sins only speak; murder shrieks out."
—John Webster, 1580-1625

The horror hit Dulcie at a visceral level. She instinctively covered her heart with her hand, shielding it from the pain Rafe's words were inflicting. Learning her parents had died in a freak yachting accident and were never coming home again had been a crushing blow for a girl of sixteen. But learning their deaths had not been a tragic accident and had instead been perpetrated by her father's beloved younger brother was a thousand times worse.

They had been murdered. Her brother, Geoff, had also been murdered. All because Guilford wanted to be the viscount. She blinked back the tears burning her eyes. "Guilford was supposed to be in Brighton when we received word of Geoff's death. Surely he didn't travel to Spain to arrange an ambush?" Her voice wobbled on the last word, but she managed to keep her composure.

"No." Rafe shook his head. "But he could have paid hirelings to do it for him or called in favors from his friends or gambling cronies to arrange it." He paused. "*If* he had the money."

"He had the money." Dulcie's voice was stronger and harsher than before. "Mavis was an heiress." Seeing the question in Rafe's face, she explained. "Guilford married a few months after my parents died. I didn't attend the ceremony because I was in mourning. His wife, Mavis, brought a small fortune into the marriage."

"So…money to pay for the ambush would not have been an obstacle."

"No," she said. "And now that you've told me about Guilford's financial situation, I understand why he was in such a rush to marry. He needed money and he couldn't get his hands on his inheritance or his regular allowance until my father's estate was settled, and my brother was granted access to the accounts. Marrying an heiress solved his problems." She frowned. "He didn't need to have Geoff murdered. With the dowry Mavis brought into the marriage, Guilford could have easily paid all his debts. He didn't need the title to get money."

"It's not what your uncle *needs*, sweet Dulcie." Rafe framed her face between his hands. "It's what he *wants*. He coveted the title. He believes he is entitled to it. Guilford was a younger son who wanted what his older brother had. He spent years of his life expecting to inherit after your father. But your father married and had a son and Guilford was excluded from the direct line of succession. So he conspired to get what he felt he deserved, what was unfairly taken from him when your brother was born."

"I understand what you're saying, and I know you're telling me the truth. But it's so hard to believe Guilford would kill just to inherit a title."

"Believe it," Rafe told her. "And make no mistake, men have committed murder for a lot less."

"But three…"

"More than three," Rafe corrected in a deeply fierce voice. "Closer to a *dozen*."

"What?" Dulcie could barely comprehend three. Her stomach roiled. More *murders* by her uncle's hand were unthinkable.

"That I know of," Rafe continued. "There may be more. Your father and mother and the captain and three crewmen on your father's yacht." His Scots burr became more pronounced when he recalled that except for an earache, Dulcie would have been another victim.

The expression in Dulcie's eyes was brimming with earnestness. "I know what you're telling me is true. My head knows it. But my heart doesn't want to accept that my uncle not only murdered my family, but members of other people's families as well."

As Rafe gazed at her, a chill ran down his spine. She was so guileless. So honest, so strong, so brave, yet dependent on an uncle so filled with malice toward her. Everything she felt was written on her beautiful face. She needed a protector. She needed someone to care about her and for her. She needed someone to watch over her and keep her safe. She needed him.

A profound wave of warmth filled him at the knowledge that she was his wife. "You're a good person. An honest, moral person who tries to see the best in everyone—especially in the people you love."

Dulcie shook her head, clearly struggling to grasp everything she'd learned. "My uncle's crimes against others are damning enough, but to kill your own brother and nephew just to usurp a title and a position in society?" She shuddered. "It's barbaric. It's vile. It's..."

"Evil," Rafe finished. "And unfortunately, when Guilford gained the title he also gained immunity from prosecution. As a lord, he is beyond the reach of the law."

Dulcie knew the peerage and the nobility were immune from prosecution, but hearing Rafe confirm it came as shock. "There's nothing I can do?"

"You, sweet Dulcie, can stay out of his way," Rafe warned her. "Don't cross him. And if it comes down to a forced marriage, do your utmost to accept your uncle's choice." Rafe studied the girl facing him. She was a petite slip of a girl on the cusp of full womanhood. Guilford would crush her without a second thought if she continued to try to thwart him. "Stay out of his way and stay alive."

"What about justice?" she demanded. "How does my family ever get justice if Guilford is beyond the reach of the law?"

"I don't know," Rafe answered honestly. "If I hadn't ridden into the trap my enemy set for me at Waterloo, I would have been able to prevent Guilford from ever harming you. But…"

Understanding dawned. Dulcie stared at the man she'd married a few short hours ago. "You're a victim, too. The army is carrying out someone else's plot against you, isn't it? That's why they're going to murder you in the morning. And there's no way for me to stop it."

"I can't prove Guilford Tennant had anything to do with the judgment against me. I may be the target of someone's scheming, but I am *not* a victim. I'm responsible for what happens to me. I knew the penalties. I sealed my fate the moment I disobeyed orders," Rafe explained. "I'm an officer. The army has to make an example of me. It has no choice. It must mete out punishment in order to maintain order in the ranks. I disobeyed orders on a field of battle. And I've been sentenced to die for that infraction by a military court of inquiry. I knew I would face punishment when I led that charge." He took a deep breath and released it in a rush of air. "Unfortunately, I miscalculated how severe my sentence would be."

"What's the customary sentence?"

"A court martial, a substantial fine, and two years' confinement in a military prison."

"You've been confined here for ten months. Why was your sentence harsher than usual?" she asked.

"I made an enemy in a high position. I remembered him from our first encounter in Spain. And he remembered me."

"What happened during your first encounter?"

Rafe hesitated before he answered her question. Suddenly, acutely aware of how his answer would sound to an innocent like her. He'd spent four years killing the French and their allies in war, but he hadn't enjoyed it. He had done what he considered to be his duty to serve his country and protect his way of life, the men in his command, and the innocent villagers caught between two armies. He had learned in war that he wasn't a particularly violent man. He had an explosive temper, but he'd spent the six years since he'd become the Earl of Blackburn learning to control it. Except when he was on the field of battle, fighting for the lives of his men as well as for his own. On the battlefield he lived up to the name his men had given him. On the battlefield, he *was* 'Raging Raphael Blackburn, the Angel of Death' or 'Mad Black.' But he didn't want Dulcie to think of him that way. He didn't want her to know she'd married that man. Rafe wanted her to remember him kissing her and holding her close on a massive bed in a honeymoon cottage on their wedding night. He didn't want Dulcie to think badly of him.

She moved closer to him. "You can tell me." She offered him a teasing smile. "I can keep a secret."

Rafe clamped his jaw shut.

Dulcie responded to the challenge. "I've told you all *my* deep, dark secrets."

Rafe gave her a skeptical look.

"Well, I *would* have told you all my deep dark secrets if I had any," she amended with a shrug. "But, alas, I am an open book."

"Not so open anymore," Rafe reminded her in a deep, rumble of a voice. "I'd say you have about six and a half feet of one deep, dark, secret to keep."

"How can you expect me to keep *you* a secret? You are my husband and I'm proud of you and who you are. You are a secret too good to keep. Especially when I need to have a husband to prevent Guilford from choosing one for me."

"I can't be a husband to you *or* a protector for you when I'm dead," he said.

"Don't!" Dulcie placed her fingers against his mouth. "Please don't say it! It's bad luck."

Rafe smiled against her fingers, then kissed them. "Och, lass, saying the truth aloud doesn't bring bad luck."

"But I can't bear to hear you speak the words!"

"You can. And you must." He took her hand in his so he could plant a warm, kiss against her inner wrist and feel the steady beat of her heart. "I don't want to leave you a widow."

"I know," she sighed. "And I don't want to be your widow. I want to be your wife. I want us to have a life together, but if that cannot be, then I want to make you proud of me. And a widow has options an unmarried girl doesn't have. A widow can't be forced to marry. A widow can have a home of her own if she has income enough."

"You'll have a home of your own," he assured her. "I purchased it over three years ago as part of the jointure Geoff and I negotiated in the marriage settlements. You'll also have an income that will allow you to live quite comfortably, if not luxuriously. I've seen to that." He met her gaze. "What you won't have is someone to protect you from your uncle's greed and malice."

"But in order to have my freedom I'll have to be your widow. Otherwise, how could I explain my change in station?"

"A mother's portion?" he suggested. "A recently departed maternal great aunt who left you a house in town and the income to maintain it." Thinking of the deal he'd concluded with the Earl of Weymouth, Rafe added, "Or a maternal grandfather who bequeathed you the income from the breeding rights to an exceptional stud horse..."

"Until this morning, I was an unmarried female. I don't know anything about breeding horses. I've never even been to the horse sales at Tattersall's. Or Ascot, even though I know ladies are allowed to attend."

"You don't have to know anything about horse breeding. The Earl of Weymouth has extensive knowledge of horses and the breeding of them. He can advise you."

"And how would I explain my sudden close association with the Earl of Weymouth?"

"Through your friend, Lady Carlisle. Weymouth is her godfather. You're bound to have met him on occasion."

"It won't work, Rafe." Dulcie shook her head. "I'm not saying your suggestions are without merit, I'm simply saying they won't work because you've forgotten two important details."

"What important details?" Rafe tilted his head to study her. He liked the way she thought. She was quick-witted, intelligent, and curious. He appreciated the pertinent questions she asked and the way she gave careful thought to each of his suggestions before finding the flaws in his logic. She shared many of the same traits Rafe had admired in her brother. Traits Rafe had missed since Geoff's death.

"I'm still underage and until I reach the age of majority stipulated in my father's and in Geoff's wills, any income or property I receive will be controlled by Uncle Guilford."

Rafe frowned. She was right. He'd never considered that she might not yet be of legal age to claim her inheritances on her own. Of course, he had also never expected to hang when he had signed the marriage contracts. He did a quick calculation. "You're over twenty-one."

"Yes, I am. But I'm under twenty-five. And in order to receive my mother's portion or any other incomes or inheritances bequeathed to me, I must be married or have reached the age of twenty-five. I'm twenty-two. I'll turn twenty-three in August. As my guardian, Guilford controls everything until my twenty-fifth birthday."

Rafe rubbed his hand down his unshaven cheek and over his chin, muttering a string of oaths beneath his breath. "And at the rate he's going, you won't have much fortune left by the time you reach the age of your majority."

"So the only way I can claim my inheritance on my own is as your wife." *Or his widow.* But Dulcie couldn't bear that thought when he was living and breathing right beside her. "That's one of the reasons I chose you to be my Charlotte Society soldier *and* my husband."

"*One* of the reasons?" Rafe couldn't help wondering what her other reasons were.

The look she gave him was both flirtatious and demure. "One among several."

"For example..."

She leaned closer to him. "I wanted to see if you were as handsome as I imagined you to be from Geoff's descriptions in his letters."

"Seems reasonable." Rafe had wondered what she looked like as well. But he wasn't ready to confess it yet.

"It's *verra* reasonable." Dulcie rolled her *r*'s in a bad imitation of the way Rafe pronounced the word when his Scottish burr broke through his proper English. "What if you had been old, massively overweight, and corseted like the Prince Regent?"

"And an active cavalry officer?" He scoffed. "In a place where food was scarce? Not very—*verra*—likely."

"I suppose you're right." She pursed her lips in thought. "Then you might have been young and slim, but with a face covered in spots."

"You know better. Your brother would never have chosen a boy covered in spots to be your husband and your protector. A beautiful, intelligent, and willful young lady like you would have him tamed and wearing leading strings in no time." His smile grew even more knowing. "You're right. You *are* a terrible liar."

"Perhaps I need more practice."

"Verra well," he drawled. "Try again."

"Perhaps I was simply curious to know if you were an accomplished kisser... Open up, Raphael. You'll feel better," she whispered, before she dipped her head and traced the seam of his lips with her tongue. "I've just told you three of my secrets. Surely you can tell me one of yours."

"You've told me one secret," he said, eyeing her delectable lips hungrily as she drew away from him. "And I'm happy to see that you are still a terrible liar."

"Then we're even. One for one," she retorted. "Please. Sharing one secret can't be any worse than telling me what happened to you at the inquiry this morning."

"It was bad enough to *cause* what happened at the inquiry this morning."

Dulcie sat back. "I promise it won't be bad enough to drive me away or make me change my mind about you, Raphael Simon John Blackburn."

"You *should* stay away from me, sweet Dulcie," he warned. "My name and reputation are going to bear a black mark forever. I'm going to be tainted. You don't want to be a part of my disgrace."

"If you truly believe that, you should not have made me your wife.

Because I have no intention of staying away from you tonight. Black mark or not." She brushed his lips with hers. "Groan all you want," she whispered. "I intend to do this until you tell me your secret."

"Very well. My men call me 'Mad Black' and 'Raging Rafe, the Angel of Death'."

"That's because they've only seen you as a cavalry officer on the battlefield." She narrowed the gap between them even more by sliding onto his lap. A lap that was aching to receive her. "They don't know you the way I do."

He snorted at that. "I can assure you they know me far better."

Dulcie wrapped her arms around his neck, pulled his face down to hers, and whispered against his mouth. "They've known you *longer*. That doesn't mean they know you *better*."

Her tender torture was driving him mad. "Dulcie..."

"I'm your wife."

"Of two and a half hours," he pointed out.

"Do they know all your secrets?"

"No," he told her. "And neither do you."

"I will," she promised as she trailed a line of kisses from his mouth along the line of his jaw to his ear. "Before this night is over." She nipped his earlobe, then gently sucked it into her mouth, lavishing the bite she'd inflicted with tender ministrations.

Rafe groaned aloud as she abandoned his earlobe to trace the shell of his ear with her tongue.

"What terrible thing did you do?" she whispered.

"I lost my temper and became 'Raging Rafe'."

"On the battlefield?"

"No. In the officer's quarters when I returned from the hospital to discover that the officer who had countermanded my orders a fortnight earlier had confiscated our tent for his private use while I was at the hospital." He closed his eyes, shuddering at the memory of the day he and Geoffrey Tennant had made the best deal of Rafe's life. His bride. The woman doing her best to kiss him into spilling his secrets. Or losing his heart. He closed his eyes before she could see the memory come flooding back...

"Geoff?"

"Rafe." The relief in Geoffrey Tennant's voice had been palpable as he opened his eyes and recognized his good friend.

"I'm here." Rafe reached over to clasp Geoff's icy hand, seeking to warm it with his own.

Geoff shifted his head on his pillow, his desperate gaze searching the shadows around them. "Alone?"

"Aye," Rafe assured him.

"What I have to say is for your ears only." Geoff's handsome face contorted with pain.

Rafe furrowed his brow. "Geoff, let me call a surgeon."

"After." Geoff dug his teeth into his bottom lip, clearly struggling to master his pain. "Agreed?"

"Agreed," Rafe reluctantly said. "Now, what were you doing on that patrol?"

"Fenton." Geoff bit out the name.

"Fenton?" Rafe repeated. "What the devil does Cornelius Fenton have to do with our patrols?"

"Nothing," Geoff said. "But he's a colonel and his orders are followed."

"He ordered Woolridge to stand down?"

Geoff nodded. "And for me to take his place."

"Why you?" Rafe's frown deepened. "You were already slated for the midnight patrol. Why not someone else?"

Geoff shook his head. "Careful, Rafe."

"Me? You're the one who got himself shot by a pack of hostile guerillas."

Rafe was trying to ease Geoff's torment by pointing out that the man upon whom he most relied, his closest confidant and best friend, had managed to get himself shot by a roaming band of scavengers who used outdated weapons to fire at Army patrols on a daily basis.

"Targeted," Geoff whispered. "We rode into an ambush." He gave Rafe's hand a squeeze. "I don't know who they were, but they were well-armed and they didn't speak Portuguese or Spanish."

"And you believe you were their target?"

"I must have been," Geoff said. "Why have me take Woolridge's place otherwise? I was the only change to the detail."

Rafe slowly nodded, horrified comprehension dawning. As far as he could tell, Colonel Lord Cornelius Fenton, younger son of the twelfth Marquess of Lancaster, was more interested in the cut of his uniform and the deference his rank provided him than the men he commanded. The fact that Colonel Fenton's commission had been purchased by his father to steer Cornelius away from a life spent in a succession of bawdy houses and gaming dens was well known. Fenton had never reviewed any troops outside the regimental parade ground in London and had never accompanied his own regiment—or any other regiment—to a hostile land or ever concerned himself with the day-to-day operations of a cavalry unit. Why journey to Spain and intervene on this day? When Fenton's commission as a colonel in the cavalry had, until now, been exclusively ceremonial? "Have you had any recent dealings with Fenton?"

"No," Geoff replied. "Lancaster approached me with a business proposition before I left London, but I've never had any dealings with Fenton."

"Did you accept Lancaster's proposition?"

"No. I politely refused to consider it."

Rafe lifted an eyebrow at that. "A mere viscount dared refuse a marquess..."

The corners of Geoff's mouth turned up into a painful semblance of a smile. "You're not the only one whose reputation proceeds him."

Geoffrey's reputation as an earnest, honorable, and sober-sided peer had been well-earned. Rafe's answering smile was genuine. "I'm delighted to hear it. How did Lancaster take the rebuff?"

"Amicably."

"Did he simply appear amicable? Or did you find him to be sincere?"

"I found him to be sincere." Geoff shifted slightly and grimaced at the pain. "Once I explained my reasons, we were of an accord."

Seeing Geoff's expression, Rafe bent closer, his helplessness deepening to anguish. "Let me summon the surgeon. Please." He was not a man who begged, but Rafe would have gladly gone to his knees on his friend's behalf at that moment.

Geoff's grimace deepened. "Not yet."

"Geoff..."

"You'll be on your guard on patrol tonight?"

"Always."

"You make a big target, Rafe."

Raphael forced a smile. "Bigger than you. The guerillas' aims must be improving."

"It's nothing to joke about, Rafe," Geoff had admonished. "Look at me."

"You're going to be all right," Raphael assured him, fearing even as he spoke the words that he was making an empty promise.

"God willing," Geoff had conceded. "But you'll keep your promise about Dulcie and the ones dearest to me if I'm not?"

"Of course," Rafe said. "I gave you my word as a gentleman. And I shall keep it."

"You'll need proof." Geoff coughed; a bubble of blood stained his bottom lip. "Of everything. By the book. Their future depends on it."

"We'll make everything legal after *the surgeon."*

"Rafe..."

"No arguments, Captain."

"All right." Geoff sighed. "Summon the surgeon."

Rafe opened his eyes to find himself gazing into a pair of eyes that were almost identical to his friend's. A week later, when Geoff was strong enough to endure the process, the two men had drawn up and signed the marriage contracts. Try as he might to deny it and pretend otherwise, Rafe had been forced to accept what Geoff already knew—that despite heartfelt hopes and prayers Geoff was not going to survive his wounds, There had been no arguing or debate about the terms. Rafe had agreed to everything Geoff asked for. And there had been no celebration at the conclusion of the negotiations. Only relief and the deep, abiding understanding of their honor and duty and the love and admiration between two friends.

Rafe had sent a copy by special courier to Archibald Gunn in Edinburgh for review and had sent Geoff's copy by special courier to his solicitor, Mr. Wiley Merritt in London, along with Geoff's final letter to Dulcie. Mr. Merritt's instructions had been to review the contract and address any concerns to Archibald Gunn in Edinburgh, who had Rafe's permission to act in his stead to fulfill the terms of the contract to ensure the contract was more than generous to the bride. When the two solicitors were satisfied with the contract, Wiley was to retain the contract for Dulcie and Dulcie only. Guilford Tennant was not to be privy to the contents.

"Rafe?" Dulcie's expression was filled with concern at his sudden silence. "What happened in the officer's quarters?"

"I punched the officer in the face for causing the deaths of three of my men, broke his nose, and tossed him out of my quarters." He sucked in a ragged breath as the memories of that night receded and Dulcie nipped his earlobe before she began trailing another line of delicate kisses along his jaw and chin until she reached his mouth once again.

"See? That wasn't so bad, was it?" She pulled his bottom lip into her mouth, then released it so she could tease the seam between his lips until he opened them.

"It was very bad," he admitted. "Geoff had died a few moments before. And I walked into our quarters to find the man who caused his death sipping whisky and warming his feet at our stove."

"Oh, Raphael..." Dulcie hugged him close, then covered his face with kisses. She couldn't change his memories, but she could give him other, happier memories. She redoubled her efforts to entice him to kiss her back by slipping her tongue into his mouth and sweeping it around the interior, touching, tasting, tangling her tongue with his.

Unable to withstand the torture any longer, Rafe plunged his fingers into her hair, scattering her hairpins and holding her head at the angle he liked best as he took control of the kiss.

Dulcie thought she'd mastered the art of kissing him, but Rafe showed her how much more he had to teach and how much more she had to learn. He took her breath away, then gave it back in the most exquisite way possible, changing tempo from a deep, slow, wet, carnal kiss to hard, fast kisses that left her gasping and begging him not to stop.

"Sweet, sweet Dulcie," he murmured as he abandoned her mouth and began brushing his lips against her cheeks, her chin, the tip of her nose, the delicate skin at the corners of her eyes and eyelids. "Stop talking while I kiss you." He kissed each temple, her forehead, and the soft, wispy curls along her hairline.

"I'm trying to keep my mouth open," Dulcie said when she could form a coherent thought. "So you'll want to kiss me."

"I'll keep it open," he promised. "And you needn't worry about me wanting to kiss you. I do. And I will. For as long as I can."

CHAPTER 13

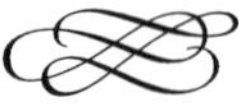

"Cato said the best way to keep good acts in memory was to refresh with new."
—Francis Bacon, 1561-1626

St. James's Street
London

The five gentlemen—a duke, two marquesses, an earl, and a viscount—meeting in the small private salon on the first floor of White's were in deep discussion about how to proceed with the implementation of the desperate plan Lord Weymouth had asked them to devise in the event his negotiations with a certain military commandant to secure the release of Major Lord Raphael Blackburn, seventh Earl of Blackburn, failed to yield positive results. Blackburn's release was the first of Weymouth's objectives. His second objective was to escort Blackburn's intended bride and her attendant and witness to the Isle of Wight to facilitate their marriage.

"I had hoped we'd have more time," Jarrod, Marquess of Shepherdston, and leader of the group, said. "But time is running out. Now that we've learned the date of the inquiry is not only set, but has been advanced, we've no choice but to go ahead with what we've got." He glanced at his compatriots. "It isn't the way we normally operate or the way we prefer to operate, but it is why we plan for all eventualities."

"The range of eventualities is considerable," Daniel, Duke of Sussex, remarked, rubbing his side. He'd been shot on his last mission across the Channel. The wound had healed and no longer pained him, but he sported a most interesting scar as a souvenir from a French patrol boat crew. "And unpredictable. And not all of them are favorable."

"Do you know who scheduled the military inquiry for this morning?" Alexander, Marquess of Courtland, wanted to know.

"Not yet," Shepherdston said. "I haven't heard from my sources yet. But I'll know shortly."

Courtland nodded. "I thank Barclay for calling the meeting this morning and for bringing his information to our attention as soon as possible. I only wish we could have alerted Lord Weymouth before he set off. As it stands, he will be fortunate to reach the island before it's over."

"We did what we could," Colin McElreath, Viscount Grantham, said. "He's sailing from my father-in-law's wharf on the *Manx Queen*, one of the newest and fastest yachts ever built. Gillian commissioned it to be our personal vessel so Weymouth will be traveling in style. We put on additional sails for extra speed and if Lord Weymouth and the two young ladies arrive at the docks on schedule, he'll have ideal conditions for tide and wind."

"Two young ladies?" Barclay was aware of Weymouth's search for Blackburn and knew that Weymouth had been asked to locate him for a specific reason. He had been involved in the planning of Blackburn's rescue should negotiations with the commandant fail, but because he

and his wife had been entertaining her grandfather all week, Barclay had been unable to attend the previous meeting at White's and had been unaware of Weymouth's decision to facilitate an elopement and clandestine marriage between Blackburn and the young lady he had promised to wed.

"Miss Dulcie Tennant," Grantham replied. "And her friend Miss Phoebe Osborne. Gillian and I met them at Lady Middleton's ball last night. Along with Courtland's friend, the Earl of Sinclair and Montleith, Alasdair Sinclair." He glanced at Courtland. "Miss Tennant is Blackburn's betrothed."

"She's the reason Lord Weymouth set out to locate Blackburn. Miss Tennant, Miss Osborne, and the new Lady Anthony Carlisle founded the Charlotte Society together." Shepherdston elaborated, explaining the purpose of that charity and Dulcie Tennant's appeal to Weymouth for help in finding Blackburn.

"He should make it to the garrison with time to spare," Grantham added. Grantham's father-in-law, Baron Davies, had been a linen merchant when he was created First Baron Davies and had built the fastest, most modern fleet of vessels in Britain or the continent. He was a pioneer in shipping, building faster, narrower ships with smaller cargo holds, but with extra room for additional sails. Davies' ships couldn't carry as much cargo as larger ships, but they were faster, more maneuverable, and less expensive to build. In addition to his cargo ships, Baron Davies and his only child, Colin's wife, Gillian, had commissioned and begun building luxury yachts and barges for those in the aristocracy who preferred water travel. Nothing on the ocean was faster than a Davies vessel.

"The devil of it is that the man's been confined in the garrison on Wight for ten months," Jonathan Manners, the Earl of Barclay, said. "And it's just happenstance that I overheard a trio of gentlemen discussing it at India's grandfather's celebration at the Admiralty last night."

Barclay and his wife, India, had attended her grandfather, Admiral Sir Harold Gregory's, reception, foregoing Lady Middleton's masked ball in order to celebrate the old man's retirement from the Admiralty.

Lady Middleton's masked ball was the first masque of the Season and the most spectacular, but Admiral Gregory was Barclay's wife, India's, only family, and she didn't consider missing Lady Middleton's ball a hardship. Missing the celebration of her grandfather's illustrious career in the British Navy had been unthinkable.

Fortunately, Barclay had recognized the name of the man a trio of gentlemen attending the Admiralty's celebration honoring Admiral Gregory were discussing as Lord Raphael Blackburn, the man Lord Weymouth had spent a sennight attempting to locate. And Barclay and his associates had spent the subsequent days after Weymouth had located him formulating a plan of rescue. But according to the snippets of conversation Barclay had overheard, Weymouth's mission to negotiate a release was destined for failure.

Barclay had attempted to report the conversation to Weymouth earlier in the morning only to learn Weymouth had left London for the Isle of Wight before dawn. Barclay had immediately sent word to the other four gentlemen—members of the Free Fellows League—who worked in secret out of the War Office with the support and guidance of the Wizard of the War Office, the Earl of Weymouth. "According to the conversation I heard, the outcome of the inquiry has already been determined."

Sussex let out an ominous groan. "This sounds like a personal or political retaliation."

"Blackburn is charged with disobeying a direct order and striking a superior officer," Courtland said. "But Wellington absolved him of the charge of disobeying a direct order when he proclaimed Blackburn a hero and rewarded him with a medal for leading the charge to save the artillery crew at Waterloo."

"But Wellington did *not* absolve him of the charge of striking a superior officer," Shepherdston pointed out. "Although reports from the witnesses unanimously upheld Blackburn's claim that he led the cavalry charge against orders but did not strike his superior."

"That's the reason for the official inquiry," Grantham added. "To hear testimony from the accused and witnesses in order to pronounce discipline for Blackburn."

"Discipline other than the ten months he's already been confined to quarters at a military prison?"

"Precisely," Barclay said. "He's an earl. He should have been released immediately, if confined at all. I agree with Daniel. This situation smacks of retaliation." He heaved a sigh. "In which case, the fellow is doomed."

"Did you recognize any of the gentlemen?" Courtland asked. "You and Sussex know everyone in the ton."

"I recognized the Marquess of Lancaster—" Barclay began.

"It's political then," Shepherdston interrupted. "Why else would Lancaster be there? He has no connection to the Admiralty."

"He has a connection to the Army," Sussex reminded Shepherdston.

"That's right." Barclay snapped his fingers together in a eureka moment. "And Viscount Tennant was standing beside a man in a cavalry uniform, though what Tennant was doing at an Admiralty affair is beyond me."

Grantham drew his brows together in a fierce frown, then reached for the coffee pot on the tray to the right of his chair and refilled his cup. "If I'm not mistaken, the current Lord Tennant's nephew served in the cavalry on the Peninsula with Griffin." Grantham was an original Free Fellow. He, Shepherdston, and Weymouth's eldest son, Griffin Abernathy, the current Duke of Avon, had started the Free Fellows League as schoolboys at the Knightsguild School for Gentlemen. Grantham glanced at Shepherdston for confirmation.

Shepherdston nodded. "They served in different units, but he was in the battle of *Fuentes de Oňoro* where Griff was wounded. If Griff was here, he could tell us what he knows of Geoffrey Tennant's service in Spain, but Griff elected to remain in the country while his wife and mother continue their recovery from the births of their children so Lord Weymouth could travel to Wight. I understand the previous Viscount Tennant was mortally wounded during a routine patrol several months later. He was Blackburn's second-in-command

and there is some confusion as to why young Tennant was leading the dawn patrol when he'd just returned from a midnight patrol and had been assigned to the subsequent midnight patrol. When Geoffrey Tennant died, the current Viscount Tennant, the ninth, I believe, succeeded him." Shepherdston steepled his fingers against his bottom lip. "There was talk at the time when Geoffrey Tennant's name appeared in the casualty lists that it might not have been a coincidence. Foul play could have been involved. It's hardly commonplace to lose two viscounts in one family in the span of one year. It was rumored someone helped clear the path so the younger brother of the seventh viscount and the uncle of the eighth could become the ninth Viscount Tennant."

"The *current* Viscount Tennant," Courtland pronounced, "who has proven very unlucky at the tables in the gaming dens."

"Exactly." Shepherdston nodded. "Fortune appeared to favor him when those untimely deaths made him a wealthy viscount. But has since deserted him and has left him swimming in debt."

"Who was the third man?" Daniel, Duke of Sussex asked. "The one in the cavalry uniform."

"I've no idea," Barclay said. "His back was to me the entire time. I didn't hear his name called or recognize his voice." Barclay shrugged. "I suppose I'm out of practice at ferreting out information."

"We're all out of practice," Shepherdston replied. "That's what concerns me."

"We?" Sussex was surprised. "I was involved in Courtland's mission. While the three of you were waltzing in Vienna, I was avoiding the night watchman while scrambling over the city's rooftops and waking up jewelers." He glanced at Courtland. "For a good cause, of course."

"For an *excellent* cause," Courtland retorted. "I could not have married her without you."

"The war's been over for months now," Sussex said. "We've been able to stay home with our wives and tend to our estates without the constant threat of Bonaparte hanging over our heads. We've devoted our lives to saving our country from tyrants, but it seems we've plenty of tyrants in England to turn our attention and our talents to. And the commandant of the military prisoners' garrison on the Isle of Wight is one of them. There is much more to this situation than Lord Weymouth knows. He arranged a meeting with the commandant and an inspection of the garrison and interviews with the prisoners for the War Office."

"Including an interview with a man facing a military inquiry tomorrow morning?" Grantham asked.

"That would be my guess," Sussex said.

"How many of us are going?" "And when do we leave?" Courtland and Barclay asked simultaneously.

"That depends on Grantham," Shepherdston said. "We'll need to borrow another of the fastest yachts ever made. As soon as possible." He arched an eyebrow at Grantham. "Have you another boat?"

"No," Grantham said. "But my wife has a fleet of them. I'll see that we have one made ready."

THE MAN BOUNDING UP THE STAIRS TO THE PRIVATE SALON WHERE THE Free Fellows were meeting didn't bother to knock but simply burst through the door. He breathed a sigh of relief at seeing Courtland. "Thank God!"

"Dare!" Courtland came halfway out of his seat.

"Where would Weymouth go by boat? And where do I get a boat?"

"Who the hell are you? And what do you know about Weymouth?" Shepherdston demanded.

Shepherdston's roar was generally sufficient to quell any man, but the man Courtland called Dare didn't flinch or back down. "Alasdair Sinclair, fourteenth Earl of Sinclair and Montleith, and I'm here to find out why Weymouth drove away with the woman I love shortly after daybreak this morning."

The five men exchanged glances.

Shepherdston focused his attention on Courtland. "Alex? This is the friend you were telling us about?"

"Yes. We were at Eton together."

"Do you trust him?" Sussex asked.

"With my life," Courtland swore.

"It could be if we reveal what we know to the wrong person," Grantham reminded him.

"I trust him the way you and the others trusted Jonathan and me not so long ago," Courtland said, pinning Grantham with a meaningful gaze.

Shepherdston nodded. "All right then, we can always use a trusted ally." He turned to Alasdair. "I'm Shepherdston. He's Sussex. He's Barclay. And you met Grantham last night. We're the Free Fellows League."

"I don't gi' a ha'penny who ye are or what ye do," Alasdair told him. "I want to know where Weymouth is and why Phoebe is with him."

"He's on a secret mission for the government. Miss Osborne is helping."

"And her friend?" Alasdair demanded.

"Miss Tennant is marrying a man who is scheduled to be executed tomorrow," Sussex added.

"She's marrying a condemned man?" Alasdair asked.

"Yes," Sussex said.

"Why?" Alasdair asked.

"To protect her from the man we suspect is guilty of a far worse crime than the one for which her intended is accused," Shepherdston said.

Alasdair exhaled. "I dinna care about yer secrets or yer condemned man. I just want Phoebe."

"Lord Weymouth will bring her back safe and sound after the wedding."

"But why is she there?" Alasdair asked.

"We needed a witness to the marriage. Miss Osborne was the logical choice."

"Why do you want Miss Osborne?" Grantham asked. "Enough to burst in here like a madman?"

Alasdair looked at Colin McElreath as if he'd fallen from the moon. "I need to tell her I love her before I marry her."

Shepherdston grinned. "Oh well, that's different..."

"Congratulations, Dare!" Courtland clapped him on the shoulder, guiding him toward the door as he did so. "Now, come on. We've a great deal to do before we sail for the coast." He smiled. "Have you a special license?"

Alasdair shook his head.

"Then we'll have to make a brief stop to visit Uncle Canterbury," Courtland said.

"Courtland will see that you're properly married," Sussex assured him. "While the rest of us see to the mission at hand." He pinned Sinclair with his sharp gaze. "All we ask of you is that you keep mum about the conspiracy you just became a part of..."

"We leave separately," Grantham reminded the other Fellows. "And meet at the docks. We sail in one hour."

"Courtland and Sinclair first," Shepherdston ordered. "Because they've a lot to accomplish." He looked at Courtland. "We'll need Lady Courtland and everything else you're to furnish for your part of the mission."

"You can count on us," Courtland called back as he ushered Alasdair Sinclair out of the room and toward his destiny.

~

"MISS OSBORNE!" WEYMOUTH CALLED TO PHOEBE FROM THE FORWARD deck. "Come, my dear, we have company. My associates have come to meet us. And they've brought someone along for you."

Phoebe hurried to the rail to join him. "Oh." She stopped in her tracks at the sight of her heart's desire.

Alasdair Sinclair was waiting on the dock when the *Manx Queen* sailed into port and Weymouth and Phoebe walked down the gangplank without Dulcie.

"Alasdair, what are you doing here?" Phoebe asked. "And why are you dressed like that?"

He wasn't wearing the red coat and hat he had worn to the ball. He was wearing a formal black suit. But he was dressed as a buccaneer just the same. "I've come to commandeer this vessel and to take possession of my prize."

Phoebe frowned. "Your prize? What prize? The boat?" She looked at Weymouth, who shrugged.

"You, my love." Alasdair dropped to one knee. "You're my prize. My gift. The love of the rest of my life. But I was too stupid to see it until ye left me." Reaching into his pocket, he produced the gold band he'd purchased from Dalrymple's Jewelry. "This is for Phoebe Osborne, the woman I love."

"Oh, *Alasdair*."

"Do ye love me, lass?" He found her gaze and held it. "Even a little?"

"I love you with all my heart."

Reaching into his other pocket, Alasdair produced a flawless four carat sapphire and diamond betrothal ring. "And this is for my lady mermaid, who dared to love a Scottish buccaneer. I love ye, Phoebe, lass. Ye and no other. Will ye marry me?" He opened his arms.

Phoebe raced into them. "Kiss me senseless."

"Say yes first."

"Yes."

"Congratulations, Miss Osborne," Lord Weymouth said as he passed the happy couple on his way to greet his associates. "And to you, Lord Sinclair."

"We promised him a proper wedding," Sussex said as he walked over to speak to Weymouth.

Lord Weymouth frowned.

"We had to bring him along." Shepherdston joined Sussex and Weymouth. "He burst into our *social gathering* at White's to demand answers from Courtland."

"What sort of answers?" Weymouth asked.

"He wanted to know where you were," Shepherdston explained. "And where he could secure a boat to find you. And Miss Osborne. He claimed you drove off with Miss Osborne and Miss Tennant at dawn this morning. And that a boat was involved. He wanted to know why."

"So, you see? We couldn't leave him behind at White's to cause a stir and ask a lot of questions about your whereabouts," Sussex said.

Weymouth glanced at Sinclair and Miss Osborne, who were being congratulated by Courtland and his wife and by Barclay and Grantham. "You brought Lady Courtland?"

"Why not?" Shepherdston retorted. "You brought a bride and a witness to a wedding. We believed it only fair that we do the same." He looked around. "I see you left the bride and groom on the island, so I assume the wedding took place."

"It did," Weymouth said. "But the honeymoon in London was out of the question. The negotiations did not go well."

"We were afraid of that," Sussex told him, his face falling. "Barclay and Lady Barclay attended the reception at the Admiralty last evening honoring her grandfather. Admiral Lord Harold Gregory's fifty years of naval service. While there, Barclay overheard an interesting conversation."

"Oh?" Weymouth cocked an eyebrow.

"Lord Blackburn's name came up several times." Shepherdston waved Barclay over to join them. "Jonathan, tell Lord Weymouth what you learned while attending the reception at the Admiralty last night."

Barclay recounted the conversation he'd overheard between the Marquess of Lancaster, Viscount Tennant, and the unidentified man in the cavalry uniform.

Weymouth frowned. "Did the Prince Regent make an appearance at the reception?"

"Not while we were there," Barclay replied. "And we arrived with the guest of honor and accompanied him home afterwards."

"Did you recognize any of Lancaster's allies at the reception?"

"None of his usual boon companions or the courtiers who normally trail in his wake."

"Then what the devil was Lancaster doing at the Admiralty?" Weymouth wondered.

"I don't know," Barclay answered honestly. "I only know that what I overheard didn't bode well for Blackburn."

"How did the inquiry go?" Shepherdston asked.

"It went the way Barclay's trio of gentlemen knew it would go," Weymouth said. "He's scheduled to hang at dawn."

"Hang an earl? What did he do?" Barclay asked. "Besides lead a cavalry charge at Waterloo that made him a hero?"

"He led a cavalry charge at Waterloo that made him a hero," Weymouth said.

Sussex muttered an oath beneath his breath. "We appear to have more than one group of conspirators at work."

"I agree," Weymouth said.

"What was your opinion of the inquiry?" Shepherdston asked.

"Unfortunately, I wasn't able to form an opinion of the panel," Weymouth told him. "By the time the ladies and I arrived, the military officers had completed their investigation and pronounced the sentence."

"What about the witnesses?" Sussex asked.

"They all supported Blackburn's testimony. With the exception of the artilleryman who wasn't present at the incident, but bore witness to the fact that Blackburn led the charge that saved the artillery and the artillerymen. Had the cavalry not defended the artillery, the men would have been slaughtered. The other witnesses recounted what caused Blackburn to disobey orders. Their testimony matched his to the letter. They followed Blackburn, riding with him to the defense of the artillery unit. They also disobeyed orders, yet none of them were charged with disobeying orders. Only Blackburn."

"Do you know which officers served on the panel of inquiry?"

"According to Blackburn, the panel was made up of three officers. Captain Hutton, Major Endicott, and Colonel Traynor," Weymouth said. "Blackburn's solicitor supplied the officers' names."

"Did Blackburn serve with any of them?"

"No." Weymouth shook his head. "Blackburn wasn't acquainted with any of the panel."

Jarrod Shepherdston frowned. "That's unusual. What do we know about them?"

"Not enough," Weymouth said. "Yet. But I will as soon as I get back to London."

"And you can be on your way as soon as we get Sinclair and Miss Osborne married..." Sussex said. "I'm sure Courtland would be most agreeable to having you escort Lady Courtland home."

"As soon as we see to the wedding of the happy couple, we need to put the plan into motion. We don't have a great deal of time," Barclay said. "Imagine condemning an earl to hang on such questionable charges. And in such questionable circumstances."

"The fact that none of the other officers were charged is troubling," Shepherdston agreed.

"And worthy of further investigation," Sussex added.

Weymouth nodded. "All the more reason we must take control of the commandant's early morning gallows party."

CHAPTER 14

"The joy of love is too short and the sorrow thereof,
and what cometh
Thereof, dureth over long."
—Sir Thomas Malory, 1405-1471

"Now you're in trouble," Dulcie murmured as Rafe progressed from making love to her mouth to planting a line of tender kisses along her jawline and the slender column of her neck.

"How so?" Rafe murmured between kisses.

"Now that I know you can do this"—she shivered as waves of sensual awareness moved through her body—"I'm never going to want you to stop."

"Who said anything about stopping?" He trailed his tongue from the hollow of her throat to the tantalizing underside of her chin.

"You always stop," she complained. "Whenever I want you to keep going."

Rafe stopped kissing her long enough to fix his gaze on her face.

"See what I mean?"

"I haven't stopped," Rafe said. "I paused so I could see the expression on your lovely face."

"You stopped in the coach. You stopped when the corporal interrupted us. And you stopped to explain why you want me to keep you a secret."

"I had to stop in the coach because we'd arrived at the cottage. And I had to stop when Peavey interrupted us. And..." He flashed a grin at her before kissing the tip of her nose. "If I remember correctly, I offered to continue the moment he closed the door behind him. You..." He moved from her nose to her lips and hovered a breath away from her mouth. "Suggested we wait a bit."

"I did," she admitted. "But only because I was afraid the corporal might hear us."

"He couldn't hear us kiss," Rafe assured her.

"But he'd *know* we were kissing."

Rafe grinned. "He would know regardless. Because we're doing what all newly married couples do."

"Does that mean you're going to make love to me?"

"I *am* making love to you," he said.

"You're kissing me."

"Kissing is a part of making love," Rafe said.

"Kissing is part of making love," Dulcie said. "But not *all* of it."

"Dulcie, there's something I need you to understand—" he began.

"There's something *you* need to understand, Raphael," she interrupted. "I'm young and you're the only man who has ever kissed me, but I'm not completely ignorant. I may not know everything that takes place in the marriage bed, but I know that something does. I know that housemaids often lose their virginity and have to leave service because they are with child. I know that the only way to get a child is to lie with a man. And I know men look forward to their wedding nights because it gives them license to get an heir on their wives." She pinned Rafe with her serious gaze. "I also know our marriage vows gave you license to take my maidenhead in order to get an heir."

Rafe rubbed his hand over his eyes before meeting her gaze once again.

Dulcie rushed ahead with what she needed to say before he had a chance to say anything. "You explained passion to me and the scandal and gossip and ruination it can cause so I would recognize the feelings and understand the consequences. And you explained the urge a man has to mate with a woman, but for some reason, you don't seem to want to mate with me." She bit her bottom lip to stop its quivering. "I know you enjoy kissing me. You told me you found me to your liking, but you don't act as if you do." A single tear slipped over her bottom eyelashes and disappeared into the auburn curls that had escaped from her hairpins. "You explained everything to me except why you don't want me."

The rejection he heard in her voice sent a pang of guilt shooting straight through his heart. *"Dulcie..."*

"I know you made death bed promises to Geoff before he died. I know you took on the responsibility for me and for the other unfinished business he left behind because of your friendship with him. I know that's why you married me."

When Rafe would have spoken, she held up her hand to forestall him. "You don't have to say anything. You've proven you're a man of honor, a gentleman. No matter what the military inquiry decided." She swallowed hard. "I understand how much your honor means to you so I would appreciate it if you would just tell me..." Her lip quivered again, and she bit down harder on it.

Undone by the sight, Rafe held his breath, waiting to see if Dulcie was about to ask him to reveal exactly what he'd promised Geoff he would do besides agreeing to marry her. "Tell you what, sweetheart?" he asked gently.

She took a deep breath, then released it and her words in a rush. "Tell me if you promised my overprotective brother you wouldn't touch me."

Rafe smiled in relief. "He didn't ask that of me. And I would not have promised it if he had."

Dulcie breathed her own sigh of relief. "Thank goodness. I was afraid you'd married me and bought me a house and provided me with a generous income for naught."

Rafe lifted his brow in query.

"I read the marriage contract and I know that failure to consummate the marriage invalidates the marriage contract and makes it possible for a father or a guardian to have the marriage annulled." She met his gaze. "I may not know all the details of how we accomplish it, but I do know the consummation of our vows has to take place."

Her words hit him with the force of a blow. While he had been focused on the details of providing for her and protecting her, Dulcie had been focused on the most important detail of all. The legality of the marriage contracts he had signed. "I *was* trying to protect you," he admitted. "From becoming a widow with an infant." He shook his head. "Like my oldest sister and—" He hesitated for a second before continuing. "I was trying to prevent you from having to keep both a secret. I was trying to live up to my name and my title and be noble."

She moved closer to him, offering her mouth for his kiss. "Don't be so noble. Don't leave me untouched."

Damnation. What could he say to that? How could he resist the passion he saw in her big brown eyes? *Don't be so noble. Don't leave me untouched.*

And how could he deny himself what he wanted most? Rafe took a deep breath. He'd wanted her from the first moment he'd seen her. And he'd wanted her more once he realized who she was. Once he realized she was his. He had been fighting his fate, fighting his need, and fighting his loyalty to Geoffrey Tennant. Dulcie was his best friend's baby sister. Rafe shouldn't be lusting for her. He shouldn't be imagining her in the throes of passion, shouldn't be aching for the feel of her lips on his body. He shouldn't be burning with desire for his best friend's sister.

But he was.

Rafe pulled her into his arms, abandoning all attempts at nobility.

He was tired of fighting his desire. He had done everything else he could do to protect her. He had warned her about the consequences for her and of the danger Guilford posed.

If he died tomorrow, he would do whatever he had to do, make whatever bargain he had to make with his Maker to become her guardian angel. And if, by some miracle, he survived his death sentence, Rafe would find a way back to her.

But tonight, he would not allow Dulcie Tennant to go untouched, or feel unwanted or unloved again.

Unless she changed her mind and stopped him, Raphael Blackburn was going to make love to his wife.

"Dulcie, are you sure about this? Have you considered what it could do to your life and reputation?"

"Yes, I have." Dulcie gazed up at him. "And I believe becoming your wife is worth the risk."

Rafe plunged his fingers into her hair and held her face at the perfect angle as he lowered his head to cover her lips with his own. "Sweet, sweet Dulcie. I pray I don't give you cause to regret it."

"You won't." She snuggled close to his side, then quickly pushed away. "Ouch."

"What is it?"

"Either Madam Gabrielle left a pin in this gown or the wire in the earring you dropped down my bodice is poking me."

Rafe grinned a devilish grin. "If I remember correctly, I promised to retrieve it for you." Shifting his position, Rafe slid away from the headboard until he was lying flat on his back and Dulcie was sitting beside him. Wrapping his arms around her, he gently maneuvered her into position. "May I?"

"Of course." Loving his devilish smile, Dulcie shivered in anticipation of what he was about to do.

She felt the cool air on her bare shoulders as Rafe began unbuttoning the row of buttons running from her neckline to the small of her back. She marveled at his dexterity as he released the tiny buttons from their loops.

When the buttons were all undone, he slipped his hands inside the opening and smoothed the fabric off her shoulders and over the slope of her bosom where it pooled at her waist.

The fabric of her shift surprised him. It was a delicate, sheer lawn fabric, revealing much more than it concealed. Rafe watched with rapt attention as the cool air in the bedchamber caused her flesh to pebble. He wanted to watch the tips of her breasts harden, but the top ribbon of her short stays prevented him from seeing what was hidden behind it. He slid his hands from her shoulders to her waist.

Dulcie shivered at the trail of heat his hands generated.

"What's this?" he asked as he encountered her stays. His question was meant to provoke a response. Rafe was a man of the world familiar with women's fashions and their purposes. A girl as petite, small-boned, and as slender as Dulcie didn't need an undergarment to hold her in or as support for her bosom. She likely wore it to create cleavage or for modesty's sake. To keep the tips of her breasts from showing through the thin fabrics currently in vogue.

"My short stays." She knew his question was rhetorical, but she answered it anyway.

Rafe crooked his index finger through the loop of the ribbon and tugged until he loosened the laces. "You won't be needing them." Removing her stays, Rafe tossed them aside.

Dulcie gasped in surprise as the peridot earring he had dropped down her bodice slipped from the folds of her shift and slid over her stomach and into her lap. *"Oh."*

"Look what I've found." Bending his head, Rafe plucked the peridot earring from her lap with his teeth, nuzzling the curls covering her woman's mound with his chin as he did so.

"Ooh!" His audacity might have shocked her if she hadn't been so thrilled by it. She liked the look in his eyes as he gazed at her, his eyes heavy-lidded with desire. Her heartbeat increased, and with it, the pace of her breathing.

Rafe dropped the earring into the dish on the bedside table, then turned his heated gaze on her, watching as the delicate lawn fabric moved in cadence with her breathing, caressing her soft breasts. "I fetched your missing earring, my lady. Now I shall claim my reward."

Rafe ran the tip of his finger along the delicate edging of her sheer undergarment, and smiled as her sensitive skin dissolved into a mass of tiny gooseflesh.

She sucked in another quick breath as his knuckle brushed the slope of her breast.

Nodding approval at her reaction, Rafe reached for the first of the four tiny shell buttons fastening the garment. His hands shook as he wrestled with the buttons. He didn't ask permission to release the buttons; he simply freed them, then skimmed his hands over the straps of her shift and slid them over her shoulders, down her arms, and over her hands. Her shift pooled atop the bodice of her gown as Dulcie knelt on the coverlet beside him, naked from the waist up.

This time Rafe asked for permission. "May I?"

She nodded, trembling in anticipation of his next move.

Burning with the desire to see all of her, he rolled off the bed.

Dulcie murmured a protest as he left her.

"Shh, sweetheart." Hurrying around to her side of the bed, Rafe pressed a kiss against her hair, her forehead, and the corner of her mouth. "Lie back." He guided her back down until she lay against the coverlet and carefully worked her dress and shift over her slim hips and down her legs, leaving her in a very brief pair of almost translucent silk drawers that could only be of French design and her peridot necklace. After removing her slippers, Rafe rolled her stockings and garters down her legs and dropped them on the floor beside her shoes.

Dulcie felt the heat rise in her cheeks as Rafe gazed down at her. Her first instinct was to cover her nakedness, but she didn't. The expression on his face and the gleam in his dark eyes emboldened her to keep her arms at her sides and allow him to see her. She shivered beneath the heat of his gaze.

"Are you cold?" he asked.

"No." She trembled again even as she denied being cold. There *was* a chill in the air. The prominence of her nipples proved it, but Dulcie was too enthralled by what was happening to feel it.

"Frightened?"

"A little," she admitted.

"Of me?"

"Not of you," she said. "But of what you're thinking when you look at me like this."

"That's easy." He smiled a devastatingly tender smile. "I'm thinking what a fortunate man I am because you, beautiful Dulcie, consented not only to be my bride, but to allow me to see you and to touch you the way no other man has."

"Raphael." Dulcie's heart filled with emotion. She held her arms out to him.

Rafe shoved the bed hangings aside, climbed onto the upholstered bench at the foot of the bed and over the footboard, making his way along the length of her body until he reached her arms.

"Kiss me," she ordered.

"With pleasure," he murmured.

Dulcie wrapped her arms around his neck, pulled his face down to hers, and closed her eyes as Rafe plundered her mouth with his warm, rough tongue, tasting, devouring, wanting, as he gently cupped her left breast in his hand and held it, measuring the weight while he caressed the nipple with the pad of his thumb. She kissed him back, tangling her tongue with his as he deepened the kiss. Rafe continued to kiss her as he shifted his focus from her left breast to her right one, where he lavished it with the same tender caresses, he had given to her left one.

Dulcie squirmed against him with each stroke of his tongue and caress of his thumb against her breast. Rafe broke the kiss long enough to murmur against her lips. "Do you like this?"

"Hmm."

He gave a little chuckle. "Is that a yes or a no? Or have I managed to render you speechless?"

She opened her eyes and smiled up at him.

"You're very beautiful." He caressed her cheek, marveling at the softness of her flawless, ivory-colored skin that contrasted with her auburn hair and her brown eyes. She wasn't the typical blond-haired, blue-eyed English beauty, but she was beautiful nonetheless. Rafe skimmed his hand from her cheek down her neck, over her chest, and over her ribs to her waist.

Rafe knitted his brows together at the sight of his tanned skin against the ivory of her tender flesh. Her waist was tiny and her hips small. He was a big man, and she was so petite. A frisson of something akin to fear went through him at the possibility of her conceiving and carrying his child to term. But it was a fear wrapped in a fierce pride. He had always known his family depended on his willingness to marry and produce an heir, but the reality had seemed far removed from his daily life. He had never looked at any of the women who had shared his bed and imagined one carrying his child. Until now...

"What's wrong?" she asked.

"Nothing."

"You're frowning."

"Am I?" He met her concerned gaze with one of boyish innocence.

"You know you are."

"I was thinking how much you remind me of Titania, Queen of the Fairies in *A Midsummer Night's Dream*."

"Small, but mighty?"

He recognized the note of hopefulness in her voice. "Diminutive and perfectly made."

"She's rather haughty," Dulcie said.

"She has a great deal of which to be proud." He lowered his head and planted a kiss on her midriff. "And so do you."

"Such as?"

"This." He dipped his head and blew a stream of hot air through the translucent silk above her belly button. "See how responsive you are?"

Her creamy skin pebbled at the feel of his hot breath against her stomach.

Rafe considered exploring the tempting region south of her navel, but remembered she was an innocent and headed north instead. "Here. And here. And here." He counted her ribs with kisses as he made his way to the underside of her breast and slowly licked it, tasting the tiny beads of perspiration there before he moved upward and covered the sensitive tip with his mouth and applied the perfect amount of suction.

Dulcie gasped and her body bucked from the exquisite sensation.

It was all the encouragement he needed. Rafe pulled her into his arms. Dulcie felt the heat from his body, but it was nothing compared to the heat of his mouth. Her whole body quivered as he lavished attention on her breasts, licking, kissing, suckling first one and then the other, applying suction before he gently laved the nipple and the circle surrounding it with the tip of his tongue, repeating the process until Dulcie thought she would faint from the sensation. Unable to withstand his devilishly delightful torture, Dulcie buried her fingers in his hair and pulled him from her bosom back to her mouth.

She felt the rasp of his tongue against her teeth once again as Rafe slipped it between her lips and into her mouth. Recognizing his urgency, she responded in kind, moving her lips under his, encouraging him to deepen the kiss.

She moved her own tongue, experiencing the jolt of unadulterated pleasure as it found, and mated with Rafe's. She ran her fingers through his hair, dislodging the ribbon of his queue, separating the thick strands of his hair until it hung loose over the collar of his red tunic and skimmed his wide shoulders. She clutched at his tunic, kneading the fabric before she plunged her fingers in his thick, dark hair once more.

Rafe caressed her bare back, smoothing his hands over her soft flesh, warming her, dispelling the tiny bumps that pebbled her ivory skin. He pressed her against him as he followed the line of her spine, over her silk covered buttocks, to the back of her smooth, slim thighs and back up again. Rafe halted his sensuous exploration resting the palm of his hand against the curve of her bottom while his mouth devoured hers. Over and over again.

He stopped kissing her mouth only long enough to press warm, wet kisses against the curve of her jaw, her neck, and beneath one ear.

Hot, breathless, and light-headed, Dulcie turned her face toward his and sought his mouth once more.

Rafe's kiss became bolder, more fervent.

"What are you doing?" she murmured against his lips as he left her mouth and began planting a line of hot, wet kisses from her lips to the hollow of her throat. Rafe traced the outline of her necklace with the tip of his tongue until Dulcie's body was taut and straining for more. He left her necklace and moved to the underside of her breasts and beyond, sliding down her body until he was kneeling between her legs.

"Going on a treasure hunt."

"A *treasure* hunt?"

"With you as the treasure, sweet Dulcinea," he murmured against her flesh, his hot breath promising more delight. "I'm going to touch you and taste you and kiss you and spend the night, or what's left of it, discovering all your hidden treasure..." He captured the end of the drawstring of her silk drawers with his teeth and tugged, then slid his hands up her thighs, over the silk legs of her undergarment, widening the opening so he could slip her drawers over her hips and buttocks and whisk them down her legs and over her feet.

"Rafe?" she breathed.

He answered her by placing a tender kiss on her stomach before testing the depth of her navel with his tongue. Rafe moved back a fraction to gaze at her and his grin was so devilishly handsome and wickedly inviting Dulcie knew she wasn't going to deny him anything as long as he continued to kiss her.

Breathing heavily, fighting to retain control of his raging desire, Rafe said the first thing that came to mind. "Lady Blackburn, did I remember to tell you how lovely you looked in your wedding dress?" He glanced at the puddle of green silk lying on the floor beside the bed.

"No, Lord Blackburn." Dulcie gazed at him from beneath the cover of her eyelashes, trying to encourage him to kiss her again. She was learning she craved his kisses like she craved air to breathe. "But you told me I was beautiful when you took it off me."

Rafe's breath caught in his throat at the innuendo he heard in her voice. "You are," he said hoarsely when he had regained his ability to speak.

"You're the only man who has ever called me beautiful," she whispered.

"I'm the only man to ever see you like this. Or to kiss you..." He stretched his legs out and gazed at her over the landscape of her body. "Like this..."

CHAPTER 15

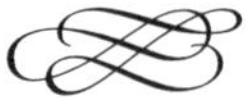

"Love me little. Love me long."
—Christopher Marlowe, 1564-1593

Dulcie's eyes widened in surprise as Rafe pressed a hot kiss on the russet curls covering her woman's mound. *"Raphael?"*

He recognized her nervousness when she spoke his name in a slightly higher pitch than her normal husky tone and realized he might be moving too fast for her. Although Dulcie had allowed him numerous liberties with her body, she was still a virgin and fearful of the unknown. This was a first for her. Her first time making love with a man and his first time making love to a virgin. "Will you trust me?"

"I already do," she whispered.

"Then trust me to give you pleasure." He inhaled the rose scent of her bath soap, then slowly blew a stream of hot breath over her, rustling the same curls he had kissed.

Dulcie shivered uncontrollably.

Seeing it, feeling it, Rafe smiled. "If I do anything you don't like, tell me and I promise I'll stop." *And he would stop. Even if it killed him.*

"All right."

Praying she wouldn't stop him, Rafe gently traced the folds of her labia with his tongue.

The first touch of Rafe's mouth on her was electric. Ripples of fire, like the fire of a glass of sherry on an empty stomach, shot through her, but the ripples of fire he evoked were a million times better than anything that could be found in a decanter of sherry. Dulcie gasped as her body reacted. Her breasts seemed to swell, the tips of them tightening into hard, little nubs, and her whole body began to ache for something she couldn't name but knew only Rafe could give her.

She arched her back and began filling the air around them with soft incoherent sounds she made deep in her throat. Squirming in his arms, Dulcie moved steadily closer until she finally reached down, clamped her fingers in his thick, dark hair and held him pressed against her. She whimpered hoarsely as Rafe teased her with his wicked tongue, delighting in creating ever-expanding waves of hot desire that surged throughout her body.

Her voice quavered with emotion as she called his name. "Rafe…"

"Do you like it?" Rafe asked.

"Yes," she gasped.

"Good," he murmured, trailing his tongue over her labia and across her upper and inner thighs, leaving kisses in his wake as he returned to the delta between her thighs and delved deeper. "Because I intend to broaden my search for treasure."

Dulcie shivered in anticipation.

And because he was a man who kept his promises, Rafe did just that.

Dulcie sucked in a ragged breath as he discovered the little nub hidden within the triangle of soft hair. Placing her hands against his shoulders, she pushed, then squeezed her thighs together.

Rafe broke the kiss and gazed up at her. "Do you want me to stop?"

"No." She opened her thighs again to give him access. "Don't stop."

"Did I hurt you?"

"Yes," she whispered. "No."

"Yes, or no?"

"I want..." Her words came out in a sob. "I want..." She thrust her hips upward, seeking release from the pleasure-pain he was creating with each touch of his tongue. "I need..." She searched for a word to explain but she couldn't concentrate on words when she could feel his breath against her. *"Something."*

"It's all right, sweetheart." Rafe's voice was tender and reassuring. "I know what you need." He kissed her again, teased her some more, harder, faster, softer.

"Please, don't stop."

Rafe smiled against her. He wasn't going to stop. Not until she found her release.

"Raphael?"

He had never particularly liked his given name until he heard it in her low, husky voice. He heard the question in the way she said his name and the urgency behind it and knew she was close to finding what she needed, what her body was seeking. He knew she needed reassurance, knew she couldn't understand what was happening to her until it happened.

Rafe paused to reassure her. "It's all right, Dulcie, my sweet. Don't fight it. Let go. Let it happen. I'm with you. I'll catch you." Plunging his tongue inside her, he lavished the sensitive button with attention and pushed her over the edge of her body's endurance and into bliss.

Her muscles relaxed, then tightened, quivered, and finally relaxed completely as she cried out his name.

Rafe moved up to hold her close, pressing his face against her hair, cradling her against his body as she shuddered in the aftermath of her stunning climax.

Dulcie opened her eyes to find Rafe gazing down at her with the tenderest expression she had ever seen on his face. "What happened? Did I faint again?"

"Yes," he said. "But it's a different kind of fainting that happens in lovemaking. Physicians call it an orgasm. The French call it 'the little death.'"

"I call it *magnificent*," Dulcie said.

Rafe laughed. "Well, I aim to please."

"Does it happen every time you make love?"

"Only if you do it right."

"Then we must have done something *very* right." She sighed. "I thought it was going to be embarrassing and painful and messy."

"Where did you get that idea?" Rafe was curious to find out how much she knew about the intimacies men and women shared while making love.

"I've heard the housemaids talking." She shrugged. "And I paid attention."

"I'll wager you did," Rafe said.

"And later, while sitting with the chaperones and matrons on the edges of ballrooms, I listened to the older ladies talking about what was expected of a young lady when she married. They never talked about what you just did to me. They always talked about the pain and embarrassment, the mess, and the fact that they weren't allowed to say no." She met Rafe's gaze. "Why would they say things like that when what you did to me was surprising and a bit embarrassing and overwhelming at first, but felt so incredibly wonderful?"

"Not everyone has the same experience," Rafe explained. "I was taught, and I believe, that making love should be pleasurable for both parties. But I've been told that's rarely the case for women. Apparently, what we shared is not common practice among our peers. Men are generally in a hurry to satisfy themselves without regard for their partner's pleasure. And women usually need more time and coaxing to reach satisfaction than men do."

"Who taught you?" Dulcie asked.

"I was fortunate to have a father who saw to my sexual education. He explained the rules and the responsibilities for gentlemen and saw that I was introduced to the art of lovemaking by a very special lady. And other ladies have contributed to my education." Rafe was surprised to find himself having such a frank conversation with his bride, but the woman who had seen to his education had warned him that young English misses were woefully ignorant and unprepared for the intimacies of the marriage bed. Dulcie was a perfect example of that.

Of course, Rafe understood that things were different for young ladies because there was no way for them to gain experience without suffering social ruination or pregnancy. He said as much to Dulcie.

"What are the rules for gentlemen?"

"To be kind, considerate, and generous to one's partners. To give pleasure before taking it. To never deliberately cause pain. That a gentleman does not seduce housemaids or governesses or other women in his employ. A gentleman is discreet. He doesn't kiss and tell or engage in gossip or boast about his conquests. A gentleman does not seduce or engage in flirtations with other men's wives. A gentleman does not engage in seduction of a virginal young lady unless he intends to marry her. A gentleman takes responsibility for his actions inside and outside the bedchamber. A gentleman doesn't drink or gamble to excess. A gentleman's word is his bond," Rafe recited. There were other rules his father had taught him that he chose not to share with Dulcie about the unsavory business of keeping mistresses and the sins of indulging in repugnant sexual practices with unwilling partners, children, or animals. Rafe didn't consider it necessary to share those rules with Dulcie since he had never indulged in either sin. But they were rules his father had taught him and Raphael Blackburn had always remembered and lived by them.

"Your father sounds like a wonderful man."

"He was," Rafe said.

"He would be very proud of the man you've become."

He gazed at her. "I could say the same about your parents. And about Geoff. They would be proud of the woman you've become."

Dulcie giggled. "I'm not sure they would approve of my current state of dress—"

"It's your wedding night," Rafe reminded her. "I'm certain they would understand and make allowances."

"Even if they didn't, I know they would approve of my choice of a husband."

Touched by the earnest expression in her eyes, Rafe lifted her chin, then bent his head and kissed her tenderly. "I suppose it would be too much to hope your mother explained human reproduction to you?"

"I'm afraid so," Dulcie confirmed. "Ada, the upstairs maid, explained about my monthlies, fed me some of Papa's brandy with my tea, told me what to do and brought me what I needed the first time it happened." She blushed a bright pink as she shared that intimate information with Rafe. Although why she blushed was beyond her. After all, she was lying naked in her husband's arms with her face pillowed on his shoulder after he had performed the most intimate act she could never have imagined on her.

"Why a housemaid?"

"Maman and Papa had been called back to town for the opening of Parliament. I remained in residence at our country house," she explained. "I'm sure Maman would have explained everything to me before I married or would have had Papa recommend a book for me to read, but I didn't receive any offers my first Season so there was no reason to, and she and Papa died before my second Season."

"So young ladies *do* indulge in spirits on occasion," Rafe teased.

"Only for medicinal purposes," she reminded him primly. "Like you said this morning." She smiled at Rafe. "I thought your kisses and your touches were the most wonderful things I had ever felt, but that… I don't know how to describe *that*. Or how to thank you…"

Rafe smiled a self-satisfied smile. "There's no need to thank me, Dulcie. I enjoyed it almost as much as you did."

"But how…"

"It gave me pleasure to give you pleasure."

"You didn't—" She frowned. "What did you call it? Orgasm?"

Rafe laughed. "Not this time. That was more of a prelude before the main movement to help alleviate some of your worries and misconceptions about lovemaking."

"If that was a prelude, there must be more to follow," Dulcie reasoned.

"There is," he confirmed. "But only if you're ready for it."

"More like before?" Dulcie asked.

"If you want more," he told her. "But there might also be some unavoidable pain."

"Why?"

"It's not physically possible for me to dispense with your maidenhead without causing you some discomfort," Rafe explained.

She bit her bottom lip. "That's the part the older ladies always talk about."

"Probably to discourage curious young ladies from anticipating their wedding vows with the first fellow who hints of a marriage proposal to try to persuade her."

"In that case, and since we're married, I'm perfectly willing to give myself over to your excellent tutelage." She smiled up at Rafe. "On one condition."

Rafe arched an eyebrow. "My lady," he reminded her. "You are hardly in a position to set conditions."

"You haven't heard my condition," she drawled.

"I'm listening."

He wasn't just listening, Dulcie realized. He was also caressing her breast, rubbing his thumb against her in a soothing, almost hypnotic, motion the whole time he'd been holding her close. "My condition is that you allow me to explore your body the way you've explored mine."

The smoldering look he gave her spoke volumes.

"I did promise to love and cherish you and worship you with my body," she reminded him. "I prefer to worship you sans clothing." She managed a stern look. "*All* clothing."

"Do tell," he invited.

"I wish to further my sexual education," Dulcie told him. "And since I've never seen a naked man, I should like my husband to be my *first* naked man." She eyed him from beneath the cover of her eyelashes. "Or are you unwilling to accept my condition?"

Rafe pinned her with a mischievous look. "It depends on the situation."

Dulcie heaved an exasperated sigh. "The situation is your wedding night and your bride is lying naked in bed waiting for you to join her."

"And I'm in bed holding her beside me."

"Your bride is eager to feel your naked flesh against hers. Unfortunately, you're still wearing your dress uniform. Everything except your boots and the ribbon you used to tie your queue—"

"Your point being?" Rafe couldn't resist prodding her to see what she would do next.

"I want you beside me in this bed as naked as the day you were born."

"You're wearing a jeweled necklace and an earring..."

Reaching up, Dulcie unfastened her precious necklace and placed it on the pottery dish on the nightstand before she removed her remaining earring and laid it beside the necklace and its twin. "There," she pronounced. *"Satisfied?"*

"Not yet. But I will be." Rafe bit the inside of his cheek to keep from smiling. *There she was. There was the brave, opinionated, bossy girl her brother had talked about.* It had taken a few precious hours, but Rafe had finally met her. And he liked her. He liked having her make demands rather than expressing her gratitude to him for marrying her. She needn't thank him for that. No man could have forced him to do what he didn't want to do. Not even a dying Geoffrey Tennant.

He may not have met her before today, but Rafe knew Dulcie. He knew her from the letters and gifts she'd sent to her brother. Letters her brother had called epistles. Rafe knew her from the thousands of times her adoring brother had described her. And the sister Geoff had described had been smart and saucy and confident enough to speak her mind, and sure of her place in the world. He wanted that Dulcie, not the apprehensive, timid shadow her uncle had reduced her to. Rafe wanted an equal, a partner, a confidant, a match. He didn't want to dominate or force or pressure her to be what she thought he wanted. He wanted her to be who she was meant to be. The Dulcie she would be if evil hadn't come calling in the form of her overly ambitious and foolishly rapacious uncle.

"You won't be satisfied if you don't roll off this bed and get naked," she pointed out.

Rafe laughed. "I'm not accustomed to disrobing without benefit of a valet or my batman. I may require assistance. Are you willing to meet that condition?"

"Only if you agree to meet mine."

"But of course. Touching, tasting, kissing, and exploring to your heart's content is *de rigueur*."

"Good," she said. "I've always been a stickler for proper etiquette. My governess insisted upon it. And I put it to good use when I managed my brother's household." The smile she gave him was pure temptress. "I'm sure you will benefit as well."

"I'm delighted to hear it. There are consequences for rule breaking." He pinned her with his gaze. "There is always a price to pay." He was a paying a dearer price than most. Rafe was trying to pack a lifetime of memories of making love to his bride into a few brief hours.

"Where do we begin?" Dulcie asked, changing the subject so neither of them would be reminded that this might be the only night she would ever have with Raphael Blackburn. This was the only opportunity she might ever have to worship him with her body.

Rafe rolled off the bed and stood before her. "Since I'm wearing my full-dress uniform, we'll begin the process the way my batman would do it."

"Get on with it, major," she ordered, sliding up the bed to prop against the headboard to get a better view.

Rafe grinned as he unbuckled his belt and unbuttoned his tunic. He shrugged the red wool tunic off his shoulders and hung it on a wall peg. "My batman would assist me."

"I could assist you. But in my current state, I fear it would slow the process."

"It might hasten it, my lady," he suggested with a teasing leer.

"I don't wish to deny you the pleasure of disrobing yourself in front of a most appreciative audience." She offered him an innocent smile. "Please, continue."

Rafe loved the sound of her bossy voice, just as he loved the sound of her prim and proper voice, and the sound of her surprised voice. "As you wish, my lady."

He untied his cravat, draped it over the back of the wing chair, and began removing his ivory shirt studs. He dropped the studs in the dish on the nightstand beside her necklace and earrings and gave his shirt a tug to pull the tails out of his breeches, then pulled it over his head.

Dulcie sucked in a breath at the sight of him naked from the waist up. His chest muscles were hard, well-defined, and covered in thick dark hair that surrounded the flat discs of his nipples. She was surprised to see the tips of them had hardened into little nubs that peeked through his chest hair. And the dark hair didn't end at his chest, but continued, bisecting his flat stomach, with its four rows of muscles, like the muscles on Michelangelo's *David*, and forming an arrow that disappeared into the waistband of his buff breeches. "Cold?"

"No," he assured her. "Quite the opposite."

"You're not cold?" Despite the roaring fire in the fireplace in the front parlor, there was a distinct chill in the bedchamber that kept the tips of her breasts standing at attention.

"How can I be cold when I'm admiring my beautiful naked bride?"

One of the things she'd learned since he'd held her in his arms and pressed her against him was that Rafe's body was a source of heat. She missed his warmth. "Your naked wife is freezing."

"I'll be happy to warm you, Lady Blackburn, just as soon as I shed these breeches." He unbuttoned the gold buttons of the drop-down flap of his buff breeches, then turned his back to her and shucked his breeches and his stockings along with them.

Standing naked before his bride, Rafe was struck by an unfamiliar sense of vulnerability. Now he understood the courage it took to bare oneself before someone who mattered. He understood how much courage it had taken for Dulcie to do it. Baring one's body to someone you cared about for the first time was akin to baring one's soul. Raphael Blackburn had never been shy about stripping before the women he chose to share his bed. Removing his clothing was a necessary part of the process of achieving sexual gratification. Except for his first experience, there had never been any awkwardness or embarrassment or shame. Because, aside from his initiation to the carnal delights, there had never been any risk to his pride or to his heart. All of his previous partners had understood the game. None of them had ever looked at him the way Dulcie did. None of them had ever meant as much.

Rafe realized that stripping off his clothes for Dulcie was far more important than any sexual encounter he had ever had. For him. And for her. Because it was her first. For him because the responsibility for making it good for her was his.

And that knowledge was both daunting and exciting. This sex act was more important than any of the sex games he'd ever played. Not only was he excited by the prospect of having her see him in the buff for the first time, but he was also aroused. And there was no hiding the evidence of it. Rafe only hoped she'd be attracted rather than repelled by the sight.

Dulcie watched the play of muscles on Rafe's strong back as he divested himself of his breeches. She smiled at the contrast between the suntanned skin of his arms and back and the pale flesh of his shapely buttocks. She liked the way his body was put together. His shoulders were wide. His chest and back were broad. His waist was narrow when compared to his upper body and his hips were slim. His legs were long, his thighs and calves were firm, the muscles finely sculpted from years of horseback riding. His feet were long, narrow, and beautifully arched. And that was just his backside. "Are you going to stand with your back to me while I admire the masculine beauty of your backside or are you going to let me see the rest of you?"

Rafe blew out a breath. He had been hoping the chill in the room that was turning his toes to ice would affect the most prominent part of his anatomy. Enough to lessen his arousal a bit. But that hope died a quick death because the moment she spoke in that low, provocative tone, her voice had the opposite effect. He was hard and hot and more prominent than before. "Before I turn around, I should warn you that there's nothing subtle about a man ready to mate. There's no hiding our eagerness," Rafe warned as he turned around and presented her with the proof.

Dulcie widened her eyes at the sight of him. All she could think of was how magnificent he was. He was her first naked man and Dulcie knew that as long as she lived, she would never see a more glorious specimen than this man standing tall and fully erect. He was beautiful.

"Raphael, you are gorgeous." Dulcie was delighted to find the arrow of dark hair that had disappeared into the waistband of his breeches surrounded his navel and pointed to the extraordinary appendage jutting from another nest of curly black hair.

Rafe laughed.

"You are," she breathed. "I've visited Montagu House and viewed the paintings and the ancient Greek sculptures. They're supposed to be male beauty personified, but you are far more beautiful than they are."

He laughed again. "That's because I'm considerably younger."

"Really?" she inquired. "Because I thought it was because you are living and breathing and far more beautiful than canvas or marble representations." He was beautiful and simply looking at him, imagining what it would feel like to touch, and taste and caress and explore him was having a strange effect on her. Dulcie was flushed and hot and damp and swollen in places she couldn't name. All because he was standing there, gazing at her with that look in his dark brown eyes.

Dulcie moistened her suddenly dry lips with the tip of her tongue. "I enjoy looking at you," she said. "But the truth is that I can hardly wait to look and *touch*." She nodded at his proud erection. "Starting with that."

CHAPTER 16

"What fills the eye, fills the heart."
—Celtic Proverb

Rafe's erection responded to her words and her gesture by becoming harder and even more prominent.

Dulcie crooked her finger at him in a gesture of beckoning as old as time.

"Come join me, Lord Blackburn, and let me touch, taste, kiss, and explore you to my heart's content."

It was an invitation few men could refuse. Rafe was not one of the few.

Rafe climbed into bed with her, took her in his arms, pulled her down to the mattress, then leaned down and kissed her. His kiss was hot and sweet and the essence of temptation. Dulcie wrapped her arms around his neck, pulling him closer.

Realizing she wanted him against her, Rafe lowered himself to the coverlet beside her. "I don't want to crush you with my weight."

"But I want to feel you."

"You can feel me this way." Rafe rolled onto his back and lay there in all his naked glory. "I'm all yours," he invited.

Dulcie knelt beside him and took him at his word. She buried her nose in his chest hair, loving the way it tickled her nose. Then she kissed his nipples, teasing them with her tongue until they grew hard, then gently nipping them, before kissing away the tiny hurt. She left his nipples and trailed her tongue down the center of his abdomen, following the arrow of hair leading to her destination.

Rafe's skin rippled beneath her tongue as she edged closer to her goal. Scooting down his body, Dulcie climbed over one of his legs and settled between the other. She trailed her index finger along the length of his shaft.

Rafe groaned as her delicate touch threatened his ability to maintain his control.

Dulcie halted her exploration, but Rafe reached down and covered her hand with his, holding it in place. "Don't stop. It feels good."

"I thought I'd hurt you."

He managed a reassuring smile. "And I thought I'd frightened you. Or repelled you."

"Nothing about you could ever repel me." Dulcie resumed her exploration, marveling at the unexpected velvety feel of his flesh. She satisfied her curiosity by wrapping her fist around him, gauging his length and his circumference, wondering why he was so much bigger than the sculptures and paintings she'd seen, wondering why she hadn't noticed it bulging against the front of his breeches. She frowned.

Rafe reached up and touched the furrow between her eyes. "Then why the frown?"

"You're bigger than the nude sculptures and the paintings I've seen. I was wondering how you manage to keep this in your breeches. Or how you manage to ride a horse. It must be terribly uncomfortable."

Rafe laughed. "My sweet innocent, I could tell you I'm bigger because I'm a head taller than most men, but that wouldn't be entirely true and wouldn't add much to your sexual education. You see, my penis, as it's called, isn't always like this. Most of the time it's flaccid like the ones in the sculptures and the paintings you've seen."

"Oh."

"But you are correct. When it's engorged the way it is now, it's almost impossible to keep it inside my breeches."

"What do you do when it happens?"

"I strip down until I'm in the buff, climb into bed, and invite my bride to explore me to her heart's content."

"I'm sure this isn't the first time it's happened to you," Dulcie said. "And you've never had a bride before." She bit her bottom lip. "Have you?"

He shook his head. "No. You're my first. And the cause of my engorged state."

"Me?"

"Aye." Rafe cupped her neck and brought her face to his for a torrid kiss. He kissed her until they were both aching for more.

She broke the kiss to murmur against his lips, "Raphael, teach me how to please you."

"I don't have to teach you that," he whispered. "You already please me."

"Then teach me how to make love to you."

Rafe took her hand, placed it around his erection and showed her how to grip him. "Gently," he cautioned as he taught her the motion he liked best. "Until I beg you to stop."

"What happens after you beg me to stop?" Dulcie asked.

"Then I show you how we finish what we've started," he murmured in his deep Scottish burr.

The hard male part of him throbbed with each beat of his heart. Aching to sheathe himself in Dulcie's warmth, Rafe wrapped his arms around her waist and gently rolled with her until she was on her back. Dulcie gazed up at him as he lay above her, bracing himself on his elbows. She put her hands on his shoulders, then followed the line of his spine, sliding her hands down his back and over his rear.

Rafe groaned aloud, enjoying the feel of her soft, cool hands against his buttocks, enjoying it even more as she worked her way from his rear to the front of him. She brushed him with her fingers and Rafe grew as hard and as erect as he'd ever been.

He groaned again, hot and ready, growing more so with each caress of Dulcie's fingers. "Sweetheart, I'm not going to last if you keep doing that. Release me, please, so I can pleasure you."

She let him go in order to put her arms around his neck. He kissed her again, deep and hard and with great thoroughness, then moved down her body, settling in the valley between her thighs where he made slow, sweet love to her with his mouth and tongue and breath until she came apart in his arms once again.

Rafe slid back up her body and kissed her tenderly.

"Raphael," she whispered when she recovered her ability to form coherent sentences.

"Hmm?" He licked the corner of her mouth, then kissed his way to her ear and back again.

"I'm your bride. Don't let any man put us asunder. Before you leave me, please, make it so no one can annul us."

Rafe wrapped her arms around his neck. "Hold on, sweetheart." He smoothed his hands over her thighs, then guided her legs up and over his hips. He pressed himself against her, gauging her readiness by gently probing her entrance. Dulcie lifted her legs higher, locked them around his waist and pulled him to her.

"Now." Rafe closed his eyes, threw back his head, bared his teeth, and sheathed himself inside her. He felt the barrier the moment he breached it. He'd done as she had asked and made it impossible for her uncle to annul their marriage, but unless he withdrew soon, he'd also done what he'd sworn he would never do—leave a helpless woman pregnant with his child. He'd known she wasn't experienced the first time he'd kissed her. It didn't matter that she'd asked him to take his matrimonial rights. He should have done it with more finesse.

She had tensed when he slid inside her. She hadn't cried out in pain, but he'd hurt her. And Rafe was riddled with guilt and remorse because of it.

He'd never made love with a virgin before, but that was no excuse. He'd had other lovers. He was the one with experience. He should have known better than to push past her barrier without regard to the pain he might cause.

He was paying the price for his selfishness now. His entire body shook with the effort as he fought to maintain control while he waited for some sign that she was ready to continue.

Rafe gave her as much time as he could manage, allowing her body to fit itself to his size. He waited until she began to move before he surrendered the fight and allowed her to pull him deeper inside. She squeezed her thighs, tightening her muscles, keeping him close, holding on as Rafe began to move his hips in a rhythm as old as time.

Dulcie matched Raphael's movements thrust for thrust. She disregarded the momentary pain and clung to him, reveling in the weight and feel of him as he filled her again and again, gifting her with himself in a way that made everything they'd done—all the pleasure they had given and received—seem insignificant when compared to this magnificent joining of her body with his.

She squeezed her eyes shut. She thought she'd experienced the ultimate in pleasure when Raphael had given her the most intimate of kisses and brought her to magnificent release. The ultimate in joy. The ultimate wonder. The ultimate passion. But she was wrong. *This* was so much more. Tears of joy trickled from the corners of her eyes, ran down her cheeks, and disappeared into her hair. And as she felt the first tremors of passion rush through her, Dulcinea Marjorie Rose, Lady Blackburn, gave voice to it, filling the air around them with sharp, incoherent cries as her husband, Raphael Simon John Blackburn rocked her to him, and when he moved to withdraw, she locked her legs around him, squeezed him tightly and joined him as he exploded inside her.

RAFE LAY ON HIS BACK, HOLDING DULCIE AS SHE SLEPT WITH HER HEAD pillowed on his shoulder, her arm across his chest, and her legs entwined with his. He pressed a kiss against her hair, smiling as he listened to the soft sound of her breathing, felt her breath as it stirred the hair on his chest.

He glanced out the upper half of the window above the curtain, where the sky was visible. The rain had stopped. The moon had risen, but the light from it barely penetrated the fog that had settled over the village. His time was growing short. The night was almost over. The clock on the mantel had chimed the half hour. Half past three.

Sergeant Wilson and Corporal Peavey would be relieved by the execution detail an hour or so before his scheduled appointment with the gallows. Rafe didn't want to die, but he was content to lie there listening to Dulcie's breathing as she slept in his arms.

He'd made love to her twice more during the night. The first time, he had tried to atone for the pain he had caused her when he'd relieved her of her maidenhead by making slow, tender love to her where he'd worshipped her with his body and she had worshipped him with hers. Afterwards, he had pulled on his breeches, heated a kettle of water on the stove, and gently washed away the remnants of their lovemaking, removing the drops of blood she had shed and the seed he'd spilled. Then he'd carefully soothed the abrasion his whiskers had left on her tender flesh.

After that, Rafe had bundled her in her cotton wrapper and carried her into the front parlor, where they had picnicked before the fire on the hamper of food Weymouth had provided for them, dining on cold chicken, meat pies, fresh bread and cheese, fruit, nuts, pickles, and slices of wedding cake, along with a bottle of champagne.

After finishing their meal, Rafe had continued her father's tradition of reading before the fire by reading the first chapter of *The Life and Opinions of Tristram Shandy, Gentleman* by Lawrence Sterne to Dulcie as she curled beside him on the sofa. Rafe had selected the story of Tristram Shandy as the most likely choice to entertain her from among the three books they had found on the small shelf in the parlor, the other two volumes being *The Book of Common Prayer* and *A Treatise on Toleration* by Voltaire.

Rafe closed the book and set it aside. "I think that's enough for tonight."

Dulcie sighed. "Thank you, Raphael. It was a lovely gesture."

"It's a fine family tradition," he told her. "One you treasured." *One he hoped she would continue to follow and treasure long after he was gone.*

"You have a soothing reading voice," Dulcie said. "You don't sound as English when you read."

"Don't I?" He made a face. "Then my English schoolmasters failed in their mission to eradicate the Scots influence."

"Your Scottish burr is more pronounced when you read aloud and when you..." She blushed. "I adore the sound of it."

"That's not all you adore." Rafe waggled his eyebrows at her. "I believe I have other talents you appreciate, my lady."

"You do indeed, my lord," she assured him. "Many wondrous talents."

"I've a few you've yet to sample..."

"That's something we shall have to remedy," Dulcie replied, meeting his hot gaze. "I thought there was very little of you I had yet to sample."

"Shall we remove to the bedchamber, Lady Blackburn?"

"With pleasure, Lord Blackburn."

CHAPTER 17

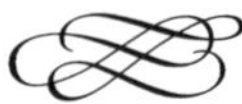

"Associate yourself with men of good quality
if you esteem your own reputation,
for 'tis better to be alone than in bad company."
—George Washington, 1732-1799

"I'd feel a bit better about this plan if the bloody fog would lift long enough for us to find our way to the cottage," Jarrod Shepherdston complained as the *Jersey Queen* anchored at the mouth of the port.

"I'd feel better about our plan if we didn't have to interrupt the man's wedding night," Alexander Courtland replied. "If anything goes wrong with the plan, it will be his first and *last* night with his bride."

"We all hate the thought of interrupting that," Jonathan Manners, the Earl of Barclay, said. "But it isn't as if we have a choice. Time is running short. If we don't implement the plan before dawn, he hangs without us."

"I'd feel better about the whole thing if we didn't have to board that skiff and row to shore." Daniel Sussex had overcome his fear of boats long ago, but they would never be his favorite form of transportation. And he'd spent over ten hours on one today. "I was shot the last time I rowed to shore in a skiff in the dead of night. We nearly avoided disaster." He took a deep breath to settle his nerves as he watched the boatswain's crew lower the first of the two small boats that would take them to shore into the water. "Let's hope everything goes according to plan," he added. "Because if it doesn't, not only do we lose a good man and an excellent officer in Blackburn, but Shepherdston and I will have to face Lord Weymouth and explain how the plan failed."

"Maybe you'll have better luck with a dory," Colin McElreath, Viscount Grantham, said. "It's larger than the skiff you used last time. And we'll all be with you." He clapped Sussex on the back. "And I don't fancy facing Weymouth to report a mission failure any more than you do. Besides, you and Shepherdston have spent nearly a fortnight planning for tonight." He exhaled. "Reporting to Weymouth with bad news is an unenviable task, but losing Blackburn—a good, brave man from all accounts, and a fellow Scotsman—would be a tragedy."

"If we arrive in time to implement the plan, we won't lose Lord Blackburn." The sixth man involved in the plan, the man wearing the uniform of a regimental surgeon, was Mr. James McGregor, physician and surgeon from Edinburgh. Weymouth had asked McGregor to join the mission because the Free Fellows plan required a physician and possibly a surgeon as well, and Mr. McGregor was a fine example of both. Weymouth trusted McGregor so the Free Fellows had decided to trust him as well. "I don't generally devise a plan of treatment for a patient in order to cause his demise."

"Ready, gentlemen." The boatswain called up from the dory in a low voice. "Come aboard."

"This blasted fog is going to present a problem," Shepherdston murmured to Sussex as they approached the rope ladder. "With navigation."

"There's nothing to be done about it now," Sussex replied. "We have to go with the plan we've formulated."

"Our ships' crews navigate these waters regularly," Grantham said, defending his father-in-law's crew. "They are experts. And entirely loyal."

"I'm not questioning your sea captain or his boat crew's ability to navigate the waters," Shepherdston said. "I have no doubt that they are the best or they wouldn't be in Lord Davies' employ. I'm concerned about *our* ability to navigate from dock to cottage and from the cottage to the garrison without being found out as frauds." Of the six of them, only McGregor had served in the military. The rest of them had served in more clandestine roles, slipping in and out of enemy lines carrying, gathering, and delivering vital information to the Wizard of the War Office, becoming whatever and whoever they needed to become to accomplish the mission.

Sussex was no coward. He'd spent his most recent mission scaling the exteriors of two Georgian houses and a veritable fortress and scrambling over rooftops with Courtland while avoiding falling and the night watchmen. He hadn't experienced any nerves on the yacht, but the memory of his last crossing of the channel in a skiff gave him pause. "I'm more concerned about alerting a fully armed garrison."

"Fortunately, it isn't a fully armed garrison," Courtland reminded him. "It's a prisoner garrison. Only the guards are armed."

"Cheer up, cuz," Barclay advised his cousin, Sussex, as he made his way to the rope ladder behind one of the crew members. "If you get shot this time, we have a surgeon aboard to stitch you up."

"No offense to the good doctor," Sussex retorted. "But I'd prefer not to collect any more holes in my birthday suit that have to be explained to my duchess. Explaining the first one was hard enough."

"No offense taken." McGregor grinned. "And I would rather not have to inspect your birthday suit *or* put myself at risk by performing repairs on it tonight. Or by having to explain to Her Grace, either."

"Just so, McGregor," Barclay approved. "Her Grace is exceedingly fond of His Grace and very protective of his person."

"So long as we keep our heads down," Courtland reminded them as he took his place descending the rope ladder after Barclay, "and keep our wits about us, we should all return home in one piece and be able to avoid having to explain to our wives."

"Courtland's right," Grantham agreed. "This is a rescue mission. We can't risk losing anyone to injury tonight. Especially the doctor."

"It's nice to be needed," McGregor said as he followed Courtland and Barclay into the first boat. Shepherdston boarded the second boat. Sussex was behind him, and Grantham boarded last. He signaled the captain of the *Jersey Queen,* who would sail to a nearby inlet to await their return.

They didn't speak as they silently rowed to shore. Sound carried across the water and none of them dared risk being overheard. They didn't fear being arrested by the guards from the garrison. Each of them carried false credentials declaring them to be the special detachment of guards sent by the Duke of Wellington to escort Lord Blackburn to his execution and to transport his body back to the mainland upon request of the Prince Regent. And because Lord Blackburn had not been charged with, or found guilty of, treason or sedition, his body would remain intact. Unlike traitors, Lord Blackburn's head would not be removed from his torso or displayed to the garrison or the guests invited to witness the execution. Once McGregor pronounced him dead, the special detachment would take possession of Blackburn's body and accompany it to London. Blackburn would not receive a hero's public funeral, but he would be allowed a private Christian burial. No announcement of his death would appear in the newspapers. As a sitting earl, Lord Blackburn had been afforded those concessions.

Now, all the Free Fellows had to do was escort Lord Blackburn to the gallows and hang him without killing him.

Rafe lifted his hand from its resting place around his bride's waist and watched as long strands of auburn hair curled around his hand. He liked the way the silky soft curls tangled around his wrist and hand when he plowed his fingers through it. He smiled at the memory. Plunging his fingers into her hair had scattered most of her hairpins all over the bed, but Rafe had kept combing his fingers through it until all the pins had been dislodged and her hair hung loose. Rafe buried his nose in it. Her hair smelled of the soap she'd used to bathe and Rafe ached with the knowledge that he would never have the opportunity to sit behind her in the evenings and brush it for her. He would miss acting as her lady's maid every day of their married life. Buttoning and unbuttoning, lacing, and unlacing, tying, and untying the fastening of her garments. His hands were large and the tiny buttons her seamstress used to fasten her garments were challenging, but the reward was worth the frustration.

Rafe had forgotten how it felt to hold a woman against his body and the pleasure he derived from the feel of female flesh pressed against him and how soft a woman's hair could be. It had been almost a year since he'd tangled his fingers in a woman's hair or pressed his nose against it to inhale the fragrance it held.

Before Waterloo.

Before he'd found himself confined to his quarters for leading a charge that had made him a hero and would ultimately cost him his freedom and his life. He barely remembered that woman. Strange that he could recall her name but couldn't seem to recall her face or her features. Nor did he care to.

His mind was filled with images of Dulcie. No woman had ever felt as good pressed against him as Dulcie did. No woman had ever made him feel the way she made him feel. She eclipsed every bedmate he had ever had in every way. No woman of experience had ever touched him the way his virginal bride had. She had held nothing back. She'd placed her trust in him and had given him everything.

Rafe hoped he had given her as much. He had made love to her in almost every way he knew. Pregnancy was still a possibility, but he had done his best to limit the risk after the first time she had taken him by surprise by locking her legs around him. He had made certain she reached satisfaction, and so had he, just not in the way he wanted most. He hoped that when she learned what he had done to protect her, Dulcie would understand and forgive him for his fear of leaving her to cope alone. He prayed she would not think less of him for his one omission in her education. And he prayed that the man who completed her education would be a good man and do so with her needs in mind rather than his own.

Rafe had spent the last few hours memorizing every inch of Dulcie's face and form. He knew the small scar on her forehead above her left eye that had been caused by a fall when she had run into a table as a child. He knew the number of freckles sprinkled across the bridge of her nose, the fact that the hole in her left earlobe that had been pierced when she turned thirteen was a fraction higher than her right one, and the fact that her right breast was plumper than her left. Rafe loved knowing she would dissolve into giggles when he trailed his tongue on the underside of her knees or blew a stream of hot air across the nape of her neck and he loved knowing how he had gained his intimate familiarity with the star-shaped birthmark beside her navel and the scent and taste of her. Rafe knew the incoherent sounds she made deep in her throat and the way his name sounded on her lips when she reached her climax. He could never forget her. He would know her anywhere. She was imprinted on his soul.

And Dulcie knew him. They hadn't made love in silence. They had talked and laughed and teased and confided secrets and shared dreams. Whatever she asked, he answered. And Dulcie had had plenty of questions on a wide range of subjects. She had asked about his family and his childhood.

He told her of his carefree childhood in Edinburgh and the names of all the horses and dogs he'd loved. He had described his two older sisters, Micheline and Giselle, and his parents. His Scottish father, Michael, who had died when he was twenty-one, and his French mother, Arielle, who had died three years later, still mourning the loss of her husband. He told her about Micheline marrying a major in service with Wellesley in India, how she had spent a year there and had returned home a widow with an infant son to find their father had died and Rafe was the earl. He confided his shock at losing his father and suddenly being responsible for the family and all the people who lived and worked on the estates. He told her it was the second biggest shock of his life. The first was being sent away to school in England at the age of seven and the teachers who had done their best to eradicate all traces of his Scottish heritage and how he had pasted drawings of Blackburn Abbey and the ruins of ancient Crags Muir Castle in the front and back covers of all his schoolbooks to remind him of what they wanted him to forsake. And then, he'd confided that those schoolbooks were shelved in the library at Blackburn Abbey.

Dulcie knew every scar on his body and how he'd gotten them. Every saber slash, every bullet wound, the bayonet scar on his ribcage, and every boyhood scrape and mishap—including the scar from a gash on the right side of his head above his hairline that had happened at the age of nine, when he had lost his grip on his hatchet, and it had bounced off his head, leaving the scar she'd uncovered when she had repeatedly finger-combed his hair off his forehead in order to kiss him there.

He had been a fortunate fellow. He'd grown up in a loving family as the adored son and heir. And despite his dismay at being sent away to school in England, he'd received an excellent education and had gone on to university and, despite the war, he had made his Grand Tour of the continent. Rafe had been privileged to serve with the best men in the regiment during his time in the cavalry and to have had Dulcie's brother as his closest friend and confidant.

As Rafe lay in bed holding Dulcie as she slept, he reflected on his life, his accomplishments and regrets, and realized they were one and the same. His greatest accomplishment had been marrying Dulcie and his greatest regret would be leaving her.

If his life ended at dawn, as he expected it to, Rafe would go to his death recalling every detail of their brief time together. He would go to his death with the taste of her kisses on his lips. He would die thanking his Maker for the gift of Dulcie Tennant and for allowing him to spend the last night of his life on earth making love to her.

His bride slept on undisturbed, pressed against his side, her head pillowed on his shoulder, her right arm draped across his chest, her right leg flung over his. Hers was the sleep of the exhausted after an eventful day of travel and a wedding and a night of lovemaking. Rafe knew he should feel a measure of guilt at his selfishness. But Dulcie had been adamant about learning everything he was willing to teach. She had been an eager, willing pupil and a most inventive one.

A smile played on his lips. After their last bout of lovemaking, he had drawn her a hot bath to help relieve some of the aches he knew she would have. After she had soaked for a bit, he had joined her in the tub and had allowed her to bathe him. She'd fallen asleep immediately after returning to bed, but he'd awakened after a brief nap and had been completely content to hold her as she slept. And while she slept, Rafe realized his little bride had taken the whole of her side of the big bed and most of his until she lay sprawled almost on top of him. And he, who had never spent an entire night with any woman, discovered he liked it.

Dulcie sighed, shifted restlessly against his shoulder, and called out, *"Raphael?"*

He recognized the note of panic in her voice and remembered she was far from home and waking up in a strange bed with a man who had been a stranger a few hours earlier. "I'm here, my sweet."

She opened her eyes. "Is it morning?"

"No, it's still dark out." Rafe brushed her hair with his lips. "We have time yet. Go back to sleep."

"You'll wake me before..."

"No, sweet Dulcie. I want to remember you like this."

"But Rafe..."

"I don't want you to remember me like that." He squeezed his eyes shut. *Dancing a jig in the air.* "I want you to remember me—remember *us*—as we are now. As we looked when we were making love to each other. I've seen the horrors of war. I've seen men die. I've seen them executed. I don't want that sight to be your last memory of me. Sweet Dulcie, I want you to remember us the way we spent our wedding night."

She pushed herself up far enough to meet his gaze. "I can't let you go alone. I can face anything as long as I'm with you." Her voice broke.

"I can't," he whispered. "I have to be strong, Dulcie. I can't falter. I can't be weak. I can't let my enemies see any weakness. I cannot be cowardly. Or less than the man I am now. I'm a man of my word, but there's a part of me that wants to take you by the hand and run. I don't want to die. But if that's my fate, I must do it as the seventh Earl of Blackburn with courage and honor and strength. And I fear I won't be able to do that if I see you with tears in your eyes."

"Oh, Rafe." Her voice wobbled but didn't break. If he had to be strong as the seventh Earl of Blackburn, she had to be equally strong as his countess. "Make me forget about morning."

Rafe did his best. He bent and kissed her. A tender, gentle kiss that said all the things he couldn't put into words. He made Dulcie forget about the dawn, while he did his best to remember every detail until it arrived.

CHAPTER 18

"Pray for me and whatsoever noise ye hear,
come not unto me, for nothing can rescue me."
—Christopher Marlowe, 1564-1593

Rafe dozed after he tiptoed out of the bedroom where Dulcie slept undisturbed, aided no doubt by the two drops of elixir Lord Weymouth had given to him to give to her. Rafe had been reluctant to follow Weymouth's instructions. He hated the idea of drugging his bride, but he had no choice but to trust the Wizard of the War Office. Weymouth deemed it necessary to protect the identities of Weymouth's associates who would be protecting her once she returned to town. Rafe told himself his sweet bride needed the sleep. Except for her fainting spell and the drowsy interludes they had shared during the night, she'd had precious little of it in the last twenty-four hours. Rafe had added the sleeping potion to the last quarter glass of the wedding champagne Lord Weymouth had placed in their supper hamper and had given it to Dulcie.

He had stayed with her until she'd fallen asleep, then slipped from the bed and gathered their scattered clothing from the bed and the floor. After dressing and tying back his hair with one of the green velvet ribbons he found in her valise, Rafe had shaken the wrinkles from her green muslin dress and matching velvet spencer and hung them up for her to find.

Bending low, he had brushed a soft kiss against Dulcie's cheek and arranged the length of black satin ribbon he'd worn the day before on her pillow. "Remember, my sweet Dulcinea," he had whispered near her ear, "that no matter what happens at dawn, I will always watch over you. The secrets I've kept, I kept because I gave Geoff my word. Please understand there were reasons I could not tell you everything. And know that my last thoughts will be of you like this and that I will always be with you."

Carrying his boots with him into the front parlor, Rafe had sat down on the sofa and pulled on his boots, then stretched out to await Wilson and Peavey and the execution detail.

RAFE AWOKE WITH A START AT THE SOUND OF A SOFT KNOCK ON THE door. He crossed the room and opened the door. A detail of six men in formal dress uniforms and tricorn hats stood outside. He didn't recognize any of the faces as being from the garrison. Keenly aware of his bride sleeping in the next room, he kept his voice low. "Who are you?"

"The Wizard's associates," the officer in charge of the detail replied.

Rafe's heart gave a jolt. Weymouth had told him the plan, but he hadn't really dared to believe it could—or would be—executed in time to save him. Still afraid to hope, he stepped aside in invitation. Four of the six men entered the cottage, crowding the small space. "Where are Sergeant Wilson and Corporal Peavey?" he asked.

"They've been relieved of duty," the officer said. He nodded toward the two soldiers who remained outside the door. "Our associates will stand watch while we prepare you."

Rafe glanced down at his uniform. It was as presentable as he could make it. "Am I not suitably turned out? Or did you bring me a fresh uniform?"

"We brought you part of one," a second soldier said.

Rafe touched a finger to his lips, then pointed to the bedroom door. "Shh. My wife is sleeping."

"Did you give her the elixir?" a soldier whose uniform bore the insignia of a regimental surgeon asked.

Rafe nodded.

"I'll check on her." The surgeon didn't ask permission. He simply eased the bedroom door open and quietly slipped inside. He returned minutes later and nodded to the commanding officer. "Her breathing and pulse are normal. She's sleeping deeply as brides are wont to do after a long wedding night. Our mission will all be over and we'll be on our way long before she awakens." He gave Rafe a knowing look. "I left a salve for the whisker burn beside the dish on the bedside table with instructions for its use."

"Thank you." Rafe ran his hand over his whiskers. "I was only allowed to shave every third day," he said. "Unfortunately, yesterday was the second day."

"One would hope the commandant would grant the courtesy of a shave to a man on his wedding day," the doctor said.

Rafe smiled when he met the doctor's gaze. "A wedding night was all the courtesy Weymouth could negotiate out of Commandant Swindell on my behalf." He shrugged. "I had hoped I'd be allowed to shave this morning."

The doctor shook his head. "It's better that you don't."

"Better for whom?" Rafe asked.

"You." The doctor stuck out his hand. "I'm Major James McGregor, Regimental Surgeon."

Rafe shook his hand. "McGregor? Do I hear Edinburgh in your voice?"

"Aye," McGregor confirmed. "University of Edinburgh Medical College. And you must be Earl Blackburn of Blackburn Abbey."

"Aye," he said.

"Pleased to meet you," McGregor told him. "I was a scholarship student thanks to your father's legacy. I'm delighted to put my education to use on your behalf, my lord."

"My friends call me Rafe."

McGregor nodded. "Now that I've seen to Lady Blackburn's welfare, let's get you ready for your appointment with destiny. If you'll remove your tunic and neck linen, please..."

Rafe unfastened his tunic, shrugged out of it, and handed it to the doctor.

McGregor nodded to the officer in charge of the detail. The man opened a heavy canvas knapsack and pulled out a red tunic, a man's corset, a pair of braces, and a stack of fresh neck linen, and set it on the chair within Rafe's reach.

The officer fixed his gaze on Rafe. "We generally use aliases in our work, but Weymouth assured us you are a man of your word and can be trusted to keep our identities secret."

"You have my word of honor." The corners of Rafe's mouth turned up in a slight smile. "Despite the fact that it won't be worth a ha'penny by breakfast once word of my disgrace gets around."

"We'll accept it." The officer offered Rafe his hand. "Jarrod, Fifth Marquess of Shepherdston, at your service. My associates and I took the liberty of replacing your original execution detail when we learned of your predicament." He glanced over at his associates. "Gentlemen..."

The other soldiers stepped forward.

"Colin McElreath, Twenty-seventh Viscount Grantham, at your service."

"Daniel, Ninth Duke of Sussex, at your service."

"And our two colleagues standing guard at the front door are Jonathan Manners, Eleventh Earl of Barclay, the slightly shorter one, and Alexander, Second Marquess of Courtland, the taller of the pair."

Rafe was momentarily stunned. The cream of London society and men from some of the most esteemed families of England were working clandestinely on his behalf. "You replaced the original detail?"

"It seemed the logical choice." Sussex shrugged. "We decided a gentleman wrongly sentenced to hang for an infraction that is clearly not a hanging offense should have a detail worthy of his position in society."

"So here we are," Grantham concluded.

"Besides," Shepherdston said, "your original detail is in no condition to escort anyone to the appointed place by the appointed hour."

Rafe's curiosity got the best of him. "What did you do?"

"We simply paid to keep the ale and the rum flowing at the local tavern where the members of the detail were dining," Sussex said. "I have heard it is customary for visitors to the island to stand the local residents a round of drinks."

"I wouldn't know," Rafe said. "I haven't had the opportunity to visit a local tavern since I've been in residence here."

"Whatever the customs, we decided not to risk offending the local populace, so we each purchased a round or two for the locals and for the soldiers of the garrison," Grantham explained. "As long as the tavern has customers drinking, we're buying."

"A method we've used on other occasions to engender good will—at least among tavern owners and their customers," Shepherdston said.

"Until morning," McGregor added. "When their heads begin to ache." He turned to Rafe. "Remove your neck linen, please."

Rafe untied his linen, pulled it off, and tossed it aside.

Grantham collected it and threw it in the fire.

Rafe pinned Grantham with his sharp gaze.

Grantham grinned in reply. "Not to worry. You won't be needing it." He picked up the braces and handed them to Rafe. "Slip these on."

"I don't wear braces," Rafe told him.

"It's a long drop with an abrupt halt," Shepherdston reminded him. "You may need them to keep your breeches and your dignity in place."

Rafe took the pair of braces Grantham held out to him and put them on, buttoning them to the buttons hidden inside his waistband for that purpose. Grantham stepped behind Rafe and adjusted the straps.

All the gentlemen in the room were over six feet tall, with the exception of McGregor, who was a fraction under six feet. Had they been Russian, Prussian, or French, they might have been recruited to serve in the special guard units made up of men over six feet tall.

"Lord Weymouth told us you were taller than usual," Grantham said. "So we used Courtland as our model. He's the tallest of us with a quarter inch on Sussex. You have a quarter inch or more on Courtland. Now, slip the straps of the braces and put this on." Grantham handed Rafe the men's corset.

"You might have been old, massively overweight, and corseted like the Prince Regent." Recalling the way Dulcie had teased him hours earlier, Rafe balked. "Not on your life."

"I'm afraid it's not on *your* life," Shepherdston remarked. "And it's essential to this mission."

Rafe looked Shepherdston in the eye, taking the measure of the man.

Jarrod Shepherdston firmed his jaw and glared back. "There are four of us and one of you. I will not jeopardize my welfare or that of my associates to indulge your pride. McGregor is the surgeon and a physician. He deems the garment necessary and you're going to wear it."

"How is a *corset* necessary?" Rafe asked. "If I were corpulent and soft, I could understand it, but I'm neither and I wish to know why it's necessary that I wear that—" He cast a disparaging look toward the offending garment that resembled the garments represented in caricatures of the Prince Regent. That of a boned waistcoat with strong laces. *"Abomination."*

"Doctor, if you please, explain it to him," Shepherdston invited.

"You already did, Lord Shepherdston, when you remarked that it is a long drop with an abrupt halt." McGregor tilted his head to give Rafe a compassionate look. "The modified waistcoat will protect the vertebra in your back from the stress of falling so far and stopping so abruptly." He offered the garment to Rafe once again. "Please...put it on."

Rafe reluctantly slipped the corset into place, then turned and presented his back so the doctor could lace it.

"I can barely breathe," Rafe complained when McGregor pulled the strings as tight as they would go.

"That's the second reason for wearing it," McGregor said. "We want to minimize your breathing." He slipped the straps of the pair of braces into place over the corset. "Hand me the neck cloth."

Shepherdston complied, handing McGregor a neck cloth half the length of the one Grantham had burned.

The doctor wrapped the linen around Rafe's neck from just under his chin to the top of his collarbones and tied it into place. "Now, the jabot."

"A *jabot?*" Rafe protested once again. "Do I look like a damned dandy?

"Not yet," Shepherdston told him. "But you will." He handed the ruffled jabot over to the doctor like an assistant handing over a scalpel. "Tall neck linen is all the rage in London this season."

"It isn't all the rage in the cavalry," Rafe pointed out.

"You'll be making a fashion statement," Shepherdston said.

"You want to look your best when you meet your Maker," Sussex said, a twinkle in his eye.

"It is the neck wear for formal occasions," Grantham added. "Especially this sort of formal occasion. According to the manual on formal attire for officers."

Rafe looked skeptical. If there was such a manual, he had never seen it.

"What are they going to do to you if tall neck linen and a jabot aren't quite cavalry regulation?" Sussex posed the question. "Court martial you? After they hang you?"

McGregor placed the jabot around Rafe's neck, positioning it over the neck cloth and fastening it into position.

"I wager *this* jabot isn't all the rage among town dandies," Rafe said. It was covered in fine fabric and a ruffle, but the jabot he was wearing fit like the iron collars worn by fighting mastiffs. Heavy collars designed to prevent the big dogs from ripping open each other's throats during their matches. Like cock fights, bull baiting, and bear baiting, the object of the fights was to wager on the outcome. Most owners had no wish to see their animals killed so they had devised protective armor for them. In Rafe's case, the protection had been covered in French linen and lace disguised as a fancy collar designed to protect his neck from the hangman's noose.

"You would win that wager," Sussex told him. "This one hasn't caught on with dandies yet. It's designed for a special clientele. I had the best blacksmith and tailor in town fashion it just for you to wear on this occasion. I even consulted your tailor to ascertain your correct neck size."

"I appreciate the effort you've gone to on my behalf, Your Grace."

"Now, the tunic," McGregor ordered.

Grantham handed the garment over and the doctor held it open while Rafe slipped his arms into the sleeves and settled the red tunic into place on his shoulders. It was larger than Rafe's previous tunic, but it had been fashioned to fit over the corset, braces, and additional neck linen.

McGregor adjusted the collar and Rafe discovered the collar of the tunic was fitted with an iron band just like the jabot. "How does it feel?" McGregor asked.

"Heavy," Rafe said. "How does it look?" Now that he understood how they were going to protect him, he wanted to make certain none of the witnesses detected a difference in fit or design from his regular uniform.

Shepherdston gave Rafe's modified uniform close inspection. "No different from any other finely tailored uniform. The modifications are undetectable."

"Except by the hangman," Rafe said. "Surely the man who puts the noose around my neck will be able to feel the difference between starched linen and iron."

"Not to worry," Sussex told him. "The hangman is one of us. He's another of our associates. Very knowledgeable and entirely trustworthy. He isn't a titled gentleman, but hangmen rarely are. He's already at the appointed place, inspecting the apparatus. You won't be introduced to him as hangmen remain anonymous for obvious reasons, but he'll take good care of you."

The doctor rubbed his hands together in a gesture of satisfaction. "All that's left is..."

Shepherdston produced a silver flask and handed it to the doctor who handed it to Rafe. "It's whiskey. You look like you could use a wee dram before we proceed."

"Aye." Lifting the flask to his mouth, Rafe took a long swallow, wiped his mouth with the back of his hand, grimaced, and did his best not to cough. "What kind of whisky is this?"

"What kind do you normally drink?" Grantham asked.

"Glenaonghais."

"This is a local tavern whiskey," Shepherdston replied. "With an added dose of the doctor's elixir."

Rafe turned his furious gaze on the doctor.

"No need to ruin good whisky with a medicinal tonic. It's a stronger concoction than the one you gave to your wife. And longer lasting. But it doesn't take effect as quickly. You'll be quite capable of making your way up the steps to the scaffold."

Grantham turned to McGregor. "Is it going to work?"

"It should. Unless his weight differs greatly from Courtland's." McGregor looked at Rafe. "How much do you weigh?"

"Just under fourteen stone."

McGregor glanced from Grantham to Shepherdston and back again. "His weight is the same as Courtland's and there is only a fraction of a difference in their heights. There shouldn't be any concerns over whether he'll fit."

"Concerns over whether I'll fit in what?" Rafe demanded.

"The coffin," Sussex replied matter-of-factly.

"The coffin?" A chill ran up Rafe's spine. It was one thing to contemplate hanging and quite another to know you had already been measured for a wooden box. He was suddenly filled with dread. He was about to hang. He was also furious with himself for allowing himself to believe he had even the tiniest chance of escaping the hangman's noose. Rafe sighed. He should have taken Dulcie, overpowered

Wilson and Peavey, and made his escape to the harbor in the coach so they could hire a boat. "Why would there be need of a coffin? I thought this was a rescue."

"It is," Sussex confirmed.

Rafe's heart pounded a bit harder. There might be a chance after all. "You're going to smuggle me off the island in a coffin? *That's* the plan?"

"No," Shepherdston told him. "We're going to remove your body from the garrison grounds in a coffin and take it off the island. After we hang you."

After we hang you. Rafe had never doubted he would hang until he'd opened the door and discovered Weymouth's associates standing the other side of it. Suddenly, he'd had hope. Hope that the men Weymouth had sent to save him would perform a miracle. And Rafe was discovering that hope was proving hard to relinquish. It didn't disappear as quickly or as easily as it had appeared. Hope was tenacious. "I thought the plan was to rescue me." His legs suddenly lost the ability to support him and he sank down hard on the sofa.

"The Wizard said you told him you suspected the moment you faced the Court of Inquiry that your punishment would be harsher than most." Grantham said gently.

"Suspecting something and knowing it for a fact are two very different things," Rafe said.

Sussex reached into his jacket and produced another silver flask. He offered it to Rafe.

Rafe took a swallow. This time the whisky was high quality, smooth, and undoctored. He returned the flask to Sussex with a nod of thanks. "I found out I was to hang an hour or so before the Wizard of the War Office arrived and mentioned a plan. Even then, I still believed I *would* hang." He swept an anguished glance over each of the men in turn—Grantham, Shepherdston, Sussex, and McGregor. "Until *you* arrived."

"I see," Shepherdston said with a brisk sympathetic nod. He clearly knew Rafe wouldn't tolerate his pity. "Hope springs eternal..."

"Something like that," Rafe said.

Sussex met Rafe's shadowed gaze. "There's no reason you should lose hope."

Rafe arched an eyebrow.

"We didn't go to the trouble of getting you all dressed up in all your military finery for nothing," Grantham said. "We learned about the plan to hang you Friday night. Before you did. Before the inquiry had decided your fate. It had already been decided by the men who planned it." He repeated the conversation Barclay had overheard while attending the Admiralty reception honoring Admiral Gregory's years of service. "Our original plan was to rescue you from the garrison, spirit you away, and hide you until such time as you were granted a full pardon."

"But that plan had to change," Sussex said. "Because securing a full pardon from Parliament and the Prince Regent would take too long. By the time we secured it, you would have been dead and buried."

"So we devised a new rescue plan," Grantham continued.

"Where I hang by the neck until dead," Rafe said.

"Yes," Shepherdston told him. "Where *we* hang you by the neck. If we hang you, we control the outcome. They don't. Hanging you *is* the rescue. So that's exactly what we're going to do."

CHAPTER 19

"See me safe up, and for my coming down,
let me shift for myself."
—Sir Thomas More, 1478-1535

Rafe preferred the original plan. The one where Weymouth's associates spirited him off the island while his neck was still intact and he was still breathing. But there was nothing he could do to stop the current one. Except survive it.

Lord Weymouth's private execution detail escorted him from the cottage and marched him to the waiting coach. Grantham and Sussex led the way. Shepherdston and McGregor followed, one on either side of Rafe, while Courtland and Barclay brought up the rear. "What about my bride?" Rafe asked. "I don't want her left alone."

"The execution detail is made up of six men. My associates and I are the six-man execution detail. I can't spare any of them. There was no one left to watch over Lady Blackburn, so the Wizard suggested I send someone to collect your solicitor, Mister Gunn, to stay with her. We hired a driver and coachman when we hired the coach. I sent

Courtland back with them to the inn where your solicitor is staying. Courtland asked him to come to the cottage. That's them now."

Rafe was surprised to see a second coach pull behind the first vehicle and stop.

Shepherdston added, "Unless you wish Mister Gunn to witness your—"

"No," Rafe cut him off. "Archibald Gunn began his profession serving as my grandfather's solicitor. He served my grandfather, my father, and me and I've asked him to stay and serve my young nephew, Simon, who will inherit. When Simon inherits, Archie will have served four generations as the Blackburn family solicitor. I would rather he not bear witness to my death. He has no wish to do so and I've no wish for him to do so. He will serve me much better by watching over my wife for me."

Shepherdston nodded. "I would want the same for my wife if I were in your situation."

"I am grateful you thought to send for him, Lord Shepherdston." Rafe extended his hand in genuine appreciation.

Shepherdston took it. "I cannot take credit for the idea. After meeting your solicitor and conversing with him, the Wizard thought it best we give him a task to occupy his mind while we carry out our mission."

"I am grateful to you both for all you've done. Including this. I feel better knowing Archie will be here with my wife when she wakes up." Rafe furrowed his brow. "Tell me, is Archie aware of the plan?"

Shepherdston shook his head. "The fewer who know the better." He opened the door of the coach and ushered Rafe inside. "And now, Lord Blackburn, I think it best for Mister Gunn's sake and for your own if you climb aboard before he sees you."

Rafe climbed into the coach, settling against the window, leaving room for Shepherdston and McGregor. Shepherdston followed him inside while McGregor escorted Rafe's solicitor into the cottage. He exited moments later and boarded the coach. Sussex and Grantham claimed the opposite seat.

Courtland traded places with the hired driver, abandoning the second coach to him as soon as Archibald Gunn and the doctor entered the cottage. Barclay elected to sit on the box beside Courtland.

Rafe didn't envy them their seats on the box despite the close confines of the interior. The air outside the coach window was thick with a low-hanging fog that blanketed the businesses along the main thoroughfare, making it nearly impossible to read the signs announcing what they were. The fog distorted the sounds of the horses' hooves on the cobblestones and dimmed the glow from the streetlamps and the coach lamps lighting the way.

They navigated the quiet streets, making their way past the coaching inn, recognizable by the size of the stable and its proximity to the garrison. Courtland pulled the coach to a halt as they reached the gates. The guard on duty demanded, "Who goes there?"

"Condemned prisoner Blackburn and his execution detail."

"Exit the coach and march the prisoner to the gallows."

The gates of the garrison swung open as the detail disembarked from the coach and lined up in formation around Rafe to march him through the gates and across the parade ground, past the garrison's mews, to the gallows built on a hill at the far end of the compound.

The sky was beginning to lighten as they marched across the compound. The fog was thicker inside the walls of the garrison. The temperature was cold and dreary. The only colors were the streaks of pink and purple in the sky above the horizon. Several coaches were parked near the commandant's office. The muffled sounds of teams of horses in harness and of the voices of the assembled witnesses penetrated the eerie silence.

There was no fanfare. No drums or fifes. No assembly of the troops. The only other sounds were the steady beat of seven men in leather boots marching in unison across the cobblestones.

A dozen chairs from the dining hall had been set up for the witnesses. Among the witnesses were the three court of inquiry judges, Commandant Swindell, Swindell's aide, Lieutenant Chasen, and other members of the commandant's staff recognized by sight, but not by name, and the three men who had testified on Rafe's behalf. Also seated among the witnesses was the Right Reverend Kendrick, who had presided over his wedding the morning before.

A lifetime ago…

Rafe wondered if the reverend would feel compelled to call upon Dulcie to offer condolences or to see how she was faring at becoming a widow less than twenty-four hours after becoming a bride.

He hoped not. Rafe wanted Dulcie safely off the island and on the way home where her friends could look out for her. Better the people she knew and loved than the total stranger who had been handsomely paid to marry them. And then, there was Ricky…

Rafe glanced at the mews. He had forgotten to ask if Weymouth had arranged to take possession of his horse. Rafe didn't want Ricky left in this garrison's stables any longer than necessary. He had reminded Archie to settle his accounts for food and lodging and stable fees and to pay in advance if Weymouth hadn't arranged transportation for the horse when Archie collected Rafe's personal effects. Rafe didn't trust the commandant not to dispose of his horse along with his personal belongings. Rafe couldn't prevent the commandant from disposing of his horse, but by paying his stable fees in advance, he could give Weymouth grounds to seek redress against Swindell if he did.

Rafe knew Archie would see to his personal items and see Dulcie safely delivered to Lady Augusta Nesbitt's house, where she was supposed to be spending a few days with her friend, Phoebe. And he trusted Weymouth would take care of his horse, but Rafe hated leaving things undone. And *unsaid*.

Rafe squeezed his eyes shut. He should have told Dulcie he loved her. He should have showered her with pretty phrases and compliments. He should have given voice to his feelings. She was an innocent. She had no way of knowing he had done his best to show her how he felt with his body. She had no way of knowing what they had shared was far deeper, far better, far more meaningful than the usual sexual congress between strangers.

He had lived his life without regrets. And had sworn he'd die without regrets or apologies for the man he was, the man he had become. Yesterday morning that had been true. But it wasn't true this morning. This morning he was filled with regrets. He should have been braver. But he had been too afraid to say the words aloud. Afraid those words would tie her to him—to his memory—more deeply than the papers that proclaimed them husband and wife. He didn't want her to spend days or weeks or months or even years mourning him. She was young and beautiful. She had her whole life ahead of her. And although he could barely stomach the thought of another man touching her, kissing her, caressing her the way he had done, Rafe wanted Dulcie to have the life she deserved. With a man worthy of her. He didn't want her pining away for him or living on memories. She was too fine, too full of life for that.

Too full of life...

He hesitated.

"Blackburn?" Shepherdston took hold of his arm. "Steady, man."

Rafe opened his eyes. While he'd been reviewing his regrets, the detail had covered the distance from the mews to Gallows Hill. He didn't remember marching, but he must have because the detail had halted before the steps leading up to the scaffold where the crossbeam and dangling rope loomed over him. Rafe took a deep breath and slowly released it in an attempt to slow his racing heart.

McGregor's kind gaze searched Rafe's face. "How do you feel?"

"Like a condemned man about to die."

The surgeon's mouth curled up at the corners. "Gallows humor is a good sign."

"That wasn't gallows humor," Rafe informed him. "It was gallows truth."

"The medicine should be taking effect," McGregor told him. "Are you able to negotiate the steps on your own or do you require assistance?"

"I'm able," he said. "Not willing, but able." He glanced at Sussex. "Are you carrying a weapon?" Rafe knew Shepherdston was the acknowledged leader of Weymouth's associates, but Sussex was a duke. He outranked a marquess. There would be fewer, if any, consequences for Sussex if he did what Rafe was about to ask him to do.

"Yes."

"Give it to the hangman."

"Why?"

"If I falter going up these bloody steps or show any sign of losing my nerve on that scaffold, have him shoot me. I'll not have it said Raphael, seventh Earl of Blackburn, showed any weakness on the gallows."

"He won't shoot you." Sussex lifted his chin to indicate the hooded man standing behind the wooden lever that operated the drop door on the platform above them. Sussex clearly knew the man well enough to know what he could and could not do.

"Will you?"

Sussex didn't flinch. "Yes."

"Thank you, Your Grace."

Sussex swallowed hard and gave a quick nod.

"Ready?" McGregor asked.

Rafe shook hands with each man and thanked them for their assistance.

Barclay, Courtland, and McGregor positioned themselves beneath the scaffold to see to Rafe as soon as he dropped through the door. Shepherdston preceded him up the steps. Sussex followed. Rafe climbed the steps with his head held high, shoulders and back straight. With the courage and dignity befitting a major in the King's Own Eleventh Blues and a hero of Waterloo.

As he reached the platform, Rafe caught sight of a private coach parked close enough to the gallows to witness his execution and to hear what was said. The curtains were drawn closed. Rafe watched through narrowed eyes as a sleeve decorated in familiar gold braid pushed the curtains open, not enough to reveal his identity, but enough to get a good look at the events taking place.

Rafe paused in front of the hangman. He didn't offer his hand when he spoke. "Whatever befalls me today is a result of my actions and the actions of the men who put me here. You bear no guilt for performing this duty. Be at peace and know that I bear you no ill will."

The silent hangman simply offered him a blindfold.

"No, thank you," Rafe said. "I want to face my murderers." He turned away from the hangman, walked to the center of the trapdoor, and stood waiting as the hangman placed the noose around his neck and carefully adjusted it.

"Try not to move, my lord," the hangman whispered as he made a final adjustment before returning to his place behind the lever.

"Raphael Simon John Blackburn, seventh Earl of Blackburn," Commandant Swindell called from the ground in front of the scaffold. "You have been sentenced to hang by the neck until dead for the crime of disobeying the order of your commanding officer in leading a cavalry charge on the battlefield at Waterloo and for the crime of striking your commanding officer in the commission of your crime. Do you wish last rites?"

"Yes." Rafe expected the garrison's chaplain to do the honors and was surprised when the Reverend Kendrick stepped forward and administered last rites for the condemned man.

Rafe thanked him.

Commandant Swindell spoke again. "Have you any last words you wish to say before your sentence is carried out?"

"I do." Rafe scanned the faces of the assembled witnesses and guests. He hadn't expected to face his accuser. Lieutenant Colonel Cornelius Fenton hadn't been man enough to face him at his Court of Inquiry or to face him at his hanging. Like the craven coward he was, Fenton preferred to hide in a closed coach and peek through the curtains, so Rafe concentrated on the commandant and the judges who had sentenced him to death knowing his actions, while deserving of a fitting punishment, were not deserving of a sentence to hang. He stared down at Commandant Swindell and spoke in a loud, clear voice. "May God have mercy on your soul and the souls of the men who conspired to have you carry out their vengeance in order to silence me and prevent the exposure of their greater sins. And if God does not see fit to grant you mercy, may you rot in hell."

Seconds later, the door beneath his feet opened and Raphael, seventh Earl of Blackburn, fell through the air toward the ground below until the rope around his neck brought him up short.

His last thought was of his bride. His last breath spent in whispering her name.

CHAPTER 20

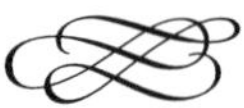

"Maid, widow, or wife."
—John Skelton, 1460-1529

"D*ulcie."*

Dulcie opened her eyes and sat up in bed at the sound of Raphael whispering her name. She reached for him, but Rafe's side of the bed was empty and cold. "Rafe?"

There was no answer.

Yet Dulcie knew she had awakened to the sound of Rafe whispering her name the way he had whispered it when he would turn to her during the night. She glanced around. The sky visible through the top of the bedroom window above the curtains had gone from dark to light with only the palest streaks of pink and purple remaining. "Oh, no." She squeezed her eyes shut. *"Rafe."*

Morning had dawned.

The wrapper that matched the nightgown Phoebe had taken from her was lying across the foot of the bed where she had left it, but the rest of the room had been put to rights. The clothes she and Raphael had left scattered on the floor the night before were gone.

The green muslin dress she had worn yesterday morning for her meeting with Rafe was hanging on a wall peg along with its matching velvet spencer, despite the fact that the last time Dulcie had seen it, Phoebe had been packing it in Dulcie's valise to bring with her to the cottage for her night with Rafe. The extra undergarments she had packed to wear home had been neatly folded and placed on the seat of the upholstered chair. Her stockings had been tucked into the tops of her half-boots, which were lined up and sitting beneath the chair. Her velvet cloak was draped across the arm of it.

But Rafe's distinctive red tunic, white linen shirt, breeches, stockings, and boots were missing.

And she was alone.

Dulcie could almost believe she'd dreamed the events of the day before, but she smelled of the citrus-scented block of soap she and Rafe had found in the bathing room and had used to bathe themselves after making love a final time. And, despite the hot bath, she ached in places she'd never used before last night. Dulcie felt the heat rise in her face. She'd done a great many things she had never done before last night. And the wee hours of this morning. She had been both exhilarated and exhausted by their lovemaking. The last thing she remembered before falling asleep was sharing the last glass of champagne and lying curled together like spoons in the silver chest, his front to her back, his muscular arm around her waist holding her close against him in a way that made her feel warm, protected, and wanted. The previous night seemed like a wonderful dream of a fairytale come true. But it was real. It had happened to her. It had *been* a fairytale come true.

Rafe had given her the wedding night she'd asked for. He hadn't left an inch of her untouched.

And now, he was gone. The only sign that he had been with her, other than the delicious marks on her body, was the indention in the feather pillow beside her where he'd laid his head. And the black satin ribbon he had used to tie his queue lying in the middle of the pillow artfully arranged in the shape of a heart.

Dulcie clutched the ribbon in her fist and pressed it to her heart and then to her lips. Unshed tears brimmed in her eyes. She ruthlessly blinked them back, refusing to let them fall. She wouldn't cry in this place where she and Rafe had shared so much and had been so happy.

The sound of china rattling nearby startled her. Her heart leapt with joy. She wasn't alone. He wasn't gone. He was here! Dulcie flipped back the covers and slid out of bed, snatching her wrapper from the foot of it as she went. Pulling it on to cover her nakedness, she tied the sash around her waist. She located her hairbrush in her valise, hurriedly brushed her hair, then twisted it up into a neat bun and began pinning it into place with the hairpins she and Rafe had retrieved from the bed covers last night and dropped into the pottery dish on the bedside table along with her peridot jewelry.

Dulcie had been so intent on securing her hair before it all came tumbling down that she hadn't noticed the note stuck beneath the dish or the small tin of lavender and comfrey salve. She snatched up the note, but her heart fell as she realized it wasn't from Rafe. It simply contained instructions for the use of the salve for the abrasions Rafe's whiskers had left on her. The note was signed not by Rafe, but by a regimental surgeon. She blinked several times. She hadn't been concerned about the abrasions, but Raphael had been concerned enough to send someone—probably Sergeant Wilson or Corporal Peavey—to get salve from the regimental surgeon for her. Her hands shook as she opened the tin, dipped her finger in the ointment, and began patting it over the visible marks.

She knew in her heart Rafe was gone. He had told her he wouldn't wake her when they came for him because he wanted to remember her in their marriage bed, not shivering in the morning cold watching as they hanged him. He didn't want her to carry that memory of him with her.

But Rafe had promised he would stay with her as long as he could, promised he wouldn't leave her alone. Her head knew he was gone, but logic didn't seem to matter where her heart was concerned. She still couldn't believe it. Perhaps he was shaving! She smiled at the thought. He had felt so badly about the way his whiskers had marked her, he was probably shaving them off before coming back to her. Dulcie had assured him that she barely felt them and that a few abrasions were nothing compared to the passion they had shared. Besides, she liked the feel of his whiskers. The way they tickled, the way they teased.

If he was shaving, Rafe hadn't left her yet. Maybe he'd been granted a reprieve. Maybe they had been given another day together. Lord Weymouth was a powerful man with powerful friends. Perhaps he had managed to sway the commandant after all. Tightening the sash of her wrapper, Dulcie made her way to the water closet in the bathing room. The room was empty. Dulcie bit her bottom lip to keep the hot tears stinging her eyes from flowing. She washed her face, cleaned her teeth, and made her way back to the bedchamber.

She shed her wrapper, rolled it up and stuffed it in her valise. She found her extra chemise in the stack of undergarments Rafe had laid out for her. After carefully threading the black silk ribbon through the eyelet lace of the garment, Dulcie pulled it over her head and tied Rafe's ribbon in a bow over her heart before picking up her short stays.

She donned the rest of her undergarments as quickly as she could and stepped into the green muslin dress, managing to button all but two of the buttons at the back as she worked the gown over her hips, twisting and turning it into place. She pulled her spencer on over the dress to hide the gap, then donned her stockings and garters. There were marks on her inner thighs. Dulcie opened the tin once again, spreading the medicine over those fresh whisker burns. When she finished, she pushed her feet into her half boots and finished packing her belongings into her valise—including her precious necklace and the tin of salve. She bit back a wistful smile as she worked the second peridot earring through the hole in her right earlobe, recalling the way Rafe had removed it—and the shockingly resourceful method he'd devised to collect it later.

Dulcie draped her velvet cloak over her arm and sucked in a deep breath… She couldn't delay any longer. Someone was moving around in the cottage. If it wasn't Raphael, she had to know who it was.

Opening the bedroom door, she stepped into the sitting room. "Rafe?"

A man emerged from the kitchen carrying a cup of tea and a packet of biscuits in a small basket looped over his arm. "Oh, my dear, Lady Blackburn, you're up and dressed. I was afraid I'd awakened you whilst I was preparing myself a cup of tea."

"Oh, Mister Gunn, it's you." Her hand flew to her heart. Suddenly, her legs would no longer support her. She sank down on the nearest chair. "I thought I heard Rafe…Lord Blackburn…"

"I'm afraid not." He slowly shook his head. "They came for him an hour or so before dawn." He gently offered her the cup of tea he'd prepared for himself.

Dulcie shook her head, fearing her churning stomach might rebel. "No, thank you. But please do go ahead and enjoy your tea."

Archie Gunn set the cup of tea and a packet of biscuits wrapped in parchment paper down on a side table. "He sent one of the members of the detail to collect me from the inn so you wouldn't be alone here." His voice cracked as he finished speaking, forcing him to swallow.

"Thank you for coming, Mister Gunn. My husband promised he wouldn't leave me by myself." She swallowed the lump in her own throat. "He kept his promise."

A ghost of a smile appeared on the solicitor's lips. "I've never known him not to. Or his grandfather or father either. They instilled that in young master Rafe."

"You've known him that long?"

"All his life." Archibald Gunn pulled a handkerchief from the pocket of his jacket and dabbed at his eyes. "Six and twenty years."

"I'm very glad you're here with me, Mister Gunn," Dulcie meant it. "I confess this is all new to me. I don't know what comes next."

"I'm to go to the garrison before we leave and collect His Lordship's personal belongings. And then I'm to see you safely to London and Lady Nesbitt's house."

"What about Lord Blackburn?" Dulcie sat up straighter and steeled her spine for what was to come. "Won't we be taking him home with us?"

"I'm not quite clear about the military rules and regulations regarding the mortal remains of condemned men," Gunn admitted. "I suspect the decision of how to dispose of a condemned man's mortal remains rests with the commandant of the garrison."

Dulcie took a deep, steadying breath. "I'm sure you will be able to obtain that information when we go to the garrison to speak with Commandant Swindell."

Rafe's solicitor was stunned. "*We*, my lady?"

"Of course, *we*, Mister Gunn," Dulcie told him. "I know you are going to the garrison to collect my husband's personal effects..." She paused to steady herself once again. "I shall accompany you to the garrison and speak with the commandant about claiming my husband's body so we can see to his proper burial."

"My lady, I don't..."

But Dulcie would brook no argument. "If you don't take me with you, I shall find my way to the garrison by myself."

"My lady, you can't!" Mister Gunn was clearly horrified by the idea. "Lord Blackburn asked me to take care of you. And a countess doesn't go about on her own."

"Then, you must take me with you. You cannot leave me in the cottage by myself. And if you go to the garrison without me, I'll follow you. Because I refuse to leave my husband's mortal remains on the island with the people who murdered him."

"You are quite correct, my dear lady," Gunn conceded with a sigh. "I cannot leave you alone here because I gave Lord Blackburn my word."

She rubbed a shaky hand over her forehead. "I can't think what else we need to do. I suppose we'll need to secure a coffin and a vehicle to transport it to the boat. And there must be other legal matters to consider... Do you think I will need my marriage lines to prove I'm Lady Blackburn?"

"You shouldn't," Mister Gunn told her. "As Lord Blackburn's solicitor I can truthfully testify that I was present at the solemnization of your union to Lord Blackburn." He reached over to pat Dulcie's hand, then frowned with concern when he realized her hand was as cold as ice. "Why don't I go make you a nice hot cup of tea. After you finish your tea and some of these delightful biscuits, we'll pay a visit to Commandant Swindell."

"I don't think I can eat or drink anything," Dulcie confessed.

"No arguments, my lady," Mister Gunn said. "You must eat something to keep up your strength." He took her hand in his and began chafing it. "Please try, my lady. For me"—he hesitated—"and for Rafe."

Dulcie slowly nodded, knowing he was right. The last thing she wanted to do was swoon from hunger in the presence of the men who had killed her husband.

"Gather your things," he instructed. "And then we'll both sit down and have our tea."

Dulcie returned to the bedchamber to gather her traveling case, then scanned the room to make certain she hadn't left anything other than precious memories of her wedding night with Rafe. She wanted to take the things that retained his scent—the citrus soap and the essence of Rafe that was unique to him. She wanted to take the sheets and the pillowslip that covered the pillow he'd slept on, but she settled for the block of soap they had used in their bath. She would never be able to smell the scent of lemons and oranges without remembering the feel of his hands slippery with soap exploring her body or the way the heat of his body gave the citrus a special tang that belonged only to him. Dulcie wrapped the block of soap in her extra pair of stockings and tucked it into her case.

She emerged from the bedchamber as Mister Gunn returned with another cup of tea. He set it on the table beside her chair. "This should warm you right up." Retrieving his own cup of tea, he sat down on the sofa opposite her chair.

"Thank you." She shivered involuntarily as the mouthful of tea she'd swallowed warmed its way to her stomach.

"I apologize for the chill in the house," Mister Gunn said. "But since we were leaving today, I thought it prudent to let the fire burn down to the coals."

"I'm certain the tea will warm me." She managed a tremulous smile to reassure him, but Dulcie doubted if she would ever feel as warm as she had felt lying next to Raphael, basking in the heat of his body.

"I hope you like it sweet. I added a rather large piece of sugar and a bit of cream."

"I do like my tea sweet. My friends will tell you that I like most everything sweet. But wherever did you learn to make it like this?" Dulcie took a sip of the tea and nibbled at a shortbread biscuit.

"I'm glad you like it. I'm an early riser. I used to make it for my missus every morning just the way I made it for you today."

"I didn't realize you were married, Mister Gunn."

"I'm a widower."

"I'm sorry."

"It happened long ago," he said. "I was a much younger man then. My missus and I shared sixteen happy years together. Then one day she became ill and died quite suddenly."

"You never remarried?" Dulcie finished her biscuit and reached for a second one without realizing it.

"I could not put another woman in my Janet's house unless she was the equal to her. Had I met such a one, I would have married again. But time passes and we grow older, and hopefully, wiser. But now that I'm an old man I ask myself who would want an aged solicitor for a husband?"

Dulcie knew his question was rhetorical, but she answered it anyway. "A lonely woman who appreciates the fine gentleman you are." She finished her tea and her biscuit and brushed her skirts to remove stray crumbs.

"One with legal matters to settle, perhaps," he joked.

She met his kind gaze, knowing there was no longer any way for her to hide the anguish in hers. "How did you go on without your Janet, Mr. Gunn?"

Archibald Gunn set his empty teacup aside and reached over to pat her hand. A hand now warmed by the tea he had prepared. "You get up each day and find something to occupy the empty hours, something about which you can be passionate. For me, it was the law. For you, it will be something else. The grief never goes away, but with time, you learn to make peace with it."

Dulcie rose to her feet.

Mister Gunn did likewise.

"May I approach you, sir?"

"Of course, my lady."

Standing on tiptoe, Dulcie, Lady Blackburn, gently kissed the older gentleman on the cheek.

CHAPTER 21

Make me to say, when all my griefs are gone,
"Happy the heart that sighed for such a one!"
—Samuel Daniel, 1562-1619

"I would like to speak with Commandant Swindell," Dulcie announced to the commandant's aide, Lieutenant Chasen, as she stood in the lieutenant's outer office, shortly after the coach Archibald Gunn had ordered the night before collected them at the honeymoon cottage and delivered them to His Majesty's Garrison on the Isle of Wight.

"Who shall I say is calling upon the commandant?" the aide asked, looking at her as if he didn't recognize her from the previous morning when she and Phoebe had accompanied Lord Weymouth to the commandant's office.

Dulcie frowned. *How could he not recognize her? For goodness' sake, she was wearing the same dress.* Drawing herself up to her full height and using the voice she had learned to use on Caroline's haughty butler at Blessing House, Dulcie announced, "You may say that Lady

Blackburn, Countess of Blackburn, and her solicitor, Mister Archibald Gunn, are calling."

Lieutenant Chasen knocked on the door that led to the antechamber where she had met with Rafe the day before and returned moments later with a reply from Swindell. "Commandant Swindell directed me to inform you that today is the Sabbath, and he does not conduct business on the Sabbath. He spends his time in private worship. He does not entertain visitors. You may make an appointment." Chasen consulted the commandant's engagement calendar. "The commandant has an opening on his calendar a fortnight from tomorrow at three in the afternoon." He glanced at Dulcie. "Shall I put your name down, Lady Blackburn?"

"No, you may not, Lieutenant. A fortnight from tomorrow at three in the afternoon is not a desirable or a convenient time for me or for Mister Gunn, who has an appointment to collect my husband's personal effects at half-past eight *this* morning."

"Commandant Swindell need not be present for that," he informed her. "I can have Major Lord Blackburn's personal effects brought to you." He rang a bell sitting on the corner of his desk. The sergeant on duty, a different one from the day before, entered the room. Lieutenant Chasen barked, "Sergeant, collect Blackburn's—"

"Major *Lord* Blackburn's," Dulcie corrected.

"*His* personal items from his quarters and bring them here for Lady Blackburn and her solicitor to take possession of."

"Yes, sir." The sergeant saluted and hurried to follow the lieutenant's order.

Chasen turned to Dulcie and brushed his palms together. "There. I've sent the sergeant to collect your husband's things. You may take possession of them as soon as he returns."

"I have an appointment with the commandant at half-past eight this morning. Sabbath or no Sabbath," Archibald Gunn spoke up. "Commandant Swindell made the appointment with me yesterday morning. And as I am here at the chosen time, I expect him to do me the courtesy of being here at half-past eight as well."

"Mister Gunn, I have explained to you that today is the commandant's day of worship and rest."

"Are you also telling me that Commandant Swindell deliberately selected a time and place for us to meet so he would have the excuse of not showing up for the meeting?" Archie Gunn demanded.

"Mister Gunn, I suggest you take Blac—" The lieutenant broke off upon seeing the look on Dulcie's face. "*Major Lord Blackburn's* personal effects and Lady Blackburn and go home."

"*I* suggest that when the sergeant returns with my husband's belongings, you send him to fetch Commandant Swindell from wherever he is hiding to avoid meeting with us. He is late for a scheduled meeting with Mister Gunn, who is here on official legal business." She met the lieutenant's gaze. "As am I."

"Commandant Swindell is the highest ranking officer at this garrison." Lieutenant Chasen was indignant. "I cannot send the sergeant to *fetch* him. He is my superior officer. He is in charge of everything that goes on here. And he does not entertain visitors or attend to business on Sundays."

"Really?" Dulcie challenged. "Then, what do you call this morning's unlawful hanging of a peer of the realm who was neither charged with, nor convicted of, high crimes and misdemeanors? Pleasure? Rest? Sunday services?"

"Madam, I will not send the sergeant to request Commandant Swindell's presence here when he is ent—" The lieutenant abruptly stopped speaking.

"Very well, I shall fetch him myself." Dulcie wasn't making an idle threat. She would search the garrison if she had to, and she would start with the office behind the lieutenant's because she was convinced that was where she would find Commandant Swindell hiding.

"Madam..."

Dulcie ignored him.

"Lady Blackburn," Chasen tried again. "This is a military prison. You are a female. You cannot wander through the corridors in search of Commandant Swindell."

"If this garrison is a military prison, the prisoners are confined to their quarters or behind bars and under guard. I shall be perfectly safe to wander the corridors under those circumstances."

"Lady Blackburn, you cannot," Lieutenant Chasen insisted.

"Watch me," she challenged once again. "I came here to speak with the commandant and I will do so before I leave. If he is the man in charge of everything having anything to do with the garrison, I shall speak to him. Not"—she raked her gaze over the lieutenant—"one of his junior officers. Now will you fetch him, or shall I?" She took a step toward the outer door, then feinted by turning in the direction of the antechamber.

Lieutenant Chasen grabbed hold of her arm above her elbow and spun her around. Dulcie let out a yelp.

Archibald Gunn snapped into action, whacking the lieutenant on the forearm with his umbrella. "How dare you put your hands on a *lady*?!"

In the midst of the scuffle, the door to the commandant's office opened and Commandant Swindell walked in. "What's going on in here?"

Lieutenant Chasen let go of Dulcie's arm and snapped to attention as his commanding officer entered the room. "Sir. This lady was threatening to search the garrison until she found you. I was endeavoring to stop her and the old gentleman was interfering with my attempt by assaulting me with a weapon."

"He struck you with his umbrella," Dulcie corrected. "To make you let go of my arm."

Commandant Swindell approached Dulcie. "Miss Susan Brown, is it not?"

Dulcie lifted her chin a bit higher to meet the commandant's condescending gaze. "It was. It's Lady Blackburn now. Mister Gunn is here to keep the meeting you scheduled for half-past eight and to take possession of my husband's belongings." She nodded toward Archibald Gunn. "And I am here to take possession of my husband's body so I can take him home for a proper burial."

Commandant Swindell stared at the solicitor. "I instructed the lieutenant to send the sergeant on duty to collect the condemned prisoner's personal effects. Once he delivers them, our meeting is no longer necessary. As I don't normally conduct business on Sunday."

"On the contrary," Gunn said. "We have quite a bit of business to discuss. I wish to settle the accounts pertaining to room, food, household items, and bathing and laundry services Lord Blackburn incurred while wrongfully incarcerated in this military installation."

"Accounts?" Dulcie asked. "He was charged for use of a room, the food he ate, and household items?"

"Of course, he was," Commandant Swindell said. "The British Army does not pay to maintain prisoners. All prisoners are required to pay for their room and board and the household goods and services they use. The fees are deducted from the monthly pay of the enlisted prisoners. Officers forfeit their army pay and are required to settle their accounts from their personal revenue."

"What sort of household goods?" she demanded.

"Sheets, a blanket, a pillow, soap, candles, a razor and shaving mug, a comb, a spoon and a dish, a tin cup. Those sorts of things." Swindell waved his hand in a gesture of dismissal.

Dulcie glanced at Mister Gunn. "Is this true? The army charged him for his keep while confining him to quarters?"

"Indeed, it is, my lady," Mister Gunn said grimly. "The army charges for everything, including the food and board for his horse and storage of his equipment. Access to pen and paper and the franking of a letter, shaving, barbering, library, medical, and burial services." He turned his attention to the commandant. "I require an enumerated accounting of Lord Blackburn's expenses for this month. And an enumeration of expenditures for his horse for this month and for next month."

Swindell blinked at him. "Next month?"

"Lord Blackburn sold the horse and all his equipment with him. The extra month's food and board is to ensure the horse is here and in fine form when the buyer sends his representative to collect him," Gunn informed him. "I've prepared a sworn statement that acknowledges the payment of the extra month's food and board for

Frederick the Great, a seal brown Prussian Trakehner seventeen-hand stallion until such time as the Earl of Weymouth, the new owner, or the owner's representative, takes possession of the horse." Archibald Gunn fixed his unyielding gaze on the commandant. "And I've other documents requiring your signature that pertain to the execution that took place on the grounds of this garrison this morning."

The commandant frowned. "I'll sign your documents and Lieutenant Chasen will provide the amounts of the total expenditures for Prisoner Blackburn."

"Amounts are not acceptable," the solicitor replied. "I require enumerated accounts of every expenditure charged to Lord Blackburn's accounts to settle his personal estate. I also require an inventory of every item returned to Lady Blackburn to compare against Lord Blackburn's inventory of items he brought with him into the army."

Commandant Swindell glanced at his lieutenant. "Make whatever Mister Gunn requires available to him."

"I have monthly amounts," Lieutenant Chasen said. "I do not have enumerated lists of every expenditure."

"Then I suggest you get started," Mister Gunn said. "I will require the entirety of the items I mentioned before Lady Blackburn and I sail this afternoon."

Lieutenant Chasen looked to the commandant for confirmation.

Swindell nodded.

"It's Sunday, sir," The lieutenant reminded him. "We do not work on Sundays."

"That isn't true," Dulcie said. "You hanged my husband this morning."

"I didn't hang him," Lieutenant Chasen protested. "I only witnessed it."

"Were you required to attend?" Mister Gunn asked.

"Of course," the lieutenant replied. "All off duty officers were required to attend."

"Do you receive pay as a lieutenant in the army?" Gunn continued.

"As a matter of fact, I do." Lieutenant Chasen's chest puffed with pride. "I'm a full-pay lieutenant."

"Then, legally, you were working this morning when you attended the hanging of Major Lord Blackburn. And *you* were working."—Gunn turned his accusing gaze on Swindell—"when you presided at the dreadful event. So I see no reason why you cannot continue to work on this most unusually sinful Sabbath for two such devout officers."

"We were doing our duty as officers in His Majesty's Army," Swindell said. "The prisoner had been condemned. We were duty-bound to carry it out at the appointed time and place."

"Of course, you were," Gunn agreed. "I am certain the good Lord makes allowances for officers who witness and preside over the murder of a wrongly accused fellow officer."

The tips of the lieutenant's ears turned a bright red.

Commandant Swindell's face turned an even angrier shade.

Archibald Gunn ignored them both. "Shall we get down to business?"

Swindell turned toward Dulcie. "Miss Brown, if you would be so kind as to wait in the antechamber until we have concluded our business…"

"I would be happy to," she said. "Once the sergeant delivers my husband's belongings."

A knock sounded on the door.

Commandant Swindell barked, "Enter."

The sergeant entered the room carrying a packed knapsack and a wooden box.

"Ah," Commandant Swindell drawled. "Here he is now." He turned to Dulcie. "The sergeant will carry the items to the antechamber for you to inspect."

Leaving the men to conduct their business, Dulcie followed the sergeant into the antechamber where she'd spent most of the previous day. *Meeting Rafe. Marrying Rafe.*

Once inside, Dulcie turned to the sergeant. "Did you get everything?"

"Everything that belonged to Major Blackburn." He indicated the rucksack and the wooden box. "It's all it here."

"What about the bed clothes, pillow, and blanket? His shaving mug and razor? His soap? His comb? Other such items?"

"No, ma'am." He shook his head. "Just his clothes and books and such."

"Tell me, sergeant, when a prisoner is first confined to his quarters, what sort of furnishings are in the room?" Dulcie asked.

The sergeant scratched his head. "A bed frame, a water bucket, and a sand bucket to..." He blushed, remembering he was speaking to a lady.

"Nothing else?" Dulcie asked.

"No, ma'am."

"Is that what Major Lord Blackburn's quarters look like now?"

"No, ma'am."

Dulcie took a deep breath and slowly released it. "Sergeant, I want you to go back and collect everything that wasn't there when Major Lord Blackburn was confined to quarters. Sheets, pillow, blanket, mattress, and everything else. I want you to leave his room the way he found it. I want his shaving mug, his razor, everything. His tin plate, his spoon and fork, and his tin cup."

His bewildered expression told her he didn't understand why she wanted those things. "I'll have to go to the barber and to the kitchen to get some of those things."

She smiled at him. "Sergeant, did you know that an officer has to pay for everything that isn't in the room when he is first confined to it?"

He shook his head. "Even a major and a lord?"

"Even so," she said. "Since my husband paid for all those things, they belong to him. And as his widow, I must confess I don't feel charitable enough toward the commandant to leave them behind."

The sergeant nodded. "I don't imagine you do, ma'am."

"Thank you, Sergeant."

"Henshaw, ma'am. Sergeant William Henshaw. And you are welcome." He lowered his voice so there was no chance of being overheard. "I liked Major Lord Blackburn. He was a good man and a good officer. A gentleman. And an outstanding cavalryman. I'll get the rest of his things packed up for you while you check all of these. You'll find pen and ink and paper in that desk." He pointed to the Georgian desk and matching chair.

Dulcie swallowed the lump in her throat and tried to thank the sergeant again, but no words would come.

DULCIE HAD COMPLETED HER INVENTORY OF ALL THE ITEMS THE sergeant had brought her, including the mattress and all the bedding and everything else he had left out the first time around. She had borrowed a sheet of paper and pen and ink from the desk and recorded each item as she searched Rafe's rucksack and the wooden box. She bit her bottom lip and blinked back tears when she came to a familiar volume of *Gulliver's Travels* that had once belonged to her father. She opened the front cover and ran her finger over the image of the Tennant coat-of-arms embossed on the title page.

She smiled. Rafe had returned all of Geoff's personal belongings to her except *Gulliver's Travels*. She wondered if he had kept it as a reminder of her brother or to add to his own personal library that consisted of Homer, Virgil, and William Shakespeare. Opening the covers of those books she saw that they bore an earlier version of the signature that appeared on her copies of her marriage contract. *Raphael, Seventh Earl of Blackburn.*

The sergeant supplied her with a placard he borrowed from the garrison's sutlery, listing the cost of each item. Dulcie faithfully recorded the price of each item beside the item. Her anger grew as she wrote the prices beside the items and realized how much Rafe had paid to be held in the garrison against his will.

Once he had finished collecting Rafe's belongings and Dulcie had completed her inventory of them, the sergeant had volunteered to load the goods on the hired coach for her. Dulcie thanked him for his hard work and for his kindness and gifted him with one of the two guineas she had brought with her to the island.

She was waiting patiently when the lieutenant knocked on the door and invited her to return to the outer office, where Mister Gunn and the commandant had concluded their business. Dulcie walked over to Mister Gunn and handed him her list. "I checked it twice against the prices in the garrison's sutlery." She shot the commandant a hard glance before continuing. "Sergeant Henshaw can verify that I added a shilling to pay for the sheet of paper, the ink, and the pen I borrowed from the desk in the antechamber. As a Blackburn, I thought it necessary to pay for the items lest I be charged with pilfering stationery and confined to my quarters to await my military inquiry and subsequent hanging."

"Very good, my lady." Biting back an admiring smile, Archibald Gunn tucked the list Dulcie had made into his accounts ledger for safekeeping. "Thank you."

"Sergeant Henshaw has loaded everything into our coach for our journey to the docks," Dulcie said.

Commandant Swindell brushed his hands together in a dismissive gesture. "Your business here is done." He pinned his gaze on the solicitor first, then on Dulcie. "You had best be on your way."

"What about my husband's mortal remains?" Dulcie reminded him.

"What about them?" he parried.

"We're taking him home with us for proper burial. We came in a coach. We need a coffin and a wagon or a dray to transport it to the boat," Dulcie explained.

"You need nothing of the kind," the commandant said. "Because your husband's mortal remains are not at the garrison."

Swindell's words hit her like a blow, but Dulcie refused to show it. "Where are they?" she demanded.

"I have no idea," he said. "I ordered the execution detail to dispose of them shortly after the regimental surgeon sent from London pronounced him dead."

"Where are the members of the execution detail?" Dulcie struggled to maintain her composure. "I would like to speak with them."

"On their way to the mainland, I suppose," the commandant replied with a dismissive shrug.

Dulcie bristled at that. "You *suppose?*"

"They were granted leave. It's customary in special cases for the members of the Court of Inquiry to request the execution detail from another military post and to grant them leave to return immediately after the deed is done," Commandant Swindell explained.

"You cannot account for Lord Blackburn's body?" Archibald Gunn's booming voice trembled with rage.

"I cannot, nor do I care to try. The man was tried, convicted, and executed for his crime. Good riddance I say. Hanging him wasn't work. It was a pleasure."

"Where does the execution detail normally take the bodies?" Dulcie clenched her fists to keep from flying at the insufferable man in a blind rage.

"Of condemned men?" Swindell drawled. "Well, once the head is removed, they usually sell the rest of the body to the anatomists at the universities or to surgeons at the hospitals for dissection." His laugh was deliberately cruel. "The Crown doesn't set high value on a condemned man's corpse. The execution detail is allowed to sell corpses for whatever price they can get. They won't get as much for a body without a head, but..."

Dulcie sucked in a breath before quickly clamping her mouth shut, determined not to let Commandant Swindell take pleasure in her reaction.

Swindell continued, "But I believe a man condemned to a traitor's death, should suffer a traitor's fate." He gave another cruel chuckle. "Especially one who uses his last words to condemn me. But he will have a difficult time condemning anyone now that he's without his head. Good afternoon, Miss Brown, Mister Gunn, and have a pleasant journey home."

"And you have a pleasant and restful remainder of your Sabbath, Commandant Swindell," Dulcie looked him square in the eye. "For I promise that you will not have another one until I learn what you did with my husband's body."

CHAPTER 22

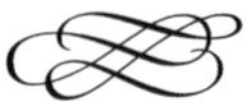

"To weep is to make less"
The depth of grief."
—William Shakespeare, 1564-1616

Dulcie was inconsolable.

She had no memory of her exit from the commandant's office or the garrison, or how she had managed to climb into the coach, but she had. And once safely inside the privacy of the closed coach, she buried her face against the cushioned seat and gave vent to the tears she'd held in check since she'd awakened to find Raphael was gone.

She might not remember the walk from the commandant's office to the coach, but Archibald Gunn did, and he was quick to assure her she had left the commandant's office uncowed with steel in her spine and with her head held high. She had made it on her own without any assistance from him.

"You were magnificent, my lady," Archie said. "The equal to my Janet."

"The equal to your Janet?" She was awed by the compliment he had paid her.

"Indeed, my lady," he confirmed. "His Lordship would be most proud of the way you comported yourself in the face of the enemy. You do the Blackburn name proud."

Dulcie turned to look at the solicitor. His kindly visage was a watery blur. "He wouldn't be proud if he saw me like this." She whisked a stream of tears from her cheek.

"Nonsense, my dear." Archie reached over and gently patted her shoulder. "There is no shame when you cry for those you love."

Unable to stop the flow of tears, Dulcie wiped her face again, this time on the back of her glove. "The commandant is monstrous."

"Yes, he is." The solicitor took a clean handkerchief from his jacket pocket and pressed it into her hand. "He is a cruel, petty man who enjoys wielding power over those who cannot defend themselves. He is a natural bully. The sort of man who pulled the wings off butterflies as a child."

"He's...filled...with...envy," she hiccupped between sobs.

"Precisely," he agreed.

"Rafe...Lord Blackburn...told...me...that...last...night..." The mention of Rafe's name produced another flood of tears and sobs. Dulcie dabbed at her face with Archie's handkerchief. "I'm sorry. I can't stop crying."

"Shh." The elderly solicitor moved from his seat to sit beside Dulcie. "Don't fret about it, my lady. You have every right to cry. And no need to apologize for it. You have been through an eventful two days and done battle with a cruel tyrant. You cry all you need to. No one will see you but me. And as your solicitor, I am bound by an oath. Everything you say to me is privileged conversation and cannot be disclosed." He managed a hint of a smile. "That includes weeping."

The sudden rush of tears blinded her. She gulped air between the sobs wracking her body because it was almost impossible to breathe through her blocked nose. The sound of her weeping filled the coach. And her agonizing cry of "They cut off his head!" broke Archibald Gunn's heart.

Fixing her blurry gaze on the middle button of the solicitor's waistcoat, Dulcie wailed, "How will I find him if they cut off his head?" Unable to bear the thought of the executioner chopping off Rafe's head, Dulcie hid her face against the upholstered seat and collapsed into another paroxysm of tears.

"There, there, my lady." Mister Gunn awkwardly smoothed the damp tendrils of auburn hair off her face. "They didn't cut Master Rafe's head off."

Dulcie lifted her head to face the solicitor. "They didn't?"

"No," he replied. "The commandant deliberately said that to torture you. Sticks and stones and all that."

"How do you know?" she asked, her voice, raw and scratchy.

"Because he's a cruel and petty man." Normally scrupulously honest, straightforward, and plainspoken, Archibald Gunn pretended to misinterpret her question. He hoped she wouldn't repeat it, but this young lady didn't miss a trick.

"No," she said. "How do you know they didn't cut off his head?"

Gunn took a deep breath and braced himself for her reaction. "Because it's customary to display the head of a traitor on the city or garrison gates. If the commandant had ordered the execution detail to remove Master Rafe's head, we would have seen it on a pike atop the gates to the garrison."

"Oh no!" Dulcie clamped her hand over her mouth to stop the scream of horror from escaping. The memory of the commandant's cruel words returned unbidden along with an image of Rafe's handsome head stuck on a pike. *Once the head is removed, they usually sell the rest of the body to the anatomists. Hanging him wasn't work. It was a pleasure.* "Why would he say such awful things?"

"To wound you."

Dulcie frowned. "But I've done nothing to him."

"On the contrary, my lady. You married the commandant's nemesis yesterday."

"What difference did that make to Swindell?" She swiped at the tears running down her face with the heels of her hands. "I mean nothing to him."

"No, you don't. But you earned his ire when you appeared at his door this morning and defended your husband's actions."

"It's a wife's place to defend her husband against his enemy."

"Indeed it is," Mister Gunn continued. "But you married a man Commandant Swindell despised. A man condemned to die by hanging. A man who disobeyed his commanding officer's direct order and was proclaimed a hero for doing so."

"But Rafe's actions saved the artillerymen and the artillery from destruction that might have cost us the battle."

"That doesn't matter to a man like Swindell. He commands a garrison of military prisoners. Orders must be obeyed without question or exception. There are no extenuating circumstances," Mister Gunn explained.

"But to be so needlessly cruel to a stranger..."

"He doesn't consider it needless. You offended him by marrying a condemned prisoner and by engaging a man of Lord Weymouth's caliber to arrange for your wedding to take place at the garrison, thereby usurping the commandant's authority, and appropriating his domain for your use. You also neglected to invite the commandant to the ceremony."

"I didn't neglect to invite him to witness the ceremony. I couldn't understand how he could be such a congenial host and fail to attend our wedding until Rafe told me that he had asked that the commandant not be invited." She met the lawyer's sharp gaze. "Not that I am criticizing my husband's decision. I agreed with him. He shouldn't have anyone at our wedding he didn't want there. Especially the man keeping him confined against his will."

"You didn't find fault with Lord Blackburn's decision, but a man like the commandant will not forgive a slight from his *inferiors.* Because Lord Blackburn was a prisoner, Swindell considered him completely inferior to him despite Lord Blackburn's title, his wealth, and his hero status. As a woman, especially a young woman, he also considers you greatly inferior to a man—especially a man of his years, experience, military service, and rank."

Dulcie's great wracking sobs had died away as he spoke, but a continuous stream of tears still rolled down her face and dripped off her chin. "It isn't fair," she said at last. "I worked so hard to find him only to lose him. We only had one day together." *And one glorious night.* It hurt so much to think of all she had lost. And it was more than the lovemaking they had shared. She'd lost a friend and a welcome confidante. A companion. A protector. Someone to keep the nightmares at bay when she slept. Someone to hold her so she wouldn't be so terribly alone. But more than all that, she had lost her dream of a life together. Dulcie glanced down at her lap and realized she'd been twisting her wedding band around and around her finger, rubbing the thin ribbon of gold the way one might rub a magic lamp in hopes a genie would emerge and grant their most fervent wish.

It seemed impossible that she could miss a man she had only known for a single day and night. But she did. And the grief was beyond bearing. With Raphael, she had experienced a glimpse of heaven, a glimpse of what they could have, the future they could build. Now she was empty, bereft of everything except tears. All she had wanted and sought and dreamed of was gone. Because *he* was gone. And she was alone again and lost. Seeking comfort in the company of a kind old gentleman mourning the same loss. "What do I do? Where do I begin? I can't abandon him. I can't leave him to be dissected by anatomists. He has a family that loves him. Sisters and nephews and nieces, friends like you, and family retainers…" Her tears flowed faster.

"And you," Mister Gunn added gently. "His wife."

"I can usually find my way, but now I can't think what to do. How to proceed…" She met his gaze, blinking through her tears. "I can't return to my old life as if nothing happened. I can't just forget him and blindly accept my guardian's choice for me."

"Is that what Master Rafe asked of you?" Mister Gunn's voice was gentle when he asked the question.

Dulcie closed her eyes and heard Rafe instructing her to go on with her life. *Tomorrow, you'll be a widow. Once, you return to London you'll continue your Season as if nothing ever happened. As if you'd never met me.*

As if having met him, she could ever forget him. Dulcie sighed. "He told me not to disobey my uncle. He told me to do my best to accept whomever my uncle chose for me. To go on with my life as if I had never met him." Dulcie searched the solicitor's face. "I promised him I would try. But I can't!" She covered her face with her hands. "Not now. Not after Rafe."

"You don't have to do anything just yet," Gunn assured her. "And you don't have to do it alone. I'm here to help you. We'll take things one step at a time and we won't stop until we find him and the people who did this to him." He brushed his hand over Dulcie's hair. "In the meantime, try not to worry. Allow me to worry for you. Try to rest for a bit, my lady. You've suffered a great shock and you need to conserve your strength for the road ahead."

The immediate road ahead took them past the honeymoon cottage. Dulcie glanced out the window and caught a glimpse of the distinctive blue front door framed by topiary, the roses blooming along the stone wall, and the white garden gate where Rafe had lifted her into his arms and told her she was in charge of opening gates and doors because his hands were full. They had made memories in that tiny cottage. Lasting memories. And those memories brought a fresh surge of tears to the surface. Dulcie kept her face to the coach window long after the cottage faded from view.

DULCIE KEPT HER FACE AVERTED FROM THE CREWMEMBERS AND BARELY acknowledged the captain of the vessel once they reached the yacht, the *Guernsey Queen,* moored alongside the dock where Lord Weymouth had told Mister Gunn it would be.

"Welcome aboard the *Guernsey Queen,* Miss Brown, Mister Gunn." The captain greeted them using Dulcie's alias, which told Archibald Gunn that he was unaware of the tragedy that had befallen the young bride. "I hope you had a pleasant stay with your relations on the island."

"It was a most pleasant night," Gunn replied. "So much so that it upset the young lady to leave them behind to return to dreary old London." He made no mention of the tears Dulcie had shed during the drive to the harbor, but allowed the captain to draw his own conclusions regarding her swollen eyes, tear-stained cheeks, and spiked eyelashes.

The captain gave Dulcie a sympathetic smile. "We've prepared staterooms for each of you if you'd like to rest. And I can have tea or coffee sent down to you once we get underway."

"Thank you, Captain," Dulcie murmured. "Tea sounds wonderful."

"If you'll follow Mister Preston, he'll show you to your rooms. We'll get underway as soon as we finish bringing your household goods and personal items aboard. If there is anything you would like delivered to your staterooms, tell Mr. Preston. He'll bring them to you first and will follow with your refreshments."

Mister Gunn glanced down at the leather portfolio he had tucked under his arm. "I have plenty of work to keep me occupied on the journey."

"What about you, Miss Brown? Is there something you wish to have brought to your stateroom?" the captain asked.

"If it isn't too much trouble, I would like the wooden box with the books in it," Dulcie replied.

"It's no trouble at all. Now, if you'll follow Mister Preston, I'll see about getting us underway."

The comfortable staterooms opened onto a small sitting room. Archibald claimed the desk by setting his portfolio on it. "I hope you don't mind, my lady, but I would like to review the inventory you made of Master Rafe's personal items." He smiled at Dulcie. "So, are you going to read Homer, Virgil, or Shakespeare?"

"None of them."

Mister Gunn frowned. "Don't tell me Master Rafe changed the books in his personal library."

Dulcie was surprised. "Did you check the list I gave you?"

"Not yet."

"Then, how did you know which books were on it?"

"It's no great secret. Master Rafe always carried his three favorite volumes of Greek, Latin, and English whenever he traveled. He couldn't choose among the three, so he always carried his petite library with him."

Dulcie smiled her first genuine smile since leaving the commandant's office. "He added a purloined volume to his little library, increasing it to four volumes."

"A purloined volume? Master Rafe stole a book?"

"He wasn't the original thief," Dulcie said. "My brother was. He took *Gulliver's Travels* from my father's library when he left for the Peninsula. Unlike Raphael, Geoff only had one favorite book. Rafe kept it rather than send it home with Geoff's other personal things." She was quiet for a moment. "My father read it aloud to my brother, my mother, and me. Of all the books my father read to us, it was Geoff's favorite."

"Is it your favorite as well?"

Dulcie shook her head. "I enjoyed it, but it isn't my favorite.

"But you're going to keep it."

"Yes," she said. "Because it belonged to the three most important men in my life."

The elderly solicitor nodded. "May I ask, out of curiosity, what is your favorite book?"

A dreamy expression covered her face. "I'm particularly partial to *The Life and Opinions of Tristram Shandy, Gentleman.*"

"Interesting choice for a young lady," Mister Gunn remarked. "Any particular reason?"

"I loved the sound of his voice as he read it aloud to me."

CHAPTER 23

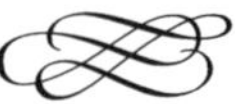

"Courage is like love, it must have hope for nourishment."
—Napoleon Bonaparte, 1769-1821

"I don't believe I've ever seen such a display of courage," Daniel, ninth Duke of Sussex, said as soon as he was comfortably seated below deck in the parlor of the *Jersey Queen* after he and the other Free Fellows came aboard the yacht that had been anchored at the rendezvous point following Blackburn's hanging and the recovery of his body. Sussex sat sipping a glass of fine Scots whisky while they congratulated themselves on a successful mission as the yacht set sail for home.

In the parlor with him were his fellow conspirators—Jarrod, Marquess of Shepherdston, Alexander, Marquess of Courtland, Jonathan, Earl of Barclay, Colin, Viscount Grantham, and Micah Beekins. Their other co-conspirator, James McGregor, was on his way to the cargo hold to check on the condition of their precious cargo.

"He was a sight to behold," Courtland agreed, raising his whisky tumbler in salute to Blackburn's stout-hearted character. "I don't know how he managed."

"His legs had to have been quaking," Sussex continued. "But he gave no outward sign of it. And not only did he not falter, but Blackburn also managed to soundly rebuke his enemy. That showed courage."

"You showed a bit of courage yourself," Shepherdston said, sipping from his own glass of whisky, "when you promised him you would shoot him if he faltered."

"I was relieved he didn't," Sussex admitted. "I've crossed this channel dozens of times, avoiding the British and the French coast watch in order to sneak in and out of France and never thought about the danger, but that..." He shuddered. "To stand without faltering while a hangman—" He glanced at Micah Beekins. "Even a *counterfeit* hangman slips a noose around your neck."

"Could you have shot him?" Barclay asked his cousin, Sussex.

"I don't know," Sussex answered honestly. "I'm glad I didn't have to put it to the test."

"We're glad you didn't have to, either," Grantham said, "For your sake and for ours because questions would have been asked about the special execution detail."

Shepherdston nodded his agreement. "Speaking of questions about the special execution detail... Micah, what did you say to Blackburn when you adjusted the noose around his neck?"

"I cautioned him not to move, your lordship," Micah replied. "I've never hanged anyone afore."

"You didn't *tell* him he was your first hanging, did you?" Barclay asked.

Micah scowled. "You know better than that, sir. The man had enough on his mind without worrying about how much practice I had as a hangman."

"You're absolutely right," Barclay said. "I apologize for asking a foolish question." As far as Barclay was concerned, Micah Beekins had earned the right to speak his mind as an equal when he had assisted Barclay in the most important mission of his life.

"I didn't mind the question, sir, so much as the idea that I would have taken this job if I didn't think I was the man for it." Micah smiled. "I like the coin ye pay me. But I'm not a greedy man. I like helping ye in your work more. I like that each mission is different. Ye've all asked me to do some strange and important jobs. But I admit that this time, I had a bout of nerves at the start. What if I made a mistake? What if I forgot to follow the doctor's instructions to the letter? What if I failed to cut through the rope just so?" He held out his hand to show it to his companions. "It hasn't been too long since it stopped shaking. I didn't want to be guilty of killing a belted earl and a war hero."

Micah Beekins wasn't a member of the Free Fellows League. He was a trusted member of a family of smugglers the Free Fellows had used to sneak them in and out of France whenever the need arose. He had proved himself a valuable ally and asset to their clandestine activities and had been the logical choice to recruit for the role of hangman. At one time or another, Micah, his brother, his father, and various trusted cousins had smuggled or assisted Grantham, Shepherdston, Barclay, Sussex, and Courtland with a secret mission or a personal one, including the one where Sussex had been shot by the French coast watch and badly wounded.

"Why should you mind?" Sussex couldn't resist teasing Micah a little. "The commandant of the garrison and his hand-picked Court of Inquiry didn't. They seemed quite eager to see it done."

"They were most eager to see Lord Blackburn hanged as soon as possible," Micah agreed. "The commandant and his man hurried out to inspect my progress as soon as they learned I had arrived. And they were curious about me and the execution detail sent from London."

"What did you tell him?" Shepherdston asked.

Micah grinned at Shepherdston. "I told him that I wore a hood for a reason. I told him that hangmen swear oaths not to reveal their identities or their home villages to anyone. As a hangman, I refused to break my oath."

"Do hangmen swear such oaths?" Grantham asked.

"I dunno, sir," Micah replied. "But if they don't, they should."

Jarrod Shepherdston smiled. "That was fast thinking, Micah."

"In the smuggling business we're taught never to give our names or put our family members at risk by revealing the name of our village," Micah said.

"You're wise to take precautions," Courtland agreed. "We also take measures to safeguard our families and homes from our enemies."

"Aye," Micah said. "I learned to think fast and come up with answers for any questions I might be asked if I was caught when I started helping my da in the family business. Ye never know when the coast watch of one side or the other will pull ye over to search your boat."

"Grantham did a grand day's work when he approached your family with our proposition that your family join forces with us," Shepherdston said, complimenting both Grantham and Beekins.

Grantham inclined his head to acknowledge Shepherdston's rare compliment. "I think so, too."

His brow wrinkled in thought, Barclay asked Micah, "Were you able to see what happened when the commandant's aide reported your response to the commandant?"

"Aye," Micah told him. "The commandant hurried to the closed black coach parked beside the scaffold and climbed inside to speak with the gentleman inside. And you could hear their raised voices from time to time."

"Did you see the gentleman inside the coach?" Sussex asked, sitting forward in his chair.

Micah shook his head. "I didn't see his face full on. But I did see him peek through the curtains a time or two."

"Did you form any impression of the gentleman?" Courtland asked.

"He was a gentleman," Micah said. "And he was powerful and important enough to have the commandant of a garrison rushing to do his bidding."

The Free Fellows exchanged glances. "It must have been one or more of the gentlemen at the Admiralty Friday night in that coach."

"They definitely wanted to see Blackburn hanged," Courtland said.

"Did the commandant's aide accompany him to the coach?" Barclay asked Micah.

"No, sir." Micah drained his whisky glass.

"Hmm," Sheperdston murmured. "Commandant Swindell didn't want his aide to see the man in the coach."

"Could you tell if there was more than one man in the coach?" Sussex picked up where Barclay had left off.

"No, sir," Micah said. "Nobody entered or left the coach except the commandant."

Shepherdston refilled Micah's glass. "Thank you, Micah. You've done an excellent job for us once again by observing our enemy for us."

"And he did an excellent job of hanging Lord Blackburn as well," Barclay said. "Everything went the way we planned."

"Blackburn's fall through the trapdoor was perfectly timed," Courtland complimented Micah. "The rope broke before the drop brought him up short. Barclay and I grabbed him and pulled down so we could pretend his neck broke on the drop."

"And to keep him from slowly strangling if anything went wrong." McGregor added as he entered the parlor. "The hanged man's jig is a ghastly way to die."

"Drink?" Shepherdston asked, lifting a glass.

"Aye." McGregor sat down at the table, took a hefty swallow of his whisky, and exhaled a sigh of relief. "What did I miss?"

"We were reviewing Micah's role as the hangman," Sussex replied.

"His timing was perfect," McGregor said. "He pulled the lever to open the trapdoor before the commandant finished giving the command."

"Your timing wasn't so bad, either, Doctor," Sussex pointed out. "You were right there to check his heartbeat and breathing and pronounce him dead. You got to Blackburn before the commandant did even though he shot out of his place in front of the scaffold like a cannon ball shot out of cannon."

Shaking his head, McGregor took another sip of his whisky.

"Blackburn's breathing was so shallow and his heartbeat so faint, I feared we'd killed him."

"The sound of the rope breaking convinced the first row of witnesses Blackburn's neck had snapped," Courtland added. "The mirror and the commandant's declaration of Blackburn's death convinced the man in the closed coach. He sped away as if the hounds of hell were after him."

"That trick with the mirror was brilliant." They had all held their own breath as McGregor had placed a mirror in front of Blackburn's mouth and nose to show the commandant there was no breath left in the body.

"It convinced me as well," Micah said, looking in need of another glass of whisky. "I was sure I'd killed him."

"It's worked in the past," McGregor said.

"You've done this before?" Barclay was clearly dumbfounded.

"I've never participated in the rescue of a condemned man," McGregor explained. But I've attended executions and declared condemned men dead on several occasions. The mirror technique has stood me in good stead since I began performing surgeries." He pinned Barclay with his sharp gaze. "Surgeons at universities like to know the corpses are actually dead before they put scalpel to flesh and begin instruction during anatomy class. And most surgeons on the battlefield use the technique as well. No one wants to begin surgery on a dead soldier when there are so many living soldiers waiting for care." He shuddered at the memory of all the battlefield surgeries he'd conducted. "I simply had to use some sleight of hand to turn the mirror away from Blackburn's mouth so there would be no fog. I may have to employ the trick once again when the inspector comes aboard to check our cargo hold," McGregor admitted. "It depends on how closely the inspector means to inspect the coffin."

"When we left we did declare we were traveling to Wight on behalf of the War Department to retrieve the body of a soldier so we could return him to his family." Shepherdston remarked. "It will behoove us to have a corpse in the coffin. So how is our corpse?" he asked the doctor.

"The elixir is slowly beginning to wear off," McGregor said. "His breathing and pulse are a bit stronger, but still shallow enough to remain undetected by inspectors who dislike dealing with corpses. I opened the door on the top of the coffin to allow him to breathe more easily. The coffin they had ordered for Blackburn had been equipped with a small, hinged door over the face to allow inspectors at the Port of London to verify their cargo was a corpse. I'll go back down and secure him before the inspectors board us."

"What if they decide to touch him?" Grantham asked. "Won't his flesh be warm?"

McGregor shook his head. "It's cold in the cargo hold. That's why I came up for some warm coffee. By the time we dock, his flesh will be sufficiently cold to convince anyone." He smiled a grim smile. "Most port inspectors recoil from corpses for fear of catching whatever it was that killed the person. Only those with a morbid fascination with the dead dare to touch."

Sussex shuddered involuntarily. "I hope you're right."

"Trust me," McGregor said. "Unless we encounter a medical student or an anatomist eager to purchase a corpse for dissection, we'll pass Custom House inspectors."

~

RAFE OPENED HIS EYES BUT WAS UNABLE TO SEE ANYTHING IN THE stygian darkness. He blinked to clear his vision, but all he saw was darkness. He tried to move and discovered he was confined—tied down or wedged into something too tight to allow freedom of movement. He opened his mouth to call for help, but no words came out.

He felt a moment of panic, believing he was trapped in a netherworld between light and dark, wakefulness and dreams, everything and nothing. He thought he was awake, but perhaps he was dreaming.

To die, to sleep—to sleep, perchance to dream—ay, there's the rub, For in this sleep of death what dreams may come.

Shakespeare's words from *Hamlet* flitted through his mind. Was he dreaming? Or was he sleeping the sleep of death? Was he awaiting entrance to heaven or to purgatory? He couldn't decide. Did souls have thoughts? Could they remember their Shakespeare? Or had he somehow slipped the veil to a place where he was able to hear the words? He couldn't see a stage or actors performing the tragedy, but he knew the play and recognized the soliloquy.

He found it strange that he should remember Shakespeare yet be unable to recall how he came to be wherever he was.

He remembered the events leading up to the nothingness. He remembered the hangman slipping the noose over his head and the words the man had whispered afterwards: "Try not to move, my lord."

Rafe thought he'd taken the hangman's advice, but he must have moved when he received his last rites or when he'd confronted the commandant and his accusers—his murderers—because he couldn't move now. He remembered the look on Commandant Swindell's face at his public indictment of the commandant and the Court of Inquiry. He recalled the visible sliver of a man's face peeking through the curtains in the black closed coach and had been certain it was the face of his nemesis, Cornelius Fenton. Rafe even recalled his surprise when the floor suddenly disappeared and he dropped into thin air.

His last thought on the way down had been of Dulcie.

And his dreams… The dreams that came were of Dulcie in all her naked splendor, and the hours they'd spent together talking, laughing, sparring, kissing, touching, and loving… *Loving.*

Suddenly forgetting his desire to awaken, Rafe closed his eyes and dreamed once again of Dulcie.

CHAPTER 24

"Love is a sickness full of woes,
All remedies refusing."
—Samuel Daniel, 1562-1619

Archibald Gunn's carriage rolled to a halt in front of Lady Nesbitt's home at Number Twelve Grosvenor Street in the wee hours of Monday morning to find the front lanterns still burning. "We're here, my lady," Gunn leaned over to rouse Dulcie, who had finally cried herself into an exhausted sleep.

She blinked. "Mister Gunn? Where are we?"

"We've arrived at Lady Nesbitt's, my lady," he told her. "The lamps are burning and the staff will be here any moment to meet us."

Dulcie pushed herself out of the seat corner and faced Rafe's solicitor. "Is there something wrong?"

"Nothing's wrong, dear lady," he explained. "Just an unpleasant duty for me." He fixed his kindly gaze on Dulcie's tear-ravaged face before glancing down at her left hand.

“Is there something I can do to help?” Dulcie drew her brows together in a show of concern.

Gunn slowly exhaled and said. “Forgive me, but I must ask you for your wedding ring.”

Dulcie gasped in horror and closed her fist around it. “My husband placed it on my finger. He gave it to me. I’m not giving it back.”

“My dear lady, you cannot be seen wearing it here.” His voice was gentle, but firm. “It’s too dangerous.”

“I wore it on the Isle of Wight,” she protested.

“You were known as Miss Susan Brown on the island. You are Miss Dulcie Tennant, ward of Viscount Tennant, here. You cannot chance your uncle learning of your marriage until the time is right.”

“Did Rafe— Did my husband ask you to keep it for me?” Dulcie swallowed her tears as she asked the question.

The solicitor shook his head. “No. I’m sure Master Rafe never considered it, but Lord Weymouth did. And he gave his word that he would keep you safe.”

Dulcie sat motionless for a moment, then slowly removed her wedding band and offered it to Mister Gunn. Fresh tears rolled down her face. “Raphael gave it to me on our wedding day. It’s all I have of him.”

“Dear lady, the ring is just a symbol. You may have far more of Master Rafe than you know. He gave you himself along with his name. Nothing can take that away.”

"You promise you won’t lose it? You promise you’ll put it in a safe place?”

“I promise on my oath.” Gunn accepted the ring and tucked it in his waistcoat pocket, then pulled out his handkerchief and offered it to her. “When your marriage is made public, I will see that it’s returned to you.” He winced as he said it. He wished he could assure her that Master Rafe would place it on her finger once again, but that was impossible. Master Rafe was gone and Gunn and Lady Blackburn would have to learn to face life without him. He straightened his shoulders. “Dry your tears, my lady. Lady Nesbitt’s staff members have come to greet us.”

The front door opened and Lady Nesbitt's longtime butler, Calder, and her footman, Randolph, hurried out to meet them.

Randolph opened the coach door and let down the steps.

"Carry her, if you will," Mister Gunn instructed Randolph.

"I can walk," Dulcie protested beneath her breath.

"Of course you can, my lady," Gunn replied. "But we need to maintain the fiction that you are ill in the event there are nosy neighbors peeking through shutters or your uncle's paid or unpaid tattlers."

"Forgive me, Mister Gunn, I forgot there is more to the fiction we are about to enact." Dulcie turned to the footman, "Randolph, do you mind?"

"Not at all, miss," he said.

"When he lifts you out of the coach, try to look faint," Gunn suggested.

Dulcie complied, forcing her body to go limp as soon as Randolph removed her from the coach. She had confessed to Raphael that she was a terrible liar and the same might be said of her acting skills. She was no Sarah Siddons, but she had fainted for the first time in her life on Saturday. And had wept her way to exhaustion after her meeting with Commandant Swindell. Dulcie knew, after hours of expressing her grief, that her feigning a mysterious illness would be convincing.

"I'm Calder," the butler said, introducing himself. "Lord Weymouth paid a call on us earlier in the evening. We've been expecting you for some time." Calder carried a lantern as he led the way to the front door. Mister Gunn walked beside him, clutching his precious portfolio against the front of his jacket. Randolph followed, carrying Dulcie.

"I'm Archibald Gunn, solicitor."

"Yes, sir, we know," Calder replied. "Lord Weymouth told us that he escorted Miss Phoebe and that you would be escorting Miss Tennant here this evening."

"I apologize for our tardiness and for keeping you up so late, but we were delayed by business on the Isle of Wight and had to wait for the tide," Mister Gunn explained.

"We certainly understand," Calder said. "Lady Nesbitt is awaiting you in the small salon and Cook is ready to prepare a simple supper or breakfast, whichever you prefer." He opened the front door, allowing Mister Gunn, Randolph, and Miss Tennant to enter first.

Turning to Randolph, Calder addressed the footman. "Please take Miss Tennant to the yellow guest room and see that she's settled." Then he said to Dulcie, "Miss Phoebe's lady's maid is waiting to assist you. Randolph will bring your bag to your room as soon as he gets it unloaded."

"Thank you, Calder," she said. "I would greatly appreciate an egg on toast and a cup of tea."

"You are most welcome, miss," Calder replied. "Lady Nesbitt asked me to relay her welcome and to tell you to make yourself at home. She will be up to see you after her visit with Mister Gunn."

"Please tell her I will look forward to it. Mister Gunn?"

"Yes, dear lady?"

"I cannot thank you enough for taking care of me today and for seeing me safely here to Lady Nesbitt's home."

Archibald Gunn took her hand and brushed his lips over her knuckles. "I was honored to do it, my la—Miss Tennant."

Dulcie gave him a sad smile. "It's difficult to know who I am anymore. Even for me."

"Och, no need to fret," he said. "You rest and recover. We'll sort it all out."

"I'll look forward to it, Mister Gunn. Goodnight."

"Goodnight, my dear," he replied.

"If you will walk this way, Mister Gunn, I will show you to the small salon where Lady Nesbitt is awaiting you." Calder led the way and Gunn followed.

"Lady Nesbitt," Calder announced. "Mister Archibald Gunn, solicitor, to see you."

Augusta Nesbitt rose from her seat to offer Mister Gunn her hand. "A pleasure to meet you, sir."

"The pleasure is mine, my lady." Archibald bowed at the waist and brushed his lips over her hand.

Augusta Nesbitt's cheeks pinkened with delight at having an older gentleman, a gentleman near her own age, displaying old-fashioned courtly manners.

Archibald Gunn straightened up to his full height. Lady Nesbitt was a tall woman with regal posture. She held her head high and met his gaze straight on. Her hair was unpowdered and a lovely silvery white. Archie had learned from Lord Weymouth that Augusta Nesbitt was the paternal great aunt of Phoebe Osborne, and the resemblance was quite noticeable. He wagered that half a century ago Lady Nesbitt had looked enough like her great niece to be her twin. And Phoebe Osborne was a beautiful young woman.

"Lord Weymouth paid us a call earlier this evening to report my great niece's whereabouts—"

"Isn't Miss Osborne here?" Archie asked. "I was delighted to make her acquaintance while attending Miss Tennant's marriage to Lord Blackburn on Saturday morning. It was my understanding that Lord Weymouth escorted her home."

Lady Nesbitt smiled a brilliant smile. "Lord Weymouth would have escorted her home to us had her young man not come to his senses and met our darling Phoebe and Lord Weymouth at the port. Lord Sinclair proposed on the spot. And Phoebe accepted. Lord Weymouth said Lord Sinclair—"

"Alasdair Sinclair, Earl of Sinclair and Montleith?"

"Why, yes," Augusta said. "Do you know him?"

"Aye, my lady. I'm Scots myself. I am proud to know him and his father before him. I've done solicitor's work for them both when they were in residence at their home in Edinburgh."

"Oh, good!" Lady Nesbitt rubbed her hands together. "Then you can review Phoebe's marriage contract to make certain it's favorable to her. I daren't present it to Mister Gorham to review. He'll quibble too much over the amount of her dowry. Weymouth assured me that Sinclair's friend, the Marquess of Courtland, drew up their marriage contract, but Courtland is no solicitor, and I want to see Phoebe properly settled. Of course, I'll see that the dowry her father set aside for her is fully paid when they return to London for their proper wedding."

"I would be happy to review the contracts for you, my lady," Archie informed her. "I drew up the marriage contracts for Miss Tennant and Lord Blackburn."

"Good. Now, I know a big, tall man like you must be hungry after traveling all day. I'll ring for Cook to bring us supper." Augusta walked over to the bellpull and rang the kitchen. "We'll talk as we eat and you tell me all about Dulcie's wedding."

"Haven't you eaten, my lady?" Archie asked.

"I had tea with Lord Weymouth, but I waited supper for you and Dul—Lady Blackburn." She invited Archie to follow her into a small morning room furnished with a sideboard and a table with room for five. "We revised our fiction about Dulcie becoming ill after Lady Middleton's ball since Phoebe didn't return with her. We decided to claim they went to the country for a weekend house party to celebrate my cousin's birthday to represent me since my horrible megrim prevented me from going, and that Phoebe decided to stay and visit longer, but Dul—Lady Blackburn—elected to return here because her guardian hadn't given her permission to stay longer. She became ill on the journey and you escorted her to my home."

"It's best if she remains Miss Tennant for the time being," the solicitor confided as he pulled Lady Nesbitt's chair out for her.

"Oh?" Augusta Nesbitt arched an eyebrow.

"We'll talk more of important matters after we eat." He echoed her earlier words as he seated himself. "I know you're completely trustworthy or Weymouth would not have involved you in Miss Tennant's secret meeting and subsequent wedding to Lord Blackburn."

They waited until a footman brought a supper of a hearty mutton stew with fresh baked bread and butter and a dessert of cherry scones with fresh cream and coffee for him and tea for her. When Archibald Gunn finished the last spoonful of stew and the last crumb of his scones, Lady Nesbitt ordered fine Scots whisky for him and brandy for her.

"That was a most delicious meal, Lady Nesbitt," he said, savoring his coffee. "My compliments to your cook."

"I always like a hot, hearty meal after a day at the seaside," she said. "I thought you might feel the same way after a day on the water."

"Aye." Archie finished his coffee and poured himself a whisky while Lady Nesbitt dismissed the footman and the butler and helped herself to a small brandy.

"Tell me what happened," she urged. "Weymouth said he escorted my niece and Miss Tennant to the Isle of Wight, but he didn't elaborate."

Archie nodded.

"Where did the wedding take place? There are several lovely old churches on Wight."

"Aye," Archie agreed. "But Miss Tennant and Lord Blackburn were married in an antechamber at His Majesty's Garrison on the Isle of Wight, near the village of Harborside," Archie replied, before relaying the details of everything that had happened during his brief stay on the island. "I have the true copy of Miss Tennant's marriage lines. I would like to give them into your care for safekeeping. I dare not risk giving them to Miss Tennant and having her guardian find them when she returns to her home. Or her wedding band." He removed the slim, gold band from his pocket and handed it to Lady Nesbitt, then retrieved his leather portfolio and handed her Dulcie's marriage lines.

"Of course. No one would expect me to keep them for her." Augusta rose and went to the writing desk on the far wall. Reaching up, she swung the Reynolds' portrait of a young boy hanging above it to one side to reveal a hidden compartment. She unlocked a small door with a key she wore on a ribbon around her neck, then tucked the precious marriage lines and Dulcie's ring inside the compartment before re-locking it. "There," she said as she returned it her seat. "They are safe. Now, tell me what happened."

Augusta had to dab at her eyes with her handkerchief after Archie related the details of his and Dulcie's visit to the garrison to collect Lord Blackburn's personal belongings...and his remains. "Oh, that poor, poor child. How is she taking it?"

"She was magnificent when she confronted the commandant,"

Archie said. "She fought like a lioness on his lordship's behalf, insisting on inventorying everything in his quarters and leaving only what was there when his lordship was first confined there." He shook his head. "But the moment we boarded the coach for the journey to the harbor, she burst into tears. She's been weeping ever since." He met Augusta's gaze. "I fear she'll make herself ill. I promised Master Rafe *I* would look after her."

"Master Rafe?"

"Lord Raphael Simon John Blackburn," Archie said proudly. "I've known him all his life and his father and grandfather before him." His voice broke. "I served them all and I cannot bear to let him down."

"Dulcie is not the only one here with a broken heart," Augusta said, rising from the table. "I'll see you to your room before I check on the poor child."

"Oh no, my lady, I cannot impose on your hospitality in such a way! I shall find lodging at the Barrister's Club."

"At this time of night? Nonsense, Mister Gunn. I've already ordered your room prepared. I will hear no arguments. You will stay the night. Besides, Dulcie is supposed to be ill. You can't leave until the doctor says she's contagion free." She paused, arched an eyebrow, and considered. "Unless you have a wife at home in Edinburgh who will object to your staying here with me..."

"Oh no, my lady, I'm a widower of many years."

"I am so sorry," she murmured. "I am a widow of many years myself."

"My sincere condolences to you, my lady. Being alone is often necessary for one's work or well-being. Living alone is simply lonely."

"Call me Augusta," she invited, her blue eyes sparkling. "And now that we're dear friends, I shall call you Archibald."

"Archibald is for business and formal occasions, my lady." He smiled at her. "My dear friends call me Archie."

AUGUSTA KNOCKED ON THE DOOR OF THE YELLOW GUEST ROOM AFTER seeing Archie to his room and bidding him a good night. "Dulcie? May I come in?"

Recognizing the voice, Dulcie called, "Yes, my lady."

Augusta walked into the bedchamber and sat down on the edge of Dulcie's bed. "Are you comfortable here?"

Dulcie nodded. "Very comfortable. Thank you for allowing me to stay."

"You are *always* welcome here, my dear." Augusta frowned at Dulcie's half-eaten egg and toast. "Aren't you hungry?"

"My eyes were bigger than my stomach," she confessed. "I haven't much of an appetite after all."

"One seldom has an appetite after a day and night spent crying." Augusta turned the bedside lamp up higher, so she could get a better look at Dulcie's face. It was tear-stained and blotchy. Her eyes were swollen almost shut. Her nose was red and congested. And her voice was rough. She looked as if she'd spent the day and most of the night sobbing. "It's exhausting. Here." Augusta reached for the teapot, found it still hot, and refilled Dulcie's cup. "Drink this. It will help soothe your throat and your spirit. I sent for the doctor to pay a call on you."

"I don't need a physician, Lady Nesbitt." Dulcie took a sip of the tea, then handed the cup back to Phoebe's great aunt.

"Oh, yes, you do," Lady Nesbitt said firmly. "It's part of the fiction that you're ill with a contagion. We want Guilford and Mavis to *believe* you are ill, but we don't want you truly ill. My physician will look you over and pronounce that you should not be around other people or moved until you are cured."

"What about you?" Dulcie asked. "What about your social obligations?"

"Pish! My physician, Mister Grimm, will pronounce me immune. He's been my physician for thirty years and despite his name, he hasn't killed me yet. Everyone in the ton knows that except for occasional megrims, I am never ill or susceptible to contagions. I come from healthy stock."

"Then I agree to have your physician attend me, but please, don't let Phoebe see me like this," Dulcie said. "I lied to her, Lady Nesbitt. And if she sees me like this, she'll know. I should be on my wedding trip." Dulcie's expression crumpled and she began to cry once again.

"There, there..." Augusta gathered Dulcie to her, soothing her by rubbing circles on her back as she wept. "It will be all right, *ma petite*," she murmured. "With time, the hurt will ease enough to be bearable."

"Phoebe would have objected to the marriage if she had known my bridegroom was condemned to hang. She would have had to in order to protect me from this. Oh, Lady Nesbitt, I didn't know it would hurt so much! I didn't know I would love him so much. Phoebe knew. Because she had lost Freddy. She was right. But please don't let her see me like this. If she does, she'll be afraid to give her heart to Lord Sinclair. And she'll never give that fine man a chance to love her."

Augusta debated the best course of action. It seemed cruel to tell Dulcie of Phoebe's wedding to Sinclair, but neither could she allow Dulcie to worry herself sick over her friend. "Don't fret about Phoebe, my dear," she advised. "Phoebe's buccaneer met her boat when she and Lord Weymouth docked. I imagine she and Lord Sinclair were celebrating their wedding night the same time you and Lord Blackburn were celebrating yours."

Dulcie lifted her head to meet the other woman's gaze. "Truly, Lady Nesbitt?"

Augusta smiled at her. "Truly, Dulcie."

"I'm so happy for her," Dulcie said, smiling through her tears. And for Lord Sinclair. They deserve a second chance at love and happiness."

"So do you, my dear," Lady Nesbitt said.

"I *was* happy," Dulcie told her. "For one day and night, I was the happiest woman alive. Because I loved Raphael Blackburn."

CHAPTER 25

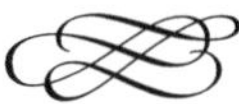

"Promise is most given when the least is said."
—George Chapman, 1559-1634

"So, you've decided to rejoin the living," McGregor said when Rafe opened his eyes a second time. "The sleeping potion I gave you should have worn off by now. Let's see if you can sit up. Can you lift your arms?"

McGregor's familiar face slowly came into focus. Rafe blinked, his bleary eyes struggling to adjust to the lantern light brightening the hold. After hours spent in the ink-black darkness, the meager glow seemed positively blinding.

"Lift your arms. First right, then left and brace yourself on the rim of the box," McGregor instructed.

Box? Rafe lifted his right arm and then his left, trying to follow the doctor's instructions without really understanding why. With his mind still scrambling to catch up, he braced his arms on the rim of the wooden box he seemed to be lying in and pushed himself into sitting position.

"Now, bend your knees. First the right and then the left and push yourself to your feet. Then hold onto me and step out of the box."

Rafe followed McGregor's instructions once again and pushed to his feet, holding onto the doctor's arm when he would have wobbled and toppled over. He carefully stepped over the side of the box, then turned back to study the wooden structure. A visceral surge of horror flooded him when he realized it was not just a long wooden box, but a coffin. It was too dark, even with the lanterns, to tell if the box showed signs of dirt or sand, but the thought of it sent shivers down his spine. "Was I buried?" His voice came out as a hoarse, barely audible, whisper.

McGregor had to lean close to hear it, then shook his head. "No, not buried, just transported from the garrison to the yacht. We'll be docking at Davies Shipping Company soon and we are not carrying you off in that coffin. You, Lord Blackburn, are a large, heavy corpse. This time you'll be wearing your uniform and marching off with the rest of us."

"How long?" Rafe croaked. "Dead?"

McGregor chuckled. "It may have felt like the sleep of the dead, but you were never a corpse, just a very realistic imitation. You certainly looked dead enough to fool the Custom House inspectors. But you are very much alive. I came to get you out of the cargo hold and bring you to the salon so I can examine you and the others can help me prepare you for the next phase of this mission."

Rafe opened his mouth to speak, but the doctor held up a hand to stop him.

"Don't try to speak any more. You may have done some damage. Just nod for yes and shake your head for no."

Rafe nodded. He was parched and his throat was aching and raw. He licked his lips, then pantomimed lifting a glass to his mouth.

McGregor nodded. "As soon as we get you upstairs."

Getting him upstairs proved more difficult than expected. The elixir McGregor had given him had done its job as a relaxing agent. As McGregor half-supported, half-carried him up the steps from the cargo hold to the first level, where the salon, state rooms, and the lavatory rooms were located, Rafe found his arms and legs were weak and unreliable, like a marionette with loose strings. But they somehow managed.

"The other gentlemen are in the salon," McGregor told him as they made their way down the narrow corridor. "It's larger than a stateroom and we have a great deal to accomplish before we leave this boat. Strong coffee will counteract the effects of the elixir. I'll have some sent in for you."

Rafe nodded.

McGregor opened the door to the salon and ushered Rafe inside.

"Welcome back!" Sussex was the first to greet him, his hand outstretched in friendship.

Rafe seized it, gripping it slightly longer than usual.

"I was afraid we'd lost you." Sussex covered their clasped hands with his free one, sealing a newfound friendship as only men who had been through hell together could do.

Rafe nodded, a sheen of tears shining in his eyes before he ruthlessly blinked them away. As he released his grip on the Duke of Sussex's hand, the other Free Fellows gathered around, clapping him on the back before shaking hands with him, congratulating him on surviving his ordeal more or less none the worse for wear. One man hung back.

Rafe met his gaze but didn't recognize him. He wasn't dressed in the red tunic and breeches of a British soldier like the others, although Courtland and Barclay had discarded their neck cloths and tunics in favor of linen shirts and waistcoats. The stranger was dressed in a black suit. Rafe tapped McGregor on the arm and pantomimed removing his neck cloth and tunic.

"Yes, of course," McGregor acknowledged. "I'm sorry I didn't think to do it earlier." He glanced around. "Will one of you give me a hand with this? Lord Blackburn is still wearing his fancy neckcloth and special occasion tunic."

The stranger stepped forward and removed Rafe's tunic so the doctor could divest Rafe of the heavy lacy jabot and carefully unwind the neck cloth.

Rafe nodded his thanks to the stranger.

Seeing the look that passed between them, McGregor made the introductions. "Lord Blackburn, you haven't met the remaining member of our acting troupe. May I introduce Mister Micah Beekins, your hangman?"

Micah tugged at his forelock and offered Rafe his hand. "I'm pleased to make your acquaintance, your lordship."

Rafe immediately recognized the voice. *Try not to move, my lord.* He took Micah's hand. The man had been wearing gloves when he'd acted as a hangman. Now that he'd discarded them, Rafe could see Micah had the rough, callused hands of a workman. He smiled at him.

Micah Beekins smiled back. "I'm relieved I didn't do ye any harm, your lordship."

Rafe nodded his reply.

"I've instructed Lord Blackburn to try not to speak until I've examined him. He appears to have temporarily lost his voice. He's also a wee bit unsteady on his feet."

Understanding the doctor's unspoken request, Grantham rose from his seat and offered it to Rafe before retrieving another chair from the stateroom that connected to the salon by a sliding door.

Rafe flashed a grateful smile and took Grantham's seat at the table.

"You must be hungry." Shepherdston rang the bell for the steward and ordered a fresh pot of coffee and a platter of sandwiches for all of them when the man arrived. Rafe quickly learned it had been over twelve hours since the Free Fellows had appeared at the door of the cottage to collect him. According to the official military report that would be delivered to Weymouth later this evening, Major Lord Raphael Blackburn had been executed and declared dead for over ten of them.

Rafe's stomach rumbled at the mention of food.

As the men gathered around the table, McGregor poured Rafe a glass of water from the pitcher on the sideboard. Rafe gulped it down, handed the empty glass to the doctor, and motioned for more. The doctor refilled the glass and Rafe drank the second glass as quickly as he'd drunk the first.

"You should be well rested," Courtland said with a friendly smile. "You've slept all day and most of the night."

"We'll get to work on him after we eat," Shepherdston announced as soon as the steward arrived with the coffee and the platter of sandwiches.

Shepherdston was as good as his word. The eight men quickly demolished the platter of sandwiches and split pea soup, and the plate of iced cakes that followed.

After the steward had cleared the table and removed the dishes, he returned with a basin and a kettle of hot water, a shaving mug, soap and brush, scissors, and a length of toweling. Shepherdston glanced at each of his friends. "Who's the best barber?"

Sussex, Courtland, Barclay and Shepherdston all looked at Grantham.

"You know I am," Grantham said. "With the exception of Micah and McGregor, the rest of you grew up with valets and servants. I didn't. I learned to shave myself and my father when his hands were too unsteady to do it for himself. I never had a valet until I shared a house with you." He pinned Shepherdston with his gaze. "I've never cut hair, though. My mother cut ours."

"I can cut hair," Micah volunteered.

"Close enough to accommodate a powdered wig?" Shepherdston asked.

Micah nodded. "I learned from my uncle, my ma's brother. He's the barber in the village next to ours."

"Very well," Shepherdston said. "Let's get started. He needs to look just like the rest of us when we leave the boat and march to the Fife and Drum Tavern. After an ale, we'll leave two by two and meet at my house by way of the back garden gate. You change clothes at my house and then I'll have two coaches waiting to take you to your own homes." He glanced at the doctor. "McGregor is staying at Viscount Selby's old town house, which now belongs to the Earl of Carlisle and his wife, the Marchioness of Blessing. As he's there by himself and still a regimental surgeon, he can wear his uniform to Selby House and return it to us tomorrow. Micah will take a coach to his usual London lodging house. Agreed?" The Marquess of Shepherdston and the Duke of Sussex both knew the name of Micah's usual lodging house, as did the butlers of both Shepherdston's and Sussex's London households, but they had never divulged it because Micah and his family were still active smugglers and too valuable to the Free Fellows for them to risk exposing his identity or his life and livelihood.

"Agreed," they answered in unison.

"Who's training Blackburn?" Sussex asked. "We haven't settled on that."

"I've narrowed it down to Henderson or your mother's butler. They're the best at what they do," Shepherdston said.

"My mother hosts too many at-home mornings during the Season with matchmaking mamas and their daughters," Sussex pointed out. "And a tall, handsome fellow is sure to attract the attention of the young ladies."

"If not their mothers..." Barclay added.

"Henderson, it is," Shepherdston decided. "Sarah and I rarely host parties at our home for obvious reasons and we decided to limit the number of invitations we're accepting this Season. After so many months spent in Vienna with its endless rounds of parties, we're spending more time at home." Shepherdston and his wife, along with the Granthams, and the Barclays, had spent half the previous year at the Congress of Vienna and were only just settling back into life in London.

"Once Henderson feels he's proficient, we'll test him in each of our households for a day or two," Sussex added. "We'll say he's temporary help replacing one of our regular staff and when he's passed the test, we implement the rest of the plan."

Unable to stand the suspense or be overlooked any longer, Rafe croaked. "Grateful. Who. Henderson? Training? What. Plan?"

McGregor glared at Rafe for disregarding his instructions not to try to speak before rummaging through his medical bag for pen, ink, and paper, which he handed to Rafe.

Rafe poured himself a second cup of coffee and began to write. When he finished penning his note, he handed it to Shepherdston.

"What did he say?" Grantham asked.

"He says he's most grateful for the rescue. He owes us his life. And thanks us for all we've done. But he wants to know who Henderson is, who he's training, and the details of the plan," Shepherdston replied.

"Henderson is Shepherdston's London butler," Sussex explained. "He will be training you for a position in the household staff."

"And the plan is to keep you hidden until you're exonerated," Courtland added, helping himself to another cup of coffee. "Hidden in a position where you will be able to protect your bride and hopefully help us identify the men who arranged your sentencing and murder in order to hide the murder of your wife's family."

Rafe scratched a name in bold, black, letters and held it up for Courtland to read: *Guilford Tennant.*

"He didn't act alone," Grantham said, his lips tightening as he nodded. "He had accomplices. Your accuser, Fenton, for one. But there is more to this conspiracy than Tennant and Fenton. Or Swindell and the Court of Inquiry judges. We mean to get to the bottom of it and see the conspirators held to account."

Rafe scrawled another word on the paper. *Why?*

"Because they conspired to have the British army hang a war hero to conceal their crimes," Barclay said grimly. "Don't you know? They did to you what should be given to them. A traitor's death."

CHAPTER 26

"We will meet; and there we may rehearse most obscenely and courageously."
—William Shakespeare, 1564-1616

In an hour's time, Rafe had been transformed into a model British soldier marching to the Fife and Drum Tavern, a busy waterfront establishment on the North side of the Thames on Coldharbour Street in Blackwall. In the company of seven other soldiers.

The multiple cups of coffee he had drank had hastened his recovery from the elixir the doctor had given him, and after a thorough examination, McGregor had pronounced him fit to march and in excellent health considering the fact he'd spent all day and most of the night as a corpse and was still *officially* a dead man. He had sustained a few bumps and bruises from the fall when the rope Micah had weakened broke. And a few more from being jostled around when the coffin was being loaded onto the yacht. The worst of the damage had been done to his throat when the rope had slipped under the steel in his lacy jabot during the drop and had bruised his neck and larynx. McGregor didn't expect the injury to be permanent, but he could not say how long it would take for Rafe to regain full use of his normal speaking voice.

Until that happened, he was essentially mute. The Free Fellows remained undaunted by that prospect and were planning to incorporate his condition into the next phase of their plan. Rafe managed a slight smile. His inability to object to anything had worked in the Free Fellows' favor. He had learned the details of three plans since Weymouth's associates had appeared at the door of the cottage and Rafe couldn't say that he would have approved of any of them. But he wouldn't be marching down Coldharbour Street if it weren't for their scheming. He wouldn't have been marching anywhere ever again.

With his hands steady, Rafe had declined Grantham's offer to shave him and had shaved himself, scraping off the rough whiskers he had worn for nearly four days, revealing his smooth countenance.

I like your whiskers. I like the way they look. And I like the way they feel. Dulcie's words came back to him as he smoothed his hand over his clean-shaven jaw and studied his reflection in the shaving mirror. She wouldn't recognize him now. He had worn the stubble so long he barely recognized himself.

"You won't recognize me once I shave."

"I'll recognize you," she'd boasted as she kissed her way down his torso. "I know every inch of you. Every mark. Every scar. Every sensitive spot." She'd flicked his nipple with the tip of her tongue and laughed her husky laugh at his reaction.

Rafe sighed, his body reacting to the tantalizing memory despite its recent trauma. He supposed he would have to actually *be* dead to remain unstirred by the memory of Dulcie's throaty laugh.

They had dressed him in his original uniform. His companions had retired his 'special occasion tunic' and Rafe had retired the braces, men's corset, jabot, and extra neck linen by tossing them at Grantham to pack in the haversack he'd taken them from.

"Are you sure you don't want to keep those?" Courtland had

teased. "You never know when there might be a special occasion when you might need them."

Micah had cut his hair. Taking Rafe's queue in one hand, Micah had untied the green ribbon binding it and tossed it on the table. While Micah snipped off the hair at his nape, Rafe quickly retrieved Dulcie's ribbon and tucked it into his waistcoat pocket, hardly daring to hope that someday he might have the pleasure of returning it to her. Once his queue was gone, Micah had cut the rest of Rafe's hair close to the scalp at the back and sides, leaving just enough to cover the hatchet scar on the top of his head. Not that anyone was in danger of recognizing it beneath the powdered wig he was going to be wearing.

"It's amazing the difference a shave and a shearing make," Sussex had said, eyeing him critically. "No one who saw you at your hanging would recognize you as a cavalry officer."

"Especially not as Raging Raphael Blackburn, the Angel of Death," Shepherdston added dryly.

"The tricorn makes all the difference." Barclay plopped a tricorn on top of Rafe's powdered wig, then tipped his own tricorn in a mock salute. "When everyone is accustomed to seeing you in a bearskin cap."

Barclay was right. Rafe had rarely worn a tricorn. The cavalry's head dress before Waterloo had been a plumed shako with visor, cords and badge of Saint George slaying the Dragon. After Waterloo, they'd adopted the tall, imposing bearskin cap worn by the French Imperial Guard to remind the world that they, not the French, had won the day and the war. In the tricorn, he resembled other foot soldiers that crowded into taverns throughout London every day.

"He needs a new name," Grantham pointed out.

"Aye, he does," McGregor agreed.

"What shall we name him?" Sussex asked.

"Something familiar so he'll remember to answer to it, but not close enough for his enemies to connect it to him," McGregor advised.

Sussex glanced at his cousin, Barclay, who'd had *Debrett's Peerage* drilled into him as a child. "What do you think?"

Barclay pursed his lips in thought. "He's Raphael Simon John Blackburn. John is familiar and probably the most common name in Britain. His father was Michael John Simon. So, John as his given name."

"And for a surname?" Shepherdston asked.

"His mother was Arielle Jean-Marie LeMarchand," Barclay continued.

"The merchant," Shepherdston translated before he began sounding out names from the letters of the name. "Merch. Archer. Hand."

"March," Sussex said. "John March. Easy to remember and it sounds like a good common English name."

"John March." Barclay nodded.

Shepherdston had smiled, tapped Rafe on each shoulder with the scissors Micah had left on the table and said, "I hereby dub thee John March."

Minutes later, the yacht had docked at the Davies Shipping Company and the eight passengers had disembarked and begun a quickstep march toward Coldharbour Street.

Rafe flinched when Shepherdston, dressed as an infantry sergeant-major, called a halt at the entrance to the Fife and Drum and barked the order. "Dismissed!"

The members of the detail paired off. First, Courtland and Barclay, then, Shepherdston and Sussex, Grantham and Beekins, and finally McGregor and Marsh filed into the Fife and Drum for much needed round of ales.

"Barkeep! A round of ales for my men!" Shepherdston ordered.

The round of ales turned into two rounds of ales before the members of the detail left the tavern, again in twos, boarding hired coaches that delivered them to different locations near Shepherdston's Park Lane residence. Shepherdston and Sussex exited first, and the others took turns departing the tavern on the quarter hour until they had all departed.

Micah Beekins bid farewell to his companions at the tavern. He left the Fife and Drum with Shepherdston after finishing his second ale and loudly announcing to his other companions that he and the sergeant had "wenches awaiting them in the sporting house down the street." They shared a hired coach that delivered them to Micah's current boarding house, where Shepherdston's own coach and driver had been awaiting his arrival.

Shepherdston gifted Micah with the bag of guineas he had placed in the locked box in the coach for that purpose before he'd left for the Davies Shipping Company docks the night before. "Safe travels, my friend," Shepherdston said to Micah as he left the coach.

"Thank ye, sir." Micah said. "I'll be leaving on the mail coach."

"Dressed like that?" Shepherdston nodded at his corporal's uniform."

Micah shook his head. "I'll be wearing yeoman's clothes. I'll wrap these up and have 'em delivered to your house afore I leave."

"I can't thank you enough."

Micah grinned. "No need to, sir. Ye paid me handsomely for a bit of adventure and for the learning of a new trade." They shook hands. "Ye know how to reach me if ye need me again."

Henderson, Shepherdston's London butler, greeted him as Lord Shepherdston approached the front door. "Welcome home, my lord."

"Thank you, Henderson. It's good to be home."

"I trust your mission was successful, sir."

"It was," Shepherdston said. "Entirely successful. Unfortunately, it isn't quite over. The other gentlemen will be coming through the garden to the back entrance shortly. There will be six, including Lords Sussex, Courtland, Barclay, Grantham, the physician, and our new guest, whom you will begin training to become a footman. Beginning tomorrow. I need him fully trained within a fortnight." Shepherdston paused before adding, "Oh, and our new guest is mute."

"Deaf?" Henderson asked.

"No, just temporarily unable to speak. He sustained an injury during the mission. See if we have a slate and chalk upstairs in the old schoolroom for him to use. If not, acquire them and hang them round his neck, so he can communicate."

"Yes, your lordship." Henderson replied.

"Our new guest will require livery beginning tomorrow and suitable evening clothes for tonight. He measures the same size as Courtland, only a fraction taller. The others will also require a change of clothing. I suggest you send footmen to each of the Fellows' houses to request attire suitable for an evening at White's. Request two sets from Courtland's valet—one for Courtland and one to lend to our new guest. I trust Lord Grantham's clothes have been cleaned and pressed?"

"Of course, my lord. They are hanging in the wardrobe in his old suite along with his shoes and the other personal items he brought." Henderson grinned. "It feels like old times, eh, my lord?" As bachelors, Shepherdston and Grantham had shared Shepherdston's residences. It was convenient for both and safer when doing the work of the Free Fellows League. But that had changed when first Grantham, and then Shepherdston, had married.

Shepherdston smiled back. "With one exception. Has Lady Shepherdston retired for the night?"

"Yes, sir. She stayed up as late as she could, but she retired to your bed nearly two hours ago."

"I'll see her before I change. Please brief our guests if I'm not down in time to do so." Leaving his butler to carry out his instructions, Shepherdston hurried upstairs to kiss his wife and to change out of his uniform.

Henderson immediately dispatched footmen to each of the other lords' houses, before preparing a tray of coffee and a bottle of Scots whisky.

With the exception of the Duke of Sussex, the other Free Fellows lived just houses down from Shepherdston's on Park Lane, so the footmen returned with the necessary clothing before the lords began arriving. But Sussex lived further away in a newly built villa in Regent's Park. The footman Henderson sent to Sussex's home took a bit longer to return, arriving at the back garden gate almost simultaneously with the duke.

Henderson greeted each lord as he arrived and handed him his suit of clothes and small clothes, directing each to the guest rooms upstairs.

McGregor was sent to Shepherdston's study to await Shepherdston and the others, who were changing out of their uniforms and the new guest was sent to the study as well to await Lord Courtland's appearance.

Rafe arrived at the back entrance of Shepherdston's town house shortly after McGregor. Henderson greeted him. "You must be our latest guest."

"Yes, I must be," Rafe replied in a barely audible whisper. "I'm John March."

Henderson nodded. "I'll show you to his lordship's study to await his lordship. You'll find Doctor McGregor waiting there as well."

"How are you feeling?" McGregor asked as soon as Henderson had ushered Rafe into the study. "Any tiredness? Lack of coordination? Dizziness?"

"Tiredness," Rafe admitted in a croaky whisper. He eased into the nearest leather chair, stretching his legs. "Although it's hard to believe I'm tired after sleeping all day and half the night."

"Not so hard to believe," McGregor replied. "How much sleep did you get the night before?"

"I dozed right before you arrived."

"And the night before?"

"Very little. I spent most of the night contemplating my appearance at the Court of Inquiry, wondering what my fate would be."

"Then it's not difficult to understand why you're still weary. Lack of exercise may also be the culprit," McGregor warmed to the subject. "How much time were you allowed to exercise each day during the months you were confined to your quarters at the garrison?"

"None."

"What?" McGregor sat up straighter in his seat, alarmed by the treatment of a peer of the realm confined to a military garrison.

"I was confined to my quarters. I wasn't allowed any time in the garden to walk about or exercise. The only exercise I got was pacing within the confines of my quarters."

"No wonder you're tired." McGregor shook his head. "You marched at least three miles today. Most of that in quick step. After ten months of little to no exercise, I'm astounded by your fitness."

"Your turn, Blackburn."

Rafe and the doctor looked up to find a grinning Alexander Courtland standing in the doorway of Shepherdston's study. "My valet sent a set of evening and small clothes for you. He assures me they've never been worn. I left them in the yellow room for you."

"Thank you, Courtland. I'm in your debt," Rafe said.

Henderson, returning to the study with a tray of bread, cheese, slices of duck leftover from the duck Cook had prepared for Lady Shepherdston's supper, and oranges and pears from the greenhouse, loudly cleared his throat in warning. "Mister March, you will begin your training tomorrow morning at half-past four."

McGregor shook his head. "He will need more sleep than that after the conclusion of this meeting." He turned his gaze on the butler. "What say he begins at half past ten?"

"Mister McGregor, footmen begin their days at half-past four in the morning. Lord Shepherdston informed me I must have him fully trained in a fortnight's time. Time is of the essence," Henderson said.

Rafe frowned. "I'm training to become a *footman?*" His voice was hoarser than before.

"Yes, Mister March," Henderson confirmed. "And when your training is over, you will be able to obtain employment with the finest families in Great Britain."

"And why shouldn't he?" Courtland quipped. "When he comes from one of the finest families in Great Britain." He pinned Rafe with his amused gaze. "Didn't you tell him?"

Rafe shook his head before saying hoarsely, "I thought I was to use John March with everyone except all of you."

"Henderson knows everything," Courtland assured him. "He is Shepherdston's courier and confidante. We report to him if Shepherdston is unavailable. He is the very soul of discretion."

"But he didn't know who I was."

"Because he was only told we were conducting a military rescue. He didn't think he needed to know the details."

Sussex appeared at Courtland's side. "We trust Henderson with our lives. And have for many years." He glanced from Henderson to Rafe. "Even so," Sussex drawled. "Henderson, may I present Raphael, seventh Earl of Blackburn?"

Henderson looked horrified. "I apologize for my impertinence, Lord Blackburn."

Rafe offered Henderson his hand. "You displayed no impertinence. You were simply showing devotion to your duty. There's no need for you to apologize. Under your tutelage, I'm sure I will learn to appreciate more fully the footmen serving in my households."

"And having said that, Lord Blackburn, you will say no more," McGregor ordered. "Your throat has endured enough for one day."

Still looking a trifle bit mortified, Henderson nodded toward Blackburn. "What happened to him?"

"We hanged him," Courtland replied, with a note of pride.

"And then we threw him in a coffin and brought him home," Sussex added.

CHAPTER 27

"Hope springs eternal in the human breast."
—Alexander Pope, 1688-1744

Sir Walter Grimm, the physician Lady Nesbitt asked to call on Dulcie, arrived shortly after sunrise the following morning to find Dulcie wan and listless from a night spent weeping into her pillow. He poked and prodded her, examined her swollen eyes, her red, stuffed-up nose, and the blotches marring her face, and pronounced her seriously ill with an ague-causing contagion. He prescribed bloodletting because it was his favorite remedy for every ill. Dulcie squeezed her eyes shut at the idea. But she needn't have worried about watching the physician bleed her because Lady Nesbitt refused to allow him.

"It must be done to cure her," Grimm insisted.

"It might be done as a last resort," Lady Nesbitt said, "but I am a firm believer that sound sleep, tasty food, and plenty of tea and hot chocolate will do more to strengthen her than draining pints of blood will."

"But, my lady, in all my years of caring for the sick, I—" Grimm began.

"I'm sure you learned a great many things and I'm grateful for your coming so promptly, Mister Grimm." Lady Nesbitt handed him a pouch of gold coins before ushering him out of Dulcie's bedchamber and toward the stairs. "I'm quite certain Miss Tennant will be cured in time to attend Lady Pepperdine's musicale this evening. There is sure to be a huge crush. Everyone who is anyone will be there. We've purchased new gowns for the event and simply cannot miss it."

The physician blanched, holding up his hands as if to ward off her words. "Oh, no, Lady Nesbitt, she cannot leave her bed for a fortnight or more for fear of spreading an aggressive contagion to Lady Pepperdine's guests. Nor should you allow her any visitors except me. And you should not go amongst a crush of people either, in the event that you catch her dreadful disease yourself."

"But I cannot keep her confined to bed during the waning days of the most important month of the Season." Lady Nesbitt argued. "She's expected to return to her home after Lady Pepperdine's musicale. Her guardian and his wife need her there as Lady Tennant is increasing with the anticipated heir. You see Miss Tennant is such a dear comfort to her aunt."

"You must keep her confined here," the physician insisted. "She must not be allowed to return to Lord Tennant's home. To allow it would be to condemn Lady Tennant's unborn child."

Lady Nesbitt threw her hands up in a gesture of surrender. "How can I possibly explain this to Lord and Lady Tennant? They will surely think she's deathly ill and that I am refusing to allow them to call upon the niece they adore. They will blame me for her illness."

"You shan't have to explain at all," Grimm promised. "I shall pay a call upon Lord and Lady Tennant and explain the situation. I will assure them she is receiving the best of care and that I will allow them to see her as soon as I've effected a cure. Until then, they must allow her to remain where she and they will be safe from certain tragedy."

"Oh, thank you, Mister Grimm. I knew you were the right physician for us." She turned to her butler. "Calder, please collect Mister Grimm's fee."

"My dear lady, you have alre—" The physician clamped his mouth shut. If the lady forgot she had already paid his fee, who was he to remind her of it? "Thank you, Lady Nesbitt," he said, when Calder presented him with his fee in coin he quickly pocketed before Lady Nesbitt could realize her mistake. "I shall call upon Viscount and Lady Tennant without delay."

"You won't forget, will you?" Lady Nesbitt's voice quavered. "I would be devastated if they should blame me."

"Consider it done, dear lady," Grimm said. "In the meantime, the young lady is to stay in bed and is barred from entertaining any visitors."

"Thank you, Mister Grimm, for your incomparable medical opinions and wise care."

"Sir Walter," the physician corrected. "I was knighted by the Prince Regent, you know, for services to the Crown."

No doubt for failing to cure the king of his madness, which had precipitated the Act of Parliament that allowed the Prince of Wales to become Prince Regent and rule in his father's stead. "Thank you, *Sir* Walter," Lady Nesbitt amended without apology for her earlier slight.

"You are most welcome, Lady Nesbitt." The physician bowed over her hand, brushing his lips against her knuckles. "Good day, dear lady."

As he straightened, Lady Nesbitt dabbed her hand with a linen handkerchief, while discreetly motioning for her butler. "Calder will see you the rest of the way."

When Calder returned after seeing the doctor out, Lady Nesbitt immediately asked for a basin of hot water.

"A basin, my lady?" The butler asked, his concern clearly evident in his voice. "Or shall I have a bathing tub and hot water sent up for the young lady's bath?"

"No." Lady Nesbitt shook her head. "I want a basin of hot water and soap so I can scrub *my* hands."

"To remove contagion, my lady?" Calder asked.

"To remove the feel of that old fool's mouth on my skin." She shuddered. "There's no contagion in this house. And that pompous nincompoop wouldn't recognize it if there was."

"But the young miss..." Calder glanced at the bedroom door. "Her face. Her swollen eyes... The physician believes she has—"

"That old relic believes she has a contagious disease when anyone with half an eye can see she spent the night crying into her pillow. The young miss isn't deathly ill. Unless love can be called a deadly illness. What she has is a broken heart."

"But he's preventing her from going out or returning home," Calder said. "Everyone will think she has an illness."

Lady Nesbitt heaved a sigh. "We want everyone to think she has an illness. We want her to stay here with us."

"I don't understand..."

"Do you recall when Miss Phoebe's young lieutenant died?"

"Of course, my lady." Calder stiffened. "Her young man's death shattered her. I feared she would never smile again."

"It took time for our Phoebe to get over Freddy Ralston. It took time for her to heal sufficiently to love again."

Calder nodded.

"Miss Tennant has been hurt in the same way. She needs time to mend her broken heart. But she won't get that opportunity if her avaricious uncle forces her to marry one of his cronies as a way to cancel his gaming debts. I won't allow that misfortune to befall our dear Dulcie any more than I would have let it happen to our darling Phoebe." She pinned her butler with her sharp gaze. "Phoebe and Dulcie are our girls, Calder. Now that Phoebe is happily married to her Scotsman, we are going see that Miss Dulcie has a chance to do the same. We are going to keep her with us for as long as we can. We're going to keep her with us until she's strong enough to put up a fight."

~

LADY NESBITT KEPT HER WORD. DULCIE REMAINED CONFINED TO THE house on Grosvenor Street for a full fortnight. Dulcie not only missed Lady Pepperdine's musicale, she also missed two weeks of parties and fetes, of dances and operas, theater opening nights, and the midnight suppers that followed in this year's abbreviated Season. Time was running out. Her sojourn with Lady Nesbitt was coming to an end. Any day now, she expected Guilford to demand her presence at home so he could present her with a Hobson's choice. But she had already made her choice and she wasn't going to change her mind.

Dulcie fingered the outline of the black hair ribbon Rafe had left on her pillow through the fabric of one of the five new dresses Madam Gabrielle had had delivered to Lady Nesbitt's house the day before. She had woven the ribbon through the lace of her chemise for safekeeping the morning she had found it. Oh, how she wished she could have strung Rafe's wedding band on it instead of turning the ring over to Mister Gunn!

For the past two mornings, Dulcie had taken breakfast with Lady Nesbitt before Lady Nesbitt left for the Returning Soldiers' Hospital, where she served tea and pastries to the patients recovering there every Monday, Wednesday, and Friday. As the patroness of the hospital, Lady Nesbitt considered her work a labor of love as well as an avenue to meet potential suitors for the young ladies she sponsored during the Season. A fair number of eligible officers, peers, and the younger sons of peers, spent time recovering from illness and wounds at the hospital.

Phoebe had met her husband, a Scottish earl, while he was recovering from wounds there when Phoebe had been serving refreshments in her great aunt's stead while Lady Nesbitt was suffering from her dreaded megrims.

Dulcie understood that her hostess was giving her time and a place to mourn her husband in private and was grateful for her kindness and understanding. Their shared morning meals had become the highlight of Dulcie's day. They breakfasted in Lady Nesbitt's set of rooms where Lady Nesbitt kept Dulcie abreast of the latest gossip and goings on of the members of the ton. She also reported the comings and goings of Viscount and Lady Tennant, who had attended the gala despite the lady's advancing pregnancy.

"Lady Nesbitt, I cannot thank you enough for the way you've taken me in and the way you've managed Mister Grimm," Dulcie had said at breakfast two mornings after the physician's initial visit. "I shudder at the thought of him bleeding me."

"I shudder at the thought of him period," Lady Nesbitt said. "He's one step below a quack and one step above an undertaker. Even so, I fear he's given the resurrection men more business than a physician ought."

"Then, why did you send for him?" Dulcie asked. "Why ask him to attend me?" She took a final bite of egg on toast and set her plate aside.

"Well, he's been my physician for over thirty years," Lady Nesbitt explained. "He knows me. He knows I take good care of myself. The only thing that plagues me are my blasted megrims. When I'm plagued by them, I usually go to bed with lavender compresses and tisane of willow bark and wait for them to go away. But occasionally, I require a stronger tonic. Grimm prepares it and promptly brings it to me." She smiled at Dulcie. "In order for our fiction to work, I needed a physician to pronounce that you were suffering from an illness that would keep you away from Guilford and his wife. And I knew Grimm would live up to his name and determine you were suffering from the most *grim* disease he could imagine. All I needed to do was plant the seeds and let them grow."

"Lady Nesbitt, you're an amazing woman."

Augusta Nesbitt blushed. "I didn't spend two score years as lady-in-waiting to Her Majesty, the Queen, without learning a thing or two about persuasion and flattery and human nature. I learned the rules of politics and power and the art of persuasion at court. Mister Grimm is pompous. He believes he is the best physician in London. He isn't, but he thinks he is and acts as if he is, so it's easy to lead him where you want him to go."

Dulcie smiled her first genuine smile since her arrival at the house on Grosvenor Street. "You wanted me confined to your house, so you insisted that I wasn't ill and simply *had* to go to Lady Pepperdine's musicale, knowing Mister Grimm would insist that as a physician, he knew best."

"I thank you for the compliment, but I can't take credit for the technique. Men have been accusing women of practicing their wiles on them since the beginning of time." Augusta laughed. "Can I help it if we are the more intelligent sex?"

"Are we?" Dulcie asked, tears brimming. "I married a man condemned to die and believed that somehow, he would be able to escape his fate. I believed we would have a life together." She tried to smile but couldn't quite manage it. "How intelligent is that?"

"You married a man you loved," Augusta said.

"But how?" Dulcie asked. "I only knew him for a day. And a night," she added, a blush warming her cheeks.

Augusta took a sip of her tea, then carefully set her cup on its saucer. "It's as plain as the swollen eyes and red nose on your face."

Dulcie touched her fingers to her nose. "Oh."

"My dear, a young lady doesn't search the whole of London for a particular soldier unless that soldier is very important to her. You knew enough about him even then to decide what manner of man he was and whether or not you wanted to meet him."

"I used to read my brother's letters over and over. I must have read them a thousand times or more. Not just to feel close to Geoff once again, but because his letters were filled with descriptions of his adventures, as he called them, in the war. And Geoff's adventures frequently involved Raphael Blackburn." She closed her eyes briefly and recalled, "At first I was curious, and then, when I met him and he spoke to me as an equal and told me he was not only willing to marry me but *wanted* to marry me, I admired him. But when he kissed me, I fell in love."

"Knowing that, I would consider your marrying a man you love most intelligent." Lady Nesbitt met Dulcie's gaze. "Perhaps you should consider that Lord Blackburn believed saving you from Guilford's nasty marriage schemes was his fate."

"Thank you, Lady Nesbitt for taking care of me. For caring *for* me."

"You are welcome, my dear," Augusta said. "I enjoy having you here. You are a pleasure to have around..."

"Even under these circumstances?" Dulcie asked. "And looking the way I look?"

Augusta reached over and patted Dulcie on the cheek. "My dear girl, you are beautiful despite the swollen eyes and the red nose. Why, I fear if you did go out in public, you would set a new fashion and every young lady in town would be using cosmetics to redden their eyes and nose." She finished her tea and toast and rose from the table. "I must be up and about. I'm taking Serenity Blakenheath to the dress-maker's for fittings. What are you going to do today?"

"I've more letters to write. I finished one to the War Office earlier and enclosed a copy of the inventory I made of the items in Raphael's room, the cost of those items, and the fact that the commandant planned to charge the next occupant of the room for the items Rafe had purchased and keep the money for himself. Mister Gunn says that is unethical and against military regulations."

Because she could not pay calls to the city's hospitals as she had when she first began her search for Rafe, Dulcie had become obsessed with writing letters to inquire if any of those institutions had purchased the body of a military man recently hanged at His Majesty's Garrison on the Isle of Wight. Her husband's body. Despite Mister Gunn's assurance that the commandant had not removed Rafe's head, Dulcie was haunted by the thought of his magnificent body lying on an anatomist's table.

"I thought you gave the inventory to Mister Gunn," Lady Nesbitt said.

"I did," Dulcie said. "I made two lists while we were conducting the inventory. One for me and one for Mister Gunn to use in settling Rafe's estate."

"Clever girl. How many letters have you written?"

"Fourteen in all. Six to the War Office in care of Lord Weymouth. Two to the Queen to ask for posthumous clemency for Rafe..."

"Surely you didn't sign your name to them?" Lady Nesbitt was concerned that Dulcie's name might be bandied about court.

"Oh, no." Dulcie shook her head. "I signed my name as Miss Susan Brown and professed to be his sweetheart."

"I would like to ask a favor."

"Of course. Anything," Dulcie replied.

"Please don't write any more letters to the Queen to petition for posthumous clemency for Lord Blackburn. She has been most concerned about His Majesty's rapidly deteriorating health, and I am afraid she may be delegating her correspondence to untrustworthy secretaries or aides. We don't want either of your names bandied about at court. Instead, I shall request an audience with Her Majesty and speak to her about clemency for Lord Blackburn personally."

"Oh, thank you, Lady Nesbitt!" Dulcie exclaimed. "I shall be so grateful."

"You are quite welcome. Now tell me, what other letters have you written?"

"One to Phoebe apologizing for missing her wedding and the celebration after—"

"Phoebe understood why you couldn't stand up for her."

"Perhaps," Dulcie said. "But will she understand and forgive me for lying to her?"

"Don't fret about it," Lady Nesbitt advised. "Phoebe loves you like a sister. She'll forgive you. Now, tell me, what other letters have you written?"

Dulcie took a deep breath and slowly exhaled it. "I wrote one to Saint Luke's Hospital, and one to Bethlehem Hospital, three to three different anatomy schools—Whitby's, Taylor's, and Easton's, and one to Mister Gunn in care of the Barrister's Club to apprise him of my progress."

"Ah, Mister Gunn..." Augusta nodded. "What a delightful man! I am quite enamored of him." She blushed. "And I haven't been enamored of a man since I fell in love with my darling, Eddie. The things that man could do with..." She blushed again, recalling the fierce passion of young love. "I tried to persuade your Mister Gunn to stay with us for the duration of his stay in London, but unlike Grimm, Archie was unpersuadable. He fears for my reputation and refuses to sully it by remaining here as a houseguest. And, he has his pride, of course. Even when tempted by feminine wiles." She chuckled. "Of course, at my advanced age, the wiles aren't what they used to be."

Dulcie's cheeks reddened until they came close to matching her eyes and her nose.

"If you are not too busy composing letters and suppling evidence against cruelly ambitious commandants, you might enjoy perusing my invitations and obligations and sorting them into 'attend' or 'don't attend' piles."

"I'll be happy to," Dulcie said.

"After the torture of enduring Serenity's fittings this morning, I'm allowing Archie to escort me to luncheon at a quaint little inn he knows." She smiled. "We might even stay for supper, but I'll return home in time to accompany Serenity and Louisa Bournemouth to whichever gathering you think most advantageous."

"Shall I respond for you? Party of three?"

Augusta nodded. "Please."

"Party of three? Or four?" Dulcie's impertinent question earned her an arched brow from Lady Nesbitt.

"Party of three, for now. I'll have to see how our Mister Gunn feels about parties, the opera, theater, and such."

"He'll endure them. It's how he feels about the woman he's accompanying that counts."

Lady Nesbitt shook her finger at Dulcie in mock admonishment. "This shall be our little secret. Archie is mortified at the thought of causing a scandal at our ages. And I'm quite certain Calder would be completely scandalized."

"You are keeping my secret," Dulcie said. "I can do no less than keep yours."

"Frankly, I would adore causing a bit of scandal, but Archie is more circumspect." Lady Nesbitt sighed. "Who knew I would be enthralled by a Scotsman?"

"It appears to be catching," Dulcie quipped. "You might even call it *contagious.*"

Lady Nesbitt gave another delightful laugh. "Good heavens!

Grimm was correct in his determination. We've been overtaken by a contagion."

Dulcie rose from the table and followed Lady Nesbitt out of her bedroom into the corridor. "Phoebe is so fortunate to have you as her great aunt." She sighed wistfully. "I wish I had an aunt like you."

"Done," Augusta pronounced as she pulled on her gloves and picked up her umbrella. "From this day forward, I declare that you are my great niece and part of my family." She patted Dulcie's face. "I'll alert the household my other great niece is in residence."

CHAPTER 28

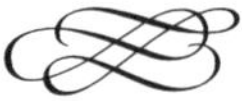

"And nothing is, but what is not."
—William Shakespeare, 1564-1616

Weymouth arrived at Shepherdston's house before breakfast.

"My lord," Henderson greeted him. "This is an unexpected surprise. Will you be breakfasting with us this morning?"

"No." Weymouth handed the butler his hat and coat. "I will have coffee, though. I cannot stay long; I've a meeting at the War Office in under an hour. But I must see Lord Shepherdston straightaway. I thought I would catch him before he and Lord Mayhew leave for their morning ride along the Row." Weymouth followed the butler into the morning room. "It's a matter of some importance."

"His lordship hasn't come downstairs yet, but he should be down shortly," Henderson said. "He nodded toward the strapping young footman setting chafing dishes of hot eggs and kidneys on the massive buffet. "When you take Lady Shepherdston's chocolate up, please inform Lord Shepherdston that Lord Weymouth is here on a matter of some importance and is awaiting him in the morning room."

The footman collected the chocolate pot and a chocolate cup and saucer, spoons, and the sugar and cream, and set them on a tray, then added two slices of toasted bread, a dish of butter, and another dish of cherry preserves with appropriate spoons and napkins and carried the tray upstairs to the master's suite.

Lady Shepherdston opened the door at the footman's soft knock. "Good morning, March."

The footman set the tray on the table, stirred the chocolate just so, and poured it into her cup. "Good morning, my lady," he whispered. "I am to inform Lord Shepherdston that Lord Weymouth is awaiting him in the morning room on a matter of some importance."

"I'll relay the message and send him right down," she promised.

Moments later, the Marquess of Shepherdston descended the stairs while buttoning the buttons of his waistcoat and carrying his riding jacket on his arm. He entered the morning room, draped his jacket over the back of his chair. "Good morning, Lord Weymouth. You wanted to see me on a matter of importance?"

"Yes," Weymouth confirmed. "Could we speak in your study? It won't take long."

"Of course," Shepherdston said. "I'll have coffee brought there." He glanced at the footman standing with his back to the fireplace and facing the dining table.

The footman nodded, then walked over to the buffet and began preparing a tray of coffee to take to the study.

Shepherdston ushered Weymouth to his study. They settled into leather wing chairs while waiting for the footman to deliver the coffee.

Rafe knocked once and entered on Shepherdston's command. He set the coffee tray down on the table between the chairs and poured coffee for Shepherdston and his guest. "Will there be anything else, my lord?"

"No, thank you," Shepherdston said. "If we do require anything else, I'll ring."

"Very good, sir." Rafe bowed slightly, backed to the door, and left as quietly as he'd come in.

Shepherdston smiled as he lifted his coffee cup. "What's so important, Lord Weymouth?"

"We must do something about the young lady," Weymouth said. "She has me quite concerned."

"What young lady, sir?"

"Lady Blackburn. Susan Brown. Miss Tennant," Weymouth replied more sharply than he intended. "Whatever you choose to call her. I've received six missives from her, all sent to me in care of the War Office, since she's been a guest at Grosvenor Street."

"Miss Tennant is confined to Lady Nesbitt's house."

"I'm aware of that," Weymouth said. "But having Grimm confine her has done nothing to stop her from writing letters. She's written me, the Queen, two hospitals, and three Schools of Anatomy, as well as Lord Blackburn's solicitor, Archibald Gunn."

"What concerns you about her letter writing campaign?" Shepherdston asked.

"Before she had my goddaughter contact me, Miss Tennant had been going around London searching for Raphael Blackburn. She had been going alone with only a footman to accompany her as she visited nearly every hospital, inn, and boarding house asking about him. And she'd also paid numerous visits to the War Office asking questions about him. We arranged for her to pretend to be ill to keep her out of the reach of her uncle. And now, she's writing letters..." Weymouth sighed. "I'm concerned that one of her letters will come to the attention of our quarry. And our whole mission will be compromised."

"What does she hope to gain from a letter writing campaign?" Shepherdston took another sip of coffee.

"She hopes to gain her husband's mortal remains."

Shepherdston grabbed a napkin to keep from spewing his mouthful of coffee all over Weymouth. "What?"

"She's seeking her husband's remains."

"Does she know we brought them—him—home?" Shepherdston

was equally alarmed. "And please tell me she's not signing her married or maiden name to the letters."

"She's not. She's using the name I told her to use. Miss Susan Brown, which happens to be the name of my goddaughter's lady's maid. I chose it because anyone looking into a Susan Brown will find dozens and among them one lady's maid to the Marchioness of Blessing and Countess of Carlisle who could easily squash the inquiries." Weymouth took a sip of his own coffee and answered Shepherdston's question before he asked it. "I asked the lady's maid for permission to use her name and she agreed to do it to help Miss Tennant throw any pursuers off the trail."

"Huzzah for the lady's maid Miss Brown," Shepherdston said wryly.

Weymouth chuckled. "Miss Brown also informed me that she has four cousins in London proper named Susan Brown who would also help if needed."

Shepherdston squeezed his eyes shut, then opened them to meet Weymouth's gaze. "We should have dug a mock grave to complete the hanging fiction."

"We couldn't take the chance that the commandant or someone else—including Blackburn's family—wouldn't have it opened in order to claim the body—a body that didn't exist," Weymouth reminded him.

"Then why didn't the commandant just tell her the army had claimed his remains for burial?"

"He did," Weymouth said. "Most cruelly."

Shepherdston frowned. "How do you know this?"

"I paid a call on Blackburn's solicitor yesterday morning at the Barrister's Club after I received another letter from Miss Tennant. He gave me an accounting of what happened after the hanging," Weymouth said.

Shepherdston sat up straighter. "I'd like an accounting of that myself."

Weymouth recounted the meeting Mister Gunn and Blackburn's bride had had with Commandant Swindell and ended by revealing that both Gunn, the solicitor, and Blackburn's wife had supplied him with an inventory of Blackburn's belongings.

"She had his quarters stripped down to the bare walls?"

"Just about," Weymouth confirmed. "She asked the sergeant to pack everything that wasn't in the room when Blackburn first arrived. She said that since her husband had paid for everything, she wasn't going to allow the commandant to resell them to the next occupant at a profit and pocket the money."

"Did she just give us evidence against the commandant that could be used to remove him?" Shepherdston was stunned.

"Gunn thinks so and so do I," Weymouth told him. "Gunn said Swindell was livid and couldn't keep from cruelly wounding Miss Tennant when she asked for her husband's remains by telling her that he had given the execution detail permission to dispose of it as they saw fit and that usually meant selling it to hospitals and schools for the anatomists to dissect. But only after they removed his treasonous head." Weymouth sighed. "Gunn reported that she threatened the commandant and marched out of his office, only to collapse in a bout of weeping once they were safely in the coach. And she hasn't stopped weeping. He's concerned she'll make herself ill. I'm concerned that she'll also stir up a hornet's nest that will wreak havoc on our mission."

"That was a cruel and contemptible thing for Swindell to do. And entirely false. We told him we had been ordered to take the body back to London. The commandant was aware that Blackburn wasn't accused of treason and there were no grounds to remove his head." Shepherdston said, his lips tightening in anger.

"Gunn explained that. But Miss Tennant was inconsolable. And still is."

Shepherdston pursed his lips in thought. "What do you suggest we do?"

"I suggest we step up our plan." He tilted his head to study Shepherdston. "How close is Blackburn to being ready?"

"You tell me." Rising from his chair, Shepherdston walked to the bellpull and rang for service. Henderson appeared almost immediately. "Ask him to come in."

There was a subservient tap on the study door moments later. "You wanted me, sir?"

"Yes, March, please come in."

A footman walked into the study with Henderson close on his heels. "Is there anything you require, sir?" The man spoke in a husky whisper, but it was easily audible.

"Lord Weymouth wishes to speak with you." He gestured toward Weymouth's chair. "Lord Weymouth, meet our newest footman, John March. March, meet Lord Trevor Weymouth."

"We've met," Rafe said. "In the commandant's office at His Majesty's Garrison on the Isle of Wight. I traded him my horse."

Weymouth sprang from his seat and gave the footman he'd barely noticed a closer look. "Blackburn? Good heavens! I didn't recognize you!"

"I recognized you," Rafe shot back. "How's Ricky? Is he settling into your stable? Or is he still confined to the garrison? Don't tell me you let them hang him, too? After all, he's the one who struck the inferior officer."

Weymouth chuckled. "Ricky is magnificent. One of Lord Davies' ships transported him for me. I've had him eight days. And no, he is *not* settling in. He's raising a ruckus. Just as I expect you expected him to do."

Rafe sighed. "I'm relieved to hear it. I was afraid they might have attempted to break his spirit." He offered Weymouth his hand. "Thank you, Lord Weymouth."

Henderson cleared his throat.

"I apologize, Mr. Henderson," Rafe said, a smile playing around his lips as he withdrew his hand.

"Very good, March," Henderson said with a nod of approval. "Do you require anything, gentlemen?"

"No," Shepherdston said.

"Then, have I your permission to withdraw?" Henderson asked.

"Yes," Shepherdston told him. "I'll ring if there's anything else we require."

Henderson moved toward the door, but Weymouth stopped him. "Henderson, you've done a magnificent job in such a short period of time. I would have never believed he is anything but a footman." He glanced at Rafe. "Without your long hair and unshaven face, and dressed the way you are, you would never be mistaken for Lord Raphael Blackburn. It's a remarkable transformation and the change in your voice is perfect."

"I cannot take credit for those things, my lord," Henderson said. "He came to me shorn and shaven and unable to speak." He glanced at Rafe. "I had excellent material with which to work. He has impeccable manners and will be ready at the conclusion of the fortnight."

"He'll be ready sooner than that," Weymouth said.

Both Rafe and Henderson stared at him.

"I must be on my way or I'll be late for my meeting. Shepherdston will explain when he returns from his morning ride." Weymouth smiled at Rafe. "Good luck, my boy. I'll be in touch."

The butler opened the study door for him, then followed Lord Weymouth to collect his hat and coat.

"What did he mean?" Rafe asked, turning to Shepherdston when they were gone.

Shepherdston grinned. "I believe it means you'll be seeing your wife sooner than we planned."

CHAPTER 29

"Now's the day and now's the hour."
—Robert Burns, 1759-1796

The news that he might be about to go into service as a footman in Tennant House had Rafe's heart racing and his palms sweating. The prospect of seeing Dulcie filled him with pure joy and sheer dread. He already hated keeping secrets from her that shouldn't be secrets at all and now he was about to slip back into her life as a fraud and a liar. But it might be worth it just to steal another glimpse of her…

He had dreamed of her every night since he'd awakened in the coffin and realized he wasn't dead. Vivid dreams where he touched and kissed and made love to her time and time again, then slept with her, their arms and legs entwined. He ached for her with a bone-deep ache like nothing he had ever experienced before. He ached to hear her low, husky voice, her infectious, tantalizing laugh, her dreams and memories, the sounds she made when he loved her, and her soft breathing when she lay against him at night. Her absence hadn't lessened his ache. It had heightened it.

Rafe managed a smile. He and Dulcie were a match in every way. Geoff had been right about that. When the door had opened and he had dropped through the floor of the gallows, Rafe's feelings for Dulcie had become crystal clear. He wanted more than just her body; he wanted all of her. Past, present, and future. He was in love for the first time in his life and the love he felt for Dulcie was forever. She wasn't a part of his life. She *was* his life.

His fight, his challenge, was to conceal those feelings, when he wanted nothing more than to reveal himself to her. But he had to stay focused on his mission. Revealing himself to Dulcie before he discovered the evidence he needed against her uncle could endanger them both. And that was the crux of his dilemma

Keeping his eyes—and hands—off the love of his life, his wife, would be the single greatest challenge of his life.

Much greater than turning himself from Major Lord Raphael Blackburn, seventh Earl of Blackburn, into John March, footman. Rafe had spent long hours every day for ten days applying himself to his training, so he had had no time to worry about whether he had the skills needed to serve with the unobtrusiveness and finesse the position of footman required. He had never imagined he would have any difficulty adopting any disguise he needed in order to protect his wife—especially masquerading as a footman in her uncle's household. Rafe had dined at formal tables since he'd left the nursery. Manners and proper deportment had been drilled into him along with arithmetic, the pianoforte, and languages, first by his tutor and then by the headmasters at school. But he had been born a leader and was accustomed to giving orders rather than taking them. Rafe had trained all his life to become the Earl of Blackburn and had only had ten days to learn the trade of footman. He was accustomed to being served; he was not accustomed to serving others—especially in the manner Henderson required.

"You are much improved, Mr. March," Henderson complimented him as Rafe stood at the sideboard folding napkins. "Your ability to convince Lord Weymouth you were a footman should go a long way in restoring your confidence in your abilities."

Rafe nodded. His voice had improved considerably. He still couldn't speak in his normal voice without pain in his vocal cords, but he could sustain a low whisper. Shepherdston's suggestion that he remain mute while a footman should work to his advantage. If he didn't speak, Dulcie wouldn't recognize his voice. If he wore livery and a wig, she wouldn't recognize him. Footmen were faceless, voiceless, and interchangeable servants.

The Free Fellows believed that a footman able to hear but unable to speak would be seen as a valuable asset in the Tennant Household. After all, Guilford Tennant had sacked his household staff and family retainers without references in order to break their attachments to Dulcie. A footman who could not speak could not carry tales or reveal what he happened to hear. He was, Shepherdston pronounced, the perfect servant for a man like Guilford Tennant.

Henderson disagreed, but the butler was seeking a different sort of perfection.

Rafe watched as Henderson unfolded the napkin Rafe had so carefully folded. The butler held the napkin aloft by one corner, shook out the folds, then placed it on the sideboard and commanded, "Try again."

Gritting his teeth in frustration, Rafe diligently refolded the napkin. Henderson inspected every crease and fold and pronounced it serviceable.

Rafe smiled.

"Footmen do not show emotion, amusement, or pride in their work," Henderson cautioned. "When you excel in your work, others will take note of it. You needn't pat yourself on the back." The butler placed a stack of a dozen napkins on a tray on the sideboard. "When you complete these, you may remove them on the tray to the butler's pantry to await my inspection."

Rafe stood at dutiful attention until the butler exited the room, then returned his attention to the napkins.

"Breathe," said a deep male voice behind him.

Rafe turned from his task to discover Shepherdston had returned from his morning ride and was helping himself to kidneys, kippers, eggs, and toast from the buffet. "I beg your pardon, my lord. I didn't hear you come in."

"I said, breathe," Shepherdston repeated. "You were lost in thought and holding your breath in anticipation of disasters that may or may not happen."

Rafe filled a cup with coffee and carried it to Shepherdston.

"Thank you, March."

Rafe returned the silver coffee pot to the warmer on the buffet. "You'll have to forgive me. I've learned to expect the worst during the past few months." Except for Dulcie. She had been the best.

Shepherdston chuckled. "I suppose you have. After spending ten months confined to your quarters in a military prison on the Isle of Wight, you get married, are granted a wedding night, are hanged the next morning, resurrected, and now, demoted from an earl to a footman." He shook his head wryly, meeting Rafe's gaze. "You've had a hellish ten days."

Rafe *had* had a hellish ten days, but when he met Shepherdston's gaze all he could think of was how lucky he was to be alive and about to see his bride again. "I'm alive," Rafe said. "And if it wasn't for the determination and courage of you and your associates I would be moldering in my grave right now and my wife would truly be a widow."

"Henderson is hard on you because he's only got a day left to complete your training." Shepherdston indicated the chair on his right. "Sit. We need to discuss what comes next."

"I can see to my duties while we talk, my lord," Rafe managed to say without a trace of mockery as he returned to folding the napkins into the precise pattern Henderson required.

Sheperdston smiled. "You'll miss Henderson when you go into service at Tennant House tomorrow."

Rafe's hands faltered. He turned from the sideboard to pin Shepherdston with his sharp gaze. "Tomorrow?"

Taking a sip of his coffee, Sheperdston nodded. "You'll be going there to interview for the position of footman first thing in the morning." Reading the unspoken question in his eyes, Shepherdston put his cup down before adding gently, "She's not there. She's still at Lady Nesbitt's house at Number Twelve Grosvenor Street. Your solicitor escorted her there in the wee hours of Monday morning following your hanging on Sunday. She's supposed to be recovering from some sort of contagious illness and confined to bed for a fortnight on physician's orders."

"McGregor?" Rafe asked, concern in his whisper.

Shepherdston shook his head. "No, not McGregor. Sir Walter Grimm, a wretched excuse for a doctor Lady Nesbitt hired to spread the word that Miss Tennant—"

Rafe narrowed his gaze at Shepherdston.

"*Lady Blackburn* had taken ill," Shepherdston conceded. "Her supposed illness is not a secret, but her position as your wife still is. I cannot blame you for wanting to claim your wife." He grimaced. "I still hate to think about how close I came to losing Sarah—Lady Shepherdston. We are all of us—Avon, Sussex, Grantham, Barclay, Courtland—even Weymouth—very happily married and madly in love with our wives. So we do understand your plight." Shepherdston took another swallow of coffee, found it had cooled and set it down. "I know it's difficult. I'm not a patient man myself, but try to be patient. We must do this properly. With no mistakes. We are playing a high stakes game and we must not lose. Understand?"

Rafe crossed to the buffet, retrieved another cup and saucer, filled it with coffee, and carried it to Shepherdston. He set the fresh coffee down and removed the other cup and saucer. "I understand."

"Lady Blackburn will be returning to her home day after tomorrow after the physician pronounces her fit to do so. Tomorrow, after your interview, you'll be offered the position and will start work immediately."

"So I'll be there when she arrives?"

"You will most likely be sent with the coach to collect her. Collecting and following ladies around is one of the duties of a footman, you know," Shepherdston said. "But, if not, you will be there when she arrives. You'll be there to collect evidence as well. But your primary assignment will be to watch over her." Shepherdston took a bite of toast and strawberry jam.

Rafe arched an eyebrow. "You don't need to tell me that."

"I don't suppose I do," Shepherdston said by way of apology, before adding, "The most recent butler at Tennant House is not as demanding as Henderson, or as hardworking and conscientious, either." Shepherdston lifted his coffee cup, took a sip of coffee, and glanced at Rafe over the rim. "Unfortunately, Guilford expects the best, but can only afford mediocre. You'll be a vast improvement over the footman about to be removed from his position and replaced with you."

Rafe looked down and pointed to his set of Shepherdston livery.

"I've arranged for you to wear a set of plain black livery to Tennant House for your interview with the current butler," Shepherdston informed him. "Normally, the butler orders the livery, but I begged a favor of the *previous* butler—"

"Hatfield?" Rafe asked.

"Yes, Patrick Hatfield. The one loyal to the seventh Viscount, his wife, and children, Geoffrey, and Dulcinea. Do you know him?"

"No." Rafe shook his head. "Know of him. From Geoff."

"Good. I sent your measurements to the man and asked him to secure you two complete sets of livery."

"How did you get my measurements?" Rafe demanded.

"I measured you."

Rafe gave him another pointed look.

"When we were moving your body from the gallows. For the official report of your death. McGregor wrote. I measured. Courtland and Barclay turned and lifted." Watching the play of the emotions cross Rafe's face, Shepherdston continued his briefing as if he hadn't just reminded Rafe of how vulnerable he had been. "By the by, you won't need a wig because you're going to wear the one you are wearing now to the interview."

"I'll need references," Rafe said. "I never engage staff without credible references."

"Henderson is working on them now," Shepherdston said. "You were most recently employed by the late Viscount Rupert Selby for four years and briefly by his successor. You stayed on another sixteen months when the current viscount took possession of the property, but financial reversals forced him to sell the London property and the new owners are bringing in their own staff. You were asked to stay on, but you've decided to seek your fortune elsewhere."

"What if Tennant verifies my references?"

"The new owner and the former butler at Selby House will verify that John March was a footman at Selby House for five and a half years."

Rafe frowned. "Why would the new owner vouch for me?"

"She is Lord Weymouth's goddaughter and one of your wife's dearest friends."

"I don't like involving Dul—Lady Blackburn's close friends in this situation. I don't want them to get hurt."

"That's a very admirable sentiment, but in this situation I fear it's necessary. They know the risks and were eager to help. Just as we are."

"Very well." Rafe took a deep breath and slowly exhaled it.

Shepherdston smiled. "Cheer up, March. By tomorrow afternoon, your bride will be within your reach."

And if her uncle had his way, Rafe would get to watch other men court her. She'd filled his dreams for the past fortnight and Rafe was aching to kiss her, to hold her, to love her. But John March, the new footman in service at Tennant House, would never be allowed to touch her...

Shepherdston seemed to read his mind. "Henderson will brief you on what he has learned about the staff and operations at Tennant House and what you need to know before you leave tomorrow. What I can tell you about Tennant House is that it's a large house with lots of nooks and crannies. Opportunities will present themselves. Take advantage of them. But be discreet. And don't get caught."

"I'm John March," Rafe reminded him. "She won't know me. I'll be a stranger to her."

"You were a stranger to her as Raphael Blackburn, too," Shepherdston pointed out. "And she married you."

CHAPTER 30

"But to see her was to love her,
Love but her, and love forever.
Had we never lov'd sae kindly,
Had we never lov'd sae blindly,
Never met—or never parted—,
We had ne'er been broken hearted."
—Robert Burns, 1759-1796

His bride had lost weight. Rafe could tell at first glance. Dulcie looked wan and listless and somewhat disheartened. His heart constricted at the thought that she had suffered during the fortnight since his hanging. She was wearing the dress she'd worn to their first meeting, the same dress he had hung up for her to wear when she left the Isle of Wight on the Sunday he was hanged. A green muslin dress with a green velvet spencer and matching bonnet. The dress had fit her perfectly two weeks ago, clinging to her compact curves in all the right places. Now, it didn't.

Her matching bonnet shadowed much of her face, but he could

see, as she approached the coach, that she was holding a handkerchief to her eyes, dabbing at tears. A handkerchief embroidered like the one she'd been twisting when they had first met. The one he'd retrieved from the floor where she'd dropped it. Rafe could recall every detail of their introduction to each other…

"Can you share your name, Miss?"

"Susan Brown."

"Miss Brown with the initials 'DMRT' on her lacy handkerchief."

"Lord Weymouth introduced me to the commandant as Miss Susan Brown. But my actual surname is Tennant."

"Tennant. *You're Geoff's little sister—"*

"Dulcie. Dulcinea Marjorie Rose Tennant."

Rafe jumped down from his perch on the Tennant coach to open the door for Dulcie and collect her bag from the footman walking behind her. It was the same valise he had carried out of the commandant's antechamber and into the honeymoon cottage. His heart leapt in his chest when she spoke to him. "Thank you, Foster."

The simple greeting spoken in Dulcie's distinctive husky tone of voice sent a surge of awareness through him. It didn't matter that she addressed him by another man's name. A fortnight ago, Rafe had believed he would never hear that voice again, never see her again, believed he would die with her name on his lips. And he nearly had. But McGregor and the members of the Free Fellows had saved him. And now, Rafe was standing before her.

"He's not Foster, miss," the coachman, Perryman, said.

Dulcie focused her gaze on the new man. Perryman was right. He wasn't Foster. Foster was tall but this man was taller, almost as tall as… She took a deep breath to steady herself. "What happened to Foster?"

Perryman shrugged, then pointed toward Rafe. "The new chap's name is John March. He hears all right, but he can't speak."

"Oh, I'm terribly sorry, March," she said as Rafe unfolded the coach steps and assisted her into the vehicle. A tingle of awareness went through him when he cupped her elbow with his gloved hand.

She felt it, too. Dulcie turned in the door of the coach and their gazes locked.

Rafe stared, drinking in the sight of her. Dulcie bit her bottom lip in consternation. He half expected her to condemn his impertinence for staring at her with impunity, but she didn't condemn him. She not only allowed him to stare at her, she stared back.

"Everything all right, Miss?" Perryman called from the box.

"Yes, thank you, Perryman," she called back, before turning and settling into her seat on the coach. She lifted her handkerchief to her eyes once again and glanced back at Lady Nesbitt's house as if loathe to leave it.

Rafe averted his eyes from her beautiful face as he hefted a valise that was considerably heavier than it had been when he had last seen it and stowed it in the boot of the coach before climbing up onto his perch beside the boot.

"Home, straightaway, miss?" Perryman called down to her once again.

"Yes," she said, before changing her mind a heartbeat later. "No. Go around the park, please. And then, to Gunter's."

Perryman gave a heavy sigh, but dutifully steered the coach away from the curb and into Grosvenor Street traffic. He circled the park, then headed to Gunter's Tea Shop in Berkeley Square. Perryman parked the coach across the street from the tea shop and confectionary. Rafe jumped down from his perch and swung open the door of the coach, then handed Dulcie a pocket-sized blank book and a Conte pencil Shepherdston had given him to carry to communicate when the slate and chalk had proved too cumbersome to carry.

She took the book and pencil from him and Rafe pantomimed the act of writing, then pointed to the entrance to Gunter's.

"Do you want me to write down my order?"

Rafe nodded. The last time he had patronized Gunter's, the shop sent waiters to the parked coached to take orders and coin and delivered the treats, but because so many coaches parked, it was often quicker to order inside. Ladies were allowed to enter the shop, but generally avoided it when they were alone.

Dulcie started to write her order, then stopped and looked at Rafe. "I have a better idea. It's perfectly proper for a lady to go in if accompanied by a footman. "Why don't you go in with me?"

Rafe shrugged, then glanced up at the coach box.

"Perryman, I wish to order an ice in Gunter's," Dulcie explained. "March is going to accompany me. I'll treat us all. What would you like?"

"A cup of tea and a currant scone, miss," Perryman said. "And I thank you for it."

"You're welcome."

"We'll make our selections inside and return shortly," Dulcie told him.

"Aye, miss."

Dulcie turned to Rafe. "Come along, March," she ordered as she started across the busy street to Gunter's.

Rafe bit the inside of his cheek to keep from smiling as Dulcie led the way inside the shop. She really was going to make a marvelous countess.

She ordered a cup of tea and a currant scone for the coachman, a dish of strawberry ice cream for herself, then turned to Rafe. "What would you like?"

Rafe studied the menu board and pointed to the orange-pineapple ice cream.

Dulcie placed the order, then opened her purse and produced a guinea for the clerk. "We'll take the scone and tea, now, please, and you may deliver the two ice creams to the third coach parked there. We'll leave the door open." She accepted the change from her coin and left a proper tip for the waiter. She started to turn toward the door, then stopped and said, "Please add another ice cream in pear and cheddar." She paid for the ice and added another tip. "Ready in half an hour," she reminded the shop clerk.

Wondering if Dulcie intended to eat another ice cream when she finished her strawberry ice, Rafe arched an eyebrow at her in question.

Dulcie narrowed her eyes at him and Rafe quickly lowered his own gaze to the floor, fearing the familiar gesture had intrigued her. She shook her head, then shrugged off her discomfiture. "It's for my aunt Mavis. She's married to my father's brother. We don't really get on well. But she adores Gunter's ices and treats and I thought…" She gave him a sheepish look. "I suppose you could call what I'm doing bribery. But Mavis is less likely to tattle on me to my uncle for coming here if I bring her something."

Rafe nodded, then pantomimed buttoning his lips.

Dulcie laughed. "Can you really not speak?"

He motioned for the book and pencil. Dulcie handed it to him. He printed the words: *Whisper some. Very painful.*

"Were you born with the condition?" Dulcie asked as they made their way to the front door through a group of customers.

A gentleman nodded in greeting and the lady accompanying him did likewise. "Good afternoon."

Rafe recognized the couple as the Marquess and Marchioness of Shepherdston.

"Good afternoon, my lord, my lady," Dulcie replied with a smile.

"Allow me." Shepherdston opened the door to allow Dulcie and Rafe to exit.

"Thank you, my lord," Dulcie said.

"You're welcome, Miss Tennant. We are glad to see you're recovering well enough from your recent illness to be released from your confinement."

"Thank you again, my lord, for your concern. I am better."

Rafe acknowledged Shepherdston with the slightest of nods as they passed.

Twice as they were crossing the thoroughfare, Rafe nearly reached for Dulcie's elbow, catching himself at the last moment. He was fortunate his hands were occupied with the coachman's tea and scone. It was heavenly being with her once again. And agonizing to know she hadn't recognized him and had no idea the footman following at her heels like an obedient puppy was the same man she'd married a fortnight ago. The same man to whom she'd given her innocence with such unbridled passion and joy.

And as he crossed the street, Rafe felt Shepherdston's gaze burning into his back. He had to admire Shepherdston's surveillance method. He was able to enjoy an outing with his marchioness at Gunter's while keeping an eye on Rafe and Dulcie. Rafe knew their meeting was not a coincidence. After seeing the casual meeting between Dulcie and the Shepherdston's, Rafe understood the importance of giving Dulcie the dose of sleeping elixir before Weymouth's associates arrived at the cottage to take him away. The members of the Beau Monde were a small community of the most fortunate who frequented the same shops, clubs, churches, cultural, and social events. It was almost impossible to attend any event of any size and not meet a relative or an old school chum or a business associate. Had she seen the faces or heard the voices of any of Weymouth's associates, Dulcie would have surely confronted them about it and unintentionally exposed the plan.

As they reached the coach, Rafe passed the cup of tea and the scone up to the coachman, then handed Dulcie into the coach. Another frisson of awareness passed between them as she steadied herself by placing her hand on the sleeve of his coat. She was wearing gloves and no flesh touched flesh, yet they both felt the electricity. As she glanced at him, Rafe did his best to steel his expression and not give anything away.

They didn't have to wait long for their ice cream. A waiter soon crossed the street carrying their treats. He handed Dulcie her dish of strawberry ice cream first, then handed Rafe his dish of orange-pineapple and retreated.

He struggled to stand at attention and eat his ice cream at the same time. Dulcie finally poked her head out of the open coach doorway. "March," she called out. "Come inside and sit."

Rafe shook his head. The last time he'd been in a coach with her they'd spent the journey kissing. It wouldn't do to get caught in a scandalous situation before he found evidence linking Guilford Tennant to the murder of his brother and nephew.

But his headstrong young mistress wasn't taking no for an answer. "You can't enjoy your ice cream that way. Come inside and sit down and eat it."

He shook his head once again.

"Very well." Dulcie climbed down from the coach, her dish of strawberry ice cream in hand, and spoke to Perryman. "I find it a bit too warm in the coach. I think I'll take my ice cream to that bench in the square and enjoy it there."

"Yes, miss."

Tilting her pert nose in the air, Dulcie headed for the empty bench just across the way.

Perryman shot Rafe a glare. "Don't just stand there, man! Take your ice cream and go with her."

Rafe followed her. Once again, he found himself biting the inside of his cheek to keep from grinning like a fool as his bride led him on a merry chase. He joined her on the bench as they ate their dishes of ice cream on one of the rare days where a sliver of sunshine shown through the clouds.

Dulcie took a bite of ice cream, then stole a glance at him. "You didn't answer my question while we were in Gunter's."

He drew a question mark in the air.

"I asked if you were born with the condition that limits your speech to a painful whisper?"

Rafe shook his head, then pulled his book and pencil out of his jacket pocket and wrote: *Accident.*

"What sort of accident?" Dulcie asked, continuing to spoon mouthfuls of melting ice cream into her mouth.

Hoping to dissuade her curiosity, Rafe quickly spooned a mouthful of orange-pineapple ice cream into his mouth. His taste buds exploded. It had been over five years since he'd enjoyed the taste of any flavored frozen cream and he had never tried this one. He closed his eyes as the cold, exotic flavors slid down his throat, soothing the pain of his raw throat and tender vocal cords. The relief was indescribable.

Dulcie was mesmerized by the sight of the footman enjoying the frozen confection of cream and sugar and the flavors of oranges from Spain and pineapples from exotic South American plantations. She had seen that look on a man's face before. It was the expression of a man in experiencing sheer ecstasy. The expression of complete and utter satisfaction. Her husband had worn that same expression in the bathtub when she'd ridden him into exhausted bliss. "You don't remember the accident?"

Rafe swallowed another bite of ice cream, sighing as the icy treat worked its magic on his throat. McGregor had prescribed hot, soothing drinks for his damaged throat, but they couldn't compare with this miracle of ice and cream. And he would be sure to enlighten McGregor the next time he saw him.

"It feels good, doesn't it?" she asked.

Rafe nodded.

"When I was a child I often had earaches and sore throats and my mother used to bring me here." She smiled. "It's one of my favorite places. And not just because of the ices and sweets. Although I'm very partial to sweets."

Rafe recalled her saying almost the same thing the day he met her.

My friends will tell you I have a terrible weakness for sweets.

Watching as she spooned the last of her strawberry confection into her perfectly bow-shaped mouth, Rafe envied the spoon. He, too, had a terrible weakness for sweets. His sweet Dulcinea.

"But when your throat aches," Dulcie was saying. "Nothing feels as good as Gunter's ices, don't you agree?"

Rafe nodded, then rubbed his throat and smiled before quickly finishing his own dish of melting ice cream. He laid his spoon in the empty dish, then reached for hers. Dulcie handed it over. Their fingers touched and the force of the attraction arcing between them rattled the spoons in the bowls.

Dulcie smiled. "I like you, March," she said. "We seem to share similar sentiments. I hope my uncle is satisfied with your work, for I should hate to lose you—"

Rafe lifted the empty dishes, then pointed to Gunter's across the street."

"We are of an accord about Gunter's, too."

Rafe shook his head. He placed the dirty dishes in a basket marked

Gunter's Tea Shop, then made a walking gesture with his fingers, and pointed to the coach.

"Goodness! You're right," Dulcie said. "It's time for the waiter to deliver Mavis's ice cream and time for us to be on our way." She shuddered. "Home. Such as it is."

~

"Welcome home, miss," Maxwell Bertram, the newest in a series of butlers at Tennant House, greeted Dulcie as soon as he opened the door for her. "We expected you earlier."

Dulcie murmured her thanks, then turned to find Mavis, Lady Tennant, descending the stairs.

"Welcome home, Dulcie," Mavis echoed. "We're so glad to see you recovered. We were expecting you early afternoon. It's almost three o'clock."

Mavis didn't approach her, but the concern in her aunt's eyes seemed genuine. Dulcie explained, "The sun was shining when I left Lady Nesbitt's and after all the rain and fog and being unable to leave the house, I decided a trip to Gunter's was in order."

"Oh." Mavis's round face fell.

Dulcie nodded toward March, who stepped forward and brought a metal dish in the shape of a pear from behind his back and presented it to Lady Tennant.

"I remembered that you like pear and cheddar ice cream from Gunter's so I had March fetch some for you."

Mavis clapped a hand to her heart, clearly shocked. "Why, thank you, Dulcie!"

"You're welcome, Mavis." Dulcie met the other woman's gaze. "I mean—Lady Tennant."

"No," Mavis told her. "Not to you. Not anymore. We're family. It's time I started acting like it." She gave Dulcie a tentative smile.

"I'd like that," Dulcie assured her. "Now, enjoy your ice cream before it melts. If you'll excuse me, I'm tired and I believe I'll go upstairs to rest."

"Will you be joining us for supper?" Mavis asked, an almost hopeful note in her voice.

"I don't think so. I ate too much ice cream. Perhaps, tomorrow night…"

"I'd like that," Mavis said.

CHAPTER 31

"The eyes those silent tongues of love."
—Miguel de Cervantes, 1547-1616

Rafe was lighting the fire in the fireplace in Dulcie's room before five o'clock the following morning when Dulcie cried out, *"Raphael!"*

His reaction was immediate and visceral. *Dulcie wanted him.* A thousand different images of their wedding night flashed through his mind. Relief swept over him. The weight of the world had been lifted from his shoulders. She had recognized him. He wasn't a stranger to her any longer. He wasn't John March, the footman. He was Raphael Blackburn, Earl of Blackburn, again and his bride knew it.

Rising from the hearth, Rafe crossed the floor to Dulcie's tiny bed in two long strides and swept open the bedcurtains. The covers and her voluminous flannel nightgown were twisted around her body. Her knees, calves, and feet were exposed. Rafe wrapped his fingers around her delicate foot. It felt like ice. She thrashed against the pillow, turning her head from side to side, trapped in the throes of a bad dream. Tears stained her cheeks and she called out for him once again.

"Cold?"

"No," he told her. "Quite the opposite."

"You're not cold?"

"How can I be cold when I'm admiring my beautiful naked bride?"

"Your naked wife is freezing."

Memories of their wedding night, when she'd been dressed in a sheer chemise and a pair of brief French silk drawers that left little to the imagination, and later when she'd been wearing nothing at all, came flooding back as he gazed down at her. She wasn't naked now, but she *was* freezing despite being draped in yards of matronly flannel.

"Shh, sweet Dulcie, I'm here." He sat on the edge of the bed, then angled his body against the headboard and gathered her into his arms, keeping one leg on the floor to avoid falling off the small bed. Pressing his lips against her forehead, he kissed her tenderly. He drew the covers over her with one hand and held her pressed against him with the other, sharing his body heat, warming her.

Dulcie's big, brown eyes fluttered open. "Rafe," she murmured sleepily. She wrapped her arms around his neck and held on. "Oh, Rafe, you still have your head. Your beautiful head."

"Yes, sweet Dulcie," he chuckled. "I still have my head." He pressed another lingering kiss against her brow.

"Thank goodness," she breathed, a note of panic returning to her voice. "I've been searching and searching, going from hospital to hospital, but I couldn't find you."

"I'm here," he assured her, holding her tighter.

"You'll stay with me?"

"Yes, I'll stay," he promised, his deep voice a raspy whisper as he smoothed away the trails left by her tears with the pad of his thumb.

She sighed deeply, then closed her eyes and drifted back into sleep in Raphael's arms.

Rafe kept his promise and held his wife in his arms until her breathing had settled into a deep and even rhythm. Only then did he ease her out of his arms and back against the pillow. He rose from the bed and tucked the covers tightly around her before kissing her lightly on the lips.

He returned to the hearth to stoke the fire, determined that when she awakened again, the room would be warm and cozy. So she cried in her sleep at night. And worried about him having his head attached to his shoulders. Rafe frowned. Why was she worried about his head? Had she heard the grisly stories of the heads of hanging victims pulling away from the neck from the force of the rope? Had someone told her that had happened to him? Rafe gritted his teeth, firming his jaw in resolution.

Her anguish had torn at his heart. Especially knowing that *he* was the one who had brought this on her. But not just him…

Someone had tried to take his life. Someone had conspired to see him court-martialed and hanged.

Rafe wanted his life back. He was grateful to be alive at all. But he would never be satisfied with the half-life he had as John March.

He wanted to return to his life as Raphael Blackburn, seventh Earl of Blackburn, and he wanted to present Dulcie to his family and friends and the world as his bride and his countess. They had married before God and witnesses. She was not meant to be kept in secret, relegated to the shadows. And neither was he. Rafe wanted to give Dulcie the life she was meant to have. The life they were meant to have together.

Don't be so noble. Don't leave me untouched.

The words Dulcie had spoken when he'd explained that he was trying to protect her from the consequences of their lovemaking flashed in his mind. Rafe swore when he resolved this situation, he would never leave her untouched again. But before he could do that, he had to figure out how he and Geoff and Dulcie fit into the puzzle.

Glancing around the room, he saw that Dulcie had unpacked. The dress she'd worn the day before was hanging up. Her bonnet was handing by its strings on the same peg. Her wrapper was lying across the foot of her bed and a pair of house slippers were neatly aligned beneath it.

Her soiled garments were lying in a basket for the maid to collect and take to the laundry. Her hair ribbons were neatly strung over a stand made for that purpose. Her hairbrush, comb, and mirror were lined up on her vanity, as was her box of hairpins, and her jewelry case was locked and stored in her armoire. He knew because he had peeked to see if her wedding dress was hanging there as well. Rafe smiled, recalling the wild disarray they had left in their wake at the cottage, the jumble of clothing lying where they had dropped them in their haste to finally bare each other's flesh and explore the mysteries and hidden treasures their clothing concealed. The passionate chaos of their honeymoon chamber was quite the contrast to this prim, virginal room.

Dulcie's writing desk was bare except for her pen and ink, seal and sealing wax, and her jar of sand. He wasn't surprised to find that everything was neatly in place. But the four books near the back of the desk, standing between heavy brass bookends bearing a seal of Saint George slaying the dragon, did surprise him. Rafe scanned the titles printed on the spines: *The Iliad and the Odyssey* by Homer in classical Greek, *The Aeneid by Virgil* in Latin, *The Complete Works of William Shakespeare* by William Shakespeare, and *Gulliver's Travels* by Jonathan Swift. No wonder her valise had been so heavy. His darling Dulcie had brought his 'petite library'—and the bookends he had received as a gift from his parents upon leaving for university—from his quarters at the garrison home with her, along with her father's copy of *Gulliver's Travels* that Geoff had carried to war with him and Rafe had kept after Geoff's death.

The large casement clock downstairs chimed the quarter hour. A quarter after five. Guilford would be staggering in from a night of losing and debauchery at any minute. And the staff would be sitting down to breakfast at half-past the hour. He still had the table to set and the buffet to lay out. But not before he did what he meant to do.

Rafe went to her vanity, plucked a blue ribbon from her ribbon holder, then returned to Dulcie's bedside and arranged the ribbon into a heart shape on her pillow.

He couldn't say it aloud. But he could show it. Bending over her,

Rafe placed his lips near her ear and whispered, "Sleep well, my love. No more tears. I love you, Dulcie." Admitting to her what he'd known when he had spoken his vows. He loved Dulcie Tennant with all his heart.

DULCIE AWOKE TO FIND A BLUE HEART ON HER PILLOW AND KNEW HER dream had not been a dream. Somehow, by some miracle, Rafe had returned to her. She knew it. She felt it. When he had gathered her into his arms, he hadn't looked the way Rafe had looked when she'd last seen him. His queue was gone, his hair was short, and his face was clean shaven. But his whisper was the same. She had heard him as clear as day. *"Sleep well, my love. No more tears. I love you, Dulcie."* Dulcie bit her bottom lip. *His whisper…*

Dulcie practically leapt out of bed. She flung off her nightgown and pulled on her wrapper, then ran across the room and tugged on the bellpull. Lennie, the housemaid, arrived within minutes with a tray of tea and toast. "I brung your breakfast, miss," she called out as she knocked on the door.

Dulcie admitted her and Lennie brought the tray in and set it down before the fire, glancing at the hearth. "Did you light the fire, miss?"

"No," Dulcie replied. "I thought you did when you opened the shutters."

"No, miss." Lennie shook her head. "It was already lit when I came in to light it."

Dulcie shrugged. "Someone must have."

"Yes, miss. Someone must have," Lennie agreed. "Can I get you anything else, miss?"

"After my tea and toast, I would like a bath," Dulcie said.

"All right, miss." Lennie heaved a tragic sigh. "I'll go put the kettles on and start lugging up the buckets of water."

"Bring the towels, too, please. Oh, and ask one of the footmen to help you carry the water," Dulcie commanded, thankful the maid wasn't the sharpest servant in the household. "He has to bring up the tub anyway."

"Yes, miss," Lennie said. "If you don't mind, I'll ask the dumb one. He may not be too bright, but he's big and strong like an ox."

Dulcie pressed her lips together to keep from grinning. "I agree. The big, dumb one has the broadest back for lifting and carrying. He will be quite suitable to the task. Thank you, Lennie."

Knowing it would take a few minutes to warm the water and haul up the heavy copper bathtub, Dulcie used the precious time wisely. After finishing her toast and taking a few sips of tea, she tended to her needs in the water closet, then sat down at her vanity and brushed her hair until it shone. She tied it up with the blue ribbon she'd found on her pillow. She dabbed a tiny bit of lip pomade in the sheerest of pink tints on her lips, taking special care to add a bit extra to the center of her bottom lip which tended to suffer abuse.

Her eyes were swollen from a fortnight of crying herself to sleep, so Dulcie employed a trick she had read in a ladies magazine years ago. After retrieving her teaspoon, Dulcie opened her bedroom window and placed the teaspoon on the windowsill to chill in the cool morning fog for a minute or two before pressing the cold bowl of the spoon against her eyes to lessen the swelling. The treatment didn't work as well as a compress of tea leaves or chilled cucumber slices, but it was faster, and Dulcie wouldn't take the chance of having the new footman catch her with tea leaves or cucumber slices on her eyes. The added effect of opening the window to the chill of the morning was clearly visible as the tips of her breasts pebbled against the smooth cotton of her wrapper.

But she ran out of time when she heard the sound of heavy footsteps coming up the stairs.

Her bedroom door flew open and a voice boomed, "Good. You've already ordered a bath."

Dulcie whirled around to face the man in the doorway, crossing her arms over her chest to preserve her modesty as she did so. "Uncle Guilford!"

The sight of her uncle framed in the doorway was shocking. Her uncle had once been a younger version of her father, but clearly, the life he was living as Viscount Tennant was a far cry from the one her father or her brother had led.

Guilford's face was bright red. His eyes were bloodshot and red-rimmed as well and the skin of his face had the appearance of wax. He seemed to be perspiring heavily after his trip up the stairs as his hair was damp and stuck to his forehead in places, ruining the effect of its fashionable styling, and he stank of bay rum mixed with an odor she couldn't identify. Guilford looked years older than her father had looked when he died, despite the fact that he had been fifteen years her father's junior and only seven years older than Geoff. He looked the age her father would be if he had lived.

"You'll have plenty of time to get ready," Guilford announced.

"Ready for what?"

"A reception at Lord and Lady Symington's at seven. Dancing at eight. Supper at ten." After making that brusque announcement, he turned on his heel to leave.

"But I have nothing to wear," she told him. "I was ill for a fortnight. My gowns will all have to be altered."

"Send a note around to Parisian Modiste Dress Shop and have someone come make alterations," Guilford ordered.

"No," Dulcie said.

Guilford turned on his heel, his face redder than before. "What did you say?"

"I said no." Dulcie stood her ground. "Parisian Modiste makes your wife's clothes. Not mine."

"Then send for whoever makes yours," Guilford barked. "I'm going to change clothes and head to my club."

"Madam Gabrielle is—"

"Madam Gabrielle is the most expensive dressmaker in town!" he roared.

"I patronize the dressmaker my mother used," Dulcie said. "My father never complained of the cost. Quite the opposite. He was happy to pay to have his girls, as he called us, beautifully dressed." Dulcie knew she was waving a red flag in front of a raging bull, but she didn't care.

"Your father no longer controls the Tennant family purse strings," Guilford snapped. "I do."

"If you're complaining about the cost of my dressmaker, you can't be very proficient at doing so," Dulcie shot back.

Guilford gritted his teeth. "Blast you! One dressmaker is very much like another!"

"Then I'm certain you won't mind shopping at Bee Clarke, Fashionable Boot and Shoe Warehouse, rather than George Hoby's for your boots." Dulcie refused to back down. "My clothes haven't cost you a penny this Season, as you well know. Lady Nesbitt sponsored me and she doesn't settle for inferior couture."

The banging of a large copper tub being carried up the narrow back stairs interrupted the argument as the new footman appeared at the end of the passageway, the tub on his back. The maid followed behind him, carrying two buckets of water. Upon seeing the viscount, they both halted at the end of the passageway.

"Your tub has arrived," Guilford snapped. "Though why you couldn't use the smaller one is beyond me." He gestured for the footman and the maid to continue their tasks.

"I requested the large tub because Lady Nesbitt's physician ordered me to luxuriate in a hot tub to prevent further chance of contagion," Dulcie lied. "I'm to soak for at *least* an hour and it's best no one else come in contact with me while I'm doing it. The physician fears my contagion might be borne in water vapor or steam. That was a condition of my returning home. I assumed you would wish me to follow his instructions. He only released me from his care a day ago and warned me that my contagion might return." She swallowed a triumphant smile as she watched over her uncle's shoulder as the cowardly maid eased her buckets of water to the floor and silently retreated down the back steps at the mere mention of the word *contagion.* "I've no wish to entertain a relapse while under your roof."

"I've never heard of such a thing!" Guilford turned his back to her, narrowly avoiding a collision with the copper tub as the footman prepared to carry it through the door.

"You may consult with Lady Nesbitt or with Sir Walter Grimm if you doubt my veracity." Dulcie addressed her uncle's back. "I'm fairly certain I understood his instructions, but Lady Nesbitt or the physician can certainly confirm them."

"Be dressed and ready by six!" Guilford shouted in reply. "And lock your door while you're *luxuriating* so you don't endanger the rest of the household!" He stabbed a finger in the footman's direction. "And you stand guard up here to make certain no one comes near her!"

The silent footman pointed to the buckets of water the maid had abandoned at the top of the stairs.

"You brought the tub, man! You fill it!"

CHAPTER 32

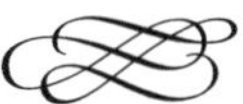

"My heart is wax molded as she pleases,
but enduring as marble to retain."
—Miguel de Cervantes, 1547-1616

Rafe turned the key in the lock and pocketed it. Lifting the last two buckets of cold water, he walked to the tub and poured them in. Crossing to the fireplace he collected the kettles of boiling water, six in all, and added them to the tub. Finished with the task, he tested the temperature, then slowly turned to face his wife. "You rang, Lady Blackburn?" His voice was almost back to normal but was still rusty from disuse.

Dulcie reached up to untie the blue ribbon holding her hair, pulled it out, and handed it to him. "I received your message, Lord Blackburn," she told him, moving closer.

"Did you, my lady?" Rafe slid his hands beneath her wrapper and smiled down at her when he encountered nothing but Dulcie's naked curves. "What did it say?"

"It said you missed me so much you came back from the dead to kiss every inch of me." Dulcie pressed against him, hugging him around the waist, and tilted her face up for his kiss.

Rafe plowed his fingers through her hair, holding her head at the best angle for kissing her. "It said all that?"

Dulcie pursed her lips. "Yes, it did. And it also said you were going to start right away."

Rafe chuckled. "No, my lady."

"No?" She gazed up into his dark brown eyes and saw her face reflected in them.

"No." Rafe bent his head and kissed her so tenderly Dulcie thought her heart might burst from the fullness of it. "My message, my lady," he said between kisses, "said much more than that."

"More?" Dulcie was breathless.

Rafe nodded. "It said I love you, Dulcinea Marjorie Rose Tennant Blackburn. With all my heart and soul. I'll love you to the end of my life and beyond. Because you are the love of my life. My lady, my dear, my better half. "

"Oh, Raphael, I missed you so much!" Dulcie wrapped her arms around his neck and held on until he lifted her. He cradled her bottom in his hands while she locked her legs around his waist.

"You only missed me?" he asked, his mouth hovering a hair's breadth from hers. "I came back from the dead and lugged all those buckets and kettles of water *and* a copper bathtub up three flights of narrow stairs to have you tell me you missed me?"

"I did miss you," she professed, her words coming out in a rush. "I missed you the way a woman misses a man who means everything to her. The man she chose to be her love and the father of her children. The man who opened her world to the possibility of being loved, of loving a very special man, of sharing his life, his home, giving him children, and loving him more than life itself." Her eyes brimmed with unshed tears. "I love you so much I thought I would die from the pain of losing you. I love you so much I wanted to die with you because I didn't want to face the prospect of life without you in it." She took a breath. "I love you Raphael Simon John Blackburn, my dear lord rogue, my better half. I will love you to the end of my life and beyond. Only you."

He kissed her. And then he carried her to her tiny bed and kissed every inch of her and once he'd covered the complete landscape of Dulcie's body from mountains to canyons and everything in between, Rafe carried her to the bathtub and bathed everything he'd kissed, then stripped off his livery and joined her in the bath.

Dulcie gasped when he removed his wig and popped it on the bedpost.

"What did they do to your hair?" she wailed as she tried to make room for him in the large tub. She ended up sitting on his lap, straddling him while she bathed him.

"They cut it off so I could wear the proper wig and uniform of a British soldier returning to his barracks in London," Rafe replied, before he told her about his escape from the garrison following his hanging. He told her everything except the identities of Weymouth's associates.

"They saved you."

"They did," he agreed. "And now, we've got to save you from whatever your uncle has in mind."

"Shh." Dulcie put her fingers to his lips. "Don't think about that now. Just love me, Raphael." She kissed him. "Besides, you've already saved me, Lord Blackburn," Dulcie reminded him "when you married me."

"And I'd do it all over again tomorrow, but neither one of us will be safe until we find out who's behind this conspiracy. I can take care of myself, but I worry about you every second we're apart."

"We know who's behind the conspiracy," Dulcie said. "Guilford. He's the one who killed my brother and my parents…"

"Sweet Dulcie, my love, it isn't that simple. We may know in our hearts that Guilford is behind their deaths, but we suspect he didn't act alone. And we still have no proof and he hasn't given up on his plans for you. You heard him." He kissed her hungrily, fiercely. "My heart dropped when I heard you challenging him. Doing what I asked you not to do. He's dangerous. And he has dangerous partners working with him, even if we don't know who they are yet," Rafe reminded her. "Someone arranged the ambush that killed Geoff because Guilford needed him dead. Just the way he must have hired, or coerced, someone to blow up your parents' yacht because he couldn't be viscount unless they were dead..."

"I don't want to think about it," Dulcie said. "Not now. I only want to love you and to have you love me while we have these precious moments together. When I realized who you were, I couldn't stand the thought of you being downstairs in the men's dormitory. So close to me, but unreachable. I want to be with you. I want us to be together."

"I want the same, sweetheart. I want my life back. *My* life. Not John March's life. I want to introduce you as my wife. I want to be Raphael Blackburn, seventh Earl of Blackburn. I want to clear my name and come back from the dead for good. I want us to have the life you dreamed of. The life I dreamed of. I can't do that as long as I'm dead."

Dulcie moved against him. "You're far from dead, Major Lord Raphael Blackburn." She gazed at him from beneath her eyelashes. "And I am about to prove it."

They made love in the tub and on her tiny bed, and finally on the carpet before they rose from the floor, toweled each other off, and began to dress.

"I don't want you to go," Rafe told her.

"And I don't want to go." Dulcie was standing in brief French drawers and a silk chemise. She positioned her short stays in place and backed up to Rafe. "Lace me, please."

Rafe complied. "Dulcie, please be careful tonight. I don't like you driving off with him."

"You'll be on the coach with me."

"I'll be on the back perch," Rafe said. "Or running along beside the coach. Either way, I won't be in a position to help you if Guilford should..."

"He won't," she insisted. "What can he do in a coach?"

Rafe arched his eyebrow, reminding her of all the things they had done in a coach.

"Symington House is two streets over from here. It's a five minute walk. If Guilford and I are gone and Mavis is asleep in the other wing, you'll have the opportunity to return and search Papa's library for proof."

"His desk is locked," Rafe told her. "I tried it last night."

"Papa always kept a spare key in the secret compartment in Maman's writing desk in the green salon. The drawer on the left has a false front. It looks exactly like the drawer on the right, but if you press the bottom, the little door will open and the key will fall into your hand. Papa had Maman's writing desk drawer modified because no one would ever expect him to hide a desk key there. Maman's writing desk never held anything except stationery and supplies. Geoff had the only other key to Papa's desk. I don't know what happened to it. It wasn't among the items the army returned."

"Neither was *Gulliver's Travels*." Rafe's voice held a husky note as he glanced at the four books between the bookends on Dulcie's desk.

"I know. You kept it because it belonged to Geoff. Just as I kept the books you treasured." She reached up and placed her palm against his smooth cheek. "I liked the stubble. It was roguish. But you're even more handsome without it." She smiled. "But I'll always be partial to the rogue—a gentleman earl and cavalry office—I met in that military prison."

"And now, a footman." Rafe gazed at her. "I still don't like the idea of you going to the Symington's with Guilford, but we need to know what he's planned and what he did. We owe it to Geoff and the men who died in the ambush, to your parents and to the others who died when your father's yacht exploded."

Dulcie shook her head, clearly confused. "My father's yacht didn't explode."

"Sweet Dulcie, there was no storm. The yacht exploded." He frowned. "Who told you the yacht sank in a storm?"

"Guilford," she breathed.

"And he never told you the port authorities determined the boat exploded?"

"No." She shook her head, then gazed up at Rafe. "I was going to check the clipping in my books of clippings, but I haven't gone up to the schoolroom to retrieve them yet."

Rafe frowned. "What books of clippings?"

"I started clipping articles of interest in the *Times* and pasting them in my books for Geoff, so he could catch up on what was happening while he was gone."

"What sorts of articles?"

She shrugged. "War news. Casualty Lists. Obituaries. Weddings. Births. The assassination of the Prime Minister Lord Perceval, the account of my parents' accident, although I didn't clip and paste that one. I just couldn't bear it, so I asked Hatfield to do it, but he must have been interrupted because when I checked later, that page was blank." She gazed up at Rafe. "The boat wasn't Papa's, you know. He wanted to buy it. That's the reason they took it out."

"He and your mother?"

"And the man who was going to sell it to Papa. He and his captain were on the boat, along with our captain. Papa never told me his name, but the man designed steamboats. Papa was so excited. And I was so disappointed not to be able to go. Papa so wanted a steam-powered yacht."

"How do you know the key to your father's desk is still hidden?" Rafe asked.

"Papa never locked his desk unless Guilford was in residence," Dulcie said. "There was never any need."

"Had he always done that?"

"No." Dulcie rummaged through her armoire. "Oh, good. Here it is." She pulled out a silk evening gown in pale yellow. "He used to trust Guilford. He was Papa's baby brother, after all." She pursed her lips in thought. "Until Papa started having his accidents. After that, Papa always locked his desk and would give the key to Maman to put away. But he always forgot to retrieve the key when he'd go to his desk to work. Maman kept the key hidden. Papa finally had the drawer in

Maman's writing desk modified by the furniture maker. Guilford doesn't know about it." She held the evening gown in front of her. "What do you think?"

"I think you will be the loveliest lady there." He pulled on his shirt. It stuck to his back where it was still damp from his bath. He tucked the tails in his breeches and slipped on his waistcoat. "Or anywhere else. But I'll always be partial to your wedding dress."

"I will, too." She pulled on the gown, then presented her back to Rafe so he could hook the hook and tie the tapes. "This dress is from three Seasons ago," she admitted. "But I was in mourning and never got the chance to wear it. Fortunately, it still fits and is still in style." She smoothed the dress over her hips and thighs, then sat down and pulled on her stockings, along with silk and lace garters adorned with tiny embroidered rosebuds. The gown still fit very well, clinging in all the right places, just like the green muslin had fit a fortnight ago.

Studying one of her shapely legs as she extended it, Rafe waggled his eyebrows at her. "I approve. But only I get to slide them off."

Dulcie's throaty giggle was provocative. "When it comes to undressing, I feel about you the way I feel about my dressmaker."

"Oh?" Rafe's raspy whisper was full of promise.

"Only the best will do." She slipped her feet into yellow silk slippers. "And you, my love, are the best."

He reached beneath her hair to cup the back of her head, then leaned down and kissed her until they were both breathless and wanting more. "You've nothing to compare me to."

"There is no comparison," she assured him. "You're the best for me." Dulcie sat down at her vanity and began piling her hair up and securing it with pins. Rafe tied his neckcloth in the serviceable style required at Tennant House and pinned it into place before handing Dulcie a yellow ribbon for her hair. Dulcie wrapped it around her bundle of curls and tied it into place. "My jewelry case is in the armoire. Will you get it for me?"

He retrieved the case and watched as Dulcie selected a topaz necklace and matching earrings from the meager selection. She hooked the earrings in her ear lobes and held the necklace in place while Rafe fastened the clasp for her.

"If you ever tire of being a footman, you'd make a wonderful ladies' maid," she teased.

"I make an even better husband." He nuzzled the side of her neck beneath her ear, then kissed the place he'd nuzzled.

"There's no question about that," shc told him.

Their gazes met in the mirror.

"Rafe, I must do this. I must know why Guilford is insisting I accompany him tonight when he's never asked me to accompany them anywhere."

Rafe replaced her jewelry case in the armoire. "I know." He didn't like it. He didn't want her alone with her uncle. He didn't want her where he couldn't see her. Not because he didn't trust Dulcie. But because he didn't trust Guilford. Rafe was terrified of losing her. "I won't be far away."

"You have to search the library," she reminded him. "You have to find something. Some note. Some scrap of paper. *Something.*"

Rafe glanced at the mantel clock. Dulcie's hour of luxuriating in the bath had turned into two and a half. Their time together was running out. It was time for him to become John March again and begin emptying the tub they'd put to such good use. He smiled. They were both exceptionally clean and smelled of citrus soap.

He pulled Dulcie into his arms, hugged her close, then let her go. "I'll search the library."

"Be careful," she pleaded. "You're not a cat, you know. You don't have nine lives. And I couldn't bear to lose you again."

"I'll be careful," he promised. "Especially since I'm down to eight lives."

"You'll be down to seven if you're caught in my bedchamber like this. I love you, Raphael."

"And I love you, sweet Dulcie. You be careful, too. If you feel unsure or uneasy about anything, plead illness, fatigue, anything at all, but make your excuses and leave."

Dulcie nodded.

"Promise me," he said as he pulled on his coat and put on his wig.

"I promise, Mister Charm."

He arched an eyebrow.

"Charm is an anagram of March," Dulcie pointed out before handing him two empty buckets so he could resume his duties as her devoted footman.

~

Rafe made seven trips from Dulcie's room to the scullery, using wooden buckets to dump her bathwater, then returned for the copper tub. Rafe deliberately splashed water onto his coat as he emptied the tub in the scullery.

"You took long enough," the butler barked at him as Rafe finished drying the interior of the tub and returning it to its customary place.

Fearing they'd been found out, Rafe's heart began a rapid tattoo. He'd checked the passageway and the backstairs when he'd unlocked Dulcie's bedroom door. And again when he'd begun bailing the dirty bathwater from the tub. But it seemed Dulcie's clever ruse had worked like a charm. There'd been no sign of any of the household staff when Rafe had made his trips up and down the stairs. The staff was giving him a wide berth and Rafe felt certain the cowardly housemaid had spread the word about the dangers of attending the young lady while she was in her bath.

While they might wonder how the young miss had managed to dress herself without help, Rafe felt certain none of the staff would volunteer to help her. He couldn't regret the time he'd spent making love to his wife, but neither could he deny the risk they had taken. Rafe wasn't afraid for himself, but of what might happen to Dulcie if they were discovered while under her uncle's roof. They would have to be more careful. He couldn't risk losing Dulcie. Couldn't risk failing her.

Rafe pointed to the empty buckets, kettles, and tub, then glanced at the housemaid who had abandoned her duties and shrugged, as if to say he'd been forced to do her job as well as his own.

"His lordship has returned and just rang from the library," the butler informed him with a sniff. "Make haste. It's your turn to attend him."

Rafe cast a sullen look at the other footman to hide the fact that he was more than happy to be summoned to *his lordship's* library. He wiped his hands on the damp towel, thrust it at the butler, and hurried out of the scullery toward the library.

"You're not presentable, March," Guilford said when Rafe stood before the man's heavy mahogany desk.

Rafe pantomimed filling and emptying the bathtub and splashing water on himself.

"Never mind," Guilford ordered. "Change your coat and waistcoat and get your hat and be on the coach in five minutes." He shoved a sheaf of papers into the top desk drawer, took out a key and locked it, then stood up from behind the desk. "I'm going upstairs to fetch my niece."

Before Guilford could reach the library door, a husky female voice said, "There's no need, Uncle. I'm here."

Rafe jerked up his head. Dulcie was standing in the passageway between the green salon and the library. She was wearing her hooded cape and was in the process of pulling on her gloves.

Guilford turned to Rafe. "You! Go change. And if you're not at the coach by the time we get there, you'll have to run to Lord and Lady Symington's."

Rafe moved toward the back stairs at the same time Dulcie moved forward. He stepped aside to allow her to pass, but she deliberately bumped into him, dropping her glove in the process.

"Oh, March, I'm sorry! I'm so clumsy." She gave her uncle an abashed look. "It was my fault, Uncle. I stepped into him."

"Next time, watch out for the lady," Guilford snapped at Rafe. "Now, pick up her glove, you oaf, and go make yourself presentable."

Rafe retrieved her glove, felt the surprising weight inside it, and neatly palmed the key. He bowed as he returned her glove.

"Thank you, March," she said.

Rafe didn't reply. He simply bobbed his head and hurried away. He didn't grin until he reached the bottom of the stairs leading to the men's dormitory. He would have to keep his eye on his countess or Weymouth would be recruiting her to convert the Charlotte Society from a needy soldier rescue into a ladies' spying operation.

CHAPTER 33

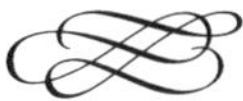

"At this hour
Lie at my mercy all mine enemies."
—William Shakespeare, 1564-1616

"You look exceptionally lovely tonight, Dulcie," Guilford said. "Although I've yet to see the gown."

"Thank you, Uncle," Dulcie murmured, uncomfortable with small talk from her uncle. He had barely taken notice of her since he'd moved back into Tennant House and taken over. She couldn't help but fear this evening was the culmination of Guilford's threat to marry her off at the end of the Season.

The Season generally lasted longer, but the weather this year had been miserable. Nothing but rain and fog and dense dark clouds. Most of the ton were packing up to return to their country houses. Lord and Lady Symington's gala heralded the end of the 'official' Season and she was attending it with Guilford. Dulcie feared that didn't bode well for the evening. And she prayed Rafe found what he needed to present as proof and that Lady Nesbitt could persuade the Queen to help them. She shuddered. At least, she didn't have to worry about locating Rafe's body. His head was still firmly attached to his body and, except for his voice, everything was in perfect working order. She smiled to herself at the memory of just how perfect.

"I trust the dressmaker made the necessary alterations to your gown," Guilford remarked.

"And I trust you had a profitable afternoon at cards," Dulcie retorted, pushing her uncle despite Rafe's warning not to, but unable to stop herself.

"What I do at my club in the afternoons is none of your affair," Guilford said. "Just as your room and board, care and clothes, will no longer be my affair soon. But tonight it is and I asked about the alterations to your gown."

"As it turned out, there was no need for alterations. This gown is from my wardrobe from three Seasons ago. I had ordered my wardrobe and Madam Gabrielle had delivered it, but I was unable to take part in the Season."

Guilford frowned. "Why was that?"

"Don't you remember?" she asked, surprised that he missed the significance of the date. "It's the year you became the viscount. The year my brother, Geoff, was murdered."

Guilford's florid face grew even redder. "Your brother was killed in the war in Spain, as you well know. He wasn't murdered."

"Wasn't he?" she challenged.

"No, he was not. He was ambushed in a raid by renegade mercenaries, along with three other men."

"I suppose it was just a terrible tragedy. Just like Papa and Maman dying when an unexpected storm caused their boat to break up and sink."

"Exactly," Guilford replied. "But that was years ago, Dulcie. It's time you put the past behind you. You're not a child any longer. You are a woman grown."

"What did you mean when you said I would no longer be your affair?" Dulcie asked.

"It means exactly what you think it means," he said. "It means I signed your marriage contracts this afternoon at my club before my card game. The gentleman asked to meet you here tonight before your engagement is made public."

Dulcie felt the color drain from her own face. "And just how much money did my sale bring into the Tennant accounts?"

"Twenty thousand pounds."

"Will that be enough to pay all your gaming debts?" Dulcie met his angry gaze without flinching.

"My gaming debts are none of your concern!"

"I'll take that as a no."

"Twenty thousand pounds is just the start. Once you're safely married, he'll be in a position to pay *all* my debts whenever I need him to," Guilford boasted.

"He must be very wealthy and well connected," Dulcie guessed.

"Not yet, but he will be very soon."

"Why would a gentleman who will soon become very wealthy be obliged to pay your debts whenever you need him to?" Dulcie didn't realize she'd spoken the question aloud until Guilford answered it.

"I did him a substantial favor a few years ago. And he repaid me by doing me one."

Dulcie slowly nodded. "And now, you're doing him another one."

"Very good, Dulcie." Guilford's answer was patronizing at best and maddening at worst. "You are more astute than I imagined."

"May I ask the name of this paragon of a financial benefactor?"

"The Earl of Halton," he crowed. "Heir to the Marquess of Lancaster."

Recognizing the name, Dulcie frowned in bewilderment. "But the Earl of Halton is dead."

"The *previous* Earl of Halton is dead. The current one is his younger brother and he is very much alive."

"I'm not acquainted with the current Earl of Halton."

"You will be," Guilford promised. "Because he's very eager to meet —and marry—you."

~

RAFE WAITED UNTIL HE HEARD THE FRONT DOOR CLOSE AND THE BUTLER, Bertram, head downstairs to the kitchen where supper was about to be dished up. If he had calculated correctly, he'd dawdled just long enough while changing out of his damp coat to miss his ride on *his lordship's* coach.

"Mister March," Bertram said as he met Rafe going up the stairs. "Cook is putting supper on the table."

Rafe shook his head, then pulled out his book and pencil and printed: *Lord Symington party. Where?*

"Ah, that's right! Lord Tennant directed you to attend the coach. He said he'd sent you to change your coat."

Rafe nodded.

The butler provided the address, then added, "You won't have any trouble finding it. There will be a long line of coaches and closed carriages and a crush of people."

Rafe wrote: *Thank you, sir.*

"Good luck, Mister March. I'm afraid you're in for a very long night with very little to do but wait," Bertram warned before continuing down the stairs.

Rafe waited until the butler was gone, then slipped into the library, unlocked the top drawer of the desk and removed the sheaf of papers Guilford had stuffed into the drawer. He quickly thumbed through the pages, searching for names and signatures.

When he found what he was looking for, he took a deep breath to calm himself. But a deep breath couldn't calm his racing heart or stifle the outrage coursing through his veins.

The papers Guilford had secured in the locked drawer were a marriage contract between the ninth Viscount Tennant, guardian of Miss Dulcinea Marjorie Rose Tennant, spinster, securing her hand in marriage to the sixteenth Earl of Halton in exchange for the sum of twenty thousand pounds, to change hands upon the announcement of the engagement. There were other conditions—dowry, pin money, property—but Rafe paid little attention to them because he intended to make certain those terms were never applied. The contracts had been signed earlier in the afternoon and witnessed by gentlemen Rafe recognized as friends of Guilford's.

Guilford Tennant's plan was to do exactly what he'd told Dulcie he would do at the end of the Season. He was going to marry her off to the highest bidder. And the contracts had already been signed. If Guilford was desperate for the twenty thousand pounds, the marriage would take place within a day or two at most.

And since he had been rescued from the hangman's noose, Rafe presented a problem for Dulcie. If she refused, her uncle could, and most likely would, do her harm. And if she agreed to the marriage as Rafe had suggested she do, she would be guilty of bigamy, which didn't create difficulties among the lower classes, but caused scandal and ruination among the upper classes. And he feared for her life if she should be blamed for causing a scandal for Guilford Tennant—especially if it cost the man twenty thousand pounds. And the scandal and ruination of the reputation of the Earl of Halton might be equally dangerous for her. Depending on who the Earl of Halton was.

Rafe slowly relaxed his hand. He had crumpled the papers in his clenched fist without realizing it. He needed help and he knew just who to ask. there was only one man for the job.

HENDERSON ANSWERED THE DOOR UPON RAFE'S FIRST KNOCK. "MISTER March."

"I need to speak with Shepherdston," Rafe said, speaking to Henderson in his normal voice for the first time. "On an urgent matter."

"I'm sorry, Mister March, but Lord and Lady Shepherdston are attending Lord and Lady Symington's gala tonight. They left a quarter of an hour ago."

Rafe swore briefly, then raked a hand through his hair. "That's all right, Mister Henderson. I'm on my way there myself."

The butler gave his attire a skeptical look. "Dressed like *that,* Mister March?"

"I'm supposed to be on the perch on Lord Tennant's coach, but something else came up. I had hoped a footman might be able to go where a gentleman cannot."

"Not unless you are wearing Symington livery. All other footmen are consigned to their coaches," Henderson told him.

"Are there any Free Fellow associates who might be able to assist me tonight?" Rafe asked.

Henderson shook his head. "*Everyone* is at Lord and Lady Symington's gala," he said. "Even Lord Wellington is attending. And the Prince Regent is expected to make an appearance." He tilted his head to study Rafe. "May I suggest that if you are going to Lord Symington's gala, you go as the gentleman you are instead of the excellent footman you've become?"

"But I haven't any formal clothes. Except in my London town house across the Park from here, but even those garments would be five years or more out of fashion."

"Follow me, my lord," Henderson invited, gesturing toward the stairs. "We kept the set of Lord Courtland's formal wear you borrowed the night you arrived. They're clean and pressed and hanging upstairs. Let's get you dressed."

Minutes later, Henderson and Rafe were on their way back downstairs with Rafe wearing Courtland's exquisitely tailored extra set of formal clothes from his small clothes to the diamond stickpin in his cravat. Even the shoes were a perfect fit.

They had nearly reached the bottom of the staircase when the doorbell rang once again. Henderson opened the door.

An elderly woman in formal evening wear stood in the doorway.

"How can I help you, madam?" Henderson asked.

"I am Lady Edward Nesbitt," she proclaimed. "I was told by Lord Weymouth that if I needed to get in touch with him, I was to contact Lord or Lady Anthony Carlisle or Lord Shepherdston or his butler." She sized Henderson up. "I presume you are the butler."

"I am," Henderson replied. "Please, come in, my lady."

Lady Nesbitt stepped into the entryway. "I should like to speak to Lord Shepherdston."

"I am afraid Lord and Lady Shepherdston are attending Lord and Lady Symington's—"

"I know," Lady Nesbitt said briskly, cutting him off. "*Everyone* is at Lord and Lady Symington's tonight. I've already been to the Carlisle's and the Tennant's."

"The Tennant's?" Rafe asked.

"Yes," Lady Nesbitt said. "I called there to speak with Miss Tennant. I have some items of hers she may need. I was told she and Lord Tennant were attending the Symington gala and I became concerned."

"Concerned how, my lady?" Rafe asked.

"For her health, of course." Lady Nesbitt leaned closer to get a good look at Rafe. "Who are you, young man?"

Rafe glanced at Henderson. "I am Raphael Blackburn, seventh Earl of Blackburn."

Lady Nesbitt took a deep breath, then let it out in a snort. "Pish! Major Lord Raphael Blackburn was hanged at His Majesty's Garrison on the Isle of Wight a fortnight ago."

Rafe nodded. "You are correct, Lady Nesbitt, But I survived the hanging and have been masquerading as a footman in the Tennant household for the past two days in order to protect my wife from her uncle after she returned from her visit with you. Guilford is scheming to force her into marriage with the Earl of Halton for twenty thousand pounds." He patted his coat pocket. "I have a copy of the marriage contract here."

"How on earth did you get it?" she asked.

Rafe answered honestly. "I pilfered Guilford's desk in the library at Tennant House while I was looking for proof that he murdered the seventh and eighth Viscounts Tennant. That's when I found the marriage agreement."

"Did you find proof of his other crimes as well?" she asked.

"Because I spent the afternoon in audience with Her Majesty, the Queen, and His Highness, the Prince Regent, securing a posthumous Petition of Clemency for Major Lord Raphael Blackburn, seventh Earl of Blackburn. If you are that man and you survived a hanging, I shall request the Queen and the Prince Regent strike the word *posthumous* so clemency is granted to the living man."

"The fact that I opened the desk with the seventh viscount's hidden key proves that Guilford conspired to murder the eighth viscount. There were only two keys. One owned by Viscount William Tennant and the other owned by his son and heir, Viscount Geoffrey Tennant. Lord William's key was in its hiding place at Tennant House until Dul—Lady Blackburn retrieved it and gave it to me. Lord Geoff's key was in his possession in Spain. It was on his person when he was ambushed and taken off of him as he lay mortally wounded. But that very same key is now in Guilford Tennant's possession. My solicitor has the enumeration of the items Geoffrey Tennant brought with him to Spain. And the enumeration of what was sent home to his family. That key, engraved with the purchaser number and the number two was listed as one of Geoffrey Tennant's possessions on the first enumeration of the personal items he took to Spain. It was absent from the enumeration of the items that were returned to his family. So how could Guilford be in possession of Geoffrey's key when Lieutenant Tennant was wearing it on a chain around his neck when he left on patrol in Spain unless Guilford arranged for it to be taken by the men Guilford paid to ambush his nephew?"

"And how do I know you are who you say you are?" Lady Nesbitt asked.

"Lord Weymouth, Lord Wellington, and the Prince Regent all know me, as well as Archibald Gunn, my solicitor, who's known me all my life." His voice softened. "And my wife knows me."

"Archibald Gunn, you say?" Lady Nesbitt echoed, tilting her head in a way that reminded Rafe of a coquettish little bird.

Rafe nodded. "He was my father's solicitor and his father's before him."

Breaking into a mysterious smile, Lady Nesbitt took hold of Rafe's arm. "Come with me, young man. We're going to the gala."

As Rafe approached her coach, Lady Nesbitt's footman opened the door and handed her into the vehicle. Rafe climbed in behind her.

As he settled onto the seat, Rafe recognized a voice from his past.

"Master Rafe! You're alive!"

CHAPTER 34

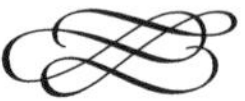

"I would not wish any companion in the world but you."
—William Shakespeare, 1564-1616

Guilford took Dulcie by the arm as their coach rolled to a stop behind a long line of carriages in front of the entrance to Lord and Lady Symington's home.

"Open the door! We'll get out here!" Guilford shouted to the coachman when the footman failed to open it. Unwilling to let go of Dulcie's arm, Guilford reached through the window and opened the door himself. He kicked the steps into place, and stepped down, pulling Dulcie with him.

She missed the top step and stumbled. Muttering curses beneath his breath, Guilford clamped his hand around her arm in a savage grip and all but dragged her to the receiving line.

Dulcie gritted her teeth against the pain as her uncle brushed past the line of guests waiting to be announced, guiding Dulcie to the head of the line and into the reception room crowded with the elite of London society.

A liveried footman approached to take her velvet cape. Dulcie glanced at him, hoping she'd find Raphael, but the footman was wearing Symington livery.

"Uncle, let go of me!" Dulcie tried to pull away, but Guilford only tightened his grip on her, digging his fingertips into her tender flesh so tightly she knew she would have bruises later. "The footman is waiting for my cape," she said through clenched teeth. "I can't remove it unless you let go of my arm." She wanted to run and would have run into the arms of the Prince Regent himself if Guilford hadn't wrenched her left arm up behind her back. The pain was agonizing, but she refused to cry out.

The Symington's butler stepped forward and asked Guilford's name, before announcing, "Lord Tennant and Miss Tennant."

Hearing the announcement, Rafe elbowed his way through the crowd of guests, while Lady Nesbitt swatted her way through the crush with her fan. Rafe had leapt out of their coach before it stopped rolling when he caught sight of a flash of the pale-yellow silk and white stockings he'd helped Dulcie put on a few hours before. He ran across the lawn, following Guilford and Dulcie past the line of guests and into the reception room.

"Let her go!" Rafe ordered.

Guilford turned, his eyes widening as he discovered that not only could his new footman talk, but that the man was garbed as a gentleman from the top of his perfectly cropped hair to the polished tips of his shoes. He blinked in disbelief. *"March?"*

"Rafe!" Dulcie tried to twist out of her uncle's grip so she could run to Rafe, but Guilford refused to let her go.

"Unhand her, Guilford," Rafe repeated, his voice stronger than before.

"Who are you to order me about?" Guilford demanded. "You're nothing but a lowly footman masquerading as a gentleman." He waved the butler over. "Call the Runners," he directed. "This man is a footman in my household and is clearly masquerading as a gentleman for nefarious purposes. Robbery perhaps, or even kidnapping."

Rafe shook his head. "No, Guilford. I am a *gentleman* who has been masquerading as a footman in your household. That's not a crime, but murder is. So do call the Runners. By all means."

"There's no need for that." Lady Nesbitt drew up beside Rafe with Archibald Gunn following at her heels. She was a bit winded, but ready to enter the fray. "The Marines are here." She directed the gentlemen's attention to the contingent of uniformed marines forming a circle around the perimeter of the reception room.

"Aunt Augusta!" Dulcie cried.

"*Aunt* Augusta?" Guilford scoffed. "This woman is nothing to you."

"I'll have you know that Dulcie is now my great niece," Lady Nesbitt declared. "I adopted her while she was recovering from her recent illness at my home when you and your wife refused to allow her to recover in yours."

"Let her go," Rafe repeated, looking Guilford in the eye. "I won't ask again."

Guilford tightened his hold. Dulcie let out a whimper of pain.

And Rafe stepped forward and punched Guilford in the face with the right cross he'd honed to perfection at Gentleman John Jackson's Boxing Parlor in his younger years.

Guilford's knees buckled. He was forced to let go of Dulcie's arm as he went down, clutching his bloody nose. Dulcie ran to Rafe.

"Are you all right?" Rafe asked, searching her face.

Dulcie nodded, then turned to kick her uncle in the chest as hard as she could with the toe of her delicate slipper.

Never one to be left out, Lady Nesbitt rapped the man on the head with her fan.

"Bravo, my dear," Gunn said, beaming his approval.

"Who are you?" Guilford wailed at Rafe, still clutching his nose, which was dripping blood all over the pristine marble floor.

"A criminal escaped from His Majesty's Garrison on the Isle of Wight. A criminal condemned to hang," said a sneering voice Rafe immediately recognized. "He is Major Lord Raphael Blackburn, seventh Earl of Blackburn."

The crowd began to buzz with excitement in anticipation of a confrontation between Raging Rafe, the Angel of Death, Waterloo's

Savior of the Fourth Horse Artillery, and Cornelius Fenton, the sitting Earl of Halton.

Rafe whirled around. "Fenton!"

"It's Halton now," Cornelius Fenton informed him. "Sixteenth Earl of Halton."

"But you were Fenton the first time I met you," Rafe said.

"Wrong," Fenton said. "I was Halton then, too. But I was forced to wait nine months before I could use the title. My late brother, the fifteenth earl, had a wife. I was forced to wait until we knew she wasn't carrying his heir. Lucky for me, he bred three little girls." He sneered at Rafe. "I thought you'd joined your friend, Tennant, in the afterlife."

"And I thought you were hiding beneath a rock," Rafe retorted. "Afraid to slither out. The way you were afraid to show your face the last time I saw you."

"I'm surprised you dare show yours," Fenton taunted. "The last time I saw you, you had a noose around your neck. A pity you'll have to repeat the experience as soon as I notify the authorities of your miraculous resurrection. You were condemned to hang by the neck until dead."

"For disobeying an order by my superior officer because he refused to lead the charge or allow any of his cavalry officers to do it."

"Precisely. You disobeyed my direct order," Fenton said, the bloodthirsty glint in his eye deepening. "On the field of battle."

"I was wrong about you, Fenton," Rafe admitted. "I thought you were simply a coward. I didn't realize you were a traitor until I spent ten months confined to the garrison and had time to think."

"Careful, Blackburn," Fenton warned, "you'll soon be going back to that garrison to be executed and this time it will be by firing squad."

"I spent ten months wondering what you had against Geoffrey Tenant and why you arranged for him to die in that ambush. Tonight, I discovered it," Rafe said.

"What did you discover? That I took a fancy to his sister? That my father approached her father on my behalf during her first Season, and that my offer was summarily refused? Or that I approached her brother once he became viscount, and I was about to become the earl and was once again refused? Fortunately, the current viscount was more amenable to my offer." Fenton turned his oily gaze on Dulcie. "And you, my dear will be fortunate to have me for I am about to become a marquess." He smiled at Dulcie. "I arrived late because tragedy has befallen my father. He was attacked by his valet earlier this evening and stabbed to death."

Dulcie was stunned. She hadn't known her father had refused an offer for her hand in marriage and she certainly hadn't known Geoff had refused a second offer from that very same suitor until now.

Rafe shook his head. "I had no idea you'd offered for the lady. Or that you bore an obvious *tendresse* for her. I followed a different trail." He smiled at Fenton. "I knew Guilford was suspect in his brother's death and his nephew's. With them gone, he would become viscount and get his hands on the money he needed to pay the gaming debts his brother and nephew refused to pay. What I didn't understand was why you were so determined to get rid of me. So I had my solicitor look into your finances. And he discovered you were in a unique position to influence the outcome of the war on the Peninsula and at Waterloo. You were being paid to make certain the only man capable of winning the war wouldn't."

A gasp went through the crowd of guests at Rafe's accusation.

Rafe continued. "I wasn't your enemy until you countermanded my orders and ordered Geoffrey Tennant to lead that patrol. I didn't know you. I'd never met you. I didn't know you were the Earl of Halton, who took money from the bankers backing Bonaparte to ensure that Lord Wellington lost."

Cornelius Fenton lunged for him.

Rafe stepped in front of Dulcie and caught Fenton with a left uppercut.

The Prince Regent leaned toward the Duke of Wellington. "More fisticuffs, sir. I'll put a hundred pounds on Blackburn."

Wellington disagreed. "I'm not a gambling man, but a hundred pounds on a man who survived a hanging? I would wager at least a thousand. After all, he led the charge that sliced the Imperial French Guard to ribbons."

"Get up, man!" the Regent shouted at Fenton. "Show us some fight." Leaning to his left, the Prince Regent complimented his hostess. "I do so adore galas and boxing. I never imagined combining the two. But now they will be all the rage." He signaled the marines who had accompanied him. "Place those two"—he pointed to Guilford and Cornelius Fenton—"under arrest for murder and treason."

"You cannot arrest me, Your Highness!" Fenton protested. "I'm an earl. I've done nothing to warrant arrest for treason. Treason is a hanging offense."

"Your Highness," Dulcie said. "My uncle and Fenton were working together. They did favors for each other. They murdered my parents and the late Earl Halton. My father was going to purchase the boat from Lord Halton. They took it out for a trial run and Lord Halton was on the boat with my parents when it exploded."

Rafe nodded. "When Earl Halton died, his younger brother became earl. When the seventh Viscount Tennant died, his son became earl. And less than a year later, that son was killed in an ambush in Spain." Rafe paused. "Fenton arranged the eighth Viscount Tennant's death for Guilford, so Guilford would become viscount. Because Guilford had arranged the explosion of the boat that killed the late Earl Halton so Cornelius could become earl." Rafe shook his head. "I'm afraid I don't know which one arranged tonight's murder of Fenton's father, the Marquess of Lancaster."

"I do." The crowd gasped again as the Marquess of Lancaster himself came strolling through their midst. Fenton took a step backward, paling as if he had seen an actual ghost. The marquess shook a finger at his son. "It was that misbegotten whelp. Unfortunately for him, my valet owed his loyalty to me instead of him and confessed that my son had paid him a handsome sum to murder me tonight. From this moment forward, I disown the murderous and traitorous whoreson." He drew nearer to take Dulcie's hand, bringing it to his lips for a gallant kiss. "I will say one thing for my son. He recognized a young lady of quality when he saw her." He glanced at the Regent. "We must find her a worthy husband."

"Thank you, Lord Lancaster," Dulcie said. "But I have already found the perfect match for me. A most worthy husband." She gazed up at Rafe, blinking back happy tears. "My love, my guardian angel, my own Lord Rogue."

The Prince Regent pinned Rafe with his piercing gaze. "What have you to say about that, Lord Blackburn?"

"I would not wish any love in the world but hers. She is my dear, my better half and I am a better man for loving her." He gazed down at Dulcie. "I could not love anyone more."

"Then it's fortunate that we have granted you amnesty from all charges," the Prince Regent announced.

"Amnesty, Your Highness?" Dulcie gazed up at the Prince Regent, her eyes shining with hope.

"Yes, dear lady," he said. "Complete and utter clemency from all spurious charges brought against him." Stepping forward, the Regent presented Rafe with the wedding band Lady Nesbitt had entrusted to him during their audience earlier in the afternoon. "I believe this belongs to your bride, Lord Blackburn. I suggest you return it to its rightful place."

Rafe slipped the gold band on Dulcie's finger, then gazed down at her beautiful face, profoundly aware of how close they had come to losing one another. "I love you, Lady Blackburn," he whispered.

"And I love you, Lord Blackburn, with all my heart."

"Kiss her, man," the Prince Regent urged.

Rafe eagerly complied with the royal command.

The Prince Regent beamed. "And now that the two of you have sealed your vows before your Regent and these worthy guests, we shall take great pleasure in making the announcement and present Lord and Lady Blackburn, the seventh Earl and Countess of Blackburn, to the guests assembled here tonight as the first Marquess and Marchioness of Blackburn."

Rafe turned to the Regent. "Marquess, sir?"

"Indeed, Lord Blackburn. Your actions at Waterloo helped save

England at great risk to your own reputation and life. And your actions this evening saved your lovely bride from the evil machinations of her murderous uncle and his ally. You've done us a very great service by ridding us of the traitorous peers in our midst. The least we could do is reward your service by elevating you to the title of marquess." The Prince Regent raised a glass of champagne into the air. "Congratulations, Lord and Lady Blackburn. May your life together be long and happy!"

The guests raised their glasses and shouted. "Huzzah! Huzzah!"

Archibald Gunn took advantage of the distraction to slip an arm around Lady Nesbitt's waist and press a tender kiss to her cheek.

Rafe gazed down at his bride, a look of complete adoration on his face. "You are everything I ever wanted and all I'll ever need. You have my heart and my soul. All I am and all I ever hope to be belong to you, my sweet Dulcinea."

"And you, my Lord Rogue, are the man I will love until the end of my life and beyond."

"Beyond, my lady?"

"Of course," she said. "It's the least I can do after you survived the hangman's noose in order to come back to me."

"I promised you, I would," He bent his head and brushed his lips against hers in the tenderest of kisses. How could I not when I knew you were waiting for me?"

"You couldn't." Dulcie beamed up at him, her love shining in her eyes. "Because you're a man of your word. You always keep your promises. I knew that the day we met. The day we wed. The day I knew I loved you."

Shouts of congratulation filled Lady Symington's reception room as the guests welcomed their latest marquess and marchioness into the ton. And in the midst of the crowd, Lord Weymouth and his associates and their wives all toasted the joyful couple and breathed profound sighs of relief that their first successful hanging had ended so happily.

EPILOGUE

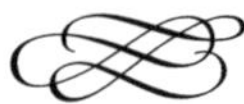

"Love is holy."
—William Shakespeare, 1564-1616

"Where are we going?" Dulcie asked her husband as they settled into their coach after attending the wedding of Lady Augusta Nesbitt to Sir Archibald Gunn.

"It's a surprise," Rafe replied.

"Not as big a surprise as Aunt Augusta and Archie's surprise wedding, I'll wager," Dulcie teased.

"I wouldn't be so sure, my lady."

It had been a momentous month, culminating in Lady Augusta and Archie's nuptials and moving into their new residence. After evicting her father, Lord Rushton and his companion, Lord Merrivale, from Blessing House, the Marchioness of Blessing and Countess of Carlisle, Lady Caroline and Lord Anthony Carlisle, had leased Blessing House to Dulcie and Rafe for one pound for a term of ninety-nine years. There would be no Blessing heirs, but because the house was entailed, it could not be sold. Caroline had decided to lease it to Dulcie for the sheer enjoyment of making Dulcie mistress of the house and its haughty butler, Tyson.

The Charlotte Society had met its goals for its first three needy soldiers and had been flooded with applications from new young ladies wishing to become society members. The first applicant had been Serenity Blakenheath, who had declared she already had her soldier in mind. And the second applicant had been Mavis, who would soon become a widow as Guilford had been convicted of murder *and* treason. Mavis and her three-week-old daughter, Jocelyn, were leaving Tennant House. It would soon have a new viscount, a stranger Dulcie had never met. Dulcie had decided to allow Mavis and Jocelyn to live in the house Rafe had bought for her until Mavis decided what she wanted to do next.

Phoebe and Alasdair were staying in Alasdair's home in Scotland. Dulcie and Rafe, Caroline and Tony, and Aunt Augusta and Archie planned to visit them soon.

In the meantime, Dulcie and Rafe were taking a wedding trip to somewhere on the *Guernsey Lady*, the yacht Raphael had purchased from Davies Shipping Enterprises. The destination was a secret, although Dulcie had begged to visit Rafe's beloved Blackburn Hall and Cragsmuir Castle.

"Are you ever going to tell me where we're going?" Dulcie asked, giving Rafe her best beseeching glance.

"No." Rafe kissed her shoulder.

They had spent the better part of the journey kissing and exploring the different ways of making love in a coach.

Dulcie knew they were heading for the coast and she was looking forward to their first long journey on the *Guernsey Lady*. She was also looking forward to exploring the different ways of making love in the massive bunk in the master's cabin.

"Not even when we get there?" She unbuttoned the buttons of his waistcoat and tugged his shirt out of his breeches.

"No." Rafe was adamant.

"How will I know?"

"Your brother will tell you."

Dulcie stopped undressing her husband and stared at him.

Rafe reached under the coach seat, pulled out a book, and handed it to her. A familiar book.

"*Gulliver's Travels.*" She smiled at Rafe. "Are you going to read it to me?"

"Probably," he admitted. "I haven't read it since Geoff died. I think this trip will be a good time to renew the Tennant family tradition."

"The Tennant-Blackburn family tradition," Dulcie corrected.

"Open it."

She did and was surprised when a pen-and-ink sketch of her at thirteen fell into her lap. Dulcie picked it up and studied it. "I gave this to Geoff."

"I know." Rafe leaned close and pressed a tender kiss on her lips. "I think I fell in love with the promise of the girl in that sketch the first time Geoff showed it to me."

"At thirteen, I was fearless, confident, and convinced I could do anything. At thirteen, we were still a family. Papa, Maman, Geoff, and me."

Rafe lifted her hand and kissed the pulse on the inside of her wrist. "I know. You were sixteen when you sent him that sketch."

"It was the only sketch I had of me. And my favorite."

"I think that's when I knew I was going to marry you as soon as you were old enough. I knew you were the girl for me. Now, go to the back of the book."

"The last page is stuck to the flyleaf."

Rafe nodded. "Open it." He had discovered Geoff's secret hiding place after Lord and Lady Symington's gala, when he'd awakened in the dead of night to the sound of Geoff's voice reminding him 'of everything by the book'. As far as Geoff was concerned there had only been one book. *Gulliver's Travels.* Whatever the answer Geoff had left for him, Rafe knew he would find it in the book. And when he found Geoff's hiding place, Rafe was surprised it had taken him so long to do so. In the secret pocket Geoff had fashioned in his favorite book, Rafe had discovered the precious items he needed to set everything right and had finally understood his friend's cryptic instructions.

There was no question of what came next. Rafe knew what he had to do.

"It's someone's marriage lines." Dulcie unfolded the marriage certificate. "Elena Maria de Marco, spinster, twenty-two, and Geoffrey William Robert Tennant, bachelor, twenty-three, united in marriage on this day, nineteenth of April eighteen hundred, eleven." She raised her disbelieving gaze to Rafe's face. "He didn't tell me. He wrote me about Elena, but he never hinted that he was going to marry her."

"He was afraid to," Rafe said. "Afraid Guilford would find out. Especially when…"

"When what?"

"Keep looking. There's more."

Dulcie checked the pocket Geoff had fashioned in the book and discovered the clipping of her parents' boating accident that hadn't been an accident after all. "He was the one who took it from my book of clippings." The names of the other victims were circled in pencil. Including Nelson, fifteenth Earl of Halton.

Rafe nodded. "Go on."

Dulcie pulled out another thick piece of paper that turned out to be a watercolor sketch of a young woman holding an infant on her lap. Her hair was as black as a raven's wing, but the infant's baby curls were a dark reddish brown. "The baby looks like Geoff," Dulcie breathed.

"He looks like you," Rafe said. "When I saw it, I pictured *our* children."

"You knew about her?"

"Of course I knew. I just didn't realize Geoff had hidden everything I needed to protect her in his beloved book. I was the one who stood up for Geoff at their wedding. And I celebrated with him when Roberto was born."

"Roberto?"

"The baby. The Honorable Robert Geoffrey Raphael Tennant." Rafe smiled. "Elena calls him Roberto. He was four on January seventeenth."

"He has your name."

"I'm his godfather," Rafe said proudly. "And you're his godmother."

"Do you know where they are now?"

"Blackburn Hall," Rafe said. "I didn't just promise to marry you. I also promised to take care of them. People think..." He shook his head. "Never mind what people think. We let them think what they will in order to protect him. Roberto is your nephew and the next Viscount Tennant. Dulcie, my darling, love of my life, I'm taking you home to meet your family."

Dulcie wrapped her arms around her husband's neck and kissed him with all the love in her heart. "Raphael Simon John, I love you so much. You're the man I dreamed of loving, of holding, of having as my husband. And this is the best wedding gift you could ever give me. Well...except a baby of our own." She blushed.

He grinned, then waggled his eyebrows at her. "We'll start with a long visit with Roberto and Elena and work on the other. And I promise you can love me to your heart's content."

The End

"The Charlotte Society" Series by Rebecca Hagan Lee
Lord Temptation
Lord Dare
Lord Rogue

Keep turning the pages for a Sneak Peek at *Barely a Bride*
by Rebecca Hagan Lee
Book 1 in her "Free Fellows League" Series

ABOUT THE AUTHOR

After arming herself with a degree in fine arts and experience in radio, television, and film, Rebecca Hagan Lee wrote her first novel *Golden Chances*. Since then, she's published numerous bestselling and award-winning novels and three novellas.

She's won a Waldenbooks Award, a Georgia Romance Writers *Maggie* Award, several *Romantic Times* awards, been nominated for an RWA *Rita* Award and has been published in nine languages.

She currently lives in Georgia with her husband, her two beloved Quarter Horses, and a miniature schnauzer named after literary icon Harper Lee.

Visit Rebecca's website http://www.rhaganlee.com

Join Rebecca on Facebook at http://www.facebook.com/rebeccahaganleeauthor

SNEAK PEEK

Barely a Bride

By Rebecca Hagan Lee

Book 1 "Free Fellows League" Series

Weymouth Hall, London
April 1810

"You sent for me, sir."

Griffin, seventeenth Viscount Abernathy, stood facing his father, the sixteenth Earl of Weymouth, in the study of his father's London town house. He was separated from his father by a wide expanse of dark, polished mahogany and a much darker, wider gulf of doubt brought about by age, familial differences, and the inherent conflict between a man and his heir.

"I sent for my heir," the earl snapped.

Griff inhaled, counted to twenty, then slowly expelled the breath. "I am your heir, Father."

"Not for much longer."

So that's how it was to be. As an only son and an only child, Griff was quite accustomed to his father's repeated attempts to use guilt as a means of manipulating him. His father's methods were tried and true, but Griff had long ago grown weary of the tactics. It would be nice to think that his father had sent for him because he wanted Griff's company. Just once.

"And why is that? Are congratulations in order?" Griff asked. "Have I an older brother I've never met?"

"Don't be ridiculous! If I had another son, you'd be the first to know about it."

"I would rather think that Mother would be the first to know about it." Griff gave his father a slight smile. "Or your mistress."

Lord Weymouth failed to find the humor in his son's remark. "However much we might like it, your mother is not increasing."

"I am disappointed to hear it."

"It isn't for lack of trying," the earl continued. "I can assure you of that. And of the fact that I have no need of a mistress. Your mother keeps me quite busy and quite satisfied in that regard. But no matter how often we try or how creative we become, we fail to accomplish our goal. Ours has never been a prolific family, and it seems that Lady Weymouth and I were quite fortunate to produce you."

"I am delighted you feel that way." Griff struggled to maintain a neutral countenance. His father had many admirable traits, but a sense of humor wasn't counted among them.

The Earl of Weymouth was a brilliant man, but careful and methodical. He was quiet and observant, paid enormous attention to detail, and rarely deviated from his planned course of action.

Griff had never heard his father mention the possibility of having intimate relations with his mother or with any other woman. Oh, he knew that his parents had had intimate relations at least once. The consummation of their union had, after all, resulted in his birth, but like most offspring, Griff didn't want to hear the details, nor could he begin to imagine his father as a lover, creative or otherwise. He blocked the mental image that threatened to ruin his perception of his parents and turned his attention back to what his father was saying.

"We are *delighted*"—Lord Weymouth used the same word Griff had used, proving to his son that he did have a fully developed sense of irony, if not a fully developed sense of humor—"enough with your presence on earth and in our lives that we've no wish to see it extinguished prematurely."

"You heard?"

"Of course, I heard. Did you expect that I wouldn't?" Lord Weymouth picked up a heavy ledger and slammed it upon the desktop.

The loud crack of leather against wood echoed through the quiet room. Lord Weymouth frowned, then pushed away from his desk and stood up.

His size was intimidating. Standing head and shoulders above almost every man he knew, Weymouth used his size to his advantage, but that tactic no longer worked with Griffin. The boy hadn't so much as flinched at the sound of the ledger hitting the desk or displayed any hint of childish emotion when his father stood up from behind his desk. Weymouth recognized the fact that his son was a grown man. Griff had sprouted up and filled out while away at university and was now able to look him in the eye. In truth, his son looked down in order to look him in the eye, a fact of which Lord Weymouth was inordinately proud. It was quite clear to Lord Weymouth that even in his stocking feet, Griffin easily bested his height by a good inch or so.

Except for age and the difference in height, the two of them were very much alike physically. Griff had his mother's brilliant blue eyes and hair a lighter shade of brown, but there was no denying that he was his father's son. His shoulders and chest were equally broad, and the earl found, much to his chagrin, that Griff was more fit. His waist was trimmer, and his hips and thighs were well muscled from hours spent in the saddle instead of behind a desk.

The earl fought to keep from grinning from ear to ear. His son was a man he could be proud of. Was proud of. But that didn't keep him from wanting to throttle him. Imagine his only son and heir choosing —choosing—to take up a commission as a major in the cavalry.

"I knew you'd hear about it," Griff admitted. "I just didn't expect you to hear about it quite so soon."

"So soon?" Weymouth came perilously close to shouting. "You accepted that commission a sennight ago. I only learned of it this morning."

"I did ask that my decision be kept quiet until I had a chance to discuss it with you," Griffin offered.

"And when did you intend our discussion to take place?" The earl's tone had taken on a biting edge, a biting edge that had been known to quell far greater men than his son.

"If you'll check your appointment calendar, sir, I believe you'll find your secretary assigned me the hours between four and six tomorrow at White's."

Weymouth reached over, flipped open his appointment book, and discovered that his son's name had, indeed, been duly noted for the hours of four to six at White's on the following afternoon. "You could have discussed this with me *before* you accepted the commission. Or did you keep it secret because you feared I would withhold my approval?"

"I have reached my majority," Griff reminded his father. "I don't fear your displeasure or require your approval."

"You are my heir," the earl replied. "My only heir. Have you no sense of duty?"

"England is at war. Father," Griffin said.

"I know England is at war!" Weymouth barked. "I see the results of it every day at the War Office, and I've no wish to see my heir's name added to the casualty lists."

Griff straightened his shoulders and stood at attention. "I had hoped that you would be pleased that I had decided to serve my country in her time of need."

"Pleased?" Weymouth snorted. "I'd be *pleased* if you would forget this nonsense. I'd be *pleased* if you'd sell your commission to someone else and let them serve in your place."

"So the Earl of Weymouth's heir can be spared? So someone else's heir's name can appear on the casualty lists?" Griff glared at his father.

Weymouth glared back. "Yes, dammit! Better theirs than mine."

"Have you so little confidence in my ability to survive?" Griffin asked.

"I have every confidence in your ability to survive," Weymouth said, "as long as you stay home where you belong. We're not talking about fox hunting or stalking stag or hunting expeditions spent traipsing across the wilds of Scotland with your friends. We're talking about war."

"I know what war is, Father."

"Do you?" Weymouth mused. "I wonder. I wonder if anyone who hasn't experienced it knows what war is."

"Then let's just say that I know where my duty lies."

"Your duty lies with your family, with tending and preserving what your mother and I have tended and preserved for you."

"And what of Bonaparte and the threat he poses to England and to our way of life?"

"What of it?" Weymouth demanded. "Bonaparte is more of a threat to our family and our way of life if you go to serve against him than he would be if you stayed home and watched him conquer the whole of England."

Griff recoiled, shocked to the core by his father's words. "I cannot believe you would forfeit your country so willingly."

"I am a great deal more willing to forfeit my country than I am to forfeit my son."

"You mean your heir," Griff corrected.

"I mean my *son*, dammit!" Weymouth glared at that son, daring him to contradict. "And I cannot believe that you would willingly forfeit your future and your family's future in order to become cannon fodder for the French." He ran a hand through his hair. "Cavalry. Bloody hell. I could understand the navy. I could even understand a commission as one of Wellesley's aides. But the cavalry..." He shook his head. "It's foolhardy. It's vainglorious. It's the most dangerous—"

"It's my strength," Griff said softly. "I sit a horse better than any man you know."

Weymouth nodded. "You sit a horse better than any man I've ever *seen* or ever hope to see."

"The army needs cavalry officers."

"Yes," the earl agreed. "And the reason the army needs cavalry officers is because we have more than our share of idiot generals who insist on getting them shot to hell. You're tall enough to be a grenadier. And you'd have a better chance of staying alive."

"I intend to serve my country," Griff said. "I mean to help defeat Bonaparte, and I have to go with my strength in order to succeed." He looked at his father, silently begging the earl to understand. "I've spent my entire life playing at soldiers, memorizing military tactics and stratagems. I may be tall enough, but I don't fancy a position in the grenadiers, lobbing grenades at the enemy lines until some sharpshooter picks me off. I prefer to take my chances with the cavalry. It's what I know best. If you were twenty years younger, what would you do?"

Weymouth nodded. “I would do exactly what you’re going to do.” He met his son’s gaze. “I would provide for the future of my family name and line by finding myself a suitable bride and getting myself an heir on that bride *before* I go off to war. And if I were you, I’d begin right away.”

“You must be joking!” Griff exclaimed.

“On the contrary,” the earl replied. “As you are quite aware, I have a considerable reputation for not having been born with a sense of humor. This isn’t a joke.”

“But, Father, be reasonable—”

“I am being reasonable,” Weymouth snapped. “Far more reasonable than you are being. I, at least, would tend to the details of the family. I, at least, would provide my parents with a grandchild to take my place as heir to the family land and tides in order that they not become extinct should something happen to their only child.”

“But to marry some poor girl and get her with child in order to leave her a widow—” Griff broke off as the magnitude of his decision and the possibility of his not returning home from war suddenly became a reality.

“I’m not suggesting you marry a poor girl or that you leave her a widow,” Weymouth told him. “An heiress will do just as well. And as long as you’re going to be a husband and a father, you might as well return from the war alive and healthy and whole.” He smiled at his son for the first time since Griffin arrived. “It’s the least you can do for your family.”

“You aren’t serious.”

“I thought that we had established that I am quite serious. I suggest you start the quest for your bride at Lady Cleveland’s soiree this evening.” Weymouth flipped through his appointment book as he spoke. “You only have two weeks.”

“I’m not going to spend my remaining fortnight attempting to locate a bride.”

“You will if you expect to be married before you leave,” his father countered. “You only have a fortnight plus four days before you’re scheduled to report to your regiment. It will take at least a day to negotiate the wedding settlement and another two days to plan and execute the wedding and a wedding breakfast for a hundred or so of our closest friends."

Griffin stood his ground. "I am not getting married."

"Fine," the earl agreed. "Sell your commission and turn your attention to Abernathy Manor. It is desperately in need of upkeep. The house and the lands are on their way to ruination."

"Abernathy Manor will have to endure a bit longer without my attention," Griffin said. "I'm joining His Majesty's Eleventh Blues."

"Then you'll want to choose a bride." His father's tone of voice and the look of steely determination in his eyes brooked no argument. "Otherwise, I shall be forced to select one for you."

"You can select a wife for me, but you can't make me repeat the vows."

"I won't have to," Weymouth said grimly. "You will repeat your wedding vows willingly, or you will find yourself summarily cashiered out of the Eleventh Blues. You'll be dishonored, disgraced, and disowned."

"You can't disown me," Griffin reminded him. "You have no other heirs."

"Then I'll cut you off without a penny."

"Fine," Griffin replied. "I'll make my own way."

"You do that," Weymouth told him. "You're young and strong and smart; you can earn a living for yourself. But that task might not be so easy for the three hundred souls at Abernathy Manor who find themselves dependent upon your income—"

"You would close the manor and turn everyone out?"

"I would tear down the manor and put sheep on the place without batting an eye," Weymouth promised. "It's less costly and a much more efficient use of the acreage." He glanced at his son, gauging Griff's reaction. "What do I need with another manor house? I have Weymouth Park, the London town house, and a hunting lodge in Scotland to keep up."

"That's blackmail."

"Of course it is," the earl agreed. "And the reason it's used so often is because it's effective. Don't look so glum," he advised his son. "While it's true that you'll be giving up your bachelor ways, you'll be able to rest easy in the knowledge that in addition to acquiring a bride and an heir, your noble sacrifice has secured the livelihoods of three hundred or so deserving souls."

"I'll have your word that Abernathy Manor and all its inhabitants will be well taken care of," Griffin demanded. "Whether or not I return from the war."

"You have my word…so long as you take a bride and get an heir on her before you leave."

"What if I take a bride but fail to leave her with an heir? I can't promise I'll be able to fulfill that duty in a few days' time."

Weymouth looked his son in the eye. "The sooner you find a bride, the more time you'll have to work at it."

"I could still fail," Griff reminded him. "You've failed to produce another child. And, as you said, not for want of trying."

"You'll have to do better than your mother and I have been able to do."

"What if I succeed, and the child is a girl?"

"Ownership of Abernathy Manor reverts to me. Our letters patent make no allowances for firstborn females."

"You could have the letters amended by parliament."

"I could," the earl said. "But I prefer that my son return to England and fulfill his duty to his family."

"Even if that means returning from the dead?"

"Whatever it takes to accomplish the deed," Weymouth pronounced. "I will accept nothing less from my son and heir."

Barely a Bride by Rebecca Hagan Lee
Book 1 in the "Free Fellows League" series

Made in the USA
Columbia, SC
20 February 2023